Olivia Goldsmith is the bestselling author of *The First Wives Club*, *Flavor of the Month*, *Bestseller*, *The Switch*, *Young Wives* and most recently, *Bad Boy*. She has contributed to *The New York Times*, *Cosmopolitan*, *In Style*, and the *Observer*, among other publications. She divides her time between her homes in upstate New York and Manhattan. For more about Olivia Goldsmith, visit her website at www.olivia-goldsmith.com.

Acclaim for Olivia Goldsmith:

'Full of wisecracks and gossip . . . Olivia Goldsmith can keep you reading'   *Cosmopolitan*

'A bubbly, fizzy story'   *Daily Mail*

'Olivia Goldsmith's forte has always been the writing of revenge novels with great good humor'
                                                                   Washington Post

'Goldsmith hands out her characters' rewards and come-uppances like Jane Austen dealing blackjack . . . You keep licking your fingers and reaching for the next page as if it were another potato chip'   *Newsweek*

'Fizzing with acerbic dialogue and high-level sexual slap-stick'   *Good Housekeeping*

OLIVIA GOLDSMITH

INSIDERS

HarperCollins*Publishers*

HarperCollins*Publishers*
77–85 Fulham Palace Road,
Hammersmith, London W6 8JB

www.fireandwater.com

This paperback edition 2002
1 3 5 7 9 8 6 4 2

First published in Great Britain by
HarperCollins*Publishers* 2002

ISBN 0 00 651438 3

Set in Transitional 521
by Rowland Phototypesetting Ltd,
Bury St Edmunds, Suffolk

Printed and bound in Great Britain by
Clays Ltd, St Ives plc

To Jack Rapke

Because you always knew how good it would be

An imprisoned creature was out of the question – my mother would not have allowed a rat to be restrained of its liberty.

Mark Twain

Book I

1

Jennifer Spencer

What is now proved was once only imagined.
William Blake, *The Marriage of Heaven and Hell*

'All rise.'

Jennifer Anne Spencer watched as Judge Marian Levitt entered the courtroom, her black robes swinging loosely from her shoulders, not concealing her dumpiness, her white hair cut in a simple bob. She climbed the three steps to the bench holding Jennifer's future in her hands.

Jennifer stood beside her lawyer and the rest of the legal team and faced Judge Levitt with what she hoped was a calm and honest gaze. She knew that the photographers would pay a great deal to have a picture of her at the time the verdict was given. But they were barred from the courtroom and for that, if nothing else, she was grateful.

Although she had been assured and reassured that the judge would see things 'their way', it was not an easy thing to stand before the woman as she leafed through her papers.

In fact, although she doubted that she would be judged guilty, she was certain that even if she was, she would be given a suspended sentence or public service or a fine.

Jennifer had to admit that she felt sick to her stomach just standing there. That she had virtually volunteered to be there didn't make it any easier. She felt a fluttering beside her and realized that Tom, her attorney, was reaching for her hand. She entwined her fingers in his and knew that he could feel her trembling. She hoped that the judge could see neither that nor the fact that they were holding hands. But she supposed it wouldn't make any difference to the outcome of the trial.

For what seemed like an interminable time, Judge Levitt paged through the notes in front of her. She had on a pair of half-glasses that were perched at the very end of her long nose. Both Donald and Tom had strongly urged Jennifer to forgo a jury trial. 'This is complicated law,' Tom had said. 'A judge would be more likely to understand the distinctions.' Donald had laughed. 'Let's face it,' he'd said. 'Civilians hate us and would be only too happy to throw the book at you.' Jennifer had nodded. 'We're the fat cats,' Donald had continued. 'We're the Wall Street smart-asses. When they make money during a bull market they resent us for making more. When they lose money they blame us. You can't win when you're on the Street. You'd never get a jury of your peers unless they could get a dozen guys from the Street, and none of them have the time to sit on a jury.' They had all laughed.

But now, looking up at Judge Levitt, Jennifer didn't feel like laughing. She told herself it was all going to be all right. Donald and Tom would see to it. This was the worst of it, and after this she'd be so well rewarded that . . .

'Jennifer Spencer. You have been accused of fraud. I find you guilty. On insider trading I find you guilty on all counts. On . . .'

A loud buzzing began in Jennifer's ears. The word 'guilty' coming from Judge Levitt's lips seemed to move from the bench to her and hit her like a blow. This wasn't what was planned. She felt dizzy and she had to close her eyes for a moment to stop the room from spinning. Tom's hand on her now clammy one did not feel comforting. She wanted to shake him off and wipe the sweat off herself. How could this be happening?

When she could hear again, the judge was intoning something about her sentence. A sentence? If she was found guilty, there wasn't supposed to be a sentence. '. . . three to five years at Jennings Correctional Facility for Women.' The judge paused, took off her glasses, and looked across the bench at Jennifer. 'You are very young,' she said. 'It's better that you learn now that this type of manipulation and illegal profiteering is unacceptable and that it could destroy your entire life.'

Jennifer couldn't respond. Even on that horrible day when the Feds came into her posh office at the prestigious Wall Street firm of Hudson, Van Schaank & Michaels to take her away in cuffs, Jennifer didn't believe that she would spend even one moment in a jail cell. The arrest made her a little nervous, of course, but that was only because she'd never been in trouble before with the law.

'This is just a publicity stunt,' her boss told her. 'They're firing shots over our heads to cool down this overheated market.' That boss was the legendary Donald J. Michaels himself, and Jennifer never questioned his judgment or authority. 'Believe me,' Donald assured her, 'these charges are going to be dropped. And even if you do go to trial, you aren't going to be found guilty of anything. Trust me,' he added with his reassuring smile.

Jennifer did trust him. After all, she *wasn't* guilty of anything. She was just taking the heat for Donald in order to deflect any further investigations into his firm's rather dubious business dealings. If the SEC – the Securities and Exchange Commission – had gone after Donald they would have thrown the book at him. 'And they've got a damn big book,' Donald had joked. 'You know how jealous, how envious, people have been over our success in the last few years.' Jennifer did know. During his Wall Street career Donald Michaels had made not only his own fortune, but had also made dozens, maybe scores – or even hundreds – of other millionaires. Jennifer herself was a millionaire at twenty-eight – but now she was a millionaire who was leaving for prison in less than an hour.

Standing in the courtroom, Jennifer cradled her right elbow in her left hand and her left in her right hand and shivered as she felt both her gooseflesh and nausea rise. How, she wondered, did it come to this? How had Tom, her lawyer, let it happen?

Thomas Philip Branston IV was the sharpest (and most handsome) young counsel on the Street. 'Nothing is really at risk,' he had told Jennifer, echoing Donald's assurances. 'It never is in cases like this. Even if you are convicted – which is virtually impossible – we'll have an appeal before the judge can pound his gavel. Donald has good friends and deep pockets,' Tom said with a knowing smile. Jennifer had no reason to doubt what he said. After all, Tom was not only a Harvard undergrad and Law Review at Yale, he was also much more than her brilliant attorney. He was her beloved fiancé.

'Think of it, Jen,' he had said days ago, 'everyone here will be in your debt. You'll not only have Donald's gratitude, but also the gratitude of the partners and all of the employees, right down to the secretaries and the mail-room staff. They'll all owe their fortunes and their jobs to you.'

'I only regret that I have but one life to give for my firm,' Jennifer had joked on that day when she, Tom, and Donald got together with Bob, the financial officer and Lenny, his assistant, to hatch their plan. There was plenty to drink and lots of laughter at that meeting as they discussed how Tom would prepare her statements, how they'd all sign them, and how Tom would 'turn her in' to the SEC. The Feds would be ripsnorting mad to miss their shot at Donald, but if she confessed they were scotched in their witchhunt, and Jennifer would be back at work within a week.

At the time their plan sounded solid; after all, Jennifer loved the heart-stopping thrill of high-risk deal-making. She loved the power of outleveraging any competitor in a buyout, and she loved the rush of watching one of their IPOs – Initial Public Offerings – burst onto the market to take the lucky or the gullible investor for the ride of his life. She loved it all – but most of all she loved the money and what it bought. She loved the Pratesi sheets on her bed, the silk Kirmans on her floor, and she loved every piece of Armani, Prada, Gucci, and Ferragamo that she kept neatly in her Biedermeier armoire. Even if her Tribeca condo was a little small, it was beautiful and in the best neighborhood in New York. (John Kennedy, Jr. had lived just around the corner.) With the very generous bonus that she was likely to get from pulling off this little charade, Jennifer was sure that she'd be able to move right on up to the penthouse.

'Jennifer, I'm so, so sorry. It's a mistake. Honestly. I thought we had Levitt in line,' Tom said to her now. Jennifer just stared at him, speechless.

The court officer began to move toward her. 'We're going to have to go now,' he said.

'What?' she asked. He must be joking. 'Go where?'

Tom looked away from her, unable to meet her eyes. 'To be transported,' he said. 'To go . . .'

'To go to jail?' she asked, and heard her voice rising. After the indictment she'd been out on bail before the desk sergeant could call the press and tip them off to her presence. 'Ridiculous,' she said, with more bravado than she felt, but the guard came at her relentlessly and when he reached her he pulled out handcuffs. Jennifer almost fainted. 'No,' she said, and it came out almost as a moan.

'Surely handcuffs aren't necessary . . .' Tom began.

'It's procedure,' the marshal said, and it was clear that there was no negotiating. He snapped the cuffs on Jennifer's wrists, then had to stop and adjust them again and again because her wrists were so small. 'Okay,' he said. 'Let's go. We have transport waiting.'

'We're going to have to go out there,' Tom told her. 'There will be a lot of photographers and journalists.' He paused. 'Look, this is only a momentary setback,' he said. 'You'll be there overnight. We'll appeal or we'll get a mistrial. Don't worry about this.'

'Let's go,' the marshal said again and took her, not gently, by the arm.

'Um, could she fix herself for a moment?' Tom asked.

Jennifer, dazed and confused, didn't know what he was

talking about, but Jane, one of the other attorneys, took out a comb and tissue and actually fussed with Jennifer's face as if she were an actor about to go before the cameras. As she was being preened, Tom stood very close to her and she felt something drop into her pocket.

'Call me sometime,' he whispered into her ear. 'Look undaunted,' Tom continued as he stepped back, while she was marshaled out to face the exploding lights and equally unsettling questions. 'Are you sorry now?' a woman's voice yelled.

'What will you do in prison?' she heard someone else shout.

'Jenny, look over here!' a husky voice intoned.

'Jenny!' echoed behind her.

'Jenny! Jenny, here!' was being chanted all around her.

Now she realized why people photographed for the newspapers always looked guilty. She, too, had to hang her head down to protect herself from being blinded by the flashbulbs and strobes. The marshal had been joined by several court officers who were pushing the media out of the way. Jennifer realized that she didn't know if Tom was still with her or not, but when they walked through the double doors and she found herself at a loading dock, Tom was right behind her, though blessedly the wolf pack was stopped in their tracks.

But right now, the idea of prison gave Jennifer another roll of nausea. She tried to quiet her fears with the confidence that she had cut quite a deal with the firm. With Tom in charge of her appeal, and Howard McBane, senior partner of the white shoe firm of Swithmore, McBane pleading it, there was – she reminded herself – essentially no risk. When all the dust was settled, Donald Michaels was going to owe her big time. She may have left the firm in cuffs, but she was certain that she would return as a senior partner.

In the days following her initial arrest, Jennifer focused her energies on practicing her testimony with Tom and deciding what to wear to court. She was charged with investment fraud, so it seemed that she should try to look as *un*fraudulent as possible. She chose Armani over Yamaguchi, because who could appear fraudulent in Armani? And for shoes she opted for Louboutin over Manolo Blahnick. Only a classic Gucci purse would do, and with a new hairstyle and makeup done to perfection, Jennifer was sure that she was dressed not only for success, but for an acquittal.

What she hadn't planned on, however, was the possibility of a female judge. For all of her success, Jennifer had never learned how to deal well with other women – especially the fat, dumpy types who prefer to cloak their femininity in the dark uniformity of robes. When Jennifer saw her judge it was like seeing the ghost of Sister Mary Margaret from St Bartholomew's school. Jennifer had looked to Tom for encouragement.

But as clever and handsome as Tom was in his own impeccably tailored suit, he had no charm over this severe incarnation of Lady Justice. The grand jury hearing was a disaster. Jennifer was indicted and brought to trial amidst a media frenzy that made national headlines. Donald had warned her that the Feds were looking for a high-profile scapegoat. They found one in Jennifer Spencer. Her story kept the tabloids churning out edition after edition, and while the humiliation of the live television coverage was considerable, what really frustrated Jennifer was the judge's inability to see that the charges against her were bogus.

At the van Jennifer cried as Tom held her close. 'This is only a little setback,' he told her. 'It's all going to blow over. We'll get an appeal. You'll get another judge. We'll get Howard McBane for the appeal. McBane is an appellate genius and every judge in the state knows him. Your case will be decided on its merits.' Jennifer tried to remind herself 'No guts – no glory.' The shame of the publicity and the shock of the verdict would be a small price to pay for a senior partnership in the firm – and a lifetime of wealth with her beloved Tom. She'd taken a gamble and if this was the downside of it, the upside was well worth a few days of a little discomfort. 'I'll call ahead,' Tom told her. 'I'll pull a few strings and make sure that you get nothing but white-glove treatment.'

Jennifer nodded as yet another horrible wave of fear, anger, and shame washed over her. She was leaving for prison! She wished Donald Michaels, the author of all this, had come to see her off, but that thought had barely registered when they moved through the doors and, as if out of nowhere, the prison transport van pulled up and two armed officers got out.

The shorter officer carried a clipboard on which various papers were signed and exchanged. Then the taller one opened the doors of the cold parking bay in which they stood. Immediately a second horde of photographers swarmed into the loading area, and in the frenzy and noise Jennifer searched their faces, hoping that Donald might be among them. He wasn't there, but Lenny Benson was. There, in the back of the crowd, Jennifer spotted good old Lenny standing all alone. He gave her a small wave good-bye just as she was told to get into the van.

'I guess I have to go,' Jennifer whispered to Tom. She felt her throat close and her eyes tear up.

'Don't worry. This is nothing,' Tom said, though he looked as pale as she must have. 'It's going to be okay, Jen. Trust me.'

'I do,' she told him, and only later thought about saying those two words in this awful context.

'Come on,' the tall officer urged.

Tom bent to kiss her, but not on the lips – only on the forehead. It made Jennifer feel like the dutiful child she had behaved as. She did trust Tom, but so far he had been wrong when he said that she wouldn't be indicted, wouldn't be tried, and then that she would get off. She looked up and tried to smile into his handsome face. 'Are you sure you're going to want to marry an ex-con?' she asked, heroically trying to joke.

Tom stared at her intently, then took her face in his hands. 'You are so beautiful,' he said in the husky voice he used when they made love. 'You know that?' he asked her. 'Think of this as just an ugly business trip. I'll take care of all the legal aspects. There will be an appeal, we'll win and it'll all be over soon. This will be completely expunged from your record when you're exonerated.'

'I love it when you talk legal,' she told him bravely, but a betraying tear slipped down one of her cheeks.

'Come on! We got a schedule to keep,' the tall officer nearly barked.

Tom looked down at Jennifer's hand. There, on the fourth finger, she wore his ring. 'Maybe you should leave the diamond with me,' he said. 'Just for safekeeping,' he added with an apologetic smile.

Jennifer was stunned. She loved her ring. When he'd put

12

it on her finger she'd planned to never take it off. But . . . well, of course it was silly, insane really, to wear a three-carat diamond to . . . She tried not to think about what she was doing, but again, like a child, she did as she was told and slipped the gorgeous emerald-cut ring from her finger and gave it back to Tom.

It was almost a relief when the van doors slid shut. As she looked out, hoping for a last glimpse of Tom, she saw nothing but photographers, and then, there in the crowd was Lenny's stricken face. She lifted her ringless hand to wave good-bye through the wire mesh. 'This Jennings place is like a country club,' she reminded herself as the van lurched forward and took her away from her job, her luxurious home, her love. And her life.

2

Gwen Harding

> *The law is the true embodiment*
> *of everything that's excellent.*
> *It has no kind of fault or flaw,*
> *And I, my Lords, embody the law.*
>
> W. S. Gilbert, *Iolanthe*

Whenever Warden Gwendolyn Harding was asked to give the occasional speech to a group of young people or a women's association, she would usually begin by telling those assembled, 'When I was a little girl and people would ask me whether I wanted to be a nurse or a teacher or a mommy when I grew up, I'd answer that question by saying, "No, *I* want to be a prison warden, because then I'll get to be all three of those things at once."' The story always got a laugh, and Gwen Harding liked to think that laughing helped people to relax a bit. If you can make someone laugh, aren't you making his or her life a little better? Isn't it giving him or her a small gift? That was why Gwen was often so disappointed with herself after a long day at Jennings. She couldn't make the lives of the inmates much better, and she most certainly could not make them laugh. She wished that she could.

She also wished that she could make the five representatives from JRU International laugh as well. They were all solemnly seated before her in her sunny but somewhat dusty office at Jennings. This wasn't the first time she'd met with Jerome Lardner, the bald little man with the protruding Adam's apple, but she didn't recognize the rest of his staff. They seemed to be interchangeable in their little suits, their little haircuts, and their little ages. They looked like they ranged between ages twenty-four to twenty-eight. Gwen Harding was used to seeing young prisoners, but her *staff* were mature. Even Jerome Lardner, whom Gwen uncharitably – but only mentally – referred to as 'Baldy', was well under forty.

'What we are hoping to achieve,' Lardner was saying, 'is not just a new level of productivity, but also a new level of profitability within a correctional facility.'

'Well,' Gwen pointed out with a smile, '*any* profitability would be a new level, wouldn't it? Prisons have never made any money.'

'Certainly,' Jerome nodded, 'certainly none of the *public* prisons make money, but the *privatized* ones do.'

That word! Gwen decided yet again that she would not argue statistics with Jerome Lardner. Whenever she called any of his 'facts' into question, he was always ready with statistics. If figures didn't lie, then liars like Jerome certainly didn't figure out anything except how to protect their own position. 'Inmate Output Management Specialists have been very effective in supervising the productivity of privatized facility workers,' Baldy droned on.

Sometimes it took Gwen as long as five minutes to figure

out what the JRU terminology meant. They seemed to avoid using straightforward words like 'prison' or 'forced labor' when they could use their multisyllabic buzzwords instead. It might fool the politicians, but it didn't fool Gwen. 'Whatever you just said, I'm sure you are right,' Gwen responded.

At last! She got a bit of a chuckle and a few laughs from the JRU staff. That would be her little gift to them. Gwen suspected that they were probably laughing *at* her, not with her. She imagined that she was probably the butt of plenty of JRU jokes. But that was nothing new. She knew, for example, that at Jennings many of the women – both the inmates and the staff – referred to her as 'The Prez' – as in 'The President'. This wasn't because of her strong image or authoritative air, but rather because of her somewhat unfortunate name. When Gwen Harding first arrived at Jennings, her nameplate had been erroneously engraved to read: WARREN G. HARDING instead of WARDEN G. HARDING. She assumed that the error was an innocent one and not a purposeful attempt to make her look silly. She had had the sign redone, but she kept the original one at home and amused friends and relatives with it at dinner parties and family gatherings – back when she gave dinner parties and had a family to gather.

Gwen could laugh about the nameplate now, but it was not the most dignified way to begin her tenure as the new warden. Fortunately, over time, Gwen had noticed that fewer and fewer of the women who were sent to Jennings even knew who Warren G. Harding was. She imagined that 'The Prez' would eventually be replaced with a new name – probably something even more offensive. Maybe it already had. The inmate population grew, changed, and became less educated and more troubled each year. She'd been shocked only last week when Flora, the middle-aged inmate in charge of the laundry detail, apparently didn't know the difference between a city and a country. 'When I get out of here, I'm going to Paris,' Flora had said.

'France?' Gwen had asked her.

'There, too!' was Flora's reply.

It would have been something to laugh about if it wasn't so sad. But Gwen would've preferred that she and Flora had something to laugh about *together*. Jennings was such a sad place, she wished that all of them – the inmates, the officers, the staff – had something to laugh about. But, after all, it was a prison, wasn't it? And she was the Warden – not a clown. And most certainly not a teacher, a nurse, or a mommy. The job wasn't what she had once hoped for. Contrary to what she (and no one else) thought of as her 'amusing public speaking anecdote', being Warden had very little to do with nurturing, medicine, or motherhood. Increasingly, it was a purely administrative position that required an expertise in staff management, food preparation, health services, and custodial care, along with – quite obviously – criminal behavior. If she had to do it all over again, Gwen Harding would've gladly chosen to be a nurse, a teacher, or a mommy. But she didn't and she couldn't.

Gwen looked at the JRU International staff seated before her. She sighed. It was a big waste of time. As she tried to concentrate on the ongoing monotone monologue of the bald one, she realized that she wasn't sure she knew *what* she was any longer; the thrust of her job had changed too much. She had more and more paperwork, less and less contact with the inmates, and virtually no programs in education and rehabilitation. The greatest focus of her work was on cost containment – especially since JRU had begun to explore the privatization of Jennings nearly a year ago.

Baldy finally stopped speaking and a member of his very young crew was now going on about a 'facilities facilitator', who would make the buildings better, stronger, cleaner, bigger, *and* more *beautiful*. It wasn't clear to Gwen how this was going to be achieved without an immense infusion of money. The Jennings infrastructure hadn't been invested in in decades. She couldn't even find money for routine maintenance.

It was very difficult for Gwendolyn Harding to comprehend how an underfunded and crumbling government-controlled institution for the so-called 'rehabilitation' of women could suddenly be transformed into a profitable subsidiary of an international corporate conglomerate. Not only did Gwen have difficulty imagining how it could happen, she was also becoming unnervingly aware that these JRU fools seemed to believe it would be up to her to see that it *did* happen. Ha! Not even *Warren* G. Harding could do the job. The job Baldy had in mind for Gwen to do required an understanding of sales, marketing, and most aspects of the private sector. She had no experience or expertise in any of these areas – nor did she want any.

What if these bozos did succeed in getting a contract from the state? When it came to the state, *anything* was possible. What kind of havoc would ensue then? Gwen envisioned management so cruel and incompetent that an armed insurrection would not be altogether unlikely. She looked at the twentysomethings gathered before her. If each and every one of them were blown away in an Attica scenario she wouldn't be sorry at all. She'd only regret that the inmates would be forced to serve more time. And as far as Gwen was concerned, it would be grossly unfair to serve time when you were just trying to perform a service for humanity.

Gwen was growing weary and angry at these jackals. What if the staff whom she had hired and trained over the years was fired so that some twenty-three-year-old 'executive' could take over? What if she herself was replaced by a 'facilities facilitator' or an 'inmate output management specialist'? Jennings was a correctional facility for women, not one of those 'country club' joints for the white-collar crooks from Wall Street.

That reminded Gwen of the intake meeting that was scheduled for that afternoon. Jennifer Spencer – the Wall Street showboater who the papers said was 'sentenced to three to five at a country club prison' was due to arrive. A country club! Someday Gwen wanted to visit one of those fabled facilities for herself. Maybe they existed somewhere for *male* white-collar criminals, but to her knowledge – which was extensive – there wasn't a correctional facility for women anywhere in the United States that was not miserably overcrowded, pathetically understaffed, and/or dangerously in need of major repairs. There was nothing at Jennings that even remotely resembled the amenities of a country club.

Gwen had all kinds at Jennings. She had women who had violently murdered, and she had a grandmother who had done nothing more criminal than to grow a little marijuana to help her grandson with his MS. And why? Because when the governor declared his war on drugs, and the legislators passed mandatory twenty-year sentences for even the most minor offense, everyone caught in the net – dolphin as well as tuna – eventually wound up on Gwen's doorstep.

And when they did, it was up to her to take care of all of them. She fed them, housed them, put them to bed, and tried to attend to their medical needs. At the same time she did her best to maintain the discipline and decorum that kept the lid on the Jennings pressure cooker of anger, resentment, and – most perilous of all – boredom. In the meantime, there were no full-time medical professionals on staff, the educational and training programs were sub-standard, there were no special facilities for family visits or overnight stays with children, and while there were a few on her staff who were hardworking men and women, Gwen also had more than a few union-protected liars and sadists who she fervently hoped would eventually end up on the other side of the bars. A country club? Gwen hardly thought so. A profit center? That was even more ridiculous. Gwen actually snorted out loud.

Quickly she took the handkerchief that she kept tucked in her sleeve and wiped her nose as if she had sneezed. Well, she thought, as long as Warden Gwendolyn Harding was still at the helm of the Jennings Correctional Facility for Women it would be neither a country club nor a corporate headquarters. It would be a place where sad, damaged, and angry women were locked away from a society that required their removal. And if she had the courage and the stamina to make it happen, when these women were released, they would leave Jennings somewhat healed, more hopeful, and partially rehabilitated and acceptable to society. That was her modest dream.

She shifted in her seat and cleared her voice. As Warden she was used to being watched and obeyed by hundreds of people. Even the slightest narrowing of her eyes usually brought a response. But in *this* meeting she could probably set her hair afire and it wouldn't stop the young woman who was now babbling on and on about telemarketing. Telemarketing?

Gwen glanced at her watch. She'd give them four more minutes and then they were out of there. She had to meet with today's new prisoner, tell her the rules, and assign her to a cell. Jennifer Spencer was going to be a tough call for Gwen. She was coming in as a 'celebrity' inmate. Everyone in America had read all about her long before she had been sent to Jennings. Her story had been in all of the newspapers and magazines, and the photos of her and her handsome young lawyer looked like something right from the society pages. Even when she was led into the courthouse in handcuffs, she held her head high and kept her nose in the air as if she was going to a meeting of the board of directors.

Gwen Harding was afraid that Jennifer Spencer was coming to Jennings to cut herself a deal. In all of the stories that she read about the arrest, the trial, the conviction, and now her imminent incarceration, Jennifer Spencer looked and sounded like a thoroughbred who always came in in first place. Jennifer Spencer was accustomed to being treated like a winner. And that meant that there were probably a lot of losers who were fashioning a knife out of a contraband piece of metal wrenched off a window frame just so they could slash the face of a woman like Jennifer Spencer. Unprovoked violence wasn't epidemic at Jennings, but it did occur and it was a constant worry to Gwen Harding. But she took her mind off it and tried to focus on the snip of a girl in front of her.

'So, in effect,' the young woman was saying, 'the telemarketing personnel could be monitored by only three shifts of management, which would give twenty-four-hour

coverage of an operation that could sell nonstop, guarantee-
ing a –'

That was enough. These people were only visitors. She
didn't report to them – yet. Gwen stood up, looked at
Jerome and nodded her head. 'Well, thank you,' she said
briskly. 'This has been most informative.'

Informative and beyond Gwen's grasp. The JRU people
began to shuffle their papers and regroup. They had no idea
what they'd be dealing with. Who was going to train the
women? And more importantly, *what* was going to *motivate*
them? All of Gwen's staffers and all of Gwen's guards
couldn't get them to do the laundry with any care, or even
to prepare meals that were anything better than slop. Many
of the inmates were content to live in squalor, and few took
any pride in their appearance or personal hygiene.

Gwen stood, opened the door of her office, and bid the
fools from JRU good-bye. They all walked out without so
much as a glance toward Gwen's receptionist, Miss
Ringling, or Movita Watson, the inmate assigned to Gwen's
office from the prisoner population. Movita was the notable
exception among the inmates at Jennings. Gwen knew she
shouldn't – really *couldn't* – afford to have favorites, but
Movita was . . . well, she was one of a kind. She was more
competent, more clever, more stylish, with more attitude,
intelligence, and tricks up her sleeve than anyone Gwen had
even known. Movita ran the tightest crew in the prison, and
perhaps ran the prison as well. Her crewmates loved and
respected her in a way that Gwen – in her more perversely
ironic moods – almost envied.

If the fools from JRU had any sense at all, Gwen
thought, they'd be talking to Movita rather than me.

3

Jennifer Spencer

They try to strip you from the very first minute . . .
When they brought me in county jail, the first thing
they did was take my wedding ring and my earrings.
Then they stripped me stark naked and made me jump
up and down on the floor in a squat position – while
they all stood around watching. They have to forget
we're human beings to treat us that way.

A woman prisoner. Kathryn Watterson, *Women in Prison*

As the prison van moved past the crowd at the courthouse
and into the city streets, Jennifer put her face up to the
smeared, barred window. As the van lumbered through
the tunnel and then through poor suburban streets it was
as if Jen was traveling back in time. She watched over-
worked women lugging laundry and groceries through the
littered blocks, the kind of low-rent neighborhood in which
she had grown up. Tears filled her eyes for a moment. Every
one of those women reminded her of her late mother. And
every staggering drunk looked like her stepfather.

Jennifer shivered again and rubbed the flesh of her arms
vigorously. She hated being in this van, she hated these
streets, and she hated the memories she was having of

living in streets like them. It had taken motivation, intelligence, and hard work to climb out of the place they were driving through. Ironically, it now seemed as if that same motivation, intelligence, and hard work was bringing her right back, or to a place even worse. Prison! She wouldn't let her tears fall. She reminded herself that this was only a temporary setback. But she was glad that her mother hadn't lived long enough to know about her trial or see her riding in a prison van.

Jennifer turned away from the window. She couldn't worry about the women on the street; she had her own problems. She'd dressed so carefully that morning – as she did every morning – but now the bench that she was sitting on was speckled with God only knew what kind of dirt. The rubber-matted floor smelled as if unspeakable things had been deposited there, and she was afraid to lean against the wall because of the nasty graffiti that was written in – what? Blood? Snot? Magic Marker? Jen thought ruefully of all the taxes that she had paid over the years. She wondered why some of it wasn't spent on keeping prison vans a little cleaner. Well, the horrible interior was probably just a show for the press. As Tom said, they were making an example of her. Things would be a lot better once she actually got to the prison. What had Tom said? It was a country club. Fine. She could handle that for a day or even two. Right now, though, the filth and the stench were permeating her hair and her clothes. Worse, Jennifer felt too tired to sit erect any longer. She gave up and leaned back. What does it matter? she thought. She would take her suit to Chris French Cleaners back on Ninth Street in a couple of days and they would work their magic on it. They would remove the smells and stains, just as Tom was working to make her

24

personal record spotless once again. She thought of pulling out her hidden Nokia and calling him, but the driver might hear and surely he couldn't have accomplished anything this soon. She should just zone out and wait.

Just as Jennifer relaxed into the ride, the driver sped up and recklessly rounded a corner. She was thrown from the steel bench onto the filthy floor. Jen struggled to get back on the bench and, in her surprise, she forgot for a moment just exactly what her situation was. 'Excuse me,' she shouted to the driver through the wire cage, 'but don't you think we're going just a little too fast in a residential neighborhood?'

His head spun around. 'I don't need no driving lessons from a convict,' he sneered. Then he looked straight ahead and drove on even faster.

Jennifer was angry and ashamed of her outburst, but still she insisted, 'It's dangerous. Your driving threw me onto this filthy floor.'

'I don't care if you fall on your ass. You ain't riding in a limo anymore, convict.'

Convict! He kept calling her a convict. She climbed back on the bench and tried to brace herself against the walls of the van. The handcuffs jangled and cut into her wrists. How in the hell had it come to this? Jennifer always followed the rules. She never smoked pot or had unprotected sex. She never took shortcuts; she never had an overdue book from the library. Hell, she never even left dirty dishes in the sink. And he'd called her a convict. Well, Jennifer thought with a shock, she was a convict. For a moment the reality – the smell, the dirt, the ugliness – broke over her in a wave. What was she doing here?

The ride continued endlessly. Jennifer went from nauseated to sleepy to hungry and then back to nauseated again.

Through it all she was frightened. At last the driver made another sharp right turn, and as Jennifer held on as best she could, the brakes screeched and the van came to an abrupt stop. Jennifer peered out the window. The prison gates were opening, and slowly the van pulled into the yard.

This wasn't like any kind of country club that Jennifer had ever seen – and the crazy-looking woman who was squatting in the flower bed was no greenskeeper. Jennifer had no way of knowing her name at the time – nor could she have ever guessed it – but 'Springtime' was the first inmate to greet her with a smile. The old woman's birth name was long lost, as was her youth. Her dark, leathery skin was pulled so tight over her skull that her death-head's grin reminded Jennifer of the cheap skeleton masks all the kids in her old neighborhood used to wear on Halloween. That grin and those loony eyes were Jennifer's first spooky glimpse of prison life. As the van continued forward, the old woman pointed to the flower bed. Jennifer couldn't see what it was that she was pointing to until they were farther away. There, in a withered garden, bright orange marigolds and faded blue argretum spelled out *Welcome to Jennings*.

Beyond the flowers Jennifer saw the terrible glint of razor wire coiled across the top of the chain-link fence. Ten feet behind it was a twin fence, also topped with the same wire. The sight stopped Jennifer's breath for a moment. What was happening to her? It looked as if she were in a Kurt Russell movie. The van approached a high concrete-block wall with garage doors that slowly opened to let them in. The doors closed behind them, the engine was turned off, and they sat in total silence. A burning bile rose in Jennifer's throat and she swallowed hard. She was soaked with sweat. What were they doing? Nobody moved or said a word. Why were they just sitting there in the dark stench of this disgusting van? It was all so unnerving. She needed air – fresh air. 'Excuse me,' she said softly, 'but what happens now?'

'Jesus Christ!' the driver sneered. 'Are you really in such a hurry to get Inside?'

Before Jennifer could answer, an alarm sounded and, as if in response, overhead lights went on. The driver and guard got out of the van, slid open the doors, and reached in to pull her from her seat. Two prison officers had come from somewhere and stood on the tarmac. 'Right this way, Miss Spencer,' the shorter officer said.

'Welcome to Jennings,' the taller one said with a leer.

Jennifer lost her footing as she made the big step down from the prison van and she nearly fell onto the slippery concrete of the Jennings garage. She blinked her eyes against the harsh fluorescent lights and tried her best to regain her balance and maintain her composure. Dizzy, she teetered on her heels.

'Can you walk on your own?' the shorter of the two officers asked Jennifer with what sounded like real concern. Although they were dressed in identical uniforms, the two men couldn't have been more different in their demeanor. While the short one seemed calm and almost caring in his work, it was clear to Jen that the taller officer was wound tight as a spring and seemed ready to explode into violence at any moment. Good cop – bad cop, thought Jennifer. She was studying the faces of her captors when she felt the tall guard's grip tighten firmly on her arm. 'You were asked if you can walk,' he sneered into her face. 'What's your answer?'

Jennifer looked at him. Who was this guy? His nameplate read KARL BYRD, but he was no bird. He was a six foot, six inch, two hundred pound hyena. 'What's your answer?' he repeated. 'Can you walk on your own?' Jennifer only nodded in response, and the officers flanked her on either side and walked her toward the prison door.

Byrd reached up to his shoulder with his free hand and snarled, 'Open One Oh Nine,' into his shoulder-mounted radio. A buzzer sounded and he pushed the door. As Jennifer twisted in an attempt to see the good cop's name-plate, she noticed that he was locking a contraption on the wall that looked like a night depository at a bank.

'It's for our weapons,' he told her, answering her unasked question. 'No guns are allowed inside Jennings.' His name was Roger Camry. Jennifer decided that she liked Roger Camry. He wasn't some vengeful sadist. He was just a short civil servant with a job to do. For the first time since she left home, Jennifer smiled. Well, this was better. The hallway didn't stink and the officers were unarmed, and one of them was even kind of nice. Maybe this was a country club after all.

But then she stepped further inside. What *was* that smell? It wasn't clinical, nor was it sterile. Before Jennifer could take another sniff, the heavy door slammed behind her with a loud and resounding *clank* of metal against metal. It made her jump, and Byrd laughed. It sounded far too final.

Jennifer looked ahead down the long, empty hallway before her. She froze. Even with Byrd's menacing 'Let's go,' she literally could not take a step. The linoleum glinted an anemic lime green. The green mile. She told herself that she wasn't going to the electric chair, but her legs were actually trembling. She needed some air. She needed just a few more minutes. Her legs were shaking so badly she couldn't walk and she didn't want to let them see. 'So, uh,' she stammered, 'I see your names are Roger and Karl.' She tried to sound casual. 'I'm Jennifer Spencer,' she said, and extended her hand.

'We know who *you* are,' Byrd said with a snort that made him sound like a horse. 'Your face has been splashed across every newspaper and TV screen in the country.' But he didn't shake Jennifer's hand as if she were a celebrity. Instead, he grabbed her elbow and jerked her forward.

Jennifer hated it when people did that. It reminded her of being herded along by Sister Imogene John back in parochial school. Byrd's touch made Jennifer flinch, and that was enough to provoke him to tighten his grip even more. Her legs were still weak. She would have paid a thousand – no *ten* thousand – dollars for just a few moments of fresh air. But it wasn't going to happen. She was locked inside. There was no way out. She took a deep breath of what foul air there was, and she knew now what she smelled. It was despair.

The guard pulled her by her upper arm. 'Please don't shove me,' Jennifer said defiantly to Byrd. He said nothing in response, but continued to shove her just the same. 'We're not getting off to a good start here,' Jennifer said, stumbling once again on the highly polished floors.

'You better take off the heels,' the officer named Roger told her, not unkindly. 'Why don't you take them off and carry them? That will help. We don't want you to fall.'

Jennifer looked down at her Louboutins and then at the long hallway before her. She didn't want to go barefoot, but Byrd drew his face right up to Jennifer's, and she could smell the hot, unpleasant combination of tobacco, chewing gum, and ... With real venom he rephrased Roger's suggestion into an order and barked, 'Get rid of the shoes. Do you understand?' His breath withered Jennifer's anger. She took off the shoes, and then, with one in each hand and a guard on each elbow, she took her first steps into the prison. Maybe it was a defense mechanism, but at that moment, all Jennifer could think about was how much those shoes had cost.

The hall seemed endless. When at last they stopped in front of a closed door, Jennifer suddenly panicked. She actually didn't want the guards to let go of her arms. She was afraid that she might collapse in fear. The sign on the door read INMATE INTAKE. With false bravado she asked Officer Camry, 'Is there another door for *Inmate Exhaust?*'

'In here,' Byrd ordered as he opened the door. Jennifer walked ahead of them and into the room alone.

Inside, a counter cut the small, gray-green space in half. Behind the check-in counter was an open door, and in that doorway lounged a tall, attractive woman. She had the palest skin and the blackest hair that Jennifer had ever seen – a sort of jailhouse Morticia Addams. If she had had a better haircut, she would've been stunning. But even here, in that ugly jumpsuit and in the hideous fluorescent lighting, she was striking. She had the high cheekbones, the long straight nose, and the pale blue eyes of a better-looking Celtic hillbilly. Well, at least now Jennifer could begin the process of getting out of this place. Without hesitation, she strode up to the counter where the desk clerk stood and asked, 'Have I received any messages?'

'Have you *what!*' Morticia asked in amused disbelief.

'Have I received any messages?' Jennifer repeated. 'I'm expecting a call from my lawyer.'

'Oh my Lord,' the woman laughed, 'she's one of *those.*'

And both officers – even the nice one – laughed right along with Morticia. Jennifer cursed herself for her foolish gaffe. Her head was swimming. But she was so accustomed to hotel check-ins, where the faxes and messages were always waiting, that only now did she realize that the jumpsuit the woman was wearing was in fact a prison uniform – she was just another inmate. Jennifer felt her face color.

Officer Camry pulled out a key chain packed more densely than the A train at rush hour and unlocked a door on the wall next to the counter. 'Please step right through here and turn to your left,' Officer Camry said.

Jennifer obliged his courteous request, and found herself in a room with nothing in it but a chair that had a bright orange jumpsuit folded neatly on the seat. She took a step closer to the chair and heard the door slam behind her just as yet another door in the far wall burst open. Jennifer spun around to see that she was alone, then she spun again to see who was about to enter. In her dizzy state she lost her balance, almost fell to the floor, and watched as her expensive shoes slid across the polished surface and into the feet of a tall, severe woman dressed in a long white lab coat.

'You'll need to strip down,' the woman said firmly. 'It's time for your exam.' Her voice was deep – as deep as her waist was wide. She wasn't really fat, but any niceties like a waistline or hips – if she'd ever had them – were long gone. 'Get on your feet, strip, and fold your clothes,' the baritone in white instructed.

'Are you a doctor?' Jennifer asked without standing.

'I'm the intake officer,' came the reply, which Jen noted was not exactly an answer but, it seemed, was all she was going to get. The intake officer pointed to a sign that read, in both English and Spanish: REMOVE ALL CLOTHING,

JEWELRY, AND OTHER PERSONAL EFFECTS, INCLUDING
CONTRABAND. HANG YOUR CLOTHES ON THE PEGS OR
PLACE THEM IN THE PLASTIC BAG YOU'LL FIND UNDER
THE GOWN. WHEN YOUR FINISHED, RING THE BUZZER.

'Can you read?' she asked in her neutral tone.

Jennifer looked at her as if she were crazy. 'Yes, I can
read,' she shot back. 'I can read well enough to see the typo.'

'What typo?' the officer asked.

'The second *your*,' Jennifer told her.

'It's not mine,' the officer sighed.

'That's the point. The *your* isn't the personal possessive.
It should be the contraction,' Jennifer continued.

'Do you understand what the sign means?'

'Yes,' Jennifer admitted.

'Fine,' the officer said. 'Then forget the spelling and do
what you're told.' Then she turned and left Jennifer alone
in the room.

Jennifer read the sign again. It might as well have read,
'Abandon all hope, ye who enter here.' God. What could she
do? On the other side of the door she could hear the guards
laughing. This was no country club and so far she certainly
wasn't receiving the special treatment that Donald and Tom
had promised she would get. This all had to be some kind of
mistake. She must be in the wrong department. That must
be it. There was probably some other area, some VIP lounge
where decent people were waiting for her. She stood up,
gave the buzzer a push, then lifted the jumpsuit and plastic
bag off the chair and sat down to wait, mindlessly stroking
the nasty synthetic texture of the jumpsuit as if it were a
kitten she held on her lap.

The door was suddenly pulled open and Officer Camry
walked in. 'Do you have a problem, Miss Spencer?'

Jennifer smiled at him as if she were a debutante who had found herself at the wrong cotillion. 'Well,' she began, 'I don't think it's really a problem. I just realized there's probably been a mistake. I don't think I'm supposed to be here. Is there someone besides the . . . intake officer you could take me to speak with?'

Camry took a deep breath, then shook his head. 'Miss Spencer, you were told to follow the directions on this sign, and while you're here at Jennings, you will not be told anything twice.' God! Even the good cop was turning nasty on her. 'Do you understand that?' he asked. Before Jen could nod she heard Byrd yell.

'She need help pulling off her panties? I'm available for a strip search,' he said and laughed.

Jennifer shuddered, then stood up. She didn't want to lose the only friend she had in the place, but she tried one more time. 'Yes,' she told Camry as calmly as she could, 'I do understand. But do *you* understand what *I'm* saying? I'm not supposed to even *be* here. I'm supposed to be in some other wing, or department, or whatever it is you call it. You've brought me to the wrong place.'

For a moment Camry looked confused. 'And just where do you think you're supposed to be, Miss Spencer?' he asked.

Jennifer used her most intimate and ingratiating smile. 'You can call me Jennifer,' she said as pleasantly as she could. 'May I call you Roger?'

The officer gave her that same look and then said, 'Just follow the rules, Spencer. Put on the smock and let the intake officer get on with her job. You've already wasted too much time. Trust me, you don't want to keep the Warden waiting.'

33

The Warden! Of course. The Warden. That must be it, Jennifer thought. She just had to get through these formalities and then her white-glove treatment would begin. She smiled again at Officer Camry and said, 'Fine. If I could have some privacy, then.'

Camry nodded and turned to leave, but just as he reached for his keys, the door flew open again and the looming hulk of Officer Byrd strode in. 'What in the hell is going on in here?' he wanted to know. 'What is taking so long?' Jennifer quickly stood and both the jumpsuit and plastic bag fell to the floor.

'Pick that up and put it on,' Byrd shouted at her. 'And leave it unbuttoned.'

'Now wait just a minute!' Jennifer said. 'I think you'll find if you check with the Warden that my lawyer has called ahead, and he has made . . .' Jennifer stopped. She could hear more than a hint of hysteria rising in her voice and she didn't want to lose control.

'Check with the Warden? Ha! I'll let you do that. You think your lawyer called ahead and he made what?' Byrd asked. He was leering at Jennifer. 'Do you think you just checked into a friggin' hotel? Do you think you have special reservations? A room with a view? A table for two?'

'Sarcasm won't get us anywhere,' Jennifer said as calmly as she could.

'That's right,' Byrd agreed. 'You're not getting anywhere until you strip naked. And that is the end of this discussion.' He looked hard at Jennifer. And Jennifer looked right back.

'Fine,' she said. 'I'm not here to make trouble. I won't be here for long, anyway.'

Officer Camry chimed in, clearly trying to make peace.

'Please just follow the directions and ring the buzzer when you are finished.'

Jennifer looked around the room again. 'Do you have any hangers?'

Byrd laughed aloud. 'Use the pegs,' he said as he exited. 'And don't hurt yourself.'

Both Byrd and Camry left the room and Jennifer proceeded with the ridiculous drill. Right, she thought. Roger Camry was right. She was wasting valuable time. Tom would've made the necessary arrangements directly with the Warden. These low-level functionaries knew nothing. The sooner Jennifer got through this Intake stuff the sooner she'd be Exhausted. She took off her Armani suit and the matching silk blouse, wincing as she hung them on the pegs. When she had removed her slacks she hung them with the jacket, only to see both pieces fall onto the floor. She stooped, picked up the clothes, and tried again. And again. The peg gave way and the clothes fell in a heap. With a shiver, Jennifer realized that the pegs were not an April Fool's joke – they were designed to swivel under weight so that no one could hang herself from them.

Not likely, Jennifer thought with a toss of her head. She hung each piece of her outfit on its own peg, then put on the nasty orange jumpsuit. The fabric was harsh against her body – probably Tercel or Herculon or something worse. And it was enormous – probably a 'one size fits all' kind of thing. She didn't want to have to meet the Warden like this. There wasn't a mirror in the room, but Jennifer did the best she could. For years she had managed to make even the drabbest Catholic school uniform look a little stylish. She slipped the alligator belt from her slacks and cinched it around her waist. After just a few tucks and a little flouncing, Jennifer rang the buzzer. She kept the phone in her bra. She was ready to meet the warden.

When Camry returned, Morticia was with him. Jennifer couldn't help but notice that *her* jumpsuit fit as though it had been made to measure. And Morticia was giving Jennifer a good looking-over, too. They both stood there, glaring at each other as only two women who have come to the party wearing the same dress can. When Morticia caught sight of Jennifer's belt, she covered her mouth to stifle a laugh. 'You ready for your close-up, Miss DeMille?' she asked. Jennifer didn't say a word.

'Cut the crap, Cher,' Camry said firmly to the woman. 'Just bag her personal effects. And Miss Spencer,' he turned to Jennifer, 'please take off the belt. It's against regulations.'

'He's afraid you're going to hang yourself,' Morticia smirked, further betraying her hillbilly origins with her accent. 'Also the brassiere and underpants if you have them.'

'What?' Jennifer asked.

'I'll have to pat you down,' Morticia said. 'Then Ms Cranston's goin' to give you an internal.'

Jennifer groaned and did what Roger Camry told her to do, but as she removed the belt she noticed that Morticia had picked up her shoes and was stroking one of them as if it were the Holy Grail. Jennifer guessed that she'd probably never seen a Louboutin before in her poor trash life. Then she turned her back and tried to carefully remove her bra without dropping the cell phone. Just as she was about to secret the phone into the sleeve of her jumpsuit she felt someone standing beside her.

'What is this?' Morticia asked as she grabbed the phone and held it up in the air for the officer to see.

'Where'd you get that?' Camry asked. 'That's what contraband is, Spencer, and it can get you into big trouble here at Jennings. Lucky for you it was found now and not later.' He tilted his head toward the personal effects bag and Morticia went over and slid the phone into the bag.

The white-coated intake officer returned and asked, 'Are we about ready to get on with this?'

'Miss Spencer is ready,' Officer Camry said, and he took hold of Jennifer's elbow. As he steered her toward the door, Jennifer saw that Cher was slipping one of the shoes onto her foot.

'Hey!' Jennifer protested. But Cher quickly pulled the shoe off and put it back on the counter before anyone could catch her.

Camry turned to look at Cher. She met his glare with the blandest look on her face. 'Get busy with that, Cher,' he said. 'Catalogue every piece of clothing and put it all away.'

'Where is she taking my things?' Jennifer asked, but she didn't get an answer from either Camry or the intake officer. Jennifer looked down at the jumpsuit she was wearing. Well, if that Cher person stole her clothes, she'd just have to ask Tom to bring something else for her to wear when he came tomorrow to take her home. She could trust Tom to select something appropriate. He had great taste in clothes and sometimes looked better in his Prada suits than Jennifer did in hers!

'All right then, let's get started,' the intake officer said in the deep voice that gave Jennifer chills.

The rest of the processing was like some kind of surreal out-of-body experience. It was almost as if Jennifer wasn't there. She became just another woman in a prison uniform, and this disassociation actually made it all a little easier to take. She was weighed, measured, and photographed. When the officer fingerprinted her she calmly watched as her fingers were rolled in the ink and then onto the paper. As her prints were being made, Jennifer asked, 'Do you have any suggestions on how to get this ink off your fingers? It's almost impossible to wash it off with just plain soap and water.'

'Well, Spencer,' the officer opined, 'maybe you might try Estée Lauder's Youth Dew.'

The sarcasm wasn't pointed or funny enough for Jennifer to laugh, but she did respond. 'I just thought that, since you worked with the stuff all the time, you might know. I'll make a note to tell our clients at Chesebrough-Ponds to develop some sort of cleansing cream for finger-print ink.'

The intake officer threw back her head and roared with laughter. 'Yeah,' she chortled, 'you can call it *Out Damn Spot!* Now get up on the table.'

Reluctantly Jennifer climbed onto the stainless steel bench. As soon as this monster was done poking and prod-ding, she would call Tom. He was probably already well on his way to getting her out of this place. Jennifer knew that everything was going to be all right. And then the officer told her to stand up.

'Bend over and open your jumpsuit,' she said matter-of-factly. She picked up a thin latex rubber glove and began to slowly and deliberately pull it over her hand. When she snapped it against her wrist, the sound sent a shiver down Jennifer's spine. 'Cavity check,' the intake officer said, and Jennifer felt her stomach start to rise.

'Why?' Jennifer whispered. This was too much. She

certainly didn't have a prostate to examine. 'Why do I need a cavity check?' she demanded more loudly. 'I'm not in here for drugs or on a weapons charge.'

'C'mon,' the officer sighed, 'it'll be over before you know it. It's a lot worse when we have to hold you down.'

4

Movita Watson

Rich women have the Betty Ford clinic; poor women have prison.

A prison commentator. Kathryn Watterson, *Women in Prison*

I declared that until I said different, this candy – a name on the Inside for a new inmate – would be known to *my* crew as *Number 71036*. 'She's just another piece of snotty white meat,' I told 'em. 'It's not like we all have to sit up and take notice just because she dragged her sorry ass into this joint. She don't mean nothin' to us.' I'm queen bee at Jennings. And while I know that might not mean much on the Outside, when you're on the Inside it's important to stay on top. Nobody wants to be on the bottom. Not the bottom bunk, not the bottom of the crew, not the bottom of *nothing* in a prison. I've always been on top, and I plan on staying there.

Cher's the funniest, smartest, and baddest in our sisterhood, and she said to me, 'Well let me tell you, that Number 71036's sorry ass was dressed in the best damn silk underwear I've ever seen.'

My crew was sitting at our usual table in the cafeteria eating lunch. Dinner is always at one of our houses but lunch is quick and gotta be in from food service. When you first see us, you might think we're kind of an unlikely group. I'm a proud and beautiful black woman, but all the rest of the women in my crew are white. Unlike men in prison, where black and white rarely mix, women inmates tend to group up based on whether or not they like each other, and what they can do to help each other out. My women make up the most organized, efficient and tight-knit crew in the joint. We're a family.

Like I said, I'm the boss. As the Warden's secretary, I hold a position of power (and opportunity) at Jennings that few, if any, can challenge. Cher McInnery works Intake, and that means that all sorts of nice things flow like a river over the desk in that room where the new inmates strip and leave all their possessions behind. Some of that river of riches, maybe just a small stream, gets diverted in Cher's direction – and some of that gets passed on to my crew.

Right now Cher had an advantage over the others in the crew. She was the only other of us who had actually *seen* Jennifer Spencer. Even though I insisted that she was 'no big fuckin' deal' to me, we had all heard and read plenty about Number 71036 in the news – the fall of 'the Wall Street Princess' – and we were all anxious to talk about her.

You see, inside a prison nothing ever changes. That's probably the worst damn thing about living Inside. Everyone's in the same uniform, Christmas looks just like the Fourth of July, the windows are too high to see out of, and the exercise yard doesn't have a blade of grass that hasn't been examined by four hundred pairs of eyes. There just isn't much to look at except the walls and each other, and women, we like to look at things. I read once in one of the Warden's magazines that the experts call it 'sensory deprivation'. I call it goddamn hard.

'What was she wearing?' Theresa LaBianco wanted to know. She's into 'How was her hair styled? Does she know how to put on makeup?' Theresa used to be at the very top of one of those big makeup sales pyramids. Had a couple of hundred housewives sellin' mascara. I could just imagine what the kites – secreted notes – would say about this new candy.

Theresa worked in the canteen and could always manage to buy us the freshest produce or the best chicken when we got to shop. It wasn't until her husband was caught cooking the books that she found herself on the Inside at Jennings. But Theresa never lost her love for life or blusher. And the bitch could dish. She especially loved to hear Cher talk about all of the new inmates. 'It's kinda like window shopping,' she would say.

'Well,' Cher began, because she knew what was expected of her, 'her shoes were the softest damn leather I ever felt.' Cher shook her head. 'Shoes like that must go for four hundred bucks if they go for a dime.'

'Well, you know what they say about shoes, don't you?' Theresa asked. 'They say, you can't know someone's sorrows until you've walked a mile in her shoes. That's what they say about shoes.' Theresa had a damn saying for everything. She lived by sayings. She said that was how she had motivated her sales force, but they drove me nuts.

'Well, I don't think 71036 has ever had too many problems walking in those shoes,' Cher sneered. 'And I plan to walk more than a mile in 'em,' she told us and laughed.

'Did you take 'em, Cher?' Suki asked, all wide-eyed. Suki Conrad was our crew's innocent – our baby. She worked in the laundry and in Suki's case it wasn't so much what she could do for the rest of us, but what we could do for Suki. I think Suki made us all better women.

'Damn right I took 'em,' Cher said proudly. 'When I saw that those shoes were a size eight, I took that for a sign.' Cher lived by signs and omens like Theresa lived by sayings. 'My parole date is comin' up, and I figure those pointy shoes were pointing directly to my getting outta here.'

'Girl,' I said with a sigh, 'you can't just keep stealin'. You're gonna get caught, lose your chance at parole and damn it, it's wrong.'

'You know what they say about stealing, don't you?' Theresa chimed in. 'They say that God helps those that help themselves. That's what they say about stealing.'

I was never sure with Theresa if she meant to support me or sass me when she said somethin' like that.

'That's not what God meant,' Suki protested. 'God said, "Thou shalt *not* steal."'

'NBD – No Big Deal – I haven't stolen from God since I used to swipe money out of the collection plate at Sunday school,' Cher laughed. 'And I never take nothin' from people who can't spare it. Won't steal from the simple minded, neither,' she added.

Cher was a thief and she didn't mind saying so. She didn't see anything wrong with what she did. What was wrong to Cher was that everyone else had more than she did, and the only way to make up the difference was for her to take what she needed. That's what she'd done to get herself incarcerated and what she did every time a new inmate was processed into Jennings. She just put the things she didn't want into a bag with the new inmate's name and number on it, and she put the good stuff into another bag with a different name and number. No one would ever reclaim the second bag, because the name and number on *that* bag belonged to a dead or released inmate. Cher had perfected the system, and now had plenty of bags hidden right out in plain sight.

'What was she wearing?' Theresa wanted to know.

'Armani!' Cher giggled. 'I've never managed to steal Armani before. It's so damned expensive that the stores usually have it wired to the rack.'

'Well, I don't think 71036 ever had to steal anything,' Suki said. 'It said in the papers that she's really rich.'

'Yeah. And greedy, too. She got busted for stealing that money on Wall Street,' Cher shot back. 'That makes her a thief just like me.'

'But did you see her on the TV news?' Suki asked. 'She looks just like a movie star.'

'Well, you know what they say about pictures, don't you?' Theresa began.

'Yeah, we all know what they say about pictures, Theresa,' I said in exasperation. 'You all act like we never had us a celebrity prisoner before. What about Jackie James, the sick little twist from Montgomery who killed her two babies on a tourist trip to New York, said they'd been kidnapped by a black brotha'? That was in all the papers.'

'Nobody likes baby killers,' Cher said.

'Or baby rapers,' Theresa added. 'Whatever happened to that teacher, Camille Lazzaro, who decided to teach one of her boy students more than geography? Didn't she just give a whole new meaning to the term "teacher's pet"? She had the baby and the daddy wasn't even thirteen years old yet.'

'Or that Carole Waters over in Unit Three?' Cher added. 'She got her boyfriend to murder both her husband *and* her mother-in-law just for the insurance and the inheritance. She was in all the papers, too.'

'I steer clear of anyone who kills for money.' Theresa shook her head. 'It's one thing if you catch your man screwin' your sister or your daughter. I say shoot 'em. But to kill someone just for money, that's cold.'

'That reminds me,' Cher said, laughing, 'any of you heard that Dixie Chicks song on the radio called "Goodbye Earl"? It reminded me of you, Movita.'

As soon as Cher said that, it got real quiet. 'We ain't gonna talk about Earl,' I said – and I meant it. Cher didn't say another word. She didn't dare to. It's an unspoken but well enforced rule that you don't never talk about anyone's life on the Outside. You specially don't never mention no one's family or her man unless you're invited to.

Most of the women on the Inside are here, one way or another, because of a man. Either she got involved in one of his illegal schemes, or he beat her until one day she fought back and killed him. It's safe to say that most of the women in Jennings wouldn't be here at all if they hadn't been hooked up with low-life no-goods like my Earl. Men are a weakness, like drinking or drugs. I know I was weak willed with my Earl, and fact is I don't like to be reminded of it.

Suki was the first one to speak up again after the silence. 'You think this Jennifer Spencer got in trouble because of her boyfriend, too?' she asked.

'I wouldn't be surprised,' I said. 'I know about book-keeping, and it doesn't matter if it's a dental office in Kew Gardens or investment banking on Wall Street. It all comes down to shifting the books and what you're allowed to get away with. Men still make the rules about that and they probably always will.'

'Well, 71036 seems to be pretty comfortable around men,' Cher said. 'You shoulda seen her flirtin' with dumb ol' Roger Camry. He was all "Miss Spencer" this and "Miss Spencer" that. It was enough to make ya' sick.'

'What about Byrd?' I asked her. 'Was that prick hittin' on her?'

'Not yet,' Cher said with a smirk. 'He'll get her eventually, but right now it looked like he was gonna let Roger have first crack at her.'

As soon as Cher said that, Suki stood up, took her tray from the table, all angry like, and said, 'I'm not gonna sit here and listen to this dirty talk. I gotta get back to the laundry.' She took her tray to the dirty dish window and left.

'Well, what's wrong with that one?' Cher asked, not that she really wanted to know.

'Maybe she's having her time of the month,' I answered, though I was afraid I knew the answer and it wasn't that.

'Well, you know what they say about women living together in prison and their periods, don't you?' asked Theresa.

'Theresa, if we all got our periods at the very same time,' I laughed, 'this ol' building would vibrate so hard from the tension that the cement blocks would all collapse and we'd be able to just walk on outta here.'

Just then old Springtime, who tends the flower gardens, was passing the table and overheard what I said. 'Is someone planning a breakout?' she asked, her voice hushed but all excited.

'Nah, old sista',' I told her gently. She's tried to escape

fifty or sixty times by now. 'We're just waiting for the place to fall down on its own so you can hop your withered old ass right over the pile of rubble and get out.' I smiled at her and she grinned back.

The whole room looked our way as old Springtime's cackle echoed off the steel and cinder blocks.

5

Gwen Harding

*Some people think that law enforcement officers are
inhumane or uninteresting. Personally, if I became
personally involved with every person sitting there
crying, I couldn't function in my job. I'm not inhumane
– I'm just removed from the emotion.*

Georgia Walton, deputy sheriff at Sybil Brand Institute.
Kathryn Watterson, *Women in Prison*

'Good morning, sir,' the new inmate began briskly as she
was ushered into the Warden's office by Officers Camry
and Byrd.

Gwen Harding didn't get many chances to laugh during
an Intake meeting, but the dumbstruck look on Jennifer
Spencer's face when she got her first look at 'sir' was almost
comical. Like so many other women, Spencer obviously
assumed that Warden Harding would be a man with whom
she might flirt. The girl was clearly more than just a little
rattled by her discovery.

Spencer was thin, taller than average, with big dark eyes
and lots of dark hair. Staring at the Warden, those eyes
went from registering surprise to embarrassment, and then
quickly to something closer to ... *manipulation*. Oh yes,
Gwen Harding thought, this girl was capable of causing

trouble. 'Too smart for her own good' was the phrase that Gwen's father would've used to describe Jennifer Spencer. 'Take a seat,' Gwen told her and pointed to the chair that sat directly in front of her desk.

There were two chairs for visitors in the Warden's office. The one beside the desk was rarely offered to inmates or even coworkers. The other chair – which was known as the 'hot seat' – was the chair intended for Jennifer's butt. But Miss Spencer seemed to be past any discomfiture, and, ignoring the 'hot seat', she slipped quite easily into the chair beside Gwen's desk. Officer Camry moved to stop her, but the Warden shook her head. She'd see how this all played out. 'You may go,' she told the officers, and they turned and left, closing the door behind them.

Gwen looked the girl over. There was no doubt that she was going to be a problem. Deciding where to put these high-profile types was always a tough call. She had to get it right the first time, because there was no good way of changing it later. Gwen thought she was a pretty good judge of character, however, and while Spencer might be high profile, Gwen didn't think she'd end up being high maintenance. Number 71036 was too proud for that.

'I trust that your trip here and your processing at Intake was not too difficult,' Gwen began. Gwen realized as she said it that it had been *very* difficult for this young woman. She could tell at a glance that Jennifer Spencer never expected to be stuck in a prison. Jennifer Spencer would've been far more comfortable heading up the JRU meeting than coping with what she was about to experience at Jennings.

'Miss Spencer,' the Warden continued as she opened her desk drawer and took out the inmate manual. 'You'll find this booklet to be indispensable during your stay here.' She handed the bright yellow pamphlet to Jennifer, who took it, set it on her lap, and folded both hands on top of it.

'Thank you,' Jennifer said. 'I –'

'You must read it completely later, but now I'd like you to turn to page three. It's headed *Inmate Responsibilities*.'

As instructed, Inmate 71036 opened the book, but only glanced at the page before she began to speak. 'It's important –'

'It's important that we read this page together,' Gwen interrupted. 'I want to touch on a few items listed here.' The Warden began to read: 'You are responsible for your behavior, actions, and attitude.' Gwen saw the girl shift in her seat.

'Warden Harding,' Jennifer said. 'May I speak frankly?'

'Please do,' Gwen said dryly, waiting for the inevitable. Often Gwen found that if she let a new inmate ramble on long enough, she would catch some pertinent detail, some insight into her personality that would enlighten Gwen on how she might help the woman to help herself. Gwen believed in rehabilitation, not punishment. But she could almost bet that Jennifer Spencer was going to put this belief to the test.

'I guess you've probably already heard from Attorney Howard McBane of Swithmore, McBane, or from Thomas Branston at Hudson, Van Schaank & Michaels,' Jennifer began. 'Or maybe Mr Michaels himself called.' Before Gwen had a chance to respond, Jennifer crossed her legs, leaned in toward Gwen, and continued. 'This situation has gotten a little out of control, I'm afraid. I wasn't meant to come here at all, and I certainly should not have had a rectal or pelvic exam. When I speak with my attorney I'm going to have to mention it and see if legal action should be taken.'

'Legal action?' Gwen asked. She was getting more than just annoyed with this woman.

'Yes,' Jennifer said flatly, 'I am neither a drug offender nor a smuggler. The invasive examination wasn't needed. And your intake officer didn't seem to have any medical education.' She took a deep breath, and Gwen saw that, in spite of her bravado, the girl was trembling. Gwen felt a stab of pity for the girl as she watched her toss her head back and continue. 'Anyway, I'd like to talk about Attorney Branston's arrangements for my special needs while my appeal is being heard.'

'Special needs?' Gwen echoed.

'Did he tell you that I would like a sunny room? And I can't have a roommate because I'll be keeping late hours. If desks and laptops are not standard issue then I'll need to get one of each.'

Gwen merely blinked.

'Also, I'll need access to a copier and hopefully some secretarial help. I don't know if you have a trained staff, but I'd be more than willing to pay for someone to come in.'

Gwendolyn Harding sat in a state of stunned disbelief as 71036 enumerated her expectations of 'white-glove treatment' and 'special considerations'. This wasn't the standard protestation of innocence, but rather a list of demands from the kind of young woman who was used to giving orders – and having them carried out. Not even when women like Margaret Rafferty – someone from a very high social position – were taken in had Gwen run into this lack of reality and misguided arrogance. Did Spencer really think Jennings would revolve around *her*? Who had led her to think such a thing? Her boss? Her success on Wall Street? Spencer's file indicated that she was clearly not from the kind of social background that would justify such an astonishing sense of self-importance.

Gwen took a deep breath. Whatever the reason for it, this was not an attitude that would allow Spencer to survive within the prison population. And it certainly was not endearing her to Gwen, either. The longer Gwen listened, the tighter the muscles cramped in her neck, jaw, and throat. All of her life she had fought a debilitating stammer when confronted with ignorance and pride. Years of speech therapy had taught her to modulate her breathing, focus her thoughts, and to speak in a rhythmic pattern that allowed no time for a stutter. She had managed to control it throughout the horrible JRU meeting, but now she felt that the stammer would return and it angered her. When she was certain that she had mastered her own emotions, Gwen placed her hands on her desk and leaned her face close to 71036. 'Your opinion to the contrary, Miss Spencer, you are not – in charge – here.'

The rhythm of the statement echoed 'On your mark – get set – go.' But the intention was not to start a race, but to stop Jennifer Spencer dead in her tracks. It worked. Spencer shut up and paled. This result pleased Gwen, and consequently she felt the spasm of anger release its grip from her throat. She would not be intimidated by this young woman, nor would she let her forget why they were both here. Jennifer Spencer *needed* Gwendolyn Harding's help.

'*You* are here – to get – help,' Gwen told her, continuing with the steady rhythm of *pa-dum, pa-dum, pa-dum*. 'I am here – to help – you.' With her anger under control, Gwen took a cleansing breath and continued in a more relaxed tone. 'You will not be given an office or a laptop, nor will you – be assigned – a desk. Or a secretary. You will work on prison work for which you will be paid. Every woman – at Jennings – works. There are no – special favors – here. Have I made – myself – clear?'

The *pa-dum, pa-dum, pa-dum* achieved the desired effect. The new inmate dumbly opened and closed her mouth a few times – kind of like a guppy – uncrossed her legs, and nodded her head with a robotlike rhythm that matched the cadence of Gwen's speech.

Fine, Gwen thought. She looked closely at Spencer's face. She had originally thought of assigning this new inmate to the library, but now she could see that Jennifer Spencer was going to need something very different than the cool and gentle hand of librarian Margaret Rafferty. This girl needed to learn values, cooperation, and probably some humility if she was going to survive incarceration.

The warden relaxed a bit, rose from her chair, sat on the edge of her desk, and continued. Jennifer in turn adjusted her attitude and sat and listened as if she were attending a lesson in the Baltimore catechism.

'First, you have to be passed through Observation for a night,' the Warden told Jennifer. This was SOP – Standard Operating Procedure. It probably wasn't needed in Spencer's case, but it was just possible that under that bravado, she was suicidal or drugged. Gwen knew Spencer wouldn't tolerate Observation well. It was an extremely dehumanizing but necessary evil. However, the real question was, after she was finished with that, where would inmate 71036 fit in?

'Miss Spencer – I assume – that you know that here – at Jennings – we all work. In addition – to the jobs – such as maintenance – there is work – to be done – in the shops.' Gwen stopped and waited to see if any of this was sinking in. She saw the girl nod.

'The pay is next to nothing. You work to help defray your cost to the taxpayer.'

'Yes,' Jennifer said calmly, 'I know. I'm in a very high tax bracket myself.'

Gwendolyn looked to see if there was any attitude or irony in the comment. It was then that she knew exactly where Jennifer Spencer needed to work. 'You will start in the laundry – for now,' the Warden told her. 'I believe that will be for the best. In due time, you may be promoted,' she added with a smile of encouragement. And then, with a deep and meaningful intake of air, Warden Gwendolyn Harding prepared for her big finale. It was a speech she had given often, to each and every new inmate that she welcomed to Jennings.

While she recited the words, she was simultaneously deciding where to put Spencer after Observation. She concluded that she must go right into the middle of Movita Watson's crew. With a good teacher like Movita, Spencer would eventually settle in and learn how to take care of herself. Gwen knew that Movita was fascinated with Jennifer Spencer. She had seen her take the papers and magazines from the library cart that was available to the inmates and read every article that was written about her.

The Warden paused for a moment, then continued both speaking and thinking. There was structure in Movita's crew. She was a good leader with an eye for talent. Of course, no one in that group had ever known the kind of wealth and privilege that Spencer knew, and if that girl looked down her nose at Movita like she had with Gwen –

well, she was likely to have that nose put out of joint. She studied Spencer's face intently. Movita would either take Spencer in – or Movita would take her out. Only time would tell. If she did take her in it would take time.

The Warden's speech was at an end, and she told Jennifer that their meeting was over. She called for Camry and Byrd to take her away to Observation.

Later, all alone in her office, Gwen couldn't help but feel disappointed with the turn of events that day. Jennifer Spencer had actually shaken her self-confidence. Or maybe it was the JRU people who had done that. Why had they all rattled her so? Gwen had seen both Spencer and the women from JRU scrutinizing every inch of her person and her clothing. They all looked like those haughty store clerks at Saks. Except with Jennifer Spencer it was even worse. She walked into Gwen's office like she was coming in for the quarterly earnings report. Gwen didn't know who made her feel the most insignificant, Spencer or Baldy from JRU.

Gwen had kept a daily journal from the first day she began at Jennings. She kept it carefully locked in the bottom left drawer of her desk – where she also kept a bottle of gin, a glass, and a jar of olives.

Most often by the time Gwen finished her journal entry for the day it was deep into the evening. She'd write and sip, sip and read. Night after night she told herself that she found both solace and inspiration in recording her thoughts and observations, but in her heart she knew that it was really the gin that kept her at the office a little later each evening. The gin and the emptiness of her house. So far, she had sternly refused to drink at home. But with her mother dead, her beloved Yorkie gone almost two years, and her husband gone for far longer than that, there was little reason for Gwendolyn Harding to rush home at night.

6

Jennifer Spencer

A cat pent up becomes a lion.

Italian proverb

When Jennifer was escorted out of the Warden's office – sandwiched between the two guards – she was flooded with a feeling of such terror that she had to sink the nails of her fingers deep into her own palms just to keep from screaming or running.

But there was nowhere to run to. Jennifer Spencer couldn't believe that she was actually being incarcerated at the Jennings Correctional Facility for Women. People like Jennifer Spencer didn't go to prison. So she'd been told by Donald and Tom and so she'd believed.

There had been only one person who had warned her not to participate in the deal with Donald Michaels. That was Leonard Benson. He was the financial officer involved, and had always seemed less than enthusiastic about the plan. As the assistant to George Gross, the CFO – Chief Financial

Officer – Lenny was privy to a lot, but not all, of the machinations at Hudson, Van Schaank & Michaels. 'Don't do this, Jennifer,' he had pleaded to her. 'When you play with the SEC, you play for keeps.'

But Jennifer was not only under the influence of too many drinks that particular night; she was also drunk on the praise and the promises that Donald had been lavishing on her. She had turned on Lenny and demanded, 'Hasn't Donald Michaels made *you* rich, too?'

'Yes,' Lenny admitted, 'but . . .'

'He took me straight from school when I had nothing – nothing but loans to pay off, and now – well, you know my net worth.'

Lenny had nodded. He prepared Jennifer's taxes and helped her keep as much of her income as the law would allow. He certainly knew how much she was worth. 'But you earned all of that,' he insisted. 'You worked hard for Don. There's no reason now to take this kind of risk.'

'But it's such a small risk,' Jennifer retorted. 'And it will save Donald. I owe him something.' She grew adamant. 'He's made you rich, Lenny. Aren't *you* grateful?'

'I work my guts out for that guy,' Lenny had protested. 'I'm available twenty-four-seven. And I *am* grateful. But that doesn't mean that I'd take the rap for him.'

'Hey, that's the point,' Jennifer had explained, as if Lenny was stupid, deaf, or not even present. 'There *is* no rap. Donald doesn't do anything that the boys at Salomon Smith Barney or Morgan Stanley or Lazard Frere don't do every day of the week.' She, who had never worked at any of those places, was only parroting back what she'd heard. 'They're envious.'

'You don't know *what* Donald has done,' Lenny had shot

back. 'Nor do I. None of us do. That guy is the most com-
partmentalized person I've ever met. He doesn't even let his
left hand know what the right one is up to.'

Jennifer put her hand on Lenny's narrow shoulder.
'Thanks for trying to look out for me,' she said. 'But you
forget that I *like* taking risks. No guts – no glory.'

The grip on Jennifer's left arm grew tighter and she was
snapped out of her reverie. Now every step she took away
from the Warden's office put Jennifer deeper into the hideous nightmare of the Jennings Correctional Facility. As she
was marched off to Observation – whatever the hell that was
– she felt that if she didn't get some fresh air to clear her
head and her lungs she might actually fall to the floor. The
meeting with the Warden had been catastrophic. How had
it gone so wrong? Was it her fault? Hadn't Warden Harding
been contacted? If not, why not? Donald Michaels was
powerful enough to get the governor on the phone in a
heartbeat at any time of the day or night. She knew that.
Why hadn't he reached the Warden? The answer had to be
because he didn't want to. So whom had he reached *instead*?
Perhaps, just this once, Donald had made a mistake and
aimed too high. If he started with the governor, or even the
State Attorney General's Office, how long might it take for
the trickle-down effect to take effect?

'This way,' Officer Camry instructed. Jennifer thought
she saw a look of pity on his bland, round face. The idea that
this thirty-eight-thousand-dollar-a-year civil servant with
the thinning brown hair, the flat brown eyes, and the plain
brown uniform – the *idea* that this pathetic excuse for a man
whose IQ probably wasn't one hundred and one in the shade
had reason to pity *her* made her feel both furious and
pitiable. She wondered whether Roger's life at home was any

better than his life in prison. Who would choose to do a job like this? You had to be nuts, stupid, or very, very limited. She glanced at Roger Camry out of the corner of her eye. He looked like he was probably all three. Officer Byrd, on the other hand, wasn't even *that* qualified. But he obviously received another kind of compensation – women to frighten or even hurt.

Jennifer tried to keep her head as they passed from the administration wing into the prison itself. It all looked oddly familiar, and Jennifer was reminded of how she felt whenever she saw a famous landmark. There's no surprise when you finally see the Eiffel Tower – it looks just like all the pictures. The same was true for Big Ben and the Statue of Liberty. But, despite the familiarity, the same was not true with prison. Sure, it looked just like every jail photo and movie she'd ever seen. But the enormous surprise was the horror that she felt at being here herself. Jen couldn't control the shakes in her hands, so she clenched her fists again. It won't be for long, she reminded herself. What had Tom said? A day. Two at the most. Not long.

The three of them – Jennifer, Roger, and Byrd – walked through one more set of doors, buzzed in this time by an observer in a glass booth, and entered the Observation Wing – at least that's what it said in chipped gray paint over the door.

Jennifer suddenly realized just how tired she was. She would've been grateful to lie down somewhere – anywhere – in the dark and just sleep. If she couldn't have fresh air, then at least give her unconsciousness. But the place she entered almost took her breath away. The room was a kind of office/reception area. It was hard to tell if the stench was more urine than ammonia, but the underscents of vomit and sweat were still strong. For a moment Jennifer thought again of Donald Michaels – this time of his penchant for his costly, custom-blended Floris aftershave and soaps – each bar close to a hundred dollars. She wondered bitterly if one of Donald's scented Floris candles would cover *this* odor.

All right, she told herself. Someday next week, she and Tom and Donald would laugh at this story. She imagined them at Fraunces Tavern or Delmonico's. Donald would laugh and shake his leonine head and wipe the corner of his eyes the way he always did and order another bottle of Veuve Clicquot.

But that would be later. Now she was steeped in this squalor and the noise would not let her mind wander. The sound of another correctional officer's heavy steps, the gruesome static and squawking of his and Camry's and Byrd's walkie-talkies, and the harsh grinding of the gates as they closed behind her chilled her more than she wanted to admit. But the noise and stench weren't the worst things. The light was so harsh it was merciless. Exhausted as she was, if she closed her eyes she could still feel the fluorescence burning through her eyelids. Sleep in this room would be impossible.

There was a lot of paperwork in triplicate and some ribald talk between Byrd and the new officer, a huge black woman. Then she was taken, at last, to Observation.

'Spencer, here,' the huge female officer told the big uniformed woman in a booth at the end of a long catwalk.

'Fourteen,' was all she said in response.

The fat woman nodded. 'How's the other freshman adjusting?' she asked.

'Just about how you'd expect a withdrawing crack whore to adjust,' the woman in the booth snapped. 'But she'll be fine in another thirty hours or so.' The woman officer motioned with her head, took Jennifer by her orange-plastic-coated shoulder, and turned her to the left into one of the cubicles.

'Let's go,' he said.

The space was one of perhaps a dozen concrete cabinets. Jesus, she thought, wasn't Hannibal Lecter confined to something like this? It was achingly bare. A blanket, a mattress, and a commode. Not that she could use the latter, since the entire outside wall of the cell was made of thick Plexiglas and she could be seen, not just from there but also from overhead. There was no ceiling to the cubicle, and as she looked up she could see an officer patrolling along the catwalk that allowed him to look down into each cell.

'Wait!' Jennifer said, and it wasn't a ploy or a power trip; she was truly terrified to be left here. 'Can I please make a phone call?'

The big woman officer laughed out loud, a guttural *haw-haw*. 'Look, this is jail, girl, and you don't have a quarter. You're in prison now,' she said. Then she softened. 'Observation is tough, but it's usually only for a day,' she added almost apologetically to Jennifer. 'After you get out of Observation you can make collect calls from your unit.'

She had barely finished speaking, when someone – or some*thing* – began to screech in a subhuman wail. It was a noise of pure rage and despair. 'I'm sorry about the noise,' the officer said. 'She's going off. But you won't be here long. Maybe twenty-four hours. So try to make the best of it.'

'Oh my God!' Jennifer wailed, then fought and won control of herself. The officer handed her a black booklet to go with the yellow one she still clutched under her arm. 'Maybe this will help,' she said, and Jennifer took it, imagining it must be some religious tract. Only a saint, a sadist, or a cult member would voluntarily work here with this stink and noise. She stepped into the cell. 'You'll get used to it,' the big woman said, and for some reason that was the thing that filled Jennifer's eyes to almost overflowing. She turned her head away. God, she certainly hoped not!

She looked over at the stained mattress and paper sheets. It was only last night – in her own home – that she'd slept in a bed made with Pratesi sheets.

Jen crouched down in the corner of the observation cell and closed her eyes. The light still beat on her eyelids but she tried to transcend to another consciousness. She could stand anything for twenty-four hours, she told herself. She thought of the nights of endless study at college and business school. She'd pulled plenty of all-nighters at Hudson, Van Schaank & Michaels, too, when she was more tired than this. So she'd pull one more now. Maybe her last. All she had to do was concentrate. But on what? Concentrating on her situation was unbearable, and without her cell phone, she couldn't check on deals, her portfolio, or her apartment. Then she thought of it: She'd spend the night concentrating on her closet and every garment in it.

Jennifer didn't have a lot of clothes; when the interior designer had discussed the bedroom Jennifer insisted that she didn't want a built-in closet, just the antique armoire. 'But it's only twenty-seven inches of hanger space,' he'd protested. She'd shrugged.

Now she sat in the corner like a child ordered to take a time out. She remembered what she'd said: 'Twenty-seven inches ought to be more than enough for any woman.' And it was. She'd always longed not for quantity but quality. Now she had it, hanging in her armoire back at home. Aside from the one she had foolishly worn today and doubted she'd ever see again, she had three other Armani suits – one black twill, one black and brown tweed and one dark brown heavy silk. Each one had been well over two thousand dollars, but she'd bought them as an investment, and every time she slipped into one she felt like a million bucks. Next she thought of the two Yamaguchi suits that made the Armanis seem cheap in comparison. She'd considered one for more than a month before she'd bought it, hoping it wouldn't be sold. That was the black one with an asymmetrical jacket; a lapel and a hem were higher on one side than the other. Jennifer couldn't wear it for a meeting that included middle managers or conservative CEOs, but it went over big with high-tech and advertising types. The other, even more costly Yamaguchi was in a neutral gray-beige miracle fiber that she could fold into her purse if she had to and it would unpack as if it had been pressed by Sister Mary Margaret herself.

Jennifer sighed. Thinking was difficult sitting on the cold concrete floor. She began a mental inventory of her drawers. When she was home she wore cashmere sweats that she'd bought at TSE. They'd been very expensive, but nothing was softer against the skin – except perhaps silk. She had a tall lingerie chest, and when she wanted to spend money foolishly she indulged herself in La Perla lace bras and matching underpants or silk wisps from any one of a dozen French and Italian stores on Madison Avenue. She moved her fingers against the tough fabric of her jumpsuit and almost shuddered. Her underwear made her feel special and secretly feminine, and she thought Tom, her fiancé, enjoyed wondering what she was wearing under the sophisticated suit when he saw her at work. Like any good girl,

Jennifer washed her panties out by hand at night – she never threw them in the machine on the delicate cycle because they were too fine for that kind of treatment.

Jen's knees and ankles and butt hurt, but she wouldn't lie on that disgusting mattress, she wouldn't use the cardboard blanket. She wouldn't eat and she wouldn't sleep. Not until she got out of this place. If there was one thing Jennifer Spencer knew about herself it was that she had a strong will. She thought back to the Cooper Corp. deal and the prolonged negotiations at the airport Marriott. Despite the grimness around her now, she almost smiled. Back then – and it seemed like years ago although it was only five months – she remembered how she had complained to Donald about having to stay in a Marriott. 'What a hell hole!' she'd told him. 'This could drag on for days, or even weeks. Couldn't we arrange for a Hyatt at least?'

'Hey, rough it,' Donald had replied. 'It's their corporate culture. Cooper executives travel coach. Even old man Cooper travels coach.' He laughed. 'If it wasn't for me, you'd probably be having this meeting in a Days Inn, so stop bitching and get your ass to sit down at the table. This is all going to be about stamina, Jennifer. I know you can outlast them, but I'm not saying it's going to be easy.' He had paused and laughed again. 'Goddamnit!' he said, 'No one ever makes it easy for you to make five hundred million dollars.'

And, to the credit of her personality and her checkbook, Jennifer and her team had outlasted old man Cooper and his whole lot of Midwestern lawyers. She had sat at that table virtually unmoving, almost unblinking, for hours and hours. Thank God for Cooper's inflamed prostate or she might have never closed the deal. But the fifteen or twenty trips to the men's room he made each day while she sat there, coolly waiting for his return, had certainly contributed to his loss of faith and confidence. Then, when she called Donald in for the kill, it had gone fairly smoothly.

And was this her reward? She opened her eyes.

The shrieking in the next cell or down the hall or wherever it was reached an inhuman crescendo but finally, mercifully stopped. For a moment Jennifer wondered if they'd killed the inmate that had been making the noise. In the blessed peace she didn't care if they had. It wasn't that she didn't feel sorry for the woman – this was a place where misery was not just natural but required and she knew everyone didn't have the self-control that she did – but this wasn't *The Oprah Winfrey Show* and there was no need to share your pain so loudly.

That thought and the relative silence strengthened Jennifer's resolve. She *would* sit here, the lights burning into her eyes. Let them observe that! She wouldn't move. She wouldn't speak. And she wouldn't sleep. It was the only way she could bring some control back to her ravaged sense of self. And then, hopefully very soon, they would take her out of here and she would call Tom and they would send a stretch limo and whatever else it took to get her the fuck out of here.

And when she returned to Hudson, Van Schaank she'd have a hero's welcome. Jennifer closed her eyes again against the unbearable glare and tried to imagine that. Tom, so tall, would be at her side, maybe just lightly holding her elbow as she entered the double-wide glass doors to the floor. She'd buy something new to wear – maybe that suit she'd seen in the window of Walter Steiger, no matter how obscenely expensive it was. Yes, and shoes to match.

And when she walked into the reception area the secretaries and support staff would be there, and they'd all stare and smile. Susan, her top secretary, would give her a big bouquet and say, 'This is from all of us. We admire you so much.' And then she and Tom would walk into the main office area and all the traders, attorneys, partners – all of them, even Dave Jacobs, who hated her – would stand up and they'd begin to clap, and the clapping would rise to a roar and then, the way they did it in European circuses, the clapping would become rhythmic, each pair of hands in perfect unison with the others. And Donald would open his office door and walk toward her and Tom. And Tom, because he was sensitive and wouldn't want to detract from her moment, would give her elbow a little push. 'Go to him,' he'd say, and she would, in front of everybody. And Donald would lift his head and say . . .

She felt wet. Jennifer opened her eyes, back to the gruesome reality of the observation cell, and jumped to her feet. Water was oozing from under the wall behind her! She looked around. In fact, all along the wall where the mattress lay, the water lapped in, much of it already absorbed by the mattress but plenty spreading across her floor. Surely this wasn't part of the punishment, some bizarre test? She ran to the door. There were roaches floating in the water! Worse, they were alive, and trying to find a perch or a nest. 'Hey!' she yelled. 'Hey, someone. What's going on? There's a flood in here.'

The sadistic Officer Byrd was at her door in a moment. He looked in at her, shook his head and yelled, 'Jesus H. Christ! Nine must have wadded the toilet.'

Then, instead of helping her or explaining, he ran off down the hall. Jennifer leaned against the Plexiglas of her door but couldn't see what was going on. She could, however, hear – and in the next moment the howls began again, this time, if anything, even louder and more ferocious than before. Jennifer kept watching, her head pressed against the glass, the water running at her feet, wondering if any of the horror was real. She'd lose her mind if the hideous noise went on for another minute. Then, after one last fiendish screech, the stranger's voice was stilled. Jennifer could still hear curses and grunts. She imagined the officers were making them and, sure enough, in another moment three burly guys were in the corridor, attempting to drag off a big black woman. She was dressed in a shameful orange jumpsuit but now it was partially obscured by the restraint jacket she had on. Though she couldn't move her arms, she was kicking out with both legs, moving her head from side to side, and furiously screaming despite the taped gag that muffled her. Her hair was wild but her face was more so.

The woman was pushed back into a hard black plastic chair that sat as low to the ground as a beach chair. Officer Byrd obstructed Jennifer's view for a few moments but, when he finally moved, Jennifer was horrified to see that the woman had been strapped into the chair at the legs. Then the straitjacket was slowly removed from the woman's body, and the straps were brought over her shoulders in much the same way that an astronaut would be strapped to his seat.

Jennifer, terrified but unable to move, watched as they struggled to wheel the woman past her window. For a moment the startling blue eyes of the African American woman gave Jennifer an intimate look, certainly not one of apology. She winked at Jennifer. Then she was gone.

Jennifer, shocked, didn't know how long she had stood there. There was a drain in the cement floor that gurgled.

She waited for a little while, hoping that the guard would return so she could demand some better conditions. But no one came. Finally she balanced on one leg and peeled off first one drenched sock, then the other. She squeezed them out over the drain. At least half a cup of water ran into the sewage hole, but Jennifer's problem wasn't solved. Now, without socks, her feet were frozen. She couldn't sit on the mattress because it was also disgustingly wet. She didn't know what the correction officer had done with the trouble-some woman. Did they have a firing squad here at Jennings? Could she scream for help or attention? She found she couldn't do it. The woman's blue, blue eye winking at her, as if they were . . . together or . . . bonded somehow had really shaken her. Then she saw, with relief, that Officer Byrd was at the end of the hall about to pass by. Finally she knocked on the glass and he turned to her.

'I'm wet,' she said. 'This whole room has been ruined. You have to help me.' The fear in her voice only made her more frightened.

But Byrd didn't have a clue. He turned his mouth to his squawk box and said something. He stepped into the room and turned around.

'*Tsk, tsk,*' he said. 'You got more than you bargained for.' Jennifer decided not to even respond. Then he looked her over. It was a sexual leer, and she could tell that he wanted her to be uncomfortable. 'I'm alone up here now,' he explained. 'They had to take that one down to the hold. It was her first day in.'

Jennifer actually shivered. 'They'll be back soon,' she said in a flat voice. What kind of man took a job in a women's prison and then tried to . . .

'Well,' said Byrd, 'I could take you down to a cell below

six. That's where the nigger was. She used her towel to stop up the toilet and caused a major flood.' Jennifer recoiled both at the word he'd used and because he'd moved toward her. His voice insinuated that . . . Just then his walkie-talkie spoke.

Roughly Byrd took her under her right arm and moved her out of her little glass box. He was rubbing up against her as they walked past the place where the mad woman had been imprisoned, then moved her to number four, a cell exactly like her previous one.

'Chow will be in a minute,' he said as he slowly released his grip and ran his hand down her arm.

'Food?' Jennifer cried. 'I can't even breathe.' Then she remembered her outfit. 'And I need a new jumpsuit. This one is wet.'

'We'll have supper for you right away,' Byrd said. 'But we can't issue another uniform. Laundry's closed.' Then he moved a little closer. 'Of course,' he almost whispered, 'you could take it off and hang it up. There's nobody here to see you.'

Jennifer looked around at the observation windows, the open ceiling, and the catwalk above. Now she was grateful for them. She wanted someone to keep their eyes on Byrd – or *Vulture*. But she had a creepy feeling that most of those eyes would get a big kick out of her standing around naked. And would they intervene if Vulture touched her?

'Maybe I could get you something else to wear,' he said now, '*if* you wanted to be friendly,' he added.

She couldn't believe what she was hearing. It was a sexual innuendo, wasn't it? 'Forget about that,' she told Byrd.

He shrugged. Had he just offered her something in return for sex? She kept her face calm but swore to herself that she'd have him reported to the governor by tomorrow afternoon. 'Too bad. You'll have to wear the damp one until morning,' he said. He locked the door on the new cubicle and left.

Jennifer was deeply grateful for that. She would have spent some time examining the cell if it hadn't been quite so obviously identical to the previous one. She'd even be willing to swear in a court of law that the stains in this mattress were shaped identically to the one on the other. Hadn't there been that blot that looked like the state of Florida on the upper left corner of the previous mattress? The wetness against her ankles was terribly cold and the rough polyester chafed, but otherwise all was the same. Except that this time, when she sat down in her corner, her stomach rumbled loudly enough for her to hear, and maybe loudly enough for the woman in the next room – if there was a woman in the next room – to hear as well.

But she was still determined that she wouldn't eat anything. And she wouldn't lie down. Even though the day seemed a hundred hours long, she wouldn't allow her hunger or fatigue to get the better of her.

She leaned her back against the wall, pulled her knees up to her chest, wrapped her arms around her cold ankles and tried, once again, to close her eyes and imagine what treats would come her way when she went back to her real life. Donald had better be especially generous with her bonus. In fact, she might not have to wait until the end of the fiscal year. Of course, after December there would be the full partnership and the big office. She took a deeper breath of the fatal air. Concentrate on it, she told herself. Think how beautiful that place will be compared with this one. She knew each partner got a generous budget to furnish and decorate his or her office, but now she thought that she might move her reproduction Beidermeyer desk from home into the office. She'd bill Hudson, Van Schaank and use the money for the dressing table she'd admired in the antique shop on upper Lexington Avenue. She'd . . . she tried once again to get into the reverie but it wasn't working.

She opened her eyes. She couldn't really imagine anything but this room, her freezing feet, the unbearable light and the hunger gnawing at her belly. She tried to remind herself that she was the hero of the Vareen takeover and the heavy lifter in the Cooper Corp. scenario, but she hadn't been cold and wet and humiliated then. Jennifer may have managed not to drink and not to use the ladies' room, but if she had had to pee then, she wouldn't have had to do it in front of a dozen pairs of eyes.

She felt her eyes begin to get wet and forced herself to stand up. Just then a noise outside the cell brought her to the front. Another guard was wheeling a trolley down the corridor. When he reached her, he didn't even look up. He merely bent toward her, his face forward, and slipped a plastic tray through the slot. It almost looked like an airplane meal.

'No,' she told herself firmly one more time. But her cold feet walked, without her permission, over to the tray. She bent and picked it up. Something green. Something brown. And something that looked like it had tomato sauce on it. Whatever it was, she took it to the bed, sat down cross-legged on the filthy mattress, and ravenously wolfed it down.

7

Maggie Rafferty

I was a prisoner long before I was an inmate.

Bonnie Foreshaw, inmate. Andi Rierden, *The Farm*

I know that it will seem a truism, but I must say that shooting your husband, accidentally or otherwise – and even more – having him die from the bullet wound, totally changes your life. The chief benefit is, of course, that he is gone, but there are other benefits, which I'll get to later. The main *drawback*, however, is that in most cases you're deprived of your liberty and might have to live in a place with a library that has only one hundred and sixteen books. That is the exact number of books in the library here at Jennings.

But back to my husband. He could have lived; he died just to spite me. The bullet only grazed his aorta. Serious? Yes – but with his will power, he might have lingered long enough for the paramedics to stabilize him. But no. He always had to get his way in the end. He could turn any situation to his advantage. This was, of course, only one of the many reasons why I hated him so fully and completely, and why the gun I was holding went off while it was pointed in his direction. At the time, I had meant to kill myself. How foolish of me.

My husband was the famous Richard Rafferty, Riff to his friends. At the very minute the bullet was nicking his deceitful heart, his latest book, *The Life of the Heart*, was being talked about on the six o'clock news. A book? On the evening *news*? How can that be? Easy. Richard was sleeping with the woman who produced the show.

And speaking of the evening news, I understand that the new arrival, this Miss Jennifer Spencer, is up in observation hell. She's certainly been news. I've been following her story with some interest, since one needs such pastimes in prison, and because both of my sons are in the same type of business as she is . . . or *was*. From the beginning I could see that she was taking the fall for someone else, probably a man. The only question that remained in my mind was, did she know what was going on? Was she complicitous? I was actually looking forward to seeing her in person, because then I would know.

How would I know? Well, let me explain another result of happening to murder your husband: It turns your brain inside out. Although this is terribly painful at the time and for a long while afterward, in the end it is a good thing. I know this sounds totally insane, but I am a better person for having killed my husband. For instance, I've become nearly as good as a dog at reading people.

Lest anyone think that I am advocating murder as a method of self-improvement, let me correct that impression at once. Yes, I am a better person, but I was a good enough person before. Riff wasn't; he wasn't worth dirtying my hands for. What he deserved from me was the indifference that I only now feel toward him. Trading life and liberty for well-deserved revenge and an enlightened mind is a very hard deal to accept. Jennings, have I said it before, is a kind of hell.

When I arrived here, I fell into despair at once. The trial, Grand Guignol though it had been, was a reason to get up, get dressed, and perform. Here there was nothing. I wanted to die. Imagine. I had been headmistress of one of the most prestigious private girls' schools on the East Coast, and had lived among the very rich and instructed their daughters. On my first day at Jennings, I was told to 'get my fuckin' ass movin'.' I had been in *Who's Who In American Education*. Here I was referred to as 'the old bitch'.

Somehow I got used to the vulgarity. It was the deprivation of every sensory pleasure that was the hardest thing for me to bear. My marriage had not been happy, but I had lived in a beautiful home, traveled to Paris and London nearly every year, spent summers in Tuscany, was a connoisseur of wines and fine foods, collected rare books and Herend, drove an immaculate '62 Mercedes Gullwing, subscribed to the ballet, shopped at Neiman Marcus.

And suddenly I was confined to one of the ugliest places on the face of the earth, twenty-four hours a day, seven days a week. I assure you, no bleaker, duller, more visually offensive place can exist. I'd rather be in Craigmore Prison, dank dark dungeon that it is. It at least has some architecture to boast of. Jennings is the kind of dull, featureless maze they put rats into when they're trying to see if they can stunt their brain development. Even crumbling ceilings or walls would add interest, but here there is no crumbling, just ugly,

1960s efficiency. Jennings was built when there was a soul-sickness plaguing the earth, probably an aftereffect of the war. Buildings were built to last, but beauty in architecture was eschewed. The style could be called 'Plainness with a Vengeance', 'Ugly is Fine', or 'Death in Life'. And I have to stay here for the rest of mine. There are no aesthetic pardons.

So I wondered how Jennifer Spencer was faring in Observation. She had a lower-middle-class youth, upper-middle-class adulthood. A transition to Jennings wasn't going to be easy for her, to say the least. But my interest in the fate and character of Jennifer Spencer was going to be limited compared to the keen interest I have in women like Movita Watson and her 'sidekick', Cher. I had never met women like them before my incarceration and I am fascinated by their unschooled intelligence.

Movita, for example, is someone I pegged as decent the minute I saw her despite her hellfire exterior. She plays tough, and sometimes dumb, but she's generous and clever, too, and has her own eye for 'attitude' in others. She will tell you that when she entered Jennings, I had no 'attitude' at all. This was why we became friends fairly quickly. She was, in her words, 'curious 'bout that weird ol' bitch'. Well, *attitude* is one of the petty attributes that I lost as a result of my husband dying at my hands, or more literally, at my feet. When I came in, I've been told by Movita, I had the look of a 'schoolteacher who'd been wiped out by a nuclear bomb'. Change 'schoolteacher' to 'schoolmistress' and her assessment was pretty much accurate.

But those credentials as a schoolteacher secured my position as the prison librarian. And since that time I have been preoccupied with thinking of ways to acquire more books. Books were always important to me. Well, they are my life's blood really. Before and after my crime.

The Life of the Heart (of which, ironically, we had two copies in the library) was Richard's sixth book. It was supposed to be about the stunning and liberated life that can be ours if we give in to our feelings of love. He'd put me and my two sons through hell while he was trying to write it, just as he had, come to think of it, when he wrote his fourth and fifth. The children were 'distractions'. Somehow I was always doing something 'stupid'. He once accused me of turning pages too loudly. Bryce and Tyler, despite their initial business success, were 'disappointments' to him. But that I could understand. How disappointing it must be for a false, humorless, and arrogant man to have two sons who could see through him and laugh. I, on the other hand – raised to be a right-minded woman – supported the bastard throughout. I fed him, excused him, pampered him, read his drafts, corrected his grammar, gave him ideas, typed his corrections, and hated his editor with him. I did it for thirty-four years. Why stop now, when he needed me more than ever?

It is only now, seven years later, that I can look back at the situation without anger. As I said above, I am a better person now.

I knew that Jennifer Spencer would be given the orientation that included a tour of the facility, a bed assignment, and a work detail. I know what's what here on my own, though I do appreciate the heads up I get when Frances delivers the ice with kites. I had to chuckle at the 'kites on ice'. There *is* no work here in the library. The prison population consists of very few readers and what they *would* read doesn't exist in the library. Needless to say, I would welcome

Miss Spencer to Jennings when she came by later in the day. Lest you think otherwise, this would not be some warm-hearted *Shawshank Redemption* nonsense where I take the girl under my wing. If I had wings, I assure you I'd fly the fuck out of here. Besides, I already have two sons – I don't need a daughter. After a quarter century of girls' schools, I know how much trouble they are.

Jennifer finally came to the library, with that Officer Camry, at about three-thirty, the time I usually fade out, having worked in schools all my life. She had the air of a young woman who was in trouble, there was no mistaking that. Her face was pale and drawn, her eyelids were swollen, and the eyes peering out from between them looked as if they'd glimpsed something horrific, but at the same time she still looked like someone whose car and driver were waiting for her. She had heavy attitude, Movita would say. But I could see right through that. The press, as usual, had gotten it wrong: Thanks to my twenty-seven years of working with schoolgirls, I could see that Jennifer had been a scholarship student. Determination to overcome obstacles was written all over her, so there had to have *been* obstacles. I could see that she had real strength to her, and that when the realization that she was going to be in here for some real time hit her, she would survive the shock.

'Hello,' I said. 'I'm Maggie.' I sounded ridiculous to myself, as if we were in some kind of meeting.

'Hi,' she answered. She was so not present that I was driven to speak to her again. 'This is our library, such as it is.'

She blinked at me, as if she didn't understand why I was talking to her. 'We have the space,' I went on, 'but we have very few books.'

'It doesn't matter to me. Don't worry about it,' she said, a little sharply. Then her expression changed. She was looking at me, wondering who I was, I expect. 'I'm sorry,' she said then. 'I don't mean to be rude. It's just that I'm not going to be *living* here. But this guard has been very nice.' I saw Officer Camry stiffen. It's funny about how prison guards refuse to be called prison guards.

'He's an officer, dear,' I said in a voice drier than the paper of my books. 'Not a guard. You call them officers or COs.'

'Correction officer,' Camry the fool added. He was harmless enough and I nodded at him.

'Oh. Thank you,' the girl said.

Jennifer Spencer surprised me in one way. I, who have met such a wide cross section of women when you consider both my students, my social circle, and my present comrades, could not tell if the girl was essentially good or bad. It's the kind of thing I almost always know at a glance yet I didn't know it then, although I do now. I could see that she was honest.

8

Jennifer Spencer

With keen, discriminating sight,
Black's not so black, – nor white
so very white.

George Canning, *New Morality*

After the night in Observation, Jennifer was ready for assignment to a cell. Though it was the relatively benign Officer Camry, rather than the brutal Byrd, who came to take her away, the relentless gloom of the institution put Jennifer into a state bordering on catatonia. If Observation had been hell for her, it was clear that the rest of the place was purgatory. It was all so grim that it was appalling to imagine that women actually lived in this hopeless drabness day after day.

'I need to make a phone call,' she managed to say to Officer Camry. Her head was pounding and she desperately needed some Tylenol – and maybe a Valium – but calling Tom was the most important thing to do right now. 'I have to make a call,' she said again. 'Is there a phone near here?'

Camry stepped back and looked at her intently. 'If there

was, you couldn't use it,' he told her. 'I'm scheduled to give you your house assignment. You can only make calls on your own time.'

Jennifer clenched her jaw and the headache intensified. She wasn't prepared for any of this. She admitted that now. How could Donald and Tom abandon her to this experience? She couldn't imagine the elegant Mr Michaels in a jumpsuit, or Ivy League Tom in the filthy hole. But that didn't matter. She squared her shoulders behind Camry's rounded ones and followed as she was instructed. She would not cry nor would she fuss. This whole ordeal was a punishment; not for the nonsense with the SEC, but for the terrible error in judgment that she had made.

'Right this way,' Camry said, leading her down a long narrow corridor. Then he stopped abruptly and opened a door. 'While we're here, this is the athletic facility,' he said.

Jennifer looked in to see a small room with a couple of flabby volleyballs and a few exercise mats that were so soiled that she had to avert her eyes. So this was the gym. She almost laughed. It was nothing at all like the Vertical Club where she and Tom worked out. Well, she'd be out of there before she needed to go to the gym. But what about the women who had to *use* the place? God almighty.

'You can use the athletic facility in your free time, but not during lockdown or after eight p.m.,' Camry told her.

Jennifer sighed. As if. Once again she turned to Camry and said with great urgency, 'Are you certain I can't use a phone? It is imperative that I get in touch with my lawyer.'

Camry lifted his eyebrows and looked up at the ceiling. He shook his head as if to say, *No, you crazy bitch, no!*

Jennifer knew then that she had made a terrible error. For the first time in her life she had been so confident that she knew everything that she needed to know that she had gone into a test completely unprepared. Prison wasn't like life on the Outside. In here, there was no multiple choice to guess at, and there was no essay that she could bluff her way through. This was all true or false – black and white. This was the test of her life, and she'd willingly come into it unprepared and ignorant.

Tom and Donald had told her that it would be easy. She didn't know why she had believed them – except that they'd never lied to her before. Christ, there was no way this could've been easy. She should've known that. Life had taught her that nothing came easy – it all took work, it all took discipline, and above everything else, it all took a willful determination not to fail. She knew that. She had always been prepared, always one step ahead of the rest.

Jennifer hung her head and looked at the orange jumpsuit that she was wearing. When she was a kid she used to lay out her school clothes before going to bed. She hated uniforms so much that she spent hours figuring out ways to make a plaid jumper and a navy blazer look like something out of *Vogue*. But she did it. She stood out from all the rest.

It was that kind of preparation and thinking ahead that were the big secrets to her success. She got into State on scholarship, and her grades there earned her a free ride into the MBA program at Wharton. When it was time to go out and get a job, Jennifer's research landed her an interview with the already legendary Donald J. Michaels. She walked into his office, clearly a girl from the working class, and she started to talk about his Gulbenkian porcelain. Donald lifted his eyebrows. He knew she was faking it, but he also knew she was *really good* at faking it. Preparation and a poker face were exactly what she needed to succeed in his

Wall Street firm. Donald Michaels not only hired Jennifer on the spot, he put her on his own team. They were known as the smartest and the most aggressive of all the Wall Street shark pool. They specialized in the highest-risk/highest-reward IPOs and some *very* leveraged buyouts. They didn't miss a trick. They were invincible.

'We go down from here,' Camry told her, and Jennifer preceded him down the stairs. She was glad she wasn't with Byrd as they made their way down the dark and damp stairwell.

The trek seemed to take forever, and through it all Jennifer mentally beat herself up. From the first moment she had gotten into the van, things had been out of her control. She tried to control the rising tide of panic that was threatening to overtake her. Why didn't the Warden know who she was? If Tom had called, whom did he talk to? And if she didn't find out, how would she be cushioned and protected from this nightmare? Who was the Warden's boss? Could she go over the stolid Warden Harding's head? She would just have to wait until this ridiculous process was over. Then she would call Tom. Or Don. Or both of them.

At long last, she and Camry entered the cellblock, and Jennifer was taken to her cell. She thought she'd seen the worst of Jennings, but no – they had saved the worst for last.

'This is your house assignment,' Camry told her.

House? This wasn't a house; it wasn't even a dormitory – and it most certainly was not a country club. It was a prison cell, plain and simple. The concrete walls were painted a color that a decorator might claim to be *Dusty Rose*, but to Jennifer's eyes it was a hideous *Battleship Pink*. The beds – four of them – were bunked and bolted against the side walls with only about ten square feet of floor space in between. There was no furniture except a tiny desk that was suspended from the wall, and, beneath it, a single chair. Jennifer wondered if she would have three cellmates, and if the four of them were supposed to share that chair.

The only other place to sit was on a toilet that was quite unlike anything Jennifer had ever seen before in her life. At first glance, the stainless steel creation reminded her of a metal miniature of the Solomon R. Guggenheim Museum. On closer inspection she saw the faucets and realized with horror that it was a monument to prison efficiency. It served as both wash basin and commode, with the seat only inches from the lower bunks. She remembered a snippet of a song parody her mother used to sing: *And my bunk is where the skunk is*. Did someone actually sleep with her head virtually in the *head*? She set her shoulders and tried not to show her dismay. After all, she only had to sit there until Tom came and took her away. She wouldn't be spending the night.

'Home sweet home,' Camry said as he rolled open the door in the fourth wall, which consisted completely of bars. The section slid open, and for a moment it doubled the bars on the left side of the cell. The shadow play they made passing reminded Jennifer of the sun through the windows of New York's elevated trains. But there was no sunshine here. The cells were on a windowless hall, and although each one did have a window, it was so high in the wall that even from the top bunk you couldn't peer through the chicken wire. Camry took Jennifer's elbow and firmly guided her into her new home.

'It's only for a few hours,' she told herself. Maybe now she could finally call Tom. She looked for a moment at Officer Camry, but decided not to ask.

'Get comfortable,' Camry instructed. 'I'll go get your cellmate so you two can get acquainted.'

'Right,' Jennifer said.

'Pardon?' Camry responded.

'I wish,' Jennifer said with a cynical sigh.

Only one of the four bunks was made up, and over it, taped to the walls, were six pictures. One was of a baby – obviously a snapshot – but the other five were clipped from magazines. There was an angel, a toddler on the beach building a sand castle, a fire engine, the Nike logo complete with *Just Do It*, and finally a picture of Jesus, looking a lot like Donny Osmond. Jennifer stood there for a moment, trying to imagine what kind of brain had arranged those particular images in that particular way.

She walked over to the desk. It was bare except for three books: the Bible, a copy of *The Pokey Little Puppy*, and a paperback Baby-Sitters Club book. Jennifer had read the Baby-Sitters Club when she was in fourth grade. Had they put her in a cell with a child or a simpleton?

On the lower bunk on the opposite wall, Jennifer found a rolled up mattress and a set of sheets. Hers, she wondered? She thought about making the bed, but was enraged at the thought of actually making herself 'comfortable' as dopey old Roger had suggested. This was no place to be comfortable. She would never sleep here, and she would most certainly never use the toilet. Anyone – even someone like Byrd – could look right through the bars and see everything that went on.

Jennifer sat on the solitary chair and wondered what time it was. Would Tom still be at home, on his way to the office, or was he already there? She knew his cell phone number by heart, but she wasn't sure if a cell phone could accept a collect call. She stood up suddenly in a rage. Goddamnit! She wasn't a convict. She had her own damn cell phone – and they had taken it. She had a Verizon credit card with no limits. Why couldn't she use it? What harm would there be in that? It had rounded corners, too. She couldn't kill anyone – or herself – with a fucking cell phone. The rage took its toll, and Jennifer wilted onto the made-up bunk. Tom had better get her out of here before the end of the day. This was worse than anything she'd imagined.

'You're sitting on my bed,' Jennifer heard a timid voice say. She jumped up to see Officer Camry standing in the door of the cell with a very small and very pretty young blonde woman.

'I'm sorry,' Jennifer said sincerely.

'It's okay,' the girl said timidly. She looked as if she was terrified of Jennifer, and she seemed to be almost clinging to the smiling Officer Camry.

'Miss Spencer, this is Suki,' Roger said as he gently guided the young girl into the cell. 'You and her will be bunking together.'

Jennifer saw the girl looking at her still damp jumpsuit.

'Were you the one who stuffed the toilet in Observation last night?' Suki asked her. Then she went over to her bunk and looked at the wet spot Jennifer had left when she sat there.

'You can use *this* bedding,' Jennifer said, pointing to the roll on the bunk meant for her. 'I won't be using it.'

'Why not?' Suki asked her.

'I'm not staying,' Jennifer replied.

'Where are you going?'

Jennifer thought she was going to scream. 'Can I just

make a phone call?' she asked, looking past this Suki and talking to Roger.

'Not until after work,' Suki told her.

'But I have to make the call *now*.'

'Miss Spencer – Jennifer – will be working with you in the laundry,' Camry told the young girl. 'Will you see that she gets there this afternoon?' he asked with a smile.

'You bet Rog – uh, sir,' Suki said, blushing.

Roger stood there as awkward as a teenager on a front porch after a first date. Was he going to kiss this girl? Jennifer wondered. But Camry finally turned and walked away. Suki watched him go until he turned for a moment and waved good-bye.

Jennifer didn't know what that was all about, and she didn't need to know. A deafening bell clanged loudly and echoed off the concrete.

'Time to go back to work,' Suki chirped brightly. 'Come on, I'll show you the way.'

Jennifer followed without question. Maybe she could find a phone in the laundromat.

9

Movita Watson

Here I am and here I stay.

Patrice de Mac Mahon

I did alotta work in the office that no inmate should be trusted with, but that was because of Miss Ringling. She was one of those state employees who felt the main function of her job was cashing her paycheck. Most work that required any intelligence was given directly to me by the Warden. The rest of it was given to me by Miss Ringling. But now I was finally shuttin' down the PC and gettin' ready to go to dinner, when Warden Harding strolled outta her office in that casual-like way that says she's got something to tell me.

'Movita?' she asked.

'Mmmm,' I kinda murmured back. You can't really diss the Warden, but by now her and me know each other good enough for me to voice a certain kind of awareness.

'I've assigned Spencer to Conrad. Do you think Suki

will mind having her as a cellmate?' the Warden asked me.

Since when did The Woman worry about what I thought? 'Why do I care what Suki minds?' I answered back. It sounded kinda snotty so I softened it a bit with, 'She'll do fine. NBD. Spencer's no suicide, if that's what you're thinking.'

'I just thought that you might have a better sense of who would be the best to match the new inmate with. You *are* the – uh – main person for the crew. I just don't want to add a problem to an already sensitive situation.'

'Hey, my policy is just like that old president's,' I told her. '"Don't ask, don't tell." That works for me, too.' I knew what she was angling for. The Warden wanted me to take that little white witch to my lovin' black bosom. That's one of the deadly things about prison; you show weakness just once and everyone is ready to prey on ya'. Just 'cause I unreasonably, uncharacteristically, and maybe unfortunately 'adopted' Suki Conrad into my crew doesn't mean I'm gonna do it for every sorrowful new piece of meat that comes to Jennings. It bugged me that The Woman even asked me.

I don't know if the *others* wanted to take Suki in, but I insisted. And when I insist, they don't have much choice. It wasn't like anybody really hated her, and face it, girls, Movita rules. Anyway, the very first day I saw Suki Conrad draggin' her pitiful little butt through Intake, I just took to her. Maybe it was that baby-fine blonde hair or the lost look in her eyes. I got me a pink-skinned baby doll with yellow hair and blue eyes for Christmas once. Didn't I love that dolly! Whatever. Sometimes, though, someone like that just tugs at your heart or some shit like that. I guess I just plain felt sorry for the little thing, and that's the truth. Just 'cause I'm in prison don't mean I got no human feelings. And I felt like we needed a baby in our crew.

Women need family. Don't matter if it's blood or not. In the crew we're like mother and daughters sometimes, and sometimes we're like sisters, and sometimes we're like other family members, too. That don't mean we don't fight and argue and stuff. But when you're in a crew you just try to keep all that to a minimum.

'Please let me know if there's any trouble with the match-up, okay?' the Warden asked me. She was lookin' me right in the eye and I knew she wanted more than a trouble report. She knew how to get at me. 'That's it for today, Movita. You better go to dinner.' She paused for a second. 'What do you and your girls have planned tonight?'

I switched off the monitor and neatened up some stacks of papers on my desk. 'Well, it's Theresa's turn to cook,' I said, 'so it's gonna be a surprise.' Sometimes I get the oddest feeling that the Warden is kinda – well – *envious* of us in the crew. It's like she'd rather come and eat with us instead of goin' to her own house. I don't know much about her life Outside, 'cept that she's divorced and that she works all the time. I doubt she's got much of a life.

When I got back to my house, Theresa was already chopping the carrots that Suki was washin'. 'You want the salad dressing sweet or you want it tart?' Theresa asked.

'I don't care as long as you're making it,' Cher told her. She was loungin' her sassy ass on the bunk, readin' a magazine, and just waitin' to eat.

If prison is the place where society thinks they can make us cons eat shit, they do a damn good job of it. Even though the Warden keeps fightin' with Ben Norton down in Food

Services, the food at Jennings never gets any better. No one
– and I mean no one – wants to eat the shit old Ben serves
up in the cafeteria. It's nothin' but starch, grease, and real
bad meat. People eat it, but only if they have to.

You can eat for free in the cafeteria. So if you're
destitute, or spend whatever you got on contraband, or if
you can't make even one friend, then you're stuck in the
cafeteria eatin' one of Ben's blue plate specials.

But if you got some sense, a little social grace, or any
initiative at all, you can buy things from the prison canteen
and cook 'em up yourself. You just need to save a little
money and get pots and pans and all. There's no real
kitchens in our houses, but Harding lets us have a hot plate
or an electric skillet. Of course, the canteen doesn't have
much variety – maybe only seven or eight kinds of things.
You can usually get a chicken, or sometimes beef. They
always got a little lettuce or some vegetable. There's
potatoes and sometimes rice. And now and then some fruit
like apples or bananas or even oranges. Theresa works down
in the dispensary, so she always knows what's comin' in. She
stashes the best for the crew, and with the money Cher gets
from sellin' some of the stuff she steals from Intake we can
buy a whole lot of good stuff. Problem is, we don't got
refrigeration, and that's why we need plenty of ice. Frances
was the lucky one to get to deliver it. Ice is like gold in
prison. Without it, lots of our good stuff goes to waste. If
we buy a chicken on our own, by the time we eat half of it
the other half is no damn good and we're so sick of chicken
that we're cluckin'. We don't wanna see no bird *ever* again.

'Hand me that pot of water, Suki,' Theresa said as I sat
down to listen to the day's bulletins. I wanted to know if
anyone had any more news on Spencer. I thought Suki

might speak up, but Cher was the first one to sound off, as usual.

'I hear she's already sashaying round here like she owns the place.' Cher smirked. 'Byrd told old Cranston down in Intake that he's gonna toss Spencer into solitary if she demands to use the phone one more damn time.'

'Well, you know what they say about asking and receiving, don't you?' Theresa said as she opened the Tupperware and measured out some pasta into the boiling water.

'Yeah, well this ain't Sunday school,' Cher shot back. 'And it ain't the movies either. You don't automatically get one call when you get here.'

'It's tough on you white girls when you don't get your way, ain't it?' I said, givin' Cher a look. She was copping some pretty amazing attitude.

'That's not very nice,' Suki said with hurt feelings.

'Movita wasn't referrin' to you, sweetie,' Cher reassured her. She got up and gave Suki a pat on the shoulder.

That was for my benefit. Back when I first took Suki in, Cher made quite a fuss. 'She can't cook, she can't steal, she can't do nothin' but cry,' Cher bitched. 'She's dumb as dirt. That's why she drove the car for her boyfriend.'

I guess Suki actually believed her boyfriend when he said he was goin' into that 7-Eleven for cigarettes. He came out with the contents of the cash register, and little Suki thought she was guilty of nothin' more than keepin' the heater running.

Theresa, on the other hand, was more understanding. 'But she lost her baby,' she said to Cher. 'She's never going to stop crying about that. You know what they say about mothers when someone takes away their babies, don't you?'

Well, nobody answered Theresa's question. It got real

quiet for a moment. You see, I don't like talkin' about children. I never talk about my little girls. Their granny is raisin' them, and that's all I can bear to say about it.

'Just what in heaven's name are you makin' there, Theresa?' I asked to break the tension. 'You trying to kill us all before Cher gets a chance to get outta here?'

'Get out of my way, Movita,' Theresa warned. 'You know what they say about too many cooks, don't you?'

I just laughed and backed off. Havin' a conversation with Theresa was like talkin' to a refrigerator door loaded with sayings. I respected that girl. The goin' never got so tough that Theresa didn't get up and go. 'People say I'm an optimist,' she'd say, lookin' all serious and stuff. 'But I don't think that's necessarily true. And do you wanna know why? I'm gonna tell you why. Because – you know what they say about pessimism and optimism, don't you?'

Theresa never really wanted you to answer her questions, 'cause she had all the answers herself.

'They say the pessimist says the glass is half *empty*, but the optimist says it's half *full*. Well, you know what I say to that? I don't say that glass is half *anything*, I say you're using the wrong damn glass. It's obviously too big. That's what I say.' Then old Theresa always waited a little and let it all sink in before she'd wind up for her big finale. 'And you know what that makes me?' she'd ask. 'That makes me a *pragmatist*! That is someone who has a practical, matter-of-fact way of solving problems. That's a pragmatist and that's what I am – a practical, matter-of-fact problem solver. If you got a problem with how much is in your glass, well then maybe you're just using the wrong glass. You understand what I'm saying here? It just doesn't matter if you think it's half empty or half full, what matters is what you *do* about it.

Get off your ass and get yourself a different glass is what I say. Always remember this: *Answer* is also a verb. You understand what I'm saying here? The door to success is labeled *PUSH!* You can't leave footprints in the sands of time if you're not wearin' work boots.'

I don't know why, but I could listen to Theresa talk for hours. I loved those speeches.

'Get up off your butt, Cher, and grab that plastic strainer for me,' Theresa told Cher, and Cher did it. 'Hold it over the bowl.'

Cher was laughing as Theresa strained her pasta and let the water go down the john. 'You think there's any symbolism here with your cookin' right next to the toilet?' Cher teased.

Theresa's specialty is her pasta. That's somethin' the canteen don't carry, but Theresa's sister sends her a lot of it. That's another thing about who you pick for crew. You want the girls who get lots of packages from the Outside. Theresa gets pasta and salamis and Italian shit like that. And you can't get better packages than Cher gets. Theft runs in her family, so they're always sendin' her stuff. Lots of it is contraband and gets taken out and sent back, but the boxes always have hand creams and shampoos and stuff like that. And now and then she'll get a big ol' canned ham with some spices. The chips and dips and stuff come in on a regular basis. Both girls are real good about sharin' with the crew.

Suki never gets a damned thing. She ain't got a family. Her little girl is in foster care. I don't care, though – we had to take her in. But if we have to take in this Spencer bitch, then that girl better be prepared to do her part.

Dinner was almost ready. Besides the pasta we were

having some lettuce and some bananas for dessert. 'All the ice is gone,' Theresa said, 'and there won't be any more until tomorrow afternoon, so get prepared to eat. I don't want anything to go to waste.'

'Speakin' of waste,' I said. 'I hear Miss Spencer had herself quite a night in Observation.'

'Did Karl Byrd give her any trouble?' Theresa asked, all concerned.

'Karl can do better than get a piece of that sorry ass,' Cher snarled.

'That's not very nice,' Suki piped up. 'I think she seems kind of nice. She's my bunkmate. But she says she's not gonna be here very long.'

Cher was laughing. 'Oh, let me guess,' she said. 'She's just another *innocent* victim, put in the slammer by mistake.'

'That's what she says,' Suki told us, all sincere. Suki doesn't get irony – you might say she has an irony deficiency. 'Jennifer says her boyfriend is coming to get her out.'

'Yeah, just like my knight in shining armor is comin' for me,' Cher snorted.

Havin' Cher as a cellmate helps the time pass. When she first hit Jennings, I couldn't imagine how I'd ever survive being locked up with a wild white woman. But she can be so damned funny. And she's honest – for a thief. She never pretends to be nobody 'ceptin' who she is. For her, everything she sees is just ripe for the pickin'. She always has her eyes wide open and on the lookout for the next chance to take what she wants. And not just for herself, either. Soon as she got here she stole me a Sony Walkman and a feather pillow, and damn it – that hillbilly girl just stole my heart. I never understood how it happened, but I was glad that it did. I love Cher. Now it isn't like we're lesbians. No one in my crew is a lesbian. I know lots of women couple up for a little sex and comfort while they're here, but nothin' like that goes on between me and Cher. But we do love each other. When I think of how I felt for Earl I almost laugh. My feelings for him were pretty shallow and pathetic when I compare 'em with the love I feel for Cher. And even for Theresa and Suki.

About the only action I get from men is from that mother Byrd. He would jump a ladybug or a polliwog as long as they were unwilling. That's what gives 'em the thrill. I keep 'em way off me by never showin' any fear and askin' him if he's got a hard three inches ready for me. Once I made the redneck bastard blush. Made my day, I tell ya'.

I just sat there on my bunk and looked at my crew. Maybe we could take Spencer in. But the thought of it made me feel like I was somehow cheatin' on Cher. Cher was gonna get paroled soon, if she kept her nose clean and didn't get caught stealin' from Intake. Even if she did, Cher had herself a good lawyer on the Outside.

It all made me feel sorta sad and cold. I didn't really resent Cher leavin' Jennings. It's just that it was gonna be a damned lonely and borin' place once she was gone. Maybe we *needed* to take another woman in.

10

Jennifer Spencer

Windows on buildings and vehicles were smashed one day after all the women in the dining room had been 'searched' for tacos as they left the cafeteria. Later the women referred to the incident as 'The Great Taco Shake'.

Kathryn Watterson, *Women in Prison*

'Mealtime,' the officer announced from the control room. 'Stay in single file and follow the brown line.'

Jennifer had absolutely no interest in eating dinner in the cafeteria, but Suki pointed in the direction that she should go and Jennifer had no choice but to follow the others. She had to admit that she was starving, but God only knew what kind of food was being served. She turned to ask Suki if she might know, but Suki seemed to have someplace else to go. Jennifer turned back and followed the woman in front of her.

As the line moved down the corridor it approached a door that was being held open by yet another officer. 'Single file, ladies, single file. Something good today. Officer Summit says it's Reubens since we had ham salad for lunch today.'

'It's about time,' spoke one inmate.

'Now you're talking,' said another.

Off to the side, a woman was having a loud argument with a doorpost. 'You no good, muthafukka,' she yelled, then paused. 'You got no right,' she answered the mute doorway. No one seemed to notice or mind.

As Jennifer finally stepped inside the cafeteria, what she saw was worse than what she had imagined. Yellow-painted concrete blocks, horrible fluorescent lights hung high from metal rafters, cold air blowing from the air-conditioning unit, and a floor that was a solid slab of poured concrete that angled down in the middle with a covered water drain grate at the center. It reminded her of the old meat market her mother used to take her to in her old neighborhood. It was like a slaughterhouse.

Jennifer mechanically imitated the inmate in front of her so that she would be sure not to mess up in mess hall. There were three drink machines: one with grape something or other, one with orange something or other, and then a much less desirable lemonade mixture that was certain to taste more like water than lemon. She took a metal cup from the inverted stack, selected the orange drink, then stepped down the line a little further only to be presented with a plastic tray covered in a clear plastic lid.

'Hey, where's the Reuben?' an inmate asked.

'Yeah, I thought someone said we were having Reubens,' another inmate intoned.

'Well, Officer Summit must have been misinformed,' the officer at the head of the line said.

Oh man, was there going to be a riot over what was served? Jennifer had been through enough already and she couldn't take any more disruption. She'd never felt so out of control in a controlled environment in her life. She took her tray and followed the woman in front of her to the table.

Jennifer stared down at her tray. She watched the other woman at the table dismantle the lid, carefully slide it under the bottom tray, and then unwrap a utensil from a napkin and let it fall in her hand. It was an abbreviated spoon – a shortened bowl with three equally short prongs extending briefly from the center. She stared at the micro landscape of food in front of her. There was a hill of instant potatoes, a wide river of grease, a dying forest of cabbage greens beside a toxic dump of gristle and gray meat. A week ago, Jennifer would have scraped something like this off her shoe in disgust. She was hungry, but eating this would be a challenge, even without the bizarre implement.

A large woman of indeterminate race with light skin, freckles, and kinky red hair pulled back into a knot at the top of her head sat down opposite and gave Jennifer a smile that lacked intelligence and the left bicuspid. 'I'm Big Red,' she said, then lowered her voice. 'You want some brew, you call Big Red.'

'What do you call *this*?' Jennifer asked her dinner companion, holding up her utensil.

'A spork,' Big Red told her, as if Jennifer was the stupid one. 'You never seen no spork before? Used to get them all the time at Kentucky Fried.'

'Are all the forks and spoons gone?' Jennifer asked.

'Get outta here, girl,' Big Red said. 'They don't give us no knives, no forks, no nothing. Don't want us to make weapons out of 'em.'

Jennifer used the spork to scoop up a little potato and gravy, but the gravy ran through the space between the two tines. 'Couldn't they give us just a spoon?' she asked in exasperation. 'You can't hurt someone with a spoon.'

'Oh, say what?' Big Red spoke up. 'Lottie J. took out Sabrina's eye with a spoon.' She was sporking up her food with the kind of relish Jennifer had rarely seen at three star restaurants. 'Lottie J. faked being sick and went to the dispensary and she got herself a spoon there and sharpened it and then when she came back and that Sabrina be botherin' her again, she just scooped out her eye like a melon ball.'

Jennifer put her spork down. The greasy taste of the gravy sat on her tongue like oil on a driveway. Her hunger turned to nausea. The glutinous gray-brown mass that passed as meat couldn't possibly be cut by the spork. 'You finished with that?' Big Red asked, eyeing Jennifer's tray.

Jennifer picked up a plastic cup of pudding and nodded. Before she could get her arm out of the way Big Red grabbed the tray and pulled it over to her, placing it on top of her first tray. She dug in and Jennifer realized that the niceties of cutting the meat were not an issue here; Big Red sporked the entire piece into her mouth and Jennifer watched as she masticated in a bovine manner for a lot longer than it took Jennifer to down the watery tapioca. This was definitely not the Four Seasons and there was no cotton candy cake with sugared violets and a candle on top for dessert.

To help calm her nausea, Jennifer tried to see what the other women were doing to get through their meals. Most of them were talking amongst themselves; some were even laughing. Then, to her absolute horror, Jennifer saw a grown woman trying to make herself a peanut butter and jelly sandwich using a spork. It would've been easier if she'd just used her fingers.

This was humiliation, not rehabilitation! Jennifer couldn't get beyond it no matter how she tried. She wondered if the population was really so dangerous that they couldn't be trusted with real eating utensils. She looked at Big Red, now mopping up the last of the food, and wondered if the story about the spoon was even true. Maybe it was one of those things they told a newcomer to scare her, like the camp story of the parked couple and the bloody hook hanging off the door of their car.

Then, even as she put the thought away, two women began screeching. In less than a second, Big Red jumped up and stood on the table, narrowly missing Jennifer's hand. 'Kill the bitch!' Big Red screamed. Jennifer wasn't sure that even in her exalted position Red could see anything. The imbroglio seemed to be on the floor, on the other side of the table, near the wall. Correction officers were on the two fighting women in an instant, and, although Jennifer didn't want to look, she couldn't help but see one of the officers – she thought it was Byrd – throw a vicious kick at an inmate who was rolling on the floor.

Just then, louder noise and movement broke out to the right. Jennifer looked over, but before she could see what was going on, she noticed a pay phone out in the corridor. This is it, she thought.

As the two women continued to shout, and as several officers rushed their table, Jennifer calmly started to walk backward to the exit. She'd walked against a crowd that way many times in New York's movie theaters when she wanted to get in to a popular show. As she made her way out, she watched the activity in front of her, but also glanced behind her to make sure she didn't disturb anyone by bumping into them. The last thing she needed was to be in a jailhouse brawl. Though she was known as the 'Warrior of Words' at Hudson, Van Schaank, the one thing she didn't know how to do was fight physically. Her path was clear – only another twelve steps before she'd be at the phone! It seemed that no one had noticed her, but her heart was thumping so loudly that she was certain that everyone could hear it, even over the ruckus.

Jennifer looked behind her again; in two more steps she reached the phone. She picked up the receiver and started to dial. She could hear the tones of the numbers in her ears and they drowned out the increasing noise from the room behind her. She dialed collect, and when the automated operator's voice asked for it she gave her name. At the other end of the line, in another world altogether, she heard the phone ring. She imagined Tom's apartment in Battery Park City overlooking New York Harbor and the Statue of Liberty. She'd looked out at the view a hundred times. She heard the phone ring again. Women were screaming and shouting from every corner of the room. It was worse than a snake pit. Jennifer couldn't help it: She instinctively put her hands over her ears, but still the noise penetrated despite her resolution. A tear began to drip from the corner of her right eye along her nose and down to her nostril. But she couldn't take her hands off her ears to wipe it away because the noise was so overwhelming.

Suddenly a squadron of guards surrounding someone was coming her way. Jennifer was bumped into by another woman who was struggling against three officers. 'Lockdown!' she heard an officer shout from the far side of the cafeteria. But Jennifer stayed where she was, listening to the distant ringing. Answer, damnit!

A shuffling line of women approached the exit, and one

woman stood directly in front of Jennifer and smiled. She was almost certain that this was the creature she had seen tending the marigolds on her way into Jennings. The black face split into a skeletal grin. 'Trying to escape this place?' the old woman asked.

At that same moment, a hand reached over and yanked the receiver away from Jennifer. 'You can't use the phone now,' a woman officer said, obviously agitated. 'Damn freshman!' She grabbed Jennifer and pushed her into line. 'Face forward!' the officer snapped. 'You too, Springtime. Step lively! Go to your houses,' the officer shouted.

Jennifer thought that she might just scream, break and run, even though the barred doors visibly truncated the long hallway ahead of her. She had to do something. She *had* to get through to Tom. He and Donald couldn't have known that this place was such a madhouse. Even one more day would be too long for her to keep her sanity. If Observation wasn't enough to make her want to kill herself, another meal like this would be.

11

Gwen Harding

*Many laws as certainly make bad men, as bad men
make many laws.*

Walter Savage Landor

Gwen Harding tightened the sash of her bathrobe, retied
the bow, and studied the papers spread before her. In her
office at Jennings she was kept busy from moment to
moment simply trying to deal with the administrative load,
employee problems, staffing, and management. Now for the
first time she looked at the JRU International information
package and the charts spread out on her dining table. JRU
had completed their proposal to the state and Warden
Harding, along with half a dozen other state correction
professionals, was being asked to write up her opinion of
their plan.

She took a preliminary look at the proposal. 'Fact: *The
private sector consistently saves government money*. In the
past decade, at least fourteen separate independent studies
have compared the costs of operating private and public

institutions. Twelve of those studies demonstrated that the cost of privately managed prisons is from two to twenty-nine percent less than that of government-managed facilities.' Gwen wondered how they managed to cut costs. Perhaps by firing outdated wardens.

She rose from her chair and passed the counter that was the only demarcation of where the dining room ended and the kitchen began. The kitchen was spotless. She crossed the blue and white tile floor to the stove, where a kettle – the only cooking implement she ever used in this kitchen anymore – sat on the one burner that she ever turned on. She took a mug from the cabinet. It had been a gift from a social-worker friend years ago. It was one of those ready-made but unpainted objects that children and women with time on their hands paint in shops set up expressly for that purpose. On it, Gwen's friend Lisa Anderson had painted BECAUSE I'M THE WARDEN, THAT'S WHY.

When she was given the gift, she and Lisa laughed over the reactions the mug stirred up among the other women at the shop where Lisa had painted it. Now Gwen filled it with hot water and dunked a tea bag into it. She was actually longing for a glass of gin, and the olives in the refrigerator seemed to be calling out to her, but she knew she had to keep a clear head. JRU was waiting and JRU came first. She crossed to the sink holding the steaming mug, opened the under-cabinet and dropped the wet tea bag into the empty trash bag. She didn't even make trash anymore. Gwen sighed. There was a different time and a different place where she used to cook and give dinner parties on a regular basis. And she'd been good – everyone praised her *coq au vin*. 'Jesus,' she thought, walking back to the dining table, 'do people even make *coq au vin* nowadays?' She hadn't

seen it on a menu or at a dinner party in years. But then . . .
she tried to think of the last dinner party she had attended
and couldn't remember one. That couldn't be! She stood
still, one hand resting on the back of a dining chair, the
other clenched around her mug. There was the dinner at
the restaurant at the close of the Eastern States Correction
Officers Association. And of course, there was always the
rubber chicken at local civic functions. But actual dinner
parties – just social time at someone's home, seemed to be
a bit thin on the ground.

Gwen took a sip of tea and wondered where her friend
Lisa Anderson was now. She smiled. They had had a lot of
fun together. Gwen had been divorced and Lisa had been in
the process of separating from her husband. The two of
them went out at least once a week, but that was . . . Gwen
put down the mug and tried to think whether it was six or
seven years ago. Could it be that long? She tried to think it
out. It had to be. It was just after she got the job at
Jennings.

At Jennings Gwen was too busy to see old friends or to
make new ones, at least in the beginning. Then, when she
had settled in, it seemed as if there were no friends to be
made. Certainly she couldn't count any of the Jennings
staff as friends. Perhaps her initial conscious distancing had
put people off, but she'd only done it because she'd been
frightened and overly sensitive about her new position and
its required authority. She supposed that by the time she
felt secure and was ready to unbend a little, no one else
seemed to be so inclined. Well, that was understandable.
She took another sip of tea and reminded herself that she'd
never been a natural extrovert.

Gwen sat down at the shining waxed dining table, only

sullied by the JRU report. She wouldn't think about anything else right now. Thinking about the emptiness of her life would surely drive her to the olives and she had to begin her response to this proposal. She looked at the inscription once again and smiled ruefully. When she first began working in the Department of Corrections it seemed to her that wardens had enormous power. Perhaps she'd been wrong or had exaggerated what she'd seen, but the position's power had certainly eroded since then. A warden's powers today were so limited, while her accountability was so vast, that Gwen often felt as trussed as a turkey before being shoved into the oven. And now this move to privatize prisons was sure to usurp whatever power she had remaining.

Privatization was a bastard trend that had been born – *mothered* – by Wall Street out of the incredible need for more prisons and taxpayers yelping at the costs of incarceration. If an aging population voted against school-board bond issues and preferred not to spend its tax dollars on educating their own grandchildren, Gwen knew all too well how they felt about spending public funds on strangers in the 'criminal population'. And yet, that population continued to grow. The only solution most agencies saw was building more places to incarcerate offenders. The ineffectual 'war on drugs', mandatory sentences, and a judiciary frightened that they might be perceived as 'soft on crime' had all contributed to a huge increase in prisoners in general, and an even larger increase in female prison statistics.

In fact, Gwen knew that women were the fastest growing sector of the prison population. Since 1980, the female inmate population nationwide had increased by more than five hundred percent. And this was not because women were involved in more violent crimes. It was because, nationwide, people were being imprisoned much more frequently for nonviolent crimes. In 1979, women convicted of nonviolent crimes were sent to prison roughly forty-nine percent of the time. By 1999, they were being sent to prison for nonviolent crimes nearly eighty percent of the time.

So privatization seemed a neat and simple answer to all these problems. Big business claimed it was ready to step in, take the risk, bear the expense, and turn prisons into moneymaking operations. Gwen of course knew that there were two major private prison corporations in the U.S. One of them, Wackenhut Corrections, owned fifty-two prisons 'employing' more than twenty-six thousand prisoners. The other, CCA – Corrections Corporation of America – had control over almost three times as many prisoners in eighty-one prisons. At the last conference for prison wardens that Gwen had attended, there had been a heated discussion over the privatization of prisons. Someone pointed out how large corporations had the incentive and the political clout to encourage the creation of a larger and larger prison population – a larger and larger cheap labor pool. This meant increased sentences and the increasing incarceration of men and women (usually from communities of color). Gwen wondered if this would turn into a new form of slavery.

She shook her head, turned another page of the proposal, and wondered what JRU International stood for. Justice Regulatory Underwriters? Jesus Really Understands? Jails 'R' Us? Jammed Rats Unlimited? Why not be honest and call it PFP: Prisons for Profit? She turned another page of the proposal before her and began to take notes in her small, neat handwriting.

*　　*　　*

There was no way this plan was going to work! Gwen looked down at the dozen pages of notations she'd already compiled. Most were written in capital letters and underlined several times. They looked like mad ravings, and weren't far from it. She'd have to somehow turn these blistering observations into cool bureaucratic reportage. She shook her head at the daunting task. What was the state thinking of?

She knew, of course, that her burgeoning budget presented nothing but trouble to them. Gwen knew that while her costs of maintaining one prisoner – including her bed, board, security, and the very limited health and education services that Jennings offered – was increasing to more than fifty-five dollars a day, private prisons claimed they could maintain prisoners at only forty-three dollars a day. She knew she couldn't compete with that.

But how was JRU going to deliver what they were promising? How were they possibly going to reduce medical staff? As it was, she had reluctantly cut the staff dramatically. When she looked at the 'Facilities Management Report' she was actually shocked. They proposed turning the visiting room into a space for a profit-making telemarketing operation. Where would the women visit with their families? They were also proposing to expand the prison itself and enclose the U of the courtyard, to provide additional housing. That meant darkening all the units facing the courtyard. Where would the women exercise? Where would Springtime plant flowers?

She had to be missing something in this ridiculous proposal. After all, though they weren't pleasant, the JRU staff didn't seem to be insane or particularly cruel. Yet the more Gwen studied the details, the more horrifying the plan seemed. It appeared that they expected to house and feed more than two hundred and thirty new inmates, who would be transferred from other facilities, facilities they would later close or would subsume into the JRU empire. Surely there must be a typo, Gwen thought as she looked at the numbers. Then she realized that the current, badly designed cells (which had four bunks but held only two prisoners) were actually going to be used to house four. The additional cells, those built in the courtyard space, would hold the balance.

Gwen did some quick calculations. It was unbelievable! Had those JRU jaspers ever read about Telgrin's experiment with rats? Decent, normal rats from good nests turned vicious – even cannibalistic – when they were overcrowded in their cages. Did they know Amnesty International's position on U.S. prison conditions? Were they so inexperienced that they didn't realize that the four bunk spaces were an error, far too small a space even for two? Clearly, JRU saw the inmates not as human beings or even rats but as a captive labor force. And based on their projection, a *profitable* force at that. How did they hope to transform this angry and sullen population of criminal inmates into chipper and cheerful telemarketers?

Gwen dropped her pen and began pacing around the dining table. This was never going to work. All of her years of experience, not just at Jennings and not just as a warden, but in social work, halfway houses, and other correctional facilities, told Gwen Harding that the plan was bound to fail. And what would happen then? Would there be protests? An uprising? And if there was violence – and with this plan there was bound to be plenty – would the inmates be blamed? Or would it be *her* head on the chopping block? If it all went up in flames – figuratively or literally – could

JRU just abandon the project, leaving the state to clean it up?

She knew very little about businesses and how they operated. She had spent her life working in the public sector. So had her father, who had been a cop, and her mother, who had been a teacher. In fact, aside from an uncle (who had run a dry goods store that failed), she couldn't think of anyone in her extended family who had any real business experience. The corporate world, with its financial realities and its politics, was a complete mystery to her. The one thing that she was sure of was that the executives who had toured her facility had been arrogant and much more prone to talk than to listen. But she'd noticed, of course, how little they wanted to hear from her. It was clear that they already felt she was an advocate of the 'prisoners'. When these people took over – if they did take over – how long would she even get to retain her job?

This situation was awful. Gwen felt the call of the olives in her refrigerator. She had to convince the Department of Corrections that this proposal should – *must* – be turned down. But Gwen had no idea how she was going to convince them that the JRU proposal was not only unrealistic, but also a recipe for failure – or for something much, much worse. She looked at the tea mug, now cold on the table, with its inscription: BECAUSE I'M THE WARDEN, THAT'S WHY. What a joke! No one at the State Department of Corrections listened to what a warden said. Especially a female warden.

She would have to sit down and put together a brilliant counterargument, complete with her own charts and graphs and projections that would not only explain why this plan was flawed but would refute JRU's assumptions. She'd also have to give the state some longer-range alternative strategy for cost-effectively handling an ever-growing prison population. She sighed and picked up the cold cup. How could she possibly do it? Gwen closed her eyes and pinched the bridge of her nose to ease the tension in her brow. In her mind she heard cries of *Attica! Attica! Attica!* Jesus Christ! This was all too much for her. She wasn't young anymore. Who was she kidding? They'd roll right over her. Gwen put the mug down, stood up and walked toward the refrigerator, only stopping on the way to grab a glass and the gin bottle.

12

Jennifer Spencer

*Remember that you are always in a better position to
ask for a job transfer if you have a good record on the
job you already have. Failure to do well on a job may
result in demotion or punishment.*

'Rules for Inmates' at the Ohio Reformatory for Women in
Marysville, Ohio. Kathryn Watterson, *Women in Prison*

Jennifer Spencer survived yet another night in prison, only
to awaken to another day of working in the laundry.

Nobody wanted the laundry detail. Undoubtedly that
was why Jennifer had been assigned to it. The laundry was a
long room in the basement with a low ceiling. Between the
steam and the pervasive smell of chlorine bleach and dirty
clothes, the place reminded Jennifer of nothing so much as
a cheap health club back in what she was beginning to think
of as her 'other life'.

There was nothing healthy about this place; the work
was heavy and dangerous. All of the prison's dirty laundry –
everything from the polyester jumpsuits to regular uniforms
to underpants, socks, sheets, and blankets – came through
this laundry. So did washrags and blood-soaked pillowcases.

In addition to the stuff that was *supposed* to be washed,

there were two other categories: detritus and contraband. Detritus included bloody gauze pads that had been accidentally wrapped in a towel and thrown into a cart, or the speculum that had been entangled in a dispensary johnny. There were hair clippings from the barbers, stale and rotting food in garment pockets, puzzle pieces, and every possible piece of unbreakable plastic dinnerware (including sporks, pepper shakers, and plastic ketchup squeezers). Jennifer had been issued heavy-gauge rubber gloves and an apron, but it wasn't enough. About the only thing she figured the gloves could protect her from were the roaches she was constantly finding in pockets, socks, or accumulated at the bottom of the bucket.

The laundry at Jennings reminded Jennifer of a blue flannel suit: it attracted everything but men and money. Only two days ago Suki had pulled out a speculum and on another day Jennifer herself had felt a lump inside the tied leg of a pair of slacks. When she untied the bottom the meticulously taped package of cocaine dropped like an iced plum into her hands. 'One day we found a scalpel,' Suki told her.

Laundry came in on industrial rolling carts that, for some reason, Jennifer kept tripping over again and again. The carts were heavy to push, and because the sheets and clothing were often water-soaked, simply untangling the garments and putting her gloved-sheathed hand into the mix seemed almost more than she could bear. The smell of sweating women, the industrial-strength liquid detergent, the cheap perfumes, and the mildew were intolerable to her. I'll call Tom and get him to charter a helicopter, she told herself.

After Jennifer unloaded the dirty linens into the huge

front loader and snapped the lock shut, she would pull the cart back and watch Suki do her magic. It was the only fun that Jennifer managed to get out of the dirty work. When Suki turned on the huge stainless steel industrial washing machines, it was as if the little blonde girl was in control of the space shuttle at Houston. She could barely reach the flip switches on the top of the machine, but she managed to snap some of them all the way up, some in the middle, some all the way down. 'You have to be careful to synchronize the water level push button with the "on" button or otherwise the water runs out over the top. It'll get you wetter than you were when you were in Observation!' Suki yelled over the noise of the tumbling drum.

Once the machine was activated, Suki and Jennifer would stand back and watch the water fill up the front of the glass and watch the bubbles consume the clothes inside.

When all the dirty clothes were sorted and washed it was time to go help out in the clean laundry. There were two black-topped Formica tables butted up against each other where women were folding the clean clothes. None of the women liked folding the jumpsuits, shirts, or undergarments. And forget about doing the socks – that was right up there with the popularity of having to wash silverware. There was always a silent contest, though, when it came to folding the towels and facecloths. It was a competition of speed, neatness, and the crispness of the crease (to insure that the stack of linens would stay vertical). The record for facecloth stacks was held by an older woman named Rory with seventy-five, while Dakota – a black teenager – held the record for twenty-five bath towels.

For Jennifer – who hadn't done laundry since college –

there was a certain fascination in watching the women work briskly, trying to outdo each other. She had to admit that the cleanliness of this part of the work area was nice, the fresh smell of the clean clothes, the heat that radiated from the sheets and towels. It was a homey kind of comfort that she couldn't quite get over.

Later in the day, just after Suki had pushed and emptied a particularly large cart loaded with wet linens, Jennifer saw the girl clutch at her stomach, grow completely pale, and then pass out. Jennifer rushed to Suki's side and caught her just under the arms. In another two seconds, Suki's head would have hit the wet concrete floor. For a moment Jennifer stood there, paralyzed, holding the tiny body upright. She couldn't lay her on the floor, nor could she let go of her grip to get a better hold and attempt to carry Suki to the infirmary. Unconscious, Suki was ninety pounds of dead weight and, unlike the wet laundry, she wasn't on wheels.

Through the din, the vapors of the room, and the jerry-built lighting system, Flora, the supervisor, a middle-aged woman who seemed to really care about her laundry staff, made a motion to another inmate to help Jennifer pick Suki up and lay her across one of the black Formica laundry tables.

A cold cloth was brought for Suki's head and a couple of aspirins were distributed. From her pocket, Flora brought out an ampule and snapped it open right under Suki's nose. Suki's eyes popped open – the bright blue color agitated by all that she could feel going on around her. When her eyelids closed again, Jennifer took a deep breath and almost choked as the supervisor cracked open another capsule of ammonia salt. Once again, Suki's head snapped back and her eyes rolled open. This time, the supervisor cradled her head in her arms and began to ask questions.

'Suki, can you hear me?'

The blonde bounced her head up and down.

'Talk to me. Talk to me, then,' Flora said.

For no discernible reason, Suki began to sing. Her voice was as petite as the supervisor but a good deal more polite 'Don't Cry for Me, Argentina' as she warbled some lines from the flat stage of the linen folding table.

'Are you on your period?' Flora asked.

Suki shook her head.

'We'd better bring her down to the dispensary,' Flora said.

'No, no!' Suki remonstrated. She struggled to sit up, then lost her strength and collapsed again on the table.

'If you take her to medical, they'll do a quick once over and take money from her canteen fund, and she doesn't have that much in it,' Springtime told Flora.

'They make you *pay* for medical treatment?' Jennifer asked in disbelief.

'Yep. A co-pay. Five bucks for a doc, four bucks for a nurse,' Flora explained.

Suki came to again and assured them she was fine. As the group broke up Suki grabbed Jennifer's arm. 'Jennifer, lean over,' she said, and Jen bent her head over the table. 'Can I tell you a secret?' asked Suki, her eyes bright with news.

'Sure,' Jennifer asked, as the supervisor left.

'I'm not on my period,' Suki giggled. 'I can't be.'

'Well, you might be weak anyway,' Jennifer told the young girl, and patted her head. 'Sometimes people are affected differently.'

'No, no, you don't understand,' Suki giggled again. 'I'm going to have a baby.'

For the first moment, Jennifer felt panic. She looked at Suki's flat stomach. Was the girl delusional? Did she think she was going to give birth here? Jennifer had seen her crumple and was sure that Suki hadn't hit her head, but somehow she was out of it. 'Suki,' Jen said gently, 'you're not having a baby. You just passed out.'

'Promise you won't tell nobody?' Suki admonished.

'Oh, I won't tell,' Jennifer told her. But how could she be pregnant? How could she *get* pregnant? Maybe she was just having some kind of seizure. Jennifer looked over at the petite blonde. She seemed to be completely recovered. 'Suki,' Jennifer went on boldly. 'You can't be pregnant, can you?'

Suki just smiled. It was the same smile that Jennifer had seen her give to Roger Camry.

When the workday was over and Jennifer had settled Suki into their cell, she realized that she had a little free time before the bell rang for dinner. One of the phones in her 'pod' wasn't being used. She approached the phone as if it were the magical port that would take her out of this forsaken place. She picked up the receiver and entered Tom's number. But as the phone began to ring on the other end, Officer Byrd came into the rec area of the unit. 'Head count,' he announced. 'Take your places.'

Jennifer kept listening to the ringing. She watched the inmates leisurely move to the entrances of their cells. She, however, was frozen in place. She *had* to get the call through.

Officer Byrd walked up to the first doorway and, with

clipboard in hand, marked off something on his papers. He moved to the next, looked over the women, and marked again. The phone rang again. When he got to Jennifer and Suki's doorway, Jennifer could see Suki leaning against the door for support. Pick up, she thought. Come on. Pick up, Tom.

'Jennifer Spencer,' Officer Byrd growled in a voice loud enough for her to hear all the way down the hall. 'Jennifer Spencer?' he repeated. 'Where is she, the infirmary?'

From her place at the phone Jennifer could see Suki's head shake strenuously and her mouth form the word 'no'. Then she smiled flirtatiously at Officer Byrd and pointed in her direction. He turned around quickly and Jennifer couldn't help but shrink back as he started toward her, though he was a long hallway away. But in what seemed like two steps he was in her face. 'Just what the hell do you think you're doing?' he asked. He grabbed her upper arm roughly. 'It's head count. You're supposed to be in your cell.'

Jen could hear the phone ring. Pick up, pick up, she silently prayed. 'I'm just trying to call . . .' she began.

'I don't care what you're doing!' he snarled. 'You stop everything – even if you're taking a leak – and get to the entrance of your house for head count.'

Then the ringing stopped. 'This is a collect call from . . .' the automated voice intoned.

'Move it,' Byrd was saying at the same time. He jerked her arm. With the receiver still to her ear, Jennifer heard Tom's voice. 'Yes, I'll accept the charges,' he said. And at that moment, Officer Byrd grabbed the phone and jammed it into the receiver.

'Get to your house, *now*, Spencer! You're being written

up for this,' Byrd said, his face flushed almost purple. 'Just two more incidents and you'll be losing visitor's privileges.'

Stricken, Jennifer did as she was told.

13

Jennifer Spencer

> *Prisoners of hope.*
> Zech. 9:12

'Back off and wait your ass like everybody else,' the skinny woman hissed at Jennifer.

Jennifer decided not to argue. She wasn't standing any closer to the woman than anybody else was, and like everyone else she'd been waiting in line for more than half an hour to use the phone. But everyone steered clear of the harsh skinny woman. Suki told her that she was from Haiti and knew voodoo. That didn't worry Jennifer, but the crazy look in the woman's eye did. Three women had already used the phone, each for a ten-minute interval, and by rights the receiver should now be handed to Jennifer. But she wasn't going to press the point with this obviously deranged, outraged woman who seemed to be getting some bad news.

Of all the facility problems at this disgusting prison, the phones were the worst. Some bastard in some state architectural office somewhere had to think long and hard in order to make placing a phone call such a humiliating experience. Two antique-looking pay phones hung side by side in the rec room, and *why* they were pay phones no one could say since inmates were only allowed to make collect calls.

Worse, they were placed just high enough on the wall so that you couldn't sit down while using them, but neither could you stand completely upright – if you did, your head was directly in front of the television set mounted on the rec room wall. If the television was on – and it was always on – you had to crouch slightly for your entire call, and then try not to bump into the person who was crouched next to you using the other phone.

Right now the volume on the TV was turned up full blast, and as the women on the phones shouted to be heard, everyone else who was trying to watch the television was shouting at the callers to 'shut the fuck up!' or 'get your goddamn fat head out of the way!' It was chaos.

At last Jennifer was just a moment away from getting to the phone. Barring a lockdown, a head count, or an act of God, she would get to talk to Tom. She stared at the receiver, now being sprayed with spittle as the angry, skinny woman shouted something. Disgusting as it was, that phone was her only lifeline to the Outside.

Jennifer called Tom's office number and heard the phone ringing. Pamela, Tom's secretary, picked it up. The moment she heard Pam's voice, Jennifer began to speak, but the automated operator interrupted her to ask whether or not Pamela would accept the charges. Jennifer felt her stomach contract tightly. My God, what if Pam said no? She held her breath for what seemed a very long moment. When her call was accepted and she heard Pam's voice say hello again, Jennifer felt actual tears of relief in her eyes.

'Pam?' she said. 'This is Jennifer. I need to talk to Tom right away.'

'Jennifer!' Pam said brightly, as if this were a normal situation. 'You're calling from –'

'Yes, yes! I need to talk to Tom right away,' Jennifer repeated.

'Oh, sure. He's in a meeting but –'

'Get him! Get him right now,' Jennifer said.

She held her breath and waited. The thirty seconds of silence seemed as long as her entire previous life. Then, when Tom's voice said hello she felt as if her heart might explode in her chest. 'Jen!' he said. 'Jen, is it you? I've been so worried.'

'Oh, Tom,' she cried, and she was shocked to hear how small and miserable she sounded. 'Oh, Tom!' She looked behind her at the line of women waiting for the phone and lowered her voice. 'Get me out of here. This is unbelievable. You just don't know.'

'What's happened?' he asked.

She realized how wide the chasm from their last good-bye to this hello was. She could never get him to understand. And she certainly didn't have the time now. 'Why hasn't *anything* happened?' she asked. 'You have to get me out of here.'

'Of course,' he said. 'God, I've been so worried. I couldn't reach you and I thought you would call me right away. Why didn't you call?'

'Why didn't I call?' How could she possibly explain to him what this place was like? 'That's all I've been trying to do,' she said. 'But it's not easy here.' Not easy! Ha! This conversation was surreal. She herself wouldn't believe what she'd been through if she herself hadn't been through it. 'Tom, what's going on? When do I get out of here?' She couldn't afford to waste her precious ten minutes on any other topic.

'Soon, real soon.'

His voice, his promise, calmed her. She breathed deeply, the first deep breath of air she'd had since she'd stepped into Jennings. 'Tomorrow?' she asked. She really didn't think she could go back to the filth of the laundry, and more meals in that wretched cafeteria would surely kill her.

Tom said something she couldn't hear. 'What?' she said.

'Tomorrow?' Tom was repeating. 'No, it's not going to be tomorrow.'

Jennifer felt panic rising. 'It has to be,' she told him. 'It *has* to be.'

'Shut the fuck up,' the woman using the phone beside her snarled. Jennifer lowered her voice and crouched even more to keep her head from blocking the television.

'You don't know what it's like here,' she said. 'You just can't imagine.'

'I know it must be rough but . . .'

'You don't know anything!' she said. 'This is no country club. And I'm not getting any special treatment.'

'Where are you?' he asked. 'I can barely hear you.'

How to describe the bedlam of the rec room? 'Never mind that,' she said. 'What's going on? How soon can I get out?'

'Look,' Tom said, his voice soothing. 'You can't expect us to engineer all this right away. You . . .'

Jennifer looked around at the rec room; inmates in grim

uniforms were playing cards, building puzzles, pacing around the room dodging the broken chairs, stopping to stare at the smudges of dirt on the walls. As usual, a clearly psychotic woman was ranting and scratching at herself, but nothing was being done to help her or shut her up. Jen took in the funky smell, the palpable anger and boredom. 'Not right away?' she asked. 'I don't understand. You said it would be just for a day or two. Remember? You said it would be a country club. And that you'd get me right out. House arrest, or a commuted sentence or . . .'

'Look, Jen, I admit it's going a little slower than we'd like,' Tom said calmly. 'You just have to trust me and accept that. We can't just bully our way through the courts on this.'

The courts? They hadn't planned on the courts. 'But what about the governor?' she asked.

'White-collar crime is a big political issue right now. And your case became pretty high profile.' He paused for a moment, and in that second or two Jen thought she'd lost him. 'You know,' he continued, 'the press is still watching us very closely, and if I move too fast they'll be all over it again. And if they are, no judge is going to take the risk of losing his bench over this case. We have to find the right time or we'll be in a worse jam than we are now.'

'We?' Jen asked and heard the bitterness in her voice. 'That must be the royal we that you're using. Because *I* am the one incarcerated, Tom. I am the one who was strip searched. I am the one who slept in a cell with a felon. I'm the one wearing the jumpsuit and eating the crap they call food here.' Then her anger left her all at once and was replaced by a sickening fear mixed with grief. She began to sob. She told herself she had to stop. She couldn't waste her phone time like this, nor let the other inmates see or hear her cry.

'Oh, Jen, I know it's tough,' Tom soothed. 'Look, just try to sit tight. I wish I could do this for you. And I wish I could do it quicker. But you have to believe me when I say that we're doing absolutely everything to get you out of there. It all takes time, Jennifer.'

Time! It already seemed as if everything in Jen's previous life had dissolved, had evaporated, and this dirty room, these miserable and frightening women were all that she knew. 'How long do you think it's going to be?' she managed to whisper.

'Two weeks,' he said. 'Three at the most. And we're already looking into getting you transferred or giving you some special treatment in the meantime.'

Jen couldn't speak. Two weeks! Another fourteen days of this! And maybe more. It was unimaginable. It was literally unbearable. She felt as if her breastbone were cracking, the pressure on her chest was so great.

'Baby?' Jen heard Tom's voice, but she could only answer him with a nod. He, of course, couldn't see her response. 'Baby, are you there?' he asked.

'I don't think I can . . .' her voice trailed off, the pain moving up to her throat and choking her.

'Don't be upset, Jen,' he said. 'You know I love you, don't you?'

'Yes,' she managed.

'Well I promise you that everything's going to be all right.' He paused and his voice became soft, really loving. 'You have to tough it out now, Jen. We're all behind you and we're playing for very big stakes. Just hang on a little while, and think of the reward.'

She clutched the receiver tightly and held it close to her. 'I just didn't know it would be this hard,' Jen whispered.

'Oh, baby. I'm so sorry,' Tom told her. 'You know I would have done it for Donald if it didn't mean I'd be disbarred. You know what *that* would have done to our future.' She nodded again. 'So, can you just hang in there?' he asked. 'Think about the penthouse we'll buy. Think about our wedding. And the cruise we'll go on.' He laughed, then lowered his voice. 'Think about lying on the sand with me on a Caribbean beach.'

'Enough, goddamnit!' Jen heard the words, jumped, and then turned to see the tall dark woman from Intake, the one who had tried on her shoes. She gave Jen a push on her shoulder. 'You've had more than ten minutes. You're not the only one who has a lawyer.'

Jen covered the receiver of the phone with her hand. 'Just another second,' she told the reptile coldly and turned back to the phone.

'Will you come for visiting day on Saturday?' Jennifer asked Tom.

'*This* Saturday?' he asked, sounding hesitant. 'Baby, I've got so much work to do. We're preparing your appeal – just in case, but we're also making a motion for mistrial and going the pardon route.'

'Please,' she begged. 'I only get an hour for a visitor. If I'm going to be here please come.'

'I'll try,' Tom promised.

'Hurry up, debutante,' the woman said, and this time she hit Jen's shoulder harder.

'I've got to go,' Jen said reluctantly, but even after they said good-bye and Tom had hung up, Jen found she couldn't let go of the receiver. She still held it to her ear.

It was Suki who finally pulled Jennifer away from the phone. 'Come on,' she said gently. 'Come away, now.' She brought Jen over to a chair. 'Bad news or good?' she asked, but before Jen had time to answer, a woman CO entered the unit and announced something. Jen didn't catch what she said, but Suki jumped up and got the look of a kid on Christmas morning. 'They're handing out the packages!' she said and grabbed Jennifer's arm, happily leading her across the rec room and into the hall where two of the guards had wheeled in a large cart laden with parcels.

'Are you expecting something?' Jen asked Suki.

'I never get a package,' Suki said, then put her hand on her stomach. 'But I got one here!' she whispered at Jennifer. 'But maybe you got a package today, Jenny,' Suki offered cheerfully. Jen shook her head, but the two of them stood with the other hopeful women.

Jennifer was shocked to see that each and every package was already torn open. Obviously the contents had been rifled through and searched for contraband, but the women all eagerly stood in line and unashamedly shouted for joy when they heard their names called as recipients of these gifts from the Outside. Jennifer watched as each inmate hungrily grabbed her package from the officers and then clutched it to her breast. Most of them scurried to their house or a far corner to examine the bounty of the contents.

Many of the women, the forgotten ones, stood silently off to the side. They knew that they would be receiving no packages today – or perhaps any day. Their looks of envy and of unspeakable sadness nearly brought Jennifer to tears. But when other women – those who were in their crews – got something, the loners gathered around the lucky member of their prison family and shared in the delight of the presents.

Jennifer thought of her mother. Up to now she had been so grateful that the woman who suffered enough in life hadn't lived long enough to witness the shame and humiliation of Jennifer's imprisonment. But right now Jennifer would give anything if she could receive a package from her mother – a package from home. She, too, wanted to open a box filled with cookies and LifeSavers and playing cards.

All around the room there were happy squeals as packages were opened and the contents were discovered. Jennifer found herself smiling as she witnessed the joy a gift of Dr Scholl's footpads could bring. Apparently inmates could buy a few generic healthcare products from the prison canteen, but real happiness was opening a box and finding Caress – Head and Shoulders – Visine – Rolaids – Jergens. The brand names were reverently whispered like the names of the gods of comfort and contentment. And as Jennifer watched she was amazed to see how nothing was taken for granted. Even Tampax and Preparation H were spoken of reverentially. The boxes and bottles were eagerly passed around, and the women, who were starved for any bit of normalcy or sign of life from the Outside examined every word, scent, and color of the products.

'Look! They've changed the Keebler elves,' one woman said with a laugh.

'Let me see.'

'Show me.'

A small chorus of voices responded to each announcement.

'Snickers bars keep getting smaller and smaller all the time,' observed Flora.

'I wish they would just make *plain* potato chips,' said a third. 'I don't think my gut can take Sour Cream and Bar-B-Que Jalapeños.'

Nutritional contents were studied and discussed, and every bit of wrapping paper and packaging was savored and saved. Many of the boxes included writing tablets and pens. One woman received an entire box of greeting cards with all of the envelopes already bearing postage stamps and preaddressed to family members. Women *oohed and ahhed* over the thoughtfulness of that, and they wanted to examine every card.

There were boxes of tissues, tea bags, and Q-tips. In some packages there were sketch pads and colored pencils – even file folders and erasers.

Jennifer's heart ached as she watched the pleasure that such a simple present could evoke. It was too easy to say this was like a birthday or Christmas; it was more important than that. These packages were more than a celebration. They were a reassurance that beyond these pink and green and gray and orange walls there were still shopping malls and pharmacies and grocery stores, all brightly lit. Each package was not only a gift from the Outside, but a momentary trip back into the world of the living. Halls Mentho-Lyptus – Sweet'n Low – Diet Coke – Chun King. Each item proclaimed, 'You're not forgotten,' 'We remember you,' 'We know what you like and what you need.' Jennifer turned away somewhat ashamed; *she* had been having a fit because she'd be here for a week or two.

No one was watching the television now that the packages had arrived, and Jennifer wondered if she should make another phone call to Tom. Maybe if she could stand up-right while talking to him it would be easier to discuss all the things that they had to discuss. She wished she hadn't hung up so abruptly. She wondered if he was still in his office. Her mind was miles away from the rec room and from Jennings, so when she heard her name being called it was as if it came to her from far away.

'Jennifer Spencer! Jennifer Spencer!' shouted one of the officers. 'Come on – use it or lose it. We don't have all day for this.'

'Jenny, you have a package!' Suki squealed, and actually jumped up and down.

Jennifer turned to see a small parcel being held out to her by the officer. It was the size of a shoebox, and in her haze Jennifer wondered who would be sending her a pair. She walked across the room and took the package. Suki had come to her side and was eagerly urging her on. 'Open it up!' she kept repeating while Jenny held the box to her chest.

'It's already opened,' Jen pointed out.

'Who do you think it's from?' Suki asked.

Jennifer didn't have a clue. Maybe Tom? But he hadn't said anything about a package while they were on the phone. Who else could it be? Who else was there? Jennifer shivered. There was no one Outside who'd send her anything.

'Let's take it to our house,' Suki half suggested, half begged. 'I never get packages to share with the crew.'

Jen smiled ruefully at the use of the word 'house'. As if that made this all homier. But she looked at Suki's radiant face and couldn't refuse.

Once they settled on the bottom bunk, Jennifer opened the box and peered inside. A tube of Crest – three Oral-B toothbrushes – Tic Tacs. She had to smile at the thought of

Tom taking the time to go to a CVS or Rite Aid to purchase all of this for her. Usually she picked up this kind of stuff for him. And she had to give him credit for remembering the products she liked to use – but Tic Tacs! She'd never used those in her whole life. Well, it's the thought that counts. There were hair care products – a shampoo, a conditioner, talcum, and other things. Tears rose in her eyes. Jennifer took out and fondled first one product then the other: her gifts. It did remind her of going through a Christmas stocking, but no stocking had ever meant so much.

Hoping to find a card, Jennifer lifted the last tissue from the bottom of the box. She saw a trifolded piece of paper. She actually sniffed it in hopes that she would be able to smell the scent of Tom's aftershave on it. With great anticipation she unfolded the Hudson, Van Schaank letterhead.

Dear Jennifer,

I thought you might need some of this. I would like to come and see you on visitor's day if that's okay with you. Because I'm neither a family member nor your attorney I have to get your approval. I've written to the Warden so she should be in touch with you directly. I look forward to seeing you. And try to keep smiling. You have such a beautiful smile.

Leonard Benson

'Who's Leonard Benson?' Suki asked, peering over Jennifer's shoulder. 'Your boyfriend?'

'No,' Jennifer responded, too surprised by the note and ny's unexpected kindness to really hear the question.

'Oh – uh, he's a guy at the office. My accountant.' She stared into the box.

Lenny Benson – her accountant – had sent her an entire box of oral hygiene and grooming products?

'Let's go to Movita's house and show the crew what you got.' Suki was so proud and enthusiastic that Jen couldn't really deny her.

Most of the crew was gathered in Movita's cell. Suki good-naturedly teased Jennifer in front of the others. 'Jenny has a new boyfriend! Jenny has a new boyfriend!' she shouted.

Suki gestured all around the tiny room. 'This is Jenny,' she said.

'Jennifer,' Jennifer corrected.

'And this,' Suki continued without taking in the correction, 'is Theresa, the best cook in Jennings.'

'Hi,' Theresa said.

'And Movita,' Suki said. 'She's the boss.'

'She's not *my* boss,' Cher said.

'That's Cher. Did you meet her at Intake?' Suki asked.

Of course Jennifer remembered the Morticia character from Intake. And she remembered her from the telephone line. But she opted to play dumb. 'No, I don't remember,' Jennifer said. Cher sneered lightly in response.

'Jenny got a big load of stuff from her boyfriend. She gave me a new toothbrush,' Suki said. 'Look at it all.'

Cher demanded to 'have a look at what ya' got,' and took the box from Jen. Then she expertly appraised each and every item. 'These Oral-B toothbrushes are top of the line,' she admitted. She looked down at Jen. 'But tell 'em to send ya' something mintier than Crest the next time,' she advised, handing the box back to Jennifer.

'Never look a gift horse in the mouth,' Theresa calmly advised, 'especially this one.'

Movita smiled. 'This boyfriend seems to be a little pre-occupied with her mouth already,' she said and smiled at Jennifer.

'He says she has a beautiful smile,' Suki said, as proud as if it were about her.

A little embarrassed, Jennifer shook her head. 'He's just a friend from work.'

'You know what they say about smiles, don't ya'?' Theresa asked. 'Everybody smiles in the same language. Smiles are the same everywhere ya' go in this world. You can smile in English and it means the same damn thing in Thailand. You know what I'm saying?'

'Would my smile mean the same thing in Poland?' Cher asked, smirking.

'If it was *my* smile, yes. But not if it was yours. You don't smile,' Theresa told her. 'You've got a shit-eatin' grin. Uh, pardon my French,' she said to Jennifer.

'Would anyone like the Tic Tacs?' Jennifer asked. She wound up giving them to Theresa. The hair spray went to Cher and a tube of hand cream was given to Movita. Jennifer was happy to be able to share her package with these women. It made her feel like a popular girl in high school.

The crew was waiting for their dinner to heat up. Theresa told Jennifer that she had received real goodies in her package from home: salami, some cheese, a six-pack of Sprite and a bag of Oreos. Tonight they would feast on store-bought, brand-name junk food. 'Well, afterwards you can all brush with Crest,' Jennifer offered.

'So back in New York City what do you usually make for dinner?' Theresa asked Jennifer.

'Reservations!' Jennifer replied.

Suki laughed. 'Get it? Reservations – like making reservations for dinner. Ya' get it?'

Movita looked at Jennifer. 'I have something for you, too,' Movita said, reaching into her pocket. 'It's from the Warden.' She handed Jennifer an envelope.

'Two in one day,' Jennifer said as she opened it and unfolded the note inside. As she silently read what it said, she felt her stomach tighten into a knot. Then she looked up at Movita and asked, 'Is this true? Can we only have one visitor on visitor's day?'

Movita shrugged. 'Not exactly. Ya' get one hour. Ya' decide how ta break it up. Half hour for each or whatever. You'll have to let ol' Gwen know who ya' wanna see,' Movita told her, 'your attorney – who can come any time – or the guy that sent the package. It's up to you.'

'I'd go for the one who makes you smile,' Theresa suggested.

Jennifer wondered which one that would be and decided she'd see both but give more time to Tom.

The bell rang for dinner and Jennifer left the crew to go once again, all alone, to the horrors of the cafeteria.

14

Gwen Harding

*Justice should remove the bandages from her eyes long
enough to distinguish between the vicious and the
unfortunate.*

Robert G. Ingersoll

The Warden was drunk, but not so drunk that she didn't
know it. More than drunk, she was lonely, and she was
afraid that she was going to lose her job. As she locked away
her bottle and journal in the bottom drawer of her desk, she
considered the irony of her situation. She was probably the
only woman in Jennings who didn't want to leave the place;
not tonight – not ever. She rose unsteadily and looked out
the window at the ugly coils of razor wire and the illuminated double rows of fences. She ran her fingers through
her hair, out of place and hanging over her eyes. She had
to move.

She stepped through the door of her office, irrationally
hoping that Movita would be there, sitting at her desk. She
~~ted~~ – no *needed* – to talk. But Watson was safely in her

cell. And Miss Ringling had her coat on at a quarter to five and wouldn't stay a moment past the hour even if the entire prison staff was being held hostage.

Gwen returned to her desk and wished that she had even one person she could confide in, or laugh with. Gin was not a friend. Gin didn't listen and gin, most certainly, never answered any of her questions or calmed her fears. In fact, Gwen knew that the gin, once a useful painkiller, had become her enemy. JRU, of course, was also her enemy, and Gwen was very much afraid that the State Department of Corrections might also become her enemy. The administration was sick of her and her years of fighting for better conditions and bigger budgets. And the inmates were not, could not, be her friends. Yet all of them – JRU, the Department of Corrections, and the inmates – they all wanted Gwendolyn to be a friend to them.

She looked down at her report to the State Department of Corrections. She prepared it at home and actually went to an outside typing service and Kinko's to do the word processing and graphics. That was because she didn't want anyone within the prison – staff *or* inmates – to read either the proposal or her response to it. It would only breed unrest, fear, and rumors. All her prison experience told Gwen that rumors were one of her biggest foes of all.

She ran her hand across the big report. She'd dropped one copy at the FedEx office herself, and now she had to take this copy and lock it away safely. Along with all of her charts, graphs, and cost projections, which clearly illustrated how and why the proposed prison privatization by JRU International was destined to fail. Gwen had summed up the moral issues with strong harsh words:

In addition to the practical, humane, and financial considerations summarized above, there is a political and ethical issue that must also be addressed. The work of those incarcerated, when exploited for commercial purposes, can easily be interpreted as a form of slave labor. In my opinion, the inmate population of this – or any other – correctional facility cannot and should not be exploited as a homogeneous pool of potential laborers. Their incarceration may void their right to vote, but it does not revoke their humanity.

The new century has brought with it new social and related penal problems. Without doubt, the explosion of the female prison populations has created a daunting difficulty and a major tax burden. But to convert this from a problem to an opportunity for profit-making would, without a doubt, be taking the wrong turn. The myriad and complex problems that these women bring to us must be the focus of our future correctional efforts. To propose the reverse is an invitation for disaster.

Drunk as she was, Gwendolyn was proud of her report and of her work at Jennings. She decided to take a walk through the cellblocks. The lockdown bell had sounded more than an hour earlier, so no one would see her – or get close enough to smell her breath. Just to be safe she turned and entered the bathroom that adjoined her office. Gwendolyn flipped the light switch, grimaced at her reflection, and then rinsed her mouth with Listerine. She splashed some cold water on her face, brushed her hair, put on her suit t, and then walked a very straight line out of the door ard the row upon row of quiet cells.

After the lockdown bell sounds, the inmates have only minutes to return to their 'houses' before the bars slide shut and the guards do the nightly bed check. They are given but a half hour to prepare themselves for bed before being plunged into a sudden darkness that – except for the muffled cries – brings with it an eerie and forbidding silence. Only the click of the Warden's heels sounded against the floor amidst the snores, the sex, the sighs – and the sobs. There was always sobbing.

And the sobbing would get a lot worse if this JRU takeover happened, Gwen thought. The burgeoning population of women's prisons created a bizarre business opportunity. Building prisons, staffing them, and exploiting the situation was something corporate America viewed as a growth industry. And communities, loath in the past to accept prisons, now often welcomed them because of the construction work and longer-term staffing positions they created in towns with failing economies. Who would have ever conceived of prisons as profit centers?

So much was going to be changing all around her that Gwendolyn Harding wondered if it might be wiser to simply resign before she was asked to leave. Every meeting with the men from JRU was more baffling than the last, and as she tried to articulate the folly of many of their proposed changes at Jennings, she herself could hear the defensive and petulant tone that crept into her voice. The men simply smiled and nodded as she voiced her concerns, all of them smirking in that way men smirk just before they accuse you of hysteria.

In the dimness, her feet shuffled along the uneven floors. It took only a split second for her toe to catch a ridge, and she was suddenly pitched forward. She felt herself toppling, but was helpless to stop herself. She managed to twist her shoulder to protect her face before she hit the floor, but the blow was a hard one. She hit the side of her forehead and knocked the wind out of herself. She tried to gasp for help, but couldn't as she blacked out.

The next thing Gwen knew, a pair of capable hands was holding her firmly and helping her up. 'You okay, Warden?' Movita Watson asked.

Gwen was dazed but managed to speak. 'I'm okay, but what are you doing out of your cell?'

'Infirmary visit. That time of the month,' Movita replied.

Gwen raised her hand to her head and felt the bump and the sticky wetness of blood. 'I guess I slipped,' she murmured.

'Just lean on me. It's okay,' Movita said.

Gwen leaned. She saw the young, white face of Roger Camry standing there looking useless. She felt dizzy and there was a sharp pain on the side of her neck.

'I'm all right,' she lied. 'Thank you. I'm all right.' She wasn't sure if that was true, but she hoped so. She found that her legs were steady. The lubrication of the gin had probably cushioned her fall. She tried to stand alone.

'I'll help you to the office,' Movita offered. 'She'll be fine,' she told Camry. 'Just fine. Come on,' Movita told Gwen.

'Warden, can I help you?' Camry asked as he approached them.

'I'm just fine,' Gwen lied, really shaken now. She sup- posed she was lucky that it was Roger Camry who had seen her fall rather than Doug Slavitz or that bastard Byrd, who would tell the entire prison and state management before morning. Camry was a good sort and would keep his mouth shut. But she was ashamed that she needed to depend on him and his kindness.

Both reluctant and grateful, Gwen went along with Movita. Did she know? Could she smell the gin? It was not far to her office and they walked in silence, Gwen feeling more pain with each step. At the door she fumbled in her pocket for her keys, but as she pulled them out, Movita took them from her hand and unlocked the office door. A total violation, but so was walking alone through the prison under the influence. Movita turned on the light with her left hand while still supporting Gwen with her right. Then the inmate helped the Warden to a chair.

'You sit here,' Movita said. 'I'm gonna get you some ice for that bang you got on the side of your head.'

Gwen again put her hand up to her forehead. It hurt, but was it also visible? Had Officer Camry seen it? How embarrassing! She listened to Movita's retreating steps. She knew how precious ice was for the inmates; it would take Movita some time to get some. Gwen wasn't so naive to what happened in her prison. All she needed was Frances to deliver kites on the rocks tomorrow and the whole population would know of her indiscretion. There was time; she reached into her drawer for the gin bottle, for just a small drink. She needed it.

When Movita came back with the ice, Gwen was slumped over her desk, the injured side of her face resting on a pile of folders. She felt no pain but she couldn't move. The last drink had done her in. 'I'm sorry,' she said to Movita. 'I'm not feeling well.'

Gently Movita lifted the Warden's head, removed the folders, and positioned the ice on the bump. 'I'll make you some coffee,' she said. 'Just a minute.'

Gwen's face was now against the ice. At first it felt good, then it began to burn and hurt. But she couldn't lift her head at all. If Movita was making coffee she must have realized that Gwen wasn't sober. She should know how hard I work, Gwen thought, what stress I'm under. I'm doing it for every inmate – Movita included. When Movita returned, Gwen spoke. 'There's something really terrible happening,' she said to Movita. 'That's one of the reasons I'm not feeling well.'

'I'm sorry,' Movita said casually, busy making a space on the desk and putting down the coffee.

'No, you don't understand,' Gwen continued. 'There's something new, something really terrible that might happen here at Jennings.'

'It's okay, Warden,' Movita said patiently, as if Gwen were a fretful child. 'Ain't nothin' gonna happen while I'm here.'

Gwen tried to raise her head. It was so frustrating. 'I'm not drunk,' she said. 'I'm being serious.'

Movita lifted the coffee cup and set it close to Gwen's head. 'Even the smell will help,' she said. 'Jus' inhale it. Then see if you can drink some.'

'Jennings may be privatized,' Gwen blurted out. 'The state will sell us all.' She heard the melodrama in her voice and she fell silent. She wasn't supposed to tell anyone this. What was she doing?

Movita stopped fussing and looked at her directly for the first time. 'Privatized?' Movita said. 'What d'you mean?'

With a huge effort Gwen managed to lift up her head. It felt good to talk to Movita. 'There's a company called JRU. They're the strangers who have been through here. They want to take over Jennings.' Damn it, she thought. I am drunk. She knew she shouldn't go on, but some lousy devil in her head was intent on blabbering everything. 'And conditions are going to get so much worse . . . It's just a terrible thing.' She felt tears rise and tremble on her lower lids. 'I can't stand it,' she said. She put her head back down, her face against the ice.

'Is this for sure?' Movita asked.

'No, but there's a good chance. They'll run the place like a factory. You and the other inmates will be the machinery and I'll be the oil.'

'Jesus Christ,' Movita muttered, sitting down in the chair next to Gwen. 'Jesus Christ.'

15

Cher McInnery

When Rebecca Cross was sent to prison, it was nine years before her children's first visit with her, because the trip . . . cost more money than she had.

Kathryn Watterson, *Women in Prison*

Cher McInnery shook her head, and her long dark hair flowed. 'Every time it's visitor's day here,' she said, 'you dumb bitches remind me of my daddy's huntin' dog.'

Floyd McInnery liked to kick his dog just to make a point. 'Ya' see that?' he'd ask his beer-drinking cronies. 'Ya' can kick Betty and she jist comes a-crawlin' back and licks your hand like she wants some more.' He'd laugh, take another guzzle and let out a belch; then with a sneer of what looked to Cher like unspeakable sadistic pleasure, he'd land his filthy old boot right in the middle of the poor dog's gut. There'd be a loud yelp, the old honey-brown coon dog would run about ten yards away, and then Floyd would holler, 'Get back here, ya' bitch.' Sure enough, the dog would come crawlin' back, her tail between her legs, her ears erect with hope for somethin' better from the drunken

son-of-a-bitch. Most often he'd just kick her again. Sometimes Floyd would even suggest that one of his friends
should try the trick. 'Go ahead,' he'd urge, 'kick the bitch.
She likes it.'

At first, little Cher pitied the dog. She could barely stand
to hear the thud, the yelp, and the laughter, but she
couldn't turn away either. She'd stand and watch, and then
wait for her father and his friends to leave so that she could
go to old Betty and comfort her with a stew bone and some
petting.

'Why do you let 'em do that, Betty?' she'd ask, searching the old dog's eyes for an answer. 'Bite 'em the next
time,' she'd urge. She tried to retrain Betty to fight. 'Bite
me!' she'd snarl at the cowering animal. 'Don't lick my
hand, bite it! Fight back, ya' stupid damn dog!' Just once,
Cher wanted old Betty to come back snarling with her fangs
bared. Just once she wanted that dog to take a bite out of
Daddy Floyd's ass.

But the next time would be the same, and so would the
time after that, and eventually Cher's pity for the dog
turned to anger, then to disgust, and finally to loathing.
Cher couldn't help but think of old Betty every time she
saw the women at Jennings preparing for visitor's day. She
just shook her head when week after week after week they
would get their hopes up and be all excited. They'd talk
about how their boyfriends or their husbands – or even their
daddies – were coming to see them, how the foster mother
taking care of their kids swore that *this* time she was going
to bring them. And then week after week after week they'd
get kicked in the gut when not one of the bastards showed
up. But they always went back for more.

'Kick the bitch, she likes it,' Cher would think as she

watched the anxious women rouge their cheeks with dried grape juice and line their eyes with eyeliner made from burnt matchsticks. Week after week after week the women would do their best to look their best for their men – the men who never showed up.

Cher never had a visitor on visitor's day, nor did she fool herself into thinking that she would. Her family was too scattered to come for a visit. But she didn't mind. Hell, with everyone else so damn distracted and actin' crazy it made it easier for her to do a little stealing. For Cher, visitor's day was like a day at the shopping mall. She didn't care if no one ever came to see her; she'd rather lift a few goodies from some dumb bitch who was downstairs getting her heart kicked out while waiting for some shiftless, useless man. As far as Cher could see, they were no smarter than old Betty. At first she had pitied them, too – but then came the disgust and the anger.

When the women came back to the cellblock crying about how disappointed they were, Cher just wanted to kick them and scream, 'Fight back, you stupid damn dog.' But instead, she stole from them, because when Cher was stealing she didn't have to think or feel bad. She remembered her mama and how pretty she used to look back when she and Cher used to go visit Uncle Silas at the Little Rock jail. They never missed one visitor's day all the while he was in there, but even back then Cher couldn't remember ever seeing a male visitor at that prison. No. Cher learned at an early age that the only visitors you can count on are mothers, sisters, and maybe a brave daughter now and then. So it pissed her off when women came back crying because some damn man hadn't showed up. They should be happy that they got to see anyone at all.

The only women Cher did feel sorry for were the ones with kids. Visitor's day was miserable for these inmates whether their kids came to see them or not. If someone did bring them, the babies were usually screaming and crying in fear, and the slightly older ones always asked too many questions like, 'Why are you wearing those clothes, mama?' or 'Why didn't you come to my birfday?' and the worst one: 'When are you coming home?' The older they got, the more ashamed they were to be coming to the prison at all. Since most of them had to grow up without their mothers, as they got older they glared at women they hardly knew, doing nothing to mask their anger, embarrassment, and discomfort. It would've been better if they hadn't come at all.

That's why Cher didn't understand why Movita went through worlds of trouble to arrange for visits with her little girls. Cher couldn't remember for sure the last time they had actually come to Jennings to see their mother. Since Movita hardly ever talked about them, or even showed anyone a picture of them, you sometimes forgot that she had any children. Cher always figured that's what Movita herself was trying to do and respected her for it. But Movita was acting real different lately. Cher could tell that something was bothering her – something was on her mind. When the lights-out alarm rang the night before visitor's day, Cher could tell that Movita was way too nervous to go to sleep. 'Ya' think it's such a good idea for those girls to come here?' Cher whispered to her.

'I'm gonna read 'em a story,' Movita answered. 'Went to the library today and had old Maggie pick me out a book for 'em.'

'That's nice,' Cher said simply. 'My mama used to read me stories.'

'Yeah,' Movita whispered. 'That's what a mama should do. A mama should read stories to her babies.'

Babies? How long since Movita had seen her girls? Cher didn't sleep that night, either. She worried about Movita. She was worried that the kids wouldn't show, or if they did, she worried about what Movita would see when she looked across the visitor's table. Cher sighed and knew there wasn't much she could do. She just hoped Movita would learn her lesson and not turn into a Betty. Then she decided that she'd steal something real nice for Movita. Maybe she could find a new hairbrush or some perfume. Movita loved a nice scent.

The cafeteria was always noisy at breakfast on visitor's day. Theresa in particular seemed to get especially loud when she knew she was having a guest – and Theresa always had a guest. Cher couldn't keep track of how many sisters Theresa had – it might be five, six, or seven – and sometimes there were also women who used to work for Theresa in the cosmetics business who still came for advice and motivation. But it didn't matter who came to see her or who didn't come to see her. As far as Theresa LaBianco was concerned, visitor's day was an occasion for great celebration.

'But don't it make you sad when it's over?' Suki asked her. 'It always makes me so sad when everyone leaves. It makes me lonelier than ever.'

'Well, you know what they say about loneliness, don't you?' Theresa began. 'Loneliness is what we call it when it's *painful* to be alone. But you know, there's another word – and that's *solitude,* and that's the word we use when we *want* to be alone. So when visitor's day is over, I just tell myself that I need a little solitude, that's all.' Theresa struck a dramatic pose and did a very bad imitation of Greta Garbo: 'I *vant* to be alone.'

'You're full of shit,' Cher said with a laugh. 'I love ya' – but you're full of shit.'

'Well, you know what they say about shit, don't you?' Movita asked.

'No,' Theresa said, falling for it like she did every time, 'I don't know. What do they say about shit?'

'Well if *you* don't know, then no one knows,' Movita said good-naturedly, causing the others to laugh.

Theresa laughed with them. Theresa could take a joke. Hell, Theresa *lived* for jokes. 'So is that good-looking lawyer coming to see you today, Cher?' she asked, batting her eyes.

'Yeah. Ain't it a pity that the only guy who comes to see a hottie like me is paid by the hour and doesn't stay long,' Cher chuckled.

'Lawyers are just like whores,' Movita said, picking up a spork full of grits. 'They're both paid by the hour and don't stay long.'

Theresa spoke up again. 'Hey, I *do* know a shit joke. What do you have when you have a lawyer buried up to his neck in shit?' she asked. She looked around the table to see if anyone had the answer. 'You don't have enough shit, that's all!'

The bell rang to signal the end of breakfast, and the crew stood up to return their trays to the conveyor belt. Cher winced when she noticed that Movita was carrying her damn storybook with her along with lollipops from Sally in Unit B. Now as they made their way toward the visitor's room, she stopped Cher. 'You gonna be down there for long today?' she asked.

Cher shook her head. 'Nah,' she answered, 'no reason to. And besides, I got me some errands to run,' she added with a wink.

Movita only nodded, then turned and followed the others out of the cafeteria. After they were out of sight, Cher followed as well. She guessed she wanted to be there to see Movita's face when she saw her little girls.

Cher wrinkled her nose as she entered the visitor's room, which always reeked of body odor and too much perfume as the crowd of nervous women quietly waited, watched, and listened for their names to be called out. Cher stayed at the back, where none of the crew would notice her. She wasn't alone. While most of the women who didn't have visitors stayed as far away as possible from the grim reminder of their loneliness, others – like Cher – stood and watched the more fortunate women with their guests. Cher was nearly on tiptoe, straining to see what was going on, but she could see no sign of Movita.

'Are you expecting someone, Cher?'

The question startled Cher and she spun around to face the debutante. 'Ain't none of your business who's coming,' she snapped at the newcomer. Then Cher caught sight of Movita on the other side of the room. A guard was handing her an envelope, and Cher could see it trembling in Movita's hand. She pushed the rich bitch aside and made her way through the crowd of waiting women.

By the time she got to Movita, the envelope was torn open and was lying on the floor at her feet. Movita was frozen into a statue. With one hand she held a crumpled wad of paper, and with the other she grasped two colorful crayon drawings to her breast, along with the storybook that she had brought with her from the library. Her face was a blank stare. Cher was relieved to see there were no tears; no visible anger. She had simply frozen.

'What happened, Mo?' Cher asked her gently. It wasn't necessary for everyone to see her in her moment of weakness. 'Where are your girls?'

'They ain't comin',' Movita said quietly. 'They ain't comin'.'

Cher took the crumpled letter from Movita's hand and read it. 'Goddamn bastards,' she hissed. 'Fuckin' cruel sons-of-bitches.'

'Watch yer mouth,' Movita shot back at her. 'I'm sick to death of yer filthy talk.'

At that moment Jennifer walked over with her tray of breakfast. Like Mo needed the sympathy of one more friggin' white girl. 'Suki told me you had it all arranged,' Jennifer said to Movita.

'Just who the hell are you to talk to me? Did I say ya' could speak to me? And I don't care what Suki told ya',' Movita snapped. 'Ya' thought I had it all arranged, huh? Well I ain't got nothin' arranged. Ya' got that? I ain't got nothin'.' She moved to push her way past Cher.

'Come on, honey,' Cher tried to comfort her. 'Come on. We'll go get ya' somethin' nice and new. Come on with Cher.'

'Just get your damn hands off me!' Movita suddenly shouted. 'Just keep away from me.' As she tried to push her way past them, the drawings and the storybook fell from her grasp and Movita collapsed onto the floor with them. One of the religion pimps – the churchgoing cranks who were always selling their brand of Jesus to the limp and the lost – started up with 'Sister, it's not too late to see the Lord's work in everything.'

'Shut the fuck up,' Cher told her, and in the moment she turned away the debutante was there kneeling beside Movita trying to help her. But when this Jennifer picked up one of the drawings Movita violently slapped her hand away from it. 'Keep your hands off it,' she snarled. 'That's from my baby. My baby drew that picture for her mama, and you keep yer hands off it. That's from my baby.'

With the paper shaking in her hand, Jennifer gave the drawing back to Movita as Cher helped the now sobbing woman to her feet. For a moment everyone else in the hot and crowded room was deadly silent.

Cher assured everyone that she had everything under control. She looked directly at Jennifer. 'She's my responsibility. I'm takin' her back to the cell,' she said protectively, and the crowd parted to let them pass. At the same time, a guard stepped over to where they were and said firmly, 'Miss Spencer, you have a visitor.'

16

Jennifer Spencer

> *Everywhere there is one principle of justice, which is the interest of the stronger.*
>
> Plato, *The Republic*

Tom hadn't disappointed her! Jennifer was actually going to see him, hold his hand. When she heard the officer say her name, her heart began to thump wildly and she almost ran to the guards to be processed and searched.

But when Jennifer walked into the visiting room, Tom wasn't sitting at any of the empty tables. She looked around, a little panicky; the noise from the inmates, the kids, and the other visitors seemed overwhelming. Then she saw her visitor. Her guest was not Tom Branston, it was Leonard Benson.

He was sitting at a large table, his dark head bent over a copy of *Forbes* magazine. He looked up, smiled, and took off his reading glasses. Jennifer tried to mask her disappointment as she crossed the room to welcome him, but her heart was still racing from excitement at being called. She actually felt the room tilt a little and start to spin. She held on to the corner of the Formica table and tried to take a deep breath. Lenny stood up and gestured to the seat opposite him. 'Lenny, what a surprise!' she managed to say.

'Yes,' he said. 'Thanks for giving me permission to visit. You don't mind that I came?'

'Of course not,' she said, and sank into the chair across from him. 'It's really good of you to come.' The words sounded forced and rather formal for a prison visiting room.

Jennifer's mind began to race. She only had one hour of visiting time. Where was Tom? Was he coming as well? She hadn't heard a confirmation or, for that matter, a decline from Tom, so she knew nothing.

'You look okay,' Lenny said, as if surprised. 'I mean, it's a shock to' – he gestured to her outfit, and to the room – 'you know, to see you here with all this.' He looked toward the officers and bars. 'But you look okay. Healthy, I mean.'

Jennifer looked around without searching for Tom. The room was stuffy and noisy. Most inmates sat across from other women. Children ran back and forth from tables to vending machines, making noise as they argued over soda selections and gobbled down candy bars. Some of the women cried, and so did some of the children. The rare male visitor, dressed in jeans and sneakers, seemed ill at ease.

'I'm all right. But not for long. It's . . . hard.' She didn't want to begin to cry so she forgot to be polite. 'Where's Tom Branston?' she asked Lenny. 'If I'm only allowed one visitor it should be him.'

It was Lenny's turn to mask his disappointment. 'I'm sorry,' he offered and shrugged. 'Tom couldn't make it, I guess. All I know is that I got a call from the Warden's office yesterday. My request for a visit had been approved, so I came.'

'But you've seen Tom at the office?' Jennifer said. 'Did you tell him you were coming? Did he say he was? Or did he give you a message for me?'

Lenny shook his head. 'I haven't told him and I haven't seen him,' Lenny said. 'He hasn't been at the office, or if he was, he kept a real low profile.'

Once again Jennifer searched the room for any signs of her fiancé. 'Well, when I spoke to him he told me he was really busy with my appeal, or even a pardon.' She looked at Lenny directly. His brown eyes seemed to brim with pity for her. Jen hated that so much that she pulled herself together. She couldn't bear to be the object of Lenny Benson's pity.

'Um . . . is there anything you need?' Lenny tried again. There was a long pause. 'Did you get the package I sent?'

Jennifer's eyes, which had been skidding like a rat from table to table, suddenly focused on Lenny's face and his question. 'Yes,' she replied, turning her gaze directly to his. His eyes were kind. 'Yes I did receive it. Thank you,' she said simply. 'Your gifts were wonderful.'

On his side of the table, Lenny blushed. 'I did a little research and read a magazine article about women in pris –' He stopped abruptly, embarrassed. 'About women in . . . places like this. It said that getting packages is very important. It also gave me some ideas about what to send.'

'Where did you read an article like that?' Jen asked, and almost giggled. 'Did they run it in *Forbes*?'

'I looked it up on the Internet,' he said. 'I didn't know if you used toothpaste or gel, so I got both.'

'Listen, it was great to get anything.' She thought of the

day the package came and how touched she'd been. 'It helped me make friends,' she said. 'I certainly didn't expect it or . . .' She was going to say 'deserve it' but she also didn't deserve the punishment she was getting, either. So they were both silent again.

'Did you know that you're not allowed to have dental floss?' he asked nervously.

'No. Why not?'

'I guess you can use floss with an abrasive kitchen cleanser like Comet and actually saw through the metal. I read that online, too,' he admitted. Then he shrugged. 'I'm so sorry for babbling,' he apologized. 'I guess I'm a little nervous.'

Jennifer nodded and another silence hung between them. Jennifer looked around at the gate through which visitors came.

'Do you want me to go?' Lenny asked. 'If you're expecting Tom or anyone else I . . .'

'No. That's fine,' Jennifer assured him. 'I'm sorry I'm so distracted. One of the women here just had a disappointment, a kind of breakdown. It was hard to watch. And I was really hoping Tom would come and, well . . .' She stopped and looked across at him.

'Does everyone miss me at Hudson, Van Schaank?' Jennifer asked lightly.

Once again Lenny colored. Then he shrugged and looked away. Lenny could not tell her anything that was not true. 'You know how people at the firm are,' he said, and Jennifer nodded in resignation. Most of her coworkers were extremely competitive. Selfish. Self-absorbed. Jealous. Vindictive. They hadn't enjoyed watching her huge success.

Still, Jennifer couldn't quite accept or believe what he

seemed to be telling her. Then it hit her. Donald Michaels, of course. He wouldn't just abandon her. He was concerned about her welfare, he wanted to know that she was all right. But he certainly wasn't free to come to the prison, not if he was under the media scrutiny that Tom had described. He must have been the one who had asked Lenny to send the package. And he must have sent Lenny now to try to take care of her until they got this all straightened out. 'Did Donald ask you to come?' she whispered.

'No,' Lenny told her, but perhaps he was being overly cautious.

'It's all right, Lenny. You can tell me.'

Lenny leaned in to the table, put both his elbows on it, and extended one hand across to her. Very gently he touched her forearm, and then held it. His hand was surprisingly big and his fingers wrapped around her wrist like a bracelet. 'Listen, Jennifer,' he said, his voice even more gruff than usual and his eyes – such a deep, deep brown – staring directly into her own. 'Listen,' he repeated, 'I think you're going to be really disappointed if you expect much from Donald. I've been around him longer than you have. I admit that when things go well for him he's a generous guy. But when they don't, or when they get complicated . . . well, let's just say that if he's the general partner and you're the limited partner when the deal gets audited *he's* not going down.'

Jennifer felt her arms go gooseflesh, even where Lenny was holding her. She pulled back from him. 'Don't tell me that Donald has forgotten me,' she said, and realized that her voice had risen. A few of the people at the other tables turned to look. She forced herself to stay calm. 'Tom told me that things are going slower than they expected but that it will be fine. Donald is one hundred percent behind me on this.'

Lenny shook his head. 'Jennifer, I'm afraid Donald is ahead of you. That's my point.' He took his arms off the table.

She felt fury mixed with fear rise in her. She wanted to slap his face right then, throw his glasses onto the floor and stomp on them. 'Donald isn't going to renege. And even if he wanted to, Tom won't let him. He's taking care of everything,' she hissed.

Lenny looked away and nodded. 'I'm sure you're right. I just don't want you to be disappointed,' he said. 'And I want you to know that you can call me anytime, day or night. You have my cell phone number, right?'

Jen shook her head. Why would she need his cell number? She realized that she hated Lenny Benson, with his long nose and his five o'clock shadow and his damned wet eyes. She just wished this negative, boring man would leave. He probably meant well, but he was frightening and upsetting her. She wouldn't tell him to shove off, but she just sat there, silently waiting for him to do it.

'So?' he asked, finally standing up. 'Is there anything else I can get for you or send to you?'

'I'm not going to be here that long,' Jennifer said defiantly. She stared intently at Lenny for some reassurance, but he said nothing. 'I'm *not*. Tom says I'm going to be out of here in just a couple of weeks.'

Lenny nodded, then handed her his card. 'I know the office number,' she said and smiled.

'It has my home and cell on the back. Call me anytime. I mean it,' he said, and he walked away.

17

Maggie Rafferty

*Good laws lead to the making of better ones; bad ones
bring about worse.*

Jean Jacques Rousseau, *The Social Contract*

I looked up from the letter that I was writing to my son to
see Movita Watson standing in the doorway. Movita didn't
come to the library often. She'd probably read any of the
books worth reading before I arrived here. Also, she already
had the job in the Warden's office, which gave her something comparatively interesting to do. So when I saw her
there, coming to see *me* rather than to get a book, I was
pleased.

She glowered. 'You're lookin' glad to see me,' she said.
'Don't make me feel bad. I ain't got no good news.'

I had, of course, heard about the incident in the visitor's
room. When you're as high-profile and respected as Movita
Watson, something like that doesn't go by unnoticed.

'Brought back some books,' Movita said, and pushed

Make Way for Ducklings and *Sarah, Plain and Tall* across my makeshift desk.

I laughed – something I rarely do anymore. 'I don't expect good news,' I told her. 'I'm imprisoned, not crazy.'

Movita smiled. She had the most beautiful mouth – I'd once seen those lips on the Thanos Venus. 'I got a couple a questions, and you're the only one might have answers. You don't mind, do ya'?'

'Please,' I said. 'Of course not.' I've always respected Movita Watson. When I first came here I was viewed as a thing, a celebrity. She was the only one who looked at me as if I were a person. The other women's eyes glossed over me as if I were invisible. Because I'm old, of course. An older woman brings to prison neither looks nor style, nor anything from the Outside that is of interest to the incarcerated. The one thing that caused unfailing interest among my social peers, the fact that I shot my husband, wasn't an interesting point to anyone at Jennings: It was no big deal as a crime.

Now Movita sat down in the only other chair in the library and frowned at the floor. She didn't usually mince words. When she started to speak, she did so very slowly.

'The first thing I wanna know is, what exactly is "privatization"?'

I almost laughed again. Was Movita thinking about investing in East German railroads? 'It depends,' I said, 'on the circumstances. There's always talk about possibly privatizing the U.S. Post Office, for instance. That means that it would no longer be run by the government but would be purchased by a private company or different companies, and run by them.'

Movita nodded. 'Why do they do it?'

'Well, sometimes it's assumed that the government lacks the skill and ability to run the business efficiently but that private enterprise could.'

'But why would they *wanna*?' Movita asked me, crossing her legs and settling back into the chair.

'For the same reason they do anything. They think that they can make a profit on it.'

'A profit, huh?' Movita frowned at me, then looked back at the floor and was silent for several seconds. I could tell she was torn, something rare in her strong personality. 'Yer sons know all 'bout this stuff, don't they?' she asked.

'As a matter of fact, yes, they do.'

Movita frowned again. I had to admit that I was curious. 'What's this about?' I finally asked.

Movita looked around the empty room, leaned forward and reached into her jumpsuit. For a moment I was afraid that she had contraband, and I was relieved when she took out a sheaf of papers.

'You'd betta take a look at these,' she said, handing the papers to me. They were still warm from her body. 'There's somethin' happenin' here, and from what ya' say, it's a real bad thing.' She looked past me across the room and spoke as if to herself. 'Profit? I didn't understand. Jesus Christ!'

I unfolded the thick pile of papers and saw the business logo at the top of the first sheet. *JRU.* I had never heard of them, but what did that mean? I had a large portfolio, not that it did me any good, but my sons managed it.

I quickly read the first few pages. It was, indeed, a proposal for privatization. I continued to read.

Movita was right. From the beginning it sounded very bad. The way they talked about Jennings, as if it were a poorly run factory or a chicken farm that didn't produce enough eggs, was shocking. In the dozen pages that I quickly read there was no indication at all that there were human beings living in Jennings. I guess JRU didn't consider prisoners people.

'My god,' I said, looking up from the white pages. I'm sure my face was equally white. 'I'm waiting for them to suggest trying out experimental drugs on us as a profit center. Except that there's no mention of us yet.'

'And it gets worse,' Movita told me. She stood up. 'I gotta go back to work,' she said. 'I ain't gonna tell ya' that I never seen that and neither have you.' I nodded my understanding. 'I'm gonna leave it with ya' to read. I'll come back. 'Cause we gotta talk about it.'

I gathered the papers off my desk and put the proposal on my lap. Then I looked up at her. I didn't know what to say.

'It looks bad, don't it?' she asked. I nodded. 'You got it for two hours.'

I took out a legal pad and my fountain pen. I began to read from the beginning, jotting down notes as I went. It seemed as if JRU had done a thorough study of the facility. Every room, including my closet of a library, was measured down to the inch. JRU had found that most of the space was 'underutilized'. The visitor's room was used once a week and sat empty the rest of the time. The cafeteria had a two-hundred-person capacity and only one hundred thirty-five inmates ate there. It also was empty for a good part of the day. The library was 'unnecessary' because books could be listed, the list given out, and then a book cart circulated throughout the cells. Human needs – like the need for air, light, privacy, a place to cry – were all disregarded. I could hardly believe what I was reading, but JRU seemed to be saying that prisoners should spend more time in their cells! When they weren't working, that is.

My chest was tightening up. For some time I've experienced a kind of mild angina-type pain but ignored it as best I could. This, however, was a vise. I waited for it to pass, for the blackness to turn to red and then clear. I took a few breaths and read on.

The plan appeared to be that the inmates must become productive. Jennings was going to become a factory! Now I am the last person to object to work, but this was not work that they were proposing. It was slavery. Pay would be minuscule. Jennings would become a concentration camp. Inmates would be either in the 'production rooms' or in their cells all but one hour of every day. Breakfast and dinner would be 'prefabricated' à la airplane meals and delivered to cells to save time! Lunch would be delivered to 'work stations' and eaten alone.

I was having trouble breathing by this time and should have stopped, but this was my future they were planning. I was sixty-four years old and had had at least my share of hell in my life. I couldn't stand to have any more. I set the proposal down on my lap and looked across the room at the books on the shelf. My eyes teared up. Pathetic of me, I know, but I loved them, even *The Power of Positive Thinking*. A most terrible thought struck me. What if I wouldn't have any time to read?

A person of my age can never experience physical distress without thinking the worst, and I am no exception. I was finding it impossible to get my breath and feared I was having a heart attack. But so what? I thought, perhaps it was better this way. I would rather die than live as a slave to an inhuman system. Every cell of my being rebelled against it. In fact, if I didn't die, I would have to kill myself, I decided, as the proposal slipped off my lap and fell to the floor. Why should I want to live on? Already it was a strain.

I started to weep, which relieved the pressure in my chest. I hadn't wept in years. What a front I kept up, even to myself! Then, to my horror, I heard a noise at the door. If it was that damnable Officer Byrd about to do another malicious shakedown, I thought I might bodily attack him. But it was Jennifer Spencer who walked in. Tears streaked my face, my hair was awry, but worst of all, the proposal was splayed all over the floor. If a CO walked in and found it, it wouldn't just jeopardize me and my position as librarian, it would also hurt Movita and anyone else who'd assisted in getting a hold of the proposal in the first place.

I tried to bend down to pick up the papers, and as I did I felt every year of my age. It isn't easy getting old anywhere, but in prison it's almost impossible. I could only manage to pull myself up to the little table that served as a desk. I must have looked dreadful, for Miss Spencer hurried over to me. 'What is it? Are you ill?' she asked.

'No. No,' I answered weakly. 'I'm just . . . very upset.'

'You're very pale. Should I take you to the nurse? Can I get you something?'

'No. I'm okay.'

Jennifer sat down across from me, where Movita had been sitting.

'Can I help in any way?'

I was touched by her manner. But I couldn't say anything.

Jennifer noticed the papers on the floor and knelt to pick them up. I made a gesture but couldn't stop her. Luckily, in her concern for me she just collected them and set them on the desk without looking at them. Then she looked back at me with a face I'm very familiar with, though I hadn't seen it in a while. It consisted of three parts: recognition and surprise, followed by embarrassment. Jennifer Spencer realized who I was. I suppose it was my ghastly look. I had looked ghastly all through the trial, in all the pictures in the newspapers.

'I see you recognize me now,' I said softly to keep her distracted while I tore the sheets with my notes off the pad and folded them. I was still feeling dreadfully bad, but I could breathe, not that I much wanted to. 'Don't be embarrassed. I'm quite used to people knowing more about me than I do about them.'

'I'm not,' she said. 'It's just a bit of a surprise.' She paused. 'I followed your case.'

'And I yours,' I told her. 'Now, can I help you?'

'Did something just happen, or are you ill? Should I call someone?'

'That's the last thing I want,' I said. 'I'll be okay.'

She nodded, and though she looked a little doubtful, went over to the bookshelves. 'I never thought you were guilty,' she said.

'But I was.'

'How long are you here for? I don't remember the sentence.'

I froze. The question was not a welcome one. It brought back the specter of more years, more and more years. 'My dear,' I said, 'I'm going to give you some advice that you will do well to follow.'

'What?' she asked.

'Never ask anyone here their crime or their time. Not unless you're looking for trouble.'

Her eyes dropped. I must say that at that moment I liked her. I pulled myself up in the chair, took the proposal off the windowsill and secreted it under me along with the notes. 'Did you want a book?'

She looked at me, confused.

'You came in here. Did you want a book?'

'Oh. Yes. I was hoping to look at some law books.' She gave the collection a doubtful look. 'Whatever you have.'

'Torts, I assume.' She nodded, and perhaps she blushed. 'We have one, and it's over there. You can't miss it. It's next to *Grow Your Own Terrarium*.'

Jennifer retrieved the book. She came back to my desk. 'Do I need to sign anything?' she asked.

Wordlessly, I handed her the sign-out sheet.

'You sure you're okay?' she asked again.

I nodded. She signed the sheet, took the book, and with one more look at me left the library.

In prison, like in life, one must learn to trust in very small things for happiness. A shaft of light that falls, just so, across the hall each afternoon. The comfort of soft slippers on the feet. A sugar cookie melting on the tongue. A smile. I sat still, waiting for some kind of clarity to return. When it did, I picked up the report again and read it through, but I didn't have the heart to take notes. As it was, I had to stop frequently to remind myself to breathe.

It seemed hours before Movita returned. When she saw me her face fell. 'So ya' read the thing,' she said.

'Yes.'

'It's bad, huh?'

I nodded.

'It's as bad as it seems?'

'No,' I told her. 'It's much worse.'

18

Jennifer Spencer

You better believe that being locked up and at the mercy
of these people is hell.

Delia Robinson, former inmate. Andi Rierden, *The Farm*

Once again, the work in the laundry was unbearably hot and
tedious. A seemingly endless train of carts filled with fouled
sheets, musty towels, and smelly uniforms was wheeled into
the room where the laundry was unloaded, sorted, and
stuffed into the huge washing machines. Then the great
heavy armfuls of steaming wet laundry were lifted into the
dryer, and finally run through the enormous ironing machines. With each new step in the process the temperature in
the room rose exponentially as the heat and the humidity
transformed the laundry into a tropical inferno.

Jennifer's rage intensified with the heat. Tom had better
have some kind of terrific explanation before she would forgive him for this hell she was in. Though she kept telling
herself that it would all be over soon, it couldn't be soon
enough. Why was it taking so long? What in the hell was he

doing? And why hadn't she been able to reach him? Three times in as many days she'd called and gotten only his voicemail.

As Jennifer summoned the physical strength to heft the heavy loads of hot, steaming laundry, she grew emotionally weaker. She thought about the surprise visit from Lenny Benson. Was he just nervous and naturally negative or had he been trying to warn her, prepare her for . . . what? Her tears began to intermingle with the steam and perspiration; her hair hung in a tangled mop of sweat on her brow.

Jennifer stopped to study her hands. They were already red and swollen from the harsh chemicals of the detergents, but at least the ink on her fingertips had finally been washed away. In a way she was sorry to see it go; it was the only enduring reminder of who she had been on the day she entered this place. She continued to stare at her hands and wondered how long it would take to get them back to normal. The chapping might heal and the color would return, but she doubted that the horror of these days and nights would ever fade from her memory.

Try as she might, Jennifer could no longer remember the justification for this gamble she'd taken and the strength of her belief that Tom and Donald were right when they told her that this was all going to be so easy. Why had she been so sure of herself? Jennifer looked over at Suki, who pulled over a canvas cart and emptied it into a dryer. Jennifer felt so sorry for herself and so pathetic that she stood there wringing her hands and mindlessly caressing the naked finger where Tom's engagement ring had once been.

'Hey you! Debutante! Wake up and get to work,' shouted Flora.

Jennifer squared her shoulders, took a deep breath, and

wiped away her tears. The astringent odor of bleach from the wet laundry burned her eyes as she continued with the soul-numbing labor.

That night, back in the cell, Suki took one of her chafed hands, looked into Jennifer's eyes, and asked why she had been crying. 'I think I must be allergic to the soaps and stuff,' Jen told her.

'Yeah? What detergent did you use at home?' Suki asked. Jen was too ashamed to tell her that she hadn't done her own laundry in almost a decade. Instead she merely blamed the red and swollen puffiness on the bleach. She wasn't going to admit to any weakness – not even to Suki. She decided that she was going to close the door on that existential chasm of anxiety threatening to swallow her. She'd trust Tom's love and Donald's respect for her. She had to. She had nothing else in which to trust or believe. There was one good thing about the work in the laundry: She would sleep tonight.

Suki was sitting quietly in the chair next to the table, patting her belly. 'You sure you're okay, Jenny?' she asked.

Jennifer mumbled only a 'Yeah' in reply. Lately, Jennifer had begun to doubt that Suki was pregnant at all. She certainly didn't appear any fatter. It could simply be a pathetic attempt to get more attention from the crew.

'Me and the girls had a pretty greasy supper,' Suki admitted. 'How was yours?' she asked as she stood up and started to get ready for bed.

Jennifer didn't answer. She didn't want to talk about her supper. She didn't want to talk at all. She turned her back to the well-meaning girl and stared at the wall, willing her eyes to pierce the dirty pink concrete and to look beyond to the walls of her own beautiful apartment. What wall is Tom looking at tonight? she wondered.

'I'm sorry,' Suki spoke in a whisper, 'but I have to use the toilet.'

Jennifer merely grunted. A moment later Suki grunted as well. Every tired and aching muscle in Jennifer's body threatened to cramp in the dank, sick chill of nausea that washed over her. She shut her eyes tightly and tried to deny the reality that Suki was suffering from diarrhea just inches from her head. Her own stomach was about to betray her as it churned the prison meal that she had so hungrily devoured.

The lights-out bell rang in concert with Suki's flush, and as Jennifer was plunged into the dark and horrifying reality of where she was, the last thing that she saw was the dirty pink paint on the wall.

'Sorry,' Suki said again as she slipped into her bunk. 'It'll be morning before you know it.'

'I'm fine,' Jennifer assured her. 'I just hate these damn pink walls, that's all.'

'Yeah, I try always to tell myself that it's the color of a sunset,' Suki said.

Jennifer let out a derisive snort of disbelief. 'Uh huh,' she sighed, 'a sunset.' She closed her eyes and tried to envision the sky; she couldn't remember the last time she had really looked at it. Somehow she was always rushing, always looking down at her computer screen or a memo or a proposal.

Jennifer stretched, and in the dark her hand reached out and brushed against something warm. It was another hand and it held hers. Then, all along her left side she felt Tom's long lean body beside her. 'Get closer,' he whispered as he often did when they made love. 'Get closer.'

Beneath her Jennifer felt the sand give and she rolled into position beside him. 'Let's stay like this all night,' he whispered, and she could feel his arms tighten around her. She couldn't speak; there was something in her throat, but she could nod and in her mind she said, 'Let's stay like this forever.'

'Yes, forever,' Tom agreed, and for a moment she wondered how he could hear her thoughts. Then she opened her eyes. 'Look,' he said. 'It's the dawn.' And she could see that they were lying on a beach and that a thin line of light was illuminated along the horizon. The sky was just beginning to color and she remembered that they'd been married and now they were on their honeymoon. How could I have forgotten that? she thought, and she felt Tom laughing beside her. Now that they were married and on this beach, she realized that she would never have to struggle again. It had all been worth it: The studying and the competition for grades and scholarships and the work on the papers she had written and all the time she'd put in on the job had paid off with this. His arms were around her and he loved her and the warm sea was beginning to turn the palest aqua as light continued to fill the sky. It was the most beautiful dawn she had ever seen and Jennifer felt her heart beating in her chest against Tom's own heartbeat. She would never have to be alone or frightened again. She felt a deep peace flow into her as if it had come in on a wave from the Caribbean and washed away all of her anxiety. She was safe. She was loved. She was not alone.

It was the smell more than the noise that woke her. The sour, stomach-rocking scent of vomit was in her nose, down her throat. She opened her eyes and realized with horror that she'd been dreaming. Tom, the sand, the sea and her

171

security were all gone. She was staring, not at the sky but up at the bottom of the bunk on top of her while Suki was making *awe, awe* noises just two feet away from her head.

'I'm sorry I woke you up,' Suki said. Jennifer began to tremble. In the confusion of waking she couldn't tell which was worse, losing that feeling of being bathed in Tom's love or remembering that she was imprisoned here. All she wanted was to close her eyes and go back to that beach and that feeling. She wanted to spend the rest of her life in that dream.

'You okay?' Suki asked. 'You were trying to talk or something in your sleep.' Jennifer knew it was hopeless to try to return to her dream, but giving it up made her feel desperately bereft. She turned her head and looked at the exhausted blonde child who sat on the floor next to the toilet. 'Do you want to talk about it?' Suki asked her.

Jennifer shook her head and turned her back to Suki. No, she still didn't want to talk to Suki about her precious dream. She wanted to live it. She wasn't one of these illiterate, victimized, stupid women. She had a future.

She heard Suki stand up. 'My grandmother said that a dream was God's way of telling the brain something that the heart already knows,' Suki told her as she rinsed the bowl of the toilet.

Jennifer did not – could not – respond. She turned her face to the wall and pulled the blanket over her head and tucked it in. If only when she opened her eyes the next time and took the blanket down she could see something other than the dirty pink paint on the cement walls of her cell. She had a terrible feeling that she would never again feel that tremendous love from Tom.

*　　*　　*

Jennifer tried to call Tom the next morning before laundry detail but no one answered his phone at home. His office number and his cell only got voicemail. She thought about the dozens of times he and she had looked at their caller ID and laughed or grimaced and refused to answer. I can't let myself get paranoid, she thought. That night Jennifer tried to remain calm as she attempted, once again, to reach Tom Branston. She got to the phone in the rec room, which was the usual zoo, but she was even more than usually agitated. She was desperate to talk with him. She *had* to. And she had to *see* him. Her heart skipped as the intense feeling from her dream moved through her. She had felt so loved, and so loving. Without the dream she actually felt abandoned. Jennifer shook her head to clear away the ridiculous feeling. Tom wasn't in the Caribbean lying on a beach with her but neither had he abandoned her. He was working to get her released.

She waited in line again and tried his office once more. This time the phone was picked up, but by a secretary whose voice Jen didn't recognize. 'Please put Tom Branston on the line,' Jennifer snapped into the phone. 'This is Jennifer.' She knew several of the women inmates were watching and listening, so she tried to keep her back to them and smile as she waited, but the smile quickly faded when the secretary responded.

'I'm sorry,' the voice said. 'He can't come to the phone.'

'What do you mean he can't come to the phone? You haven't even told him who was calling!'

'He asked not to be disturbed. Perhaps you can call back later.'

Jennifer's voice rose sharply. 'No, I can't call back later.

I'm in prison, goddamn it!' and she slammed down the phone.

Jennifer looked at the clock. She had forty-five minutes before work detail and she absolutely had to hear the sound of Tom's voice. Worse than that, she needed to be reassured that he existed – that anything Outside existed. She was watching the line of women still waiting for the phone when Movita sat down beside her. 'Tryin' to reach your lawyer or your boyfriend?' she asked her, but Jennifer didn't want to bother to explain. She just nodded her head.

'What can a goose do, that a duck can't, and a lawyer should?' Movita asked. Jennifer shrugged. 'Shove its bill up its ass,' Movita said and laughed.

To her surprise, Jennifer laughed, too. She didn't usually like vulgarity, but the joke was so unexpected that it caught her off guard. And, Jennifer thought, it wouldn't hurt to be nice to this woman, considering she could put in a good word for her with the Warden.

'Ya' gonna grind yer wheels right down to the spokes,' Movita volunteered. 'Not that you asked, and not that it's none of my bidness. Speaking of that, what exactly was it that ya' did on Wall Street? You some kinda hot shot, huh?'

'I was in venture capital and IPOs,' Jennifer told her.

'And what would that mean?' the woman asked.

'I help companies raise money to get started or to expand.'

'Any kind of company?' Movita asked.

'Just about.'

'How ya' know 'bout all kinds of companies, all kinds of bidnesses?'

The woman didn't sound hostile, exactly, but she sounded more than idly curious. Jennifer was in no mood to give a lecture on stocks, capitalism, and the American way. 'I don't know everything about every business,' Jennifer told her. 'I just know how to look at the finances of a business, compare it to its past and look at its future to decide if it's a good bet.'

Movita looked intently into Jennifer's eyes. 'Ya' usually right?' she asked.

'Usually,' Jennifer told her.

'Then how come you're here?' Movita asked.

Jennifer shrugged. 'No one seems to understand,' she said. 'I'm not *supposed* to be here.'

Now it was Movita's turn to laugh. 'Honey, ya' don't understand,' she said. 'Ain't none of us *supposed* to be here. What God of mercy would want women penned up in a place like this?'

'Yeah. And kept from your children. I'm really sorry.'

The black woman's eyes flashed. Her whole body stiffened and Jennifer could actually see her elbows, knees, and spine tremble. 'Look, forget about that. You was nice and that was fine, but I don't get visitors and I don't 'spect them. That was just unexpected, that's all. It won't happen again.'

'I'm sorry,' Jennifer said. She hadn't asked this crazy woman to sit down next to her and now she was sorry she had. She looked again at the line and realized that she wouldn't get another shot at the phone before work. Movita followed her eyes.

'Ya' really need to talk to him?' she asked. Jennifer nodded, not that it would do any good. 'Come on,' Movita said and walked to the front of the line.

Jennifer followed her. ''Scuze me, Pearl,' Movita said to the short Latina woman standing there waiting to be the next one at the telephone. 'Do ya' mind if the debutante uses the phone next? Would ya' give up yer place to her as a special favor to me?'

Pearl looked from Movita to Jennifer, then back to Movita. 'Okay,' she said, 'for you, Mo.' She gave Movita a nod and a look passed between them that Jennifer couldn't read. Pearl walked away and Movita motioned for Jennifer to take her place.

'Hey, wait a minute,' said the old crone with a long gray braid who was standing next in line. Movita raised her hand, extending her fingers out.

'Don't you talk at me, Helen,' Movita said. 'We have a situation here. Ya' had one person in front of ya' a minute ago and ya' got one person in front of ya' now. What's your beef?' Helen began to talk but Movita raised her hand again. 'Helen, don't mouth me. Ya' like to take advantage, but ya' know you've been in situations yourself. Hush now.'

And the woman did. Just like that. Jennifer waited a moment to thank Movita, but she didn't get a chance to because the woman on the phone in front of her hung up. Jennifer didn't waste a second and ran to the waiting receiver.

19

Movita Watson

I haven't seen my daughters for five years. I know I'm their mother, and I guess they know I'm their mother, but what kind of mother is that? . . . Thinking about it makes me feel dead inside.

A prisoner at the Federal Reformatory for Women in Alderson, West Virginia. Kathryn Watterson, *Women in Prison*

Even before 'the incident', I'd have to say that the Warden and I have an interesting kinda relationship. Without ever saying a word 'bout it, we help each other. She's a stickler for details and likes to do everything by the book, but she can't be blamed for that. Probably how she got the job. Anyway, she does things for me and I do things for her. It's good for me to have this, not jus' because of the benefits for me and the crew, but also 'cause it keeps me busy and gives me somethin' to think about. The thing I most hate is to have empty time to remember the past and think 'bout the future.

Anyway, the Warden hinted very strongly that she wanted me to take Jennifer Spencer into our crew. 'Movita,' she says, 'you can help that girl.' At first I think, fuck! I should help a rich white girl? What the fuck ever for? But then I'm thinkin' further that maybe she has a point. I'm no hardass mean bitch and Jennifer would probably help the crew as much as we'd help her. She's got a lot of money in the canteen – the fund for prisoners who wanted to buy extra food instead of having cafeteria crap. Of course, even so, I knew I'd have trouble with Cher. Soon as I brought the subject up I did.

It was visitor's day again, and as usual we were all tense as could be, especially Cher.

'Why the hell should we take *her* in?' Cher said, as I knew she would. 'She ain't done nothin' for us 'cept sharin' some toothpaste!' She was rubbin' red pencil on her fingernails, which I thought was ridiculous.

'That's gonna come off soon as you wash,' I said to her. 'Why you doin' it?'

'It's somethin' to do,' Cher said.

'Well, it don't even look good,' I told her, though I didn't blame her. Any stupid thing that passes the time here is worth doin'. Theresa puts together those same jigsaw puzzles and then, when she's finished, she just breaks them down and starts over. Would drive me crazy, but I don't judge her. 'Well, I say we'll benefit from Spencer bein' in crew and that's a good enough reason. It ain't no crime for her to be rich, Cher. You would be if you could.'

'Damn right I would,' Cher answered, holding out her hands. She was trying to admire them, but she couldn't do it. 'Fuck. I gotta wash this shit off.'

'Anyway,' I continued, 'it wouldn't hurt us to have her come over, check her out some more.'

'I checked her in,' Cher said, 'and I'm not interested.'

I looked at Cher, compellin' her to look back. 'Don't matter if you're interested or not,' I said to her, 'Spencer's in. I've asked Suki to bring her on over this morning.' Cher just shrugged, but I knew she was pissed.

You see, the thing is, with the JRU people breathin' down our neck, and with the Warden concerned, havin' someone like Spencer on our side might be a real good thing. Plus, the thought struck me then that once Cher was gone, which wasn't very far away, crew'd just be me and Theresa and Suki. Lord Jesus, it was a good thing the Warden had the idea to bring Spencer in. I was gonna need somebody to talk to.

Cher was still sulkin' when Suki came in with Jennifer. Yeah, I thought as I looked her over, she sure does look like a rich white girl that ain't gonna fit in. But then she says, 'Did you want to talk to me, Movita?' And then she smiled so nice and self-assured that I sorta figured that it might work out after all. Jennifer Spencer has a power attitude. And the Warden needs that right now. Maybe we can, between us, make it so this JRU thing ain't as bad as it could be.

'Sure did,' I said, real casual-like. 'I thought Suki and the rest of us could help get you all ready for visitor's day.'

Cher let out a disgusted little snort, but Suki just squealed she was so happy. 'You can borrow my curlers, Jenny,' she said.

I'm not sure Jennifer Spencer really wanted our help, but she was goin' to get it. Maybe it was kinda like an initiation or somethin'. Anyway, I went over and got Theresa to come and help, and after a lot of laughin' and havin' a good time, our new crewmate was all ready to meet her visitor.

'There. You look great now,' Suki told Spencer.

I damn near laughed out loud when that poor, little rich white girl picked up the mirror and looked at herself. She didn't look great at all. She looked like a cheap whore. After Suki was finished, all that smooth and silky dark hair of hers was a frizzy old mop. But Spencer didn't say a word.

'Great, huh?' Suki asked again.

'Oh yeah,' she told Suki.

'But that's not all,' Theresa said. 'Look what I got for you.' She opened her palm to show her a chapstick, but Spencer just looked at her.

'Open the cap,' Theresa said, but she pulled the cap off herself. Instead of the clear wax the stick was red. 'Adobe Red,' Theresa told her. 'Here,' she reached over and put it on her. 'Want some for your cheeks?' she asked.

'No. No, thanks.' Spencer stood up before Suki could get at her. I could tell that she didn't want to wipe the lipstick off right in front of Theresa, but I also knew she didn't want to wear it anymore either.

'Gosh, I wish someone was coming to see me,' Suki said. 'Even just a lawyer. Cher got some good-looking lawyers.'

'He's not just my lawyer, he's my fiancé,' Jennifer said.

'Oh, wow! Does he know about your boyfriend?' Suki asked her.

'Lenny is not my boyfriend,' Jennifer told her, looking around at the rest of us kinda embarrassed.

'Wait,' Suki said, 'your accountant is not your boyfriend and your lawyer is your fiancé.' Then she shook her head. 'And people say I'm stupid.'

We all laughed – even Cher. And Spencer laughed, too.

'You need some mascara,' Suki said, looking at Jennifer.

'I think Cher's got some,' Theresa said, all cagey-like.

'How do *you* know?' Cher asked.

'Because I saw that Diane from Unit C leaving today.

She was all dressed up, but she didn't have any makeup on.
I figure you got to it before she got her effects back.'

Cher laughed in that evil way of hers, and then leaned
over to pull a box out from beneath her bunk. 'Stand back
girls, it's my turn to help out our little debutante here.' The
box was absolutely filled to overflowing with good makeup
that Cher had swiped.

I just shook my head at her and said, 'One of these days
you're gonna be busted and you'll blow your parole stealing
shit like that.'

But nobody paid no mind to what I said. I think everybody was more worried that Cher was gonna put Spencer's
eye out with the mascara brush. But pretty soon we were all
laughing again. It was already starting to feel like Jennifer
was one of us.

20

Jennifer Spencer

*I sit here day after day dealing with all of these wounds
inside my head. The kinds of wounds that never heal.*

Bonnie Foreshaw, inmate. Andi Rierden, *The Farm*

Jennifer raced back to her cell to take a look in the mirror.
Tom would be arriving for visitor's day any minute. Did she
look all right? What a ridiculous question to even ask. How
could she look all right in this shapeless jumpsuit, with
her frizzy hair, Adobe Red lipstick, and enough mascara to
pass as a raccoon? Tom would take one look at her and
think: white trash. But it had been fun to be part of that
crew. Even so, she rubbed the cheap lipstick roughly off her
lips with the palm of her hand. How could Tom, with his
prep school upbringing and his country club expectations,
possibly look at her and love what he saw?

But he *did* love her. She took a deep breath and forced
herself to think positively. Tom loved her and despite the
ridiculous warning she'd gotten from Lenny, Tom and
Donald Michaels would do everything in their power to get

her out of this dump as soon as possible. He'd make her a lady again, and his wife.

Jennifer got to the visitor's room just as an officer called out, 'Brainard, Jackson, LaBianco, and Spencer. Visitors.' Jennifer raced inside just a step behind Theresa. She craned her neck for a first glimpse of Tom's distinguished widow's peak. Once again she was instantly overwhelmed by the noise, the smells, and the confusion.

'I made you the best chicken potpie!' a woman shrieked, attacking Theresa and enveloping her in a bear hug.

A wave of cheap Wal-Mart perfume washed over Jennifer, almost making her pass out. She pushed by Theresa – and the potpie specialist who must have been her sister, Thelma – and made her way to the center of the room to look for Tom. Everywhere little kids were hanging from their mothers' necks, while grown women tried to shout the latest news over their heads. There were absolutely no men – unless you counted the odious Officer Byrd, standing in one of the corners surveying the crowd. Two female correction officers were on the other side. Where was Tom?

Just then from the corner of her eye, she caught a glimpse of a blue Brooks Brothers suit hanging off broad shoulders. Jennifer rushed across the room and threw her arms around Tom.

'Oh, Tom. Oh . . .' she blurted out. Was it true? Was he finally there with her? This couldn't be another dream, could it? If so, please God, don't let me wake up.

'Jennifer, sweetheart, let me look at you,' Tom said, detaching himself from her and looking her over with concern. Jennifer could feel his eyes on her frizzy mop. She reached up to tame it as best she could.

'It kills me to see you like this, honey,' Tom said. 'But

you look . . . *healthy*, at least. Are they feeding you okay?'

'Oh, who cares about that, Tom? What's going on? When are you getting me out of here!'

'It's all being worked out,' Tom told her.

He reached out and took her hand. It felt so good to have contact with him. Jennifer wished she could kiss him over and over and over again. She wished they could be anywhere except in this miserable room. But most of all she wished they could talk about love and weddings and the future. Jennifer didn't want to talk about the law.

'We know the judge on this one,' Tom said as they sat down at the table, 'and he's not at all keen on holding up the governor's latest fad legislation, so –'

Jennifer cut him off. 'So, no jury trial. A summary judgment and he'll find me innocent, right? And I'll be let out of here?'

'Well . . .' Tom picked up her hand and held it in both of his.

'Well, what?' she asked.

'It's not that simple. The DA's office is being . . . difficult.'

'Difficult?' Jennifer asked. Her heart fluttered in her chest. 'Tom, you don't know what it's like here. I can't . . .' She stopped because she knew that if she went on she'd collapse. She took a deep breath. How could she explain to him how bad it was?

'Look, we feel confident that the judge will go our way this time,' Tom assured her.

Jennifer wasn't convinced.

'Well, what are you going to do to make sure of it, Tom? You've *got* to get me out of here!' Jennifer heard herself beginning to sound a little hysterical.

'Stay calm, sweetie.' He looked at her. 'That's the most important thing right now. Just keep calm and quiet – the model prisoner. Stay ladylike and let us do the dirty work for you.'

She tried to smile. 'Tom, you can't be ladylike here.'

'Oh, babe.' Tom leaned forward across the table and lowered his voice. 'You know Donald's behind you all the way on this one. Do you know the resources he's thrown behind you on this?' She shook her head. 'It's not just Howard McBane. Christ, half of Swithmore, McBane are billing their time to you. You know that Donald won't take no for an answer. So sit tight, and you'll be in the catbird seat when this is all over.'

Jennifer looked at him intently, trying to believe that it would all work out in the end. 'How much longer will it take?' she said finally.

'Oh, under a month.'

'You're sure?'

'Trust me.'

Tom leaned forward and gave her a tender kiss on the forehead. Then he pulled out a pad. 'Now tell me what you need,' he said gently. 'And we'll make sure to get it to you right away.'

'What I need,' Jennifer said, angry with his calm efficiency, 'is some fresh air and for you to get me the hell out of here.'

Tom made a gesture of annoyance with his hand, and then sighed and started speaking slowly, as if talking to a child. 'Okay. I got the point,' he told her. 'You think I enjoy spending my Saturday morning like this? We've gone over this, Jennifer. What more do you need me to tell you?'

As Jennifer looked at him, she realized with a sudden

feeling of horror that Tom had changed. His eyes, his tone of voice, the way he kissed her on the forehead . . . 'Do you still love me, Tom?' she asked abruptly. Something told her that she had to ask, that their emotional landscape had changed, but if the answer wasn't yes, she was certain her heart would stop beating.

Tom's lips tightened and he averted his eyes. 'Yes, of course. But . . .'

Jennifer heard the three-letter word and knew that those three letters shook her world.

'Jennifer, you know I care for you deeply. But, under the circumstances . . .' he stammered and began again. 'You know my family – it would be very bad publicity for them if I was involved with . . . a convict and –'

'Are you insane?' she asked. 'Are you calling me a convict? If I hadn't agreed to do this it would be you and Donald in jail!'

'Jennifer, that isn't even true,' Tom said, stiffening, 'and as your attorney I advise you not to say it again.' He paused and looked down, his eyes narrowed. 'I'm your lawyer. I think it's best if we consider our personal relationship over. When this has all blown over, I'm sure things can go back to normal, but for now it's not a good idea.'

Jennifer stared at him in disbelief. 'What are you saying?'

'I'm returning the engagement ring to the jeweler. I'll make a small statement to the press that we are no longer romantically involved – by mutual choice – but that I am still your close friend and that I will fight your case to the end.'

'Taking back the ring?' she asked. As if the jewelry was at issue.

'It's really for the best. You need to concentrate on your appeal – you don't need emotional complications –'

'But Tom, this is when I need you the most!' Jennifer felt herself on the verge of tears. 'I need your love, I need your support! You *can't* abandon me now!'

'That's not the way I see it – as abandoning. I'm still your lawyer. And really, Jennifer, you need to think of me, too. My position, my reputation.'

'Your reputation? I *made* your reputation. Without my high-powered deals, you would have been nothing. You were a nobody when I met you! And now you have the balls – or lack thereof – to leave me in the lurch? You're a lily-livered coward of a nobody!'

'You're angry, now, so maybe I should just leave. But I'll be in touch soon to talk about your case. I really do care about you, Jennifer. Be that as it may,' he began in what Jennifer had already learned to call his lawyer voice.

'I can't believe this is happening!' she interrupted. 'If you break up with me now, Tom, I swear I –' Jennifer stopped suddenly. She realized she had nothing to threaten him with – she had no leverage at all. No matter what he did, she still needed him to fight her case – he was her only card. Even now, when he was treating her like the worst doormat, she could do nothing to fight back. She felt so helpless, she wanted to attack him, to claw at his face, or at her own, to fall onto the floor and kick and scream. Instead she froze and wished her heart would stop, but it wasn't as easy as that.

'Jennifer, it might be hard to see this now but in the end everything will be okay. Don't worry,' he told her.

If she could have she would have laughed, but all she said was, 'Nothing will ever be okay again.' And then she slapped him. Firmly and soundly, right across his face.

Tom lifted a hand to his cheek. 'I'm sorry,' he said, as if that meant anything. As if saying that helped. He stood up and turned away. She watched him – his tall, graceful figure weaving through the hubbub of the room to the door.

He was gone. Just like that.

Jennifer thought she'd felt the lowest of the low in Observation and during her first meal in the cafeteria, but this was a new lowness of black despair, the kind that she'd never imagined could exist and that she wouldn't even wish on her worst enemy – who was now Tom.

Book II

21

Cher McInnery

A woman always has her revenge ready.

Jean Baptiste Poquelin (Molière)

When Jennifer Spencer finally busted up, she shattered like a bad egg hitting a brick henhouse.

Cher was in the visitor's room, meeting with her lawyer, when Jennifer bent across the table and smacked her visitor across the face with a slap that brought silence to the visitors at tables around her. Cher and her latest lawyer – Jeffery – were just about finished anyway. She bent over and said, 'Enough of this.' Cher wanted to see the fun. She got up quickly and watched Jennifer from a distance. She didn't want to get too close because when someone went ballistic you just didn't know what they might be able to pull out.

But Jennifer didn't go ballistic. She calmly stood up and left the room. Maybe Cher's instincts were wrong. Maybe the poor bitch would just cry herself to sleep. Cher followed Jennifer out of the room and was disappointed when she saw her turn into her cell. It would be hard for Cher to see what would happen next. But Cher stationed herself in the hallway and waited. Sure enough, in a moment Jennifer Spencer, her eyes blank and her face the gray-white of a blue jay's belly, walked out of her house and into the rec room. Cher smiled. Oh yeah. She could see big trouble coming.

Cher watched from the doorway while Jennifer walked to the pay phones and then just stood there and stared at them. Then suddenly she picked up the phone and made a call. Cher moved in closer. 'Collect to Donald J. Michaels,' she heard the deb say. Jesus! Donald J. Michaels was one of the biggest guys on Wall Street. He was bigger than Trump, bigger than Milken ever was. Was *he* the guy the deb had been involved with?

Cher waited, as did Jennifer Spencer. Then Cher heard her say, 'Operator, tell that secretary this is important. He *has* to accept the charges and speak to me. Make it collect and person-to-person from Jennifer Spencer.' Cher watched as nothing happened. Well, nothing happened on the other end of the line, but some huge systems crash was happening behind the deb's eyes. Slowly Jennifer began to shake, then she grasped the telephone for support. She was standing right in front of the TV but didn't hear the women's wails of protest as she blocked their view of the screen, nor did she notice the line of others who were waiting to use the phone. Angry women in the rec room continued to shout at Jennifer to 'move your fucking head, bitch,' while Cher smiled. Some stood and moved toward her to forcibly take her out of the way. It was certain that Jennifer was about to get a real walloping.

But then suddenly Spencer flew into action. She

crammed the receiver into its cradle. She was going off. Cher watched as Jennifer picked up a chair, and with a strength that Cher would not have ever expected, hurled it up and across the room. It smashed against the wall right under the clock. Half of the women were up and out of the way before it bounced to the ground. But Jennifer was moving and didn't wait for the bounce. In three long strides she too crossed the room to a table where Flora and Gloria were sitting. Jennifer slashed her arms across the puzzle they were putting together, flinging the pieces all over. Gloria screamed, and Flora slid from her chair and crouched behind it while the table followed the chair and hit the wall. Cher held back a laugh. She hated those friggin' jigsaw bitches anyway. The way Cher saw it, the debutante was finally coming out.

Meanwhile, the inmates with IQs in the three figures had hit the deck, while a few of the stupid ones were still in the 'Hey, what the fuck . . .' protest stage. Cher realized she'd better make sure she kept her nose clean, because even being a victim now might put her parole at risk. But before she could duck, she was joined at the doorway by a group of other prisoners from the unit. Movita was one of them. 'What's happenin'?' Movita asked.

'Looks like yer new crew member is goin' postal,' Cher told her, lifting an eyebrow but managing to repress a sneer. Behind her the noise in the rec room had increased while Spencer threw chairs, magazines, cards, books, and anything else she could grab hold of. Monopoly money fluttered in the air while half the tiles of a Scrabble game hit the window with hard tiny taps.

'Oh, fuck!' Movita said. Cher had to admit to herself that she was surprised. She didn't think the debutante had it in her. Cher could hear the stampede of COs running down the hall to the unit. Shit, she thought, we'll all be in lockdown in a minute!

Suki came skittering up. 'Byrd, Camry, and Rodriguez are leading a whole squad over here,' she gasped. Then, jumping like a puppy, she tried to get a look over Cher's shoulder. 'Holy shit,' she said. 'It's Jenny.' She started to push past Cher but Movita restrained her.

'Leave her be,' Movita said.

In the rec room Jennifer overturned the last standing table while the rest of the crew watched from the door. Theresa took one look, shook her head, and backed away. 'Do you know what got her goin'?' Movita asked Cher.

Cher shrugged. 'Bad news from her lawyer,' she said.

'Tom?' Suki explained. 'Her fiancé?'

'Oh, shit,' Movita murmured.

'Men. They are no good,' Cher said using a fake Latino accent.

'It's important to release your anger,' Theresa said. 'But it's just as important to do it in a positive, not negative way.'

'Thank you, Doctor Laura,' Movita said, and Cher snickered.

The noise of overturned furniture stopped, and they all froze as a long and painful wail of despair pierced the unit. They witnessed Jennifer Spencer's complete emotional meltdown. Jennifer fell to the floor and began to roll. Her horrifying wails intermingled with the blaring play-by-play broadcast of the television. Cher and the rest of the crew knew better, but one busybody – Carolyn Weltz, the recently born again – knelt beside Jennifer. 'The Lord is my shepherd,' she began, and Cher was pleased to see Jennifer lash out at her like a feral cat cornered in a dark basement.

It was then that the COs, wearing thick yellow rubber gloves, chest protectors, and clear face masks, pushed through the crowd at the doorway. The gear was needed to protect themselves against bites or contact with bodily fluids. Cher had to admit it was a good idea in this case. The debutante probably was a biter, though Cher doubted that her bodily fluids presented a health hazard to Officer Byrd or those other sons-of-bitches. Just to increase the racket, the sirens began. The team surrounded Jennifer as she continued to scream and kick, her arms brutally wrenched behind her back by the bastardly Byrd. Cher saw him knee her before he secured her arms tightly with the plastic cuffs. But the damn deb never stopped caterwauling. She was yanked to her feet but collapsed again to the floor. When she refused to stand, the officers lifted her and carried her from the room, shrieking and sobbing and demanding to see the Warden.

'Lockdown,' Officer Camry cried. 'Let's go. Show's over. Nothin' to see.'

Ha! Cher wouldn't have been surprised to see Spencer foaming at the mouth like old Betty did when she got rabies and daddy finally shot the bitch dog.

'Man, she's in trouble now,' Suki said.

'You will be too if you ain't in your cell in forty seconds,' Movita told her. 'You, too Cher.'

'Lockdown.' The cry went up and was announced over the intercom. All the sheep began moving back to their pens.

Cher wasn't going to admit it to Movita, but she was impressed with the debutante. It took all four of the officers to hold her down and she was giving them plenty of trouble.

And the noise! She could have rented out her lungs to an ambulance. It didn't seem like she ever had to stop to take a breath.

Warden Harding was already waiting at the other side of the bars at the end of the unit. 'Back to your houses, back to your houses,' Officer Camry was still telling them. Cher didn't want a write up – she was too close to parole to take any chances – but she sure did want to see what happened when the debutante passed the Warden. Cher also wondered if Spencer had anything worthwhile to steal in her footlocker. Now would be a good opportunity to go through it, since Spencer would surely get at least forty-eight hours, maybe more, in the SHU for this kind of infraction.

The inmates began moving toward their houses, but Cher tried to move as slowly as she reasonably could. She watched them carry the debutante out past the bars and up to the Warden, who ordered the officers to 'put her on her feet'. They held the panting and nearly spent Jennifer upright as the Warden firmly, but without malice, spoke to her. Cher entered her cell, luckily close to the end of the unit. She wondered if old Gwen would get to stammering but the Warden was completely in control.

'You are an inmate at the Jennings Correctional Facility for Women, Miss Spencer,' the Warden began. 'Can you get control of yourself?'

Spencer made some kind of noise, but Cher couldn't hear it.

'Show's over,' Officer Camry repeated and the bars closed on all the cells. But Cher thought the show wasn't quite over yet. Neither Spencer nor the fat lady had sung. Still, she had to be cautious. A lockdown infraction was serious.

Slowly, Cher inched her way over to the bars. Camry – no boy genius – didn't notice because he was talking with Suki. Cher cupped a hand to her ear, but it wasn't necessary. The Warden's voice carried. 'You are here to be rehabilitated for your crime and we certainly cannot accept this kind of behavior from you or from any inmate in this facility. Do you understand me, Miss Spencer?'

Cher actually heard Spencer say yes and from her tone of voice knew there wouldn't be any more kung fu fighting. She sighed, a little disappointed. But it had been an impressive performance. She had to give Movita credit: There was more to Spencer than she had given her credit for.

The warden was speaking again. 'You are financially responsible for any of the damage to state property that you have done. And you will be spending the next two nights in the Special Holding Unit.'

22

Jennifer Spencer

*I guess it used to be a whole lot worse in here. Miss
Riley, the warden before Miss Wheeler, would shave
your head bald for walking on the grass and put you in
maximum security for no less than six months.*

Becky Careway, an inmate at the Ohio Reformatory for Women.
Kathryn Watterson, *Women in Prison*

'Step back, Spencer.'

Jennifer lay sprawled on the concrete floor. 'Back, I said,'
the voice barked. 'Or I'll move ya' back.' There was real
menace in the voice. Despite her overwhelming lethargy
Jennifer forced herself to rise to a crouching position and
then managed to stand and move off to the corner of the
bare concrete space. 'That's better,' the voice on the other
side of the door said. 'Good girl.' She recognized his voice,
though she couldn't see him. It was Byrd, the creep. Even
in her dazed state, Jen could hear the sexual menace in his
voice. As if reading her mind he continued, 'Watch your
slot, Spencer. Comin' through.'

The slot at the bottom of the door rattled and a tray was
pushed inches beyond the door. Though she felt empty
inside, she was anything but hungry. She had either fallen

198

asleep or passed out from exhaustion on the bare cement, and now she had no idea how long she'd been unconscious. The muscles in her lower back and between her shoulder blades ached and one of her legs – the right one – felt sore from the knee to the upper thigh. She reached down to rub it. It was very tender to the touch. Had she been injured in the melee?

She couldn't remember much of what had happened after her attempted phone call to Don. But now, after unknown hours of screaming in rage and sorrow, followed by a deep and disorienting sleep, she just wanted to know what time it was. She took a step toward the tray. Perhaps she could figure out which meal it was by its content. But it was something she couldn't identify, perhaps lunch, perhaps dinner, or even some new brown invention for breakfast. The tray didn't have dishes or implements. It was a single piece of molded plastic with two depressions in it, one filled with the brown substance and the other filled with something that might once have been a green vegetable. But maybe not. She heard the noise of the CO moving away and called out to him. 'What time is it?' she shouted through the door.

'Not time for you to talk, unless you enjoy being in here,' the voice said, laughed, and moved away.

She looked around. No natural light, no clocks, no lights-out, no good morning. In the relentless twenty-four-hour-a-day fluorescent glare of the Special Holding Unit deep in the underground passages of Jennings, Jennifer's hands began to shake uncontrollably. Frightened, she used whatever mind she had left to try to stop them but she couldn't. She left the disgusting meal where it was and walked back to the corner, where she leaned against the wall and slowly, like a deflating pool toy with a leak, slithered down the wall into a squatting position in the corner.

After a time she heard a tiny noise, a kind of scraping. She looked up. Nothing. She heard it again. She looked carefully. And then she saw the roach, big as a waterbug, actually trying to push the plate of slop across the floor. Oh God. From across the cell the bug looked the size of a Chihuahua. She couldn't bear bugs. She felt as if she'd vomit. And then there was a noise in the hall and the bug skittered away.

Her hands kept trembling and she felt as if she couldn't get a breath into her lungs. The air in the cell was incredibly stale. It actually felt as if it were solid, some kind of gel made up in equal parts of body odor, mildew, and the spent exhalations of hundreds of previous inmates.

She still couldn't believe that she had been so unceremoniously dumped by Tom. Their relationship had been so intense, so important to her. Wasn't it true for him? How could he just let it all go? How could he walk away from the love they shared? She had never enjoyed holding, and being held by, any man the way she had enjoyed Tom. Just lying in bed with him, his left arm slid under her pillow, his right arm snaked up between her breasts, cupping one gently in his hand, was an exquisite pleasure. In response she would slide her left hand under the pillow and make a fist, lay it in his palm, and he'd curl his fingers around hers. Jennifer's head would rest just against his chin and he would lift his head a little so that his mouth rested on her ear. His whispers of 'I love you' would make her melt into his body even more.

Even now, after his dismissal of her, as she crouched here in the corner like an abandoned orphan, Jennifer could feel

Tom's body. She could feel her body burn as if his skin were pressed against her own. It was so real it made her whole body tremble. How could he give that up? How would she go on without it? What had happened to Tom since she'd been put in here? Did he fall out of love with her before all of this and just couldn't tell her? No, that couldn't be. Maybe it was pressure from Donald? Maybe it *was* his family and the hounding of the media. After all, she was locked up and had no idea what kind of hell he was going through on the Outside.

Why did he do it? It couldn't have been the publicity and trial because he had been as loving to her as usual throughout all of that. Did his parents only object once the verdict came in? She had met them only three times but they seemed to have liked her. Maybe that was an excuse. Did he see her on visiting day with the Suki hair, the cheap lipstick, and garish eye makeup and get scared away by her transformation? Did she really look like such a monster to him? How could someone who had professed eternal love, who had given her a diamond – her first – which meant 'forever', give her up so quickly and completely?

She thought back to when they first met. It was about two months after she joined Hudson, Van Schaank that she had started working on a huge deal – one that would turn out to be one of the most profitable in the history of the firm – and Tom was the lawyer assigned. They spent many nights working late, ate dinners together, even breakfasts on Saturdays and Sundays as the project neared its close. She tried not to be too attracted to him. Office romances never worked out. But this felt different. He wasn't the usual infatuation, though he was a serious person, and she wasn't a giddy girl. She wondered at first if her growing crush was mutual and began to watch him for signs. First she noticed him looking at her during her presentations to Donald and the other partners. And then there were times when they would finish each other's sentences. 'Great minds think alike,' Tom would tell her.

They were discreet with their affair for several months and were even more careful about not letting Donald know they were an item until they were sure of the seriousness of their feelings. Generally, Donald saw fraternization as a distraction from work. But he didn't have a problem with *them* breaking the rule. When they announced their engagement he was thrilled for them. 'I'll give the bride away,' he said, 'and you can honeymoon in my villa in Umbria.'

How, she wondered again, could Tom just give her up? She felt dizzy. She couldn't bear to think of it anymore. She looked around the cell for distraction. There was nothing to look at, not even graffiti. The light never changed. There was nothing to read, nothing to do, nothing to capture her imagination except her thoughts, which were unbearable. She was, for the first time she could ever remember, completely alone with herself, a self that was soul-sick, frightened, and with hands that would not stop trembling.

She sat and sat and sat. After some time – she'd never know how much – she felt herself undergoing a kind of sea change. The sensory deprivation that left her emotionally numb and staring dumbly at her hands moved her into an altered state. Her fear and anger, all her anguish, seemed to go away, and she saw her hands as if for the first time. Slowly she opened and closed her fists. They were something. They could go from giving the softest caress to the hardest punch. Jennifer opened and closed them again and thought of the marvel of human anatomy that enabled her to perform this simple task. She tried to remember high school biology and the number of bones in the hands but couldn't, though she remembered the names: carpals, metacarpals, and phalanges. She wondered if each of the phalanges had a different name. Perhaps they had numbers.

She was alive; that was all that she felt. Her love for Tom was a physical pain in her chest but all of her emotions were washed away. Maybe this was why they used the SHU. It took away your feelings and left you empty, only partly human. Because, she realized as she sat there staring at her hand, we are not our bodies or our brains. We are our feelings. Without feelings we are not human. She felt as if her humanity had waned. Her anger was spent. Her sorrow was pushed out like an ebbing tide.

Was it possible that Tom had overreacted, that he would regret what he had said and write her an apology? Would he ask to visit again? If he did, what would she do? A man who abandoned a woman in need was not a man who could be trusted. She thought of how her father had run out and what her mother went through. Jennifer had thought that *she* would escape from the bad luck that plagued her family. She had thought she would have money, position, a husband, and, eventually, a family. But she didn't think any of that would be possible now.

Oddly, at that moment, her hands stopped trembling. She had no more hopes, no more delusions of a quick release. She was simply alive in a Special Holding Unit of a prison.

There was no way for Jennifer to know how much time was passing – she could only try to mark the passing of the hours by the delivery of her meals. She counted back the meals that had been delivered. She could remember at least three, though she hadn't eaten any of them. The supper was still there, as was the breakfast and the lunch. She probably had less than twenty-four hours to go. Now, hungry and tired, she crawled over to the trays and was eating what she could when she heard the key in the door. Like a caged animal she quickly retreated to the farthest corner, pulled her knees up to her chest, and stared intently at the heavy iron door.

The door opened very slowly, and Jennifer held her breath. Then, very softly she heard someone whisper her name. 'Jennifa'?'

Jennifer did not answer, but remained frozen in abstract fear. 'Jennifa'?' the voice sounded again.

'Movita?' Jennifer whispered in response. 'Movita, is that you?' Jennifer jumped to her feet and nearly shouted for joy when she saw Movita quickly slip into the cell. 'What are you doing here? How do you get in here?'

Movita held up her hand for Jennifer to be quiet. 'I wasn't sure which of these holes they put ya' in.'

'But you have a key?' Jennifer asked.

'Don't be crazy. Let's just say a guard owes me a favor.' She raised her hand. 'We'll talk about that later. I don't have much time and if I get caught doin' this they'll transfer my tired black ass outta here.'

'What are you doing here, then?' Jen asked.

'I came to see if you're okay,' Movita answered. She looked around the cell. 'No fun, huh?' Jennifer shook her head in agreement. 'This place can break ya' forever. Or it can make ya' stronger. Which ya' think it's gonna do for you, girl?'

'I just want to get back to my cell,' Jennifer said, and realized that it was true. How pathetic. She didn't even say she wanted out of jail. She didn't say she wanted to go home. She said, with absolute sincerity, that she wanted to go back to her cell.

'Ya' certainly acted up enough to warrant bein' here,' Movita said. 'Girl, you were fierce.'

Jen nodded and flushed. 'He dumped me.'

'I guessed,' Movita shrugged. 'Ain't the end of the world. There's lots more lawyers.'

'He was my fiancé.'

Movita shrugged again, then made a noise like a sigh. 'Ain't a woman in the joint who hasn't been dumped by the man Outside.' She looked at Jennifer and, despite the hard words, her face was kind. Her deep brown eyes, virtually the same color as her skin, radiated warmth. 'Ya' still got a day and a half to do nothin' but think in here. I'm goin' to suggest that you think about others as well as yourself.' She handed Jennifer a large manila envelope. 'Since ya' probably figured out by now that you're going to be in here for a while I think ya' should read this.'

Jennifer looked down at the envelope. 'What is it?' she asked.

'It's bidness. Somethin' I don't know enough about, but I think *you* do. There's something goin' down here. It involves a company called JRU. You hear of them?'

Jennifer shook her head. Whatever Movita Watson wanted, Jen didn't care. And she certainly didn't want to be caught breaking a rule and ending up with more time in the SHU. 'I don't care about JRU,' Jennifer told Movita, handing the envelope back. 'Anyway, I may not be engaged to Tom, but he's still my lawyer. I'm not going to be in here that much longer.'

'Goddamnit, woman, face the facts,' Movita spat with a

sudden vehemence, 'you *are* gonna be in here. Ya' still think you're different? Ya' still think you're a special case? You've been fucked over like almost everyone else in this place and you *are* gonna be here.' She shook her head and lowered her voice. 'Ya' have to accept that or this place will destroy ya'.'

Jennifer remained silent in the wake of Movita's passion. The words landed like blows to her gut. 'That's not true,' she said, but for the first time she was afraid maybe it might be. 'I don't mean I'm better than everyone else, I just . . .'

'Oh, yes ya' do. Ya' think someone's gonna pull strings and ya' ain't gonna do time. Ya' think Suki is stupid, and Theresa is a joke, and I'm a gansta. Uh-uh. We're women just like you who fucked up.' She looked Jen up and down. 'Accept it,' she said. 'Live it minute by minute.'

'I can't,' Jen said, trembling. 'I can't take any more of this. I'll die.'

'Then you're gonna have to die,' Movita said simply. Jennifer's head shot up in terror. Was this woman threatening her? Was she trying to force her to do something?

Movita laughed gently at Jen's frightened response. 'Don't worry baby, I ain't here to kill ya'. I'm here to make sure ya' live.'

Jen took a deep breath. 'I don't understand what you're trying to say to me,' she said softly. 'I can't stay here. I can't stay in this place for another day. I can't.' She began sobbing quietly.

'It ain't just 'bout you,' Movita said. 'That's what I'm trying to tell ya'. Ya' ain't the only woman in this place.'

'I know that,' Jennifer responded, hearing how defensive she sounded.

'Do ya'?' Movita asked her. 'There's a difference between knowin' there are others around you and knowin' that *you* are around others. Ya' get what I'm saying, girl? We're all in this together.' She gestured with the envelope. 'It ain't 'bout any one of us, it's 'bout *all* of us. That's the only way we can make it here. Ya' understand that?' Jennifer nodded, and Movita continued. 'And it ain't about forever, either,' she said firmly. 'Ya' got that?'

'I don't know what you mean,' Jennifer told her.

Movita said nothing for a moment. She only stared directly into Jennifer's eyes, and Jennifer didn't like what she saw in them. The pain in those dark eyes was almost more than she could bear, but she sensed that she could not look away – that she *must* not look away. 'I'm gonna die in this place,' Movita finally said. 'Ya' know what that means? I'm never gettin' out of here. Never.'

'But . . .' Jennifer tried to speak.

'Shut up, girl,' Movita said, raising her hand. 'Shut up and listen, 'cause I ain't never talkin' about this again. I killed a man. My man. Earl Watson. He beat me, sure, but I hit him back plenty. One day he went for my daughter. That was it. Still, all of the reasons and justification in the world don't mean shit anymore. I killed him. And I'm gonna live the rest of my days in here. That's *my* reality. It can't be changed.'

'But they can't keep you here forever,' Jennifer protested, horrified. Somehow she hadn't thought about Movita's crime or sentence.

'That's what I'm sayin' to ya', girl. They can, but they can only keep me here one day – one moment – at a time. I just gotta stay in that moment. Ya' hear what I'm sayin' to ya'?' Jen, shocked, barely managed to nod her head. 'I don't think about tomorrow and I don't think about yesterday. I don't even think about ten minutes from now. I just stay in

207

the moment, and honey, if the moment's good, I'm happy. If the moment's bad, like the one I had over this here report, I let it pass. I just take it just one moment at a time, and that's what you have to do, too.'

Jennifer could not begin to accept the reality of a life sentence in prison. What she could sense, however, was the great strength, compassion, and wisdom that were with her in the cold, sterile holding cell. The moment was a good one – good because she was not alone. Movita was there with her. Jennifer looked deeply into Movita's eyes and nodded, and Movita saw that she understood.

'Ya' got more than twenty-four hours in here,' Movita told her, 'so I brought ya' a little readin' material.' Again, Movita referred to the envelope that Jen held in her hand.

'What is it, exactly?' Jennifer asked her, hoping it wasn't some stupid religious tract.

'It's the worst damn thing that's happened to me since the day I picked up the knife and cut Earl's throat,' Movita told her, and motioned to the envelope.

Jennifer, really curious, looked at it. She read the return address: *JRU International*. It meant nothing. 'What is this?'

'It's all in there,' Movita said quietly. 'I want ya to read it.'

'Won't they see me with this? Will I get in trouble?'

'No to both questions. It's been taken care of. I don't have no more time to talk. Shift's gonna change. Once Byrd is off, we both get our asses in a jam over this.' She looked down at the envelope. 'I don't understand all the bidness talk in there, but I do know that if what's in them pages comes true, then I can't go on here. If they do what they say they're gonna do, it *will* be 'bout forever, and I can't . . .'

She stopped and turned away toward the door. Jen wanted to reach out and hold her but knew she shouldn't. 'I gotta get outta here now,' Movita said. 'Read that up and figure out what we can do about it. I got a lollipop for you from Sally to make the readin' more enjoyable.' Jen looked down at the envelope and Movita left as quickly and mysteriously as she had come.

The moment Jennifer heard the key turn to lock her in for another twenty-four hours, she opened the wrapper of the lollipop and popped it into her mouth. The burst of flavor, of sugar, was an incredible comfort. Sugar was the legal drug in Jennings and no inmate could do without it. Tears came into her eyes at the simple pleasure flooding her, and the kindness of Movita. Then, after a few moments, she opened the envelope and began to read.

She read and read. When a meal came in she ate it without tasting it while she was reading. When she finished she didn't even pause – she went back to the first page and began again. She was appalled. JRU International couched their intentions in the politically correct verbiage of 're-habilitation and job training', but what the privatization plans really described was not unlike a slave owner's plantation in the old South. The report cited 'underutilized' beds and called for an immediate doubling of the inmate population. 'Cost per unit' would thereby be reduced, and with round-the-clock work shifts, the prison would be able to 'more fully realize existing and proposed profit centers'.

She finally looked up from the world she was in to find herself back in her cell. The proposal was an unbelievably callous and cruel assessment and Jennifer grew angrier with each and every word that she read. JRU International was going to turn the place into a factory. In the name of rehabilitation, the women – the 'units' – would be worked twenty-four hours a day. And double the population? Jennifer scanned the rest of the report. Where were the plans for increased health care and better nutrition to keep this slave labor force working? Where were the cost estimates for the repairs and modifications that would transform this hell hole into something better than a kennel? Where was the reality, the humanity in this report?

Jennifer knew she wouldn't be at Jennings for long, but Suki and Theresa and poor Springtime and Flora – all of them would. Who and what was this JRU? She would have to get in touch with Lenny and ask him to do some research. But not over the phone. Nor could she write to him – letters were read. Maybe he'd visit. They could talk about it more then. Just as these thoughts were going through her head, her eyes focused by chance on the page before her and landed on the word 'visitation'. She read the paragraph closely.

> *Research shows that inmate visitation frequently leads to unrest and deviant behavior. In addition, far too much space is dedicated to this purpose. While we cannot eliminate visitation entirely, we can reduce the magnitude of the problem by a general dispersal of the inmate population to other JRU-controlled facilities across the nation, and in turn, transfer new units into this facility. Research shows that relatives and friends will rarely travel more than three hours for a prison visit.*

People were 'units'. Visitation caused 'deviant behavior'. Jennifer could not read one more word of the report. She thought back to what Movita had told her: *'It's not about you and it's not about forever.'*

'Mealtime, Spencer,' a woman CO's voice said. Jennifer scrambled over to push her old tray out the slot in the bottom of the door. Then another meal was silently shoved into the room, without a mention of the contraband report in front of her. She was so upset, so angry, that her first impulse was to kick the damn tray. Instead, she picked it up, sat back down on the floor, picked up her spork, and started to eat. She needed to think, but not too far ahead. She had to stay in this moment.

Tom might not love her, he might not want to marry her, but he wasn't going to abandon her without counsel. But it looked as if, without possibility of an immediate action from the governor or a judge, she would be here for some time at least. Perhaps she could use the time to do some good. She looked at one of the charts in front of her. This was what she knew how to do and it would keep her busy, as well as make a difference to her quality of life. She could focus on this for distraction, and help a woman as powerful and tragic as Movita Watson.

23

Gwen Harding

A leader is a dealer in hope.

Napoleon I

Warden Harding sat in her car in the parking lot of Jennings. She looked at her watch. Her self-regulated lunch break was over and she hadn't done what she wanted to do. Nor had she eaten lunch. She had driven around town for forty-five minutes, parked outside a church for fifteen minutes, and then drove back to Jennings, stupidly passing a McDonald's and a Taco Bell without picking up anything to eat. And she was hungry. Ravenous, actually.

Angry at herself, she got out of the car, slammed the door behind her, and went inside, stopping at the employee lounge and going straight for the snack machine. She put in change and got two candy bars. The hell with it. She'd eat them and make coffee in her office.

Movita was at her desk while Miss Ringling was working at the copier. Movita looked up at Warden Harding and smiled. 'Nice lunch?' she asked. It was unusual for the Warden to go out during the day and she knew Movita well enough to know she noticed every little thing.

Gwen again felt a rush of gratitude, embarrassment, and shame. For several nights in a row she'd dreamed of her drunken tour of Jennings, and although each dream differed slightly, in all of them she was caught by COs and fired. It had been a narrow escape. How fortunate she was that Movita and Roger Camry had found her and not anyone else! But how had Movita managed to get out of her cell? Did she remember the inmate saying 'infirmary'? Well, these women were clever and resourceful. That Gwen knew for sure. She wouldn't ask and Movita wouldn't tell. At least the story wouldn't get all over the prison. She self-consciously reached up and touched the bruise on her jaw. 'Fine,' she said. 'Just a sandwich with a friend.' Movita smiled and went back to her work. Movita Watson was a fine person, Gwen thought, a very fine person. What a pity . . .

'You got one message, Warden,' Movita said. 'Somebody called from that JRU. They wanna make an appointment for a tour.'

Gwen felt her face flush. It made the bruise more tender and she hoped Movita didn't see. She turned away and tried to compose her features, but found herself instead thinking of the gin in her desk drawer. How she would've loved a drink at that moment! Don't think of it, she told herself firmly. 'Fine,' she told Movita, and turned to her office, where she'd at least have the comfort of privacy, caffeine, and chocolate.

But Movita continued. 'And there's somethin' else I expect you'd like to know 'bout.'

'What's that?' she asked, though her feet kept moving her to her office. Movita followed her and stood just inside the doorway while Gwen sat down at her desk. She could feel the gin, behind the drawer front next to her left leg.

'Well, I know what caused Spencer to go berserk. I heard all about it.'

The Warden looked at her. 'I'm interested,' she said, and meant it. It had been a disappointment to see the new, highly visible inmate so out of control. Perhaps she'd been taunted, or worse. 'What was it about?'

Movita crossed her arms and leaned back against the door. 'She had provocation.'

Warden Harding gave her a skeptical look. 'Movita . . .'

'Warden, I ain't excusin' it. You know I ain't. But she's just a kid and it was a terrible thing for her.'

'Okay Movita, I believe you,' the Warden said, folding her hands on her desk and putting the thought of a drink firmly out of her mind. 'Tell me.'

'She met with her lawyer and apparently one of the other women heard mostly everything,' Movita began. 'She said the man was very good-lookin', wearing a suit and a shirt that was starched and ironed so stiff it looked like it could cut his neck and wrists. But he was also stiff and mean lookin' too. Well, it seems he wasn't just her attorney. He and Spencer was engaged, and he comes here and breaks the engagement. He tells her he can't be involved with no convict 'cause a his family and his position so he's breakin' it off.'

Gwen Harding shook her head. 'Bad timing, I'd say. They love to kick you when you're down.'

'But there's more,' Movita added.

'Go on.'

'Well, Jennifer's sayin' to him, "but you know I didn't do nothin' except what you said I should do." Or somethin' like that. I didn't hear the whole rap, but it sounded like she took the fall for him, or someone else.'

The Warden sat very still, biting her lower lip. Her eyes were staring across the room. She was thinking. How many, what percentage of women were imprisoned because of their involvement with men? Far more women's lives were destroyed by men than the opposite, she thought. Maybe that was painfully obvious. But why? The women were often smart, clever women, women with jobs and children, educated women, women who should know better. Even in her own life she'd . . .

'Anyway, he left and she got twisted.'

'Did she love him, you think, Movita?' Gwen asked.

'How can we know that? But if I had to guess, I'd say she did. She don't seem the kinda girl to get hooked up with someone she don't love.' Movita opened the door. 'She didn't have no fight over the TV show they was watching or nothin' like that. She just went crazy.'

Gwen nodded and Movita left her alone.

She fully intended to write up a report for the file on Jennifer Spencer. That was what she always did when an inmate went into the SHU. It would, of course, affect Spencer's time and parole. After Movita's news she thought that maybe she should forgo the report. This was all disturbing, and the JRU call, and her drunken incident were all on her mind at once. Hadn't she been granted another chance? She'd never been tempted to hush up an incident before. Was she being a more responsible person or was she disintegrating? She wasn't sure.

The Warden had to call the people at JRU. No hurry on

that one. She'd eat her junk food and take a look at Spencer's file, then she'd make the phone call. There would be plenty of time, once JRU took over, for her to jump at their command.

One of the tragedies of prison was that prisoners with relatively light sentences, a year or two, increased their time through breaking rules and bad behavior. She knew that sometimes the women were provoked by others, sometimes they acted out of self-defense and, shamefully, they were occasionally egged on by COs. She'd known a woman who'd started with a twelve-to-eighteen-month sentence and ended up serving nine years because of her troubled reactions to authority. She'd tried to help that poor soul, but couldn't get through to her. She certainly didn't want the same thing to happen to Jennifer Spencer. The trouble was, it became a vicious cycle: Every punishment increased the anger and the anger led to worse behavior.

Gwen wolfed down the Butterfinger bar and felt better. With her sugar high she might be up to calling JRU and setting up an appointment. But after she'd done that her mood soured again. She looked at her watch. It was only three-thirty. She looked down at her drawer, the one with the gin. This was impossible. She took out the bottle, secreted it in her purse, and stood up. 'I have to leave early today, Miss Ringling,' she said, ignoring the surprise in Movita's face. Did the fact that she hadn't left early more than once in almost a decade mean she had to explain why? No, it didn't, she told herself.

She walked out of the office, a false front over an unquiet interior. It was okay, she told herself, for while Movita saw all, Movita didn't judge.

Back in her car she felt the same terror that she'd felt

earlier in the day. She was amazed at the deep and simple quality of the terror. She hadn't been this frightened since childhood. Then her misbehaviors had always been minor. Now, her misbehavior was not. Being drunk at work was terrible. It was shocking. And she had done it. She was so distracted by her thoughts that she nearly went through a red light. She stopped just in time. What was next? A DUI?

She rolled down her window, took the bottle from her purse, and poured it out the window. There.

She was spurred on by that act of courage to drive directly back to the church. It was important that she go. That she do something.

This time, afraid she might not go in if she didn't do it immediately, she got out of her car as soon as she had parked. Putting one foot in front of the other, she walked up the narrow path between two patches of well-kept lawn, and entered the side door of the stone building. There was a sign on the wall directing her to the basement. Not so easy. She held the rail firmly as she descended, because her trembling had increased.

She heard people talking and went toward the doorway the voices were coming from. Then she entered the smoky room and stood in the back. She was just in time to see a woman rise and hear her say, 'Hello, my name is Pat, and I am an alcoholic.' Gwen heaved a big sigh. She was where she ought to be.

24

Jennifer Spencer

Self is the only prison that can ever bind the soul.
Henry Van Dyke, *The Prison and the Angel*

Jennifer Spencer came out of the SHU a different person from when she went in. It wasn't just the rage, the disappointment, and the pain that swept through her, leaving her empty as a broom-swept New York apartment. And the change wasn't all internal either. As she was led back to her cell Jen caught sight of herself in a smudged stainless steel door: The white face, the gray around the eyes, the dark marionette lines between nose and mouth, all looked like they belonged to someone else; none of it looked like her. The face she saw looked ugly to her, but what the hell did she care? It didn't matter anymore without Tom.

When she got back to her cell, just before head count and lights-out, all she longed for was darkness. She wanted to climb into her bunk and collapse.

But Suki had other plans. She was lying on her narrow

lower bunk clutching her belly. 'Wow! You're out! We were worried about you.'

'Really,' Jennifer managed. She couldn't imagine who the 'we' was.

'Time in the SHU is tough. Are you okay?'

Jennifer shrugged, too tired to talk. 'NBD,' was all she could manage. She heaved herself into her bunk, and pulled the pillow over her face. Then she remembered Suki's condition. 'Are *you* okay?' she asked. 'How are you feeling?'

'I'm better. I haven't passed out since that once. And I'm not nauseous all the time anymore,' she explained. 'Only when I eat something my stomach don't like.'

'That could never happen at Jennings,' Jennifer said with as much sarcasm as she could muster. She replaced the pillow.

Through it she could hear Suki laugh, but Jennifer kept her face covered. Nothingness was all she wanted. The nothingness of sleep to match the nothingness inside her.

'You know something funny?' Suki asked. Apparently it was a rhetorical question because she continued. 'I keep having this appetite for German potato salad. The kind with vinegar and bacon bits. Isn't that weird?'

Reluctantly Jennifer took the pillow off. 'No,' she told Suki. 'Pregnant women crave all kinds of things. It's normal.'

'Is it? Oh, good.'

Silence reigned, for which Jennifer was grateful. But lying there she couldn't help but wonder how much Suki knew about pregnancy, childbirth, and child rearing. She assumed that the baby picture on the wall was hers. But she had never asked. Jennifer turned on her side so that she could speak quietly but Suki would be able to hear her.

'With the food here, how can you be sure you're getting enough nutrition for your baby?'

'Oh, I got some vitamins,' Suki said proudly.

'From the dispensary?' Had they finally figured out Suki's condition?

'No. I don't dare go there till it's too late for them to take the baby. Cher's sister sent 'em.'

'They're not enough,' Jennifer told her. She pulled her knees up to her chest and her blanket up to her nose and retreated back to her pillow. 'Goddamn place,' she muttered. 'I have to sleep now,' she said, and merciful darkness closed in over her.

Jen wasn't able to retreat from reality for long. It seemed only minutes before the morning bell rang. It was her time to shower, and even if it was with a group that was being watched over by an officer, she didn't care; the SHU had to be the most disgusting place she'd been in, and she had to wash all of it off. She could hardly believe that she was supposed to get up and shuffle along with everyone else as if everything were fine. As if being locked in an SHU was just one more life activity you learned to deal with. As if giving up your future and your entire former life and accepting this present one was no big deal. But she just had to stay in the moment.

The next task was breakfast. As she set her plate of reddish beige glop on the table and sat down at her place, a surge of anger made her exclaim, to no one in particular. 'Fuck!'

Theresa looked at her from across the table. 'Keep your chin up,' she said. 'Better times are coming.'

Jennifer rolled her eyes. 'How do you know that,

Theresa? Maybe *worse* times are coming.' She thought of the JRU proposal and how that would make this ghastly place so much worse.

'Can't be a pessimist, you know,' Theresa said cheerfully. 'It gives you wrinkles and makes bad things happen.'

Jennifer, expressionless, looked across the table. 'Optimism makes bad things happen, too.'

Theresa smiled nervously. 'I don't think so,' she said softly.

'Fuck! *Anything* can make bad things happen,' Cher said, joining them. She sat down across from Theresa, Movita right behind her. 'They're just out there, like accidents, only more so, waiting to happen.'

Theresa looked down at her plate.

'Shut the fuck up,' Movita barked at Cher. 'Theresa's just tryin' to make Jennifer feel better.' She looked at Jennifer. 'You might try to be grateful when someone's nice to you,' she said.

Jen made a face and took a few more stabs at the Cream of Wheat on her plate. 'What the hell is this stuff? Boiled packing peanuts?' She looked over at Suki. 'Can *you* eat this?' she asked her.

Suki shrugged. 'Sure, as long as you pour fourteen teaspoons of sugar over it.' She loaded her bowl with the sugar and so much margarine that the yellow grease made a puddle across the top of her bowl. 'It's okay,' she said with a shrug. 'I like it better than most of the stuff they serve.'

Jennifer dropped her spork on the table with disgust. The others pretended not to notice. She sat perfectly still, ate no more and said no more. Why bother?

When Suki reminded her that they were supposed to be in the laundry soon, Jen rose and followed her like a robot.

As they walked to the laundry, down one after another of the bleak institutional corridors, the vision of her life as empty and frightening came back to Jennifer, as it had when she had been down in that dreadful hole. Even if she could actually stay here at Jennings and serve her time, remain in this horrible place for years without going crazy – which she strongly doubted – there would be nothing, not a goddamn thing, waiting for her when she got out. The thought of the endless emptiness ahead made her exhale a puff of air, leaving her lungs as empty as her life. The horror of it all suddenly made her want to scream in terror, to clutch at Suki for comfort, for help. But Suki, so little as she walked in front of her, pregnant in this women's prison, couldn't help her. Suki was helpless herself.

'Are you okay, Suki?' she asked her.

'Fine. How about you?'

'Fine.'

Jennifer wouldn't have a job when she got out, no money coming in at all, and that terrified her. She wouldn't be able to go into stores and buy what she wanted. She wouldn't be able to travel. She would be poor. And she would have a criminal record.

A feeling of panic was coming over her. Poverty was like prison, she knew that. Poverty kept you from living, just like prison did. It kept ahold of you, it kept a grip on you, it said no to this and no to that, no to everything. Just like Jennings. It made you eat crap, made you sleep on an uncomfortable bed, made you wear shit, made you do without good medical care. Just like Jennings.

They'd reached the laundry room. Jen followed Suki mechanically but she was so out of it she was almost in a trance. Suki was already lifting the piles of dirty laundry into bins to sort it out while Jen just stood there, a broken machine. Then she remembered Suki's condition. Wasn't there something easier for her to work on?

'Don't!' Jen said to her, snapping out of her fog. 'Don't lift that.' Suki looked up at her. 'Come on, I mean it,' she said when Suki didn't stop immediately. 'I'll do that. You just do the sorting.'

'It's okay,' Suki assured her.

'No it's not.' Some of Jen's emptiness got filled with anger. 'Jesus! They don't give you any medical care, or tell you how to take care of yourself! Or your baby.' Then the anger was gone. 'At least let me do the lifting here, okay?' Jen asked. 'I can't stand it otherwise.'

Suki looked at her with a touch of confusion. 'Okay,' she agreed.

So Jen did the hard work, while Suki did the smaller but tedious tasks: the emptying of pockets, the sorting of colors. Still, it was hot in the laundry room and after less than an hour, when Jen looked across at her, Suki looked pale.

'Sit down,' Jen commanded. 'You're white as one of these sheets is supposed to be. I'll get Flora.'

'You are, too,' Suki said and laughed. 'But don't call Flora. I'll be okay,' Suki reassured her.

Jennifer looked down at Suki's stomach. Suki had never told her how she'd gotten pregnant, only how much she wanted the baby. She spoke about it nearly every night before she went to sleep. She was just starting to show, but the uniforms were roomy enough to camouflage her for quite a while longer. Her plan, she said, was to keep the pregnancy going until abortion wasn't possible. Jennifer sighed. Suki would never win any awards for intelligence, but she was optimistic, generous, and good hearted. She'd be a good mother. Jennifer was afraid to ask at what point they separate mothers and babies.

As they folded sheets she thought about the JRU threat. Whatever punishment Suki might get because of her pregnancy now, it would be mild compared to what JRU would probably have in store for her. Since she'd first read the proposal, Jennifer had backed off a little bit. After all, getting involved too deeply could get her into a world of trouble. But poor Suki. Jen didn't know what her sentence was, but armed robbery had to be years and years.

The shift was endless. Breaks were short, lunch inedible, and when the day finally finished Jen could barely stand. She realized it was time to go back to their 'houses' and cook something for dinner. Now that she was in the crew, it was her turn to cook. While she could manage a hostile takeover or an IPO, she didn't know how to cook very many things. This was no time to try anything new; that would only open herself up to Cher's contempt. The idea of being in the crew – something that she'd kind of liked at first – now felt like a burden. She didn't want to talk to these people today or any day. She wanted privacy. But when she thought of the cafeteria, she knew that she *had* to stay in the crew to survive. She'd just cook, eat, and not try to get involved with them beyond that. She'd have to order something decent from next week's canteen that would fit the bill for an acceptable meal.

Everybody was gathered when Jen and Suki walked in. So what? She didn't greet any of them because she wasn't thinking of anything but how the hell she was going to make dinner. Groceries were spread out on the makeshift counter. Her eyes rested on the chunks of beef and unidentifiable pale green vegetables that sat with it. It looked like she was supposed to cook Chinese, which she had never done in her life, thank you.

'What am I supposed to make out of this?' she asked bluntly.

No one answered.

'Well, if you don't know –'

'Will ya' please cut the brat attitude?' Movita suddenly shouted at her. 'We know you were in the fuckin' hole, but you're not supposed to bring it back up here to us. Do I have to tell ya' that we got it bad enough already? And that many of us been down there ourselves and don't need no revisit? Go back to ya' cell till ya' get over it.'

'I'll shut up and cook,' Jennifer said, as coldly as she could.

'Awright,' Movita said. 'Then go ahead and make somethin' good.'

Not knowing what to do, Jen started heating up the oil in the pan over the electric coil. 'Where's my knife?' she asked. She got only chuckles in reply. She tossed the meat into the smoking oil, and as soon as it started to spatter, tears started streaming down her cheeks.

'It'll be okay,' Theresa said, putting her hand on Jen's arm.

Jen didn't reply. She felt sullen and wanted to be left alone. But Movita wouldn't do it. She came up to the stove. 'You're gonna burn this meat, girl. And if you do, you're outta crew.'

Being yelled at was the last straw. Jennifer began to sob uncontrollably, but she continued to cook. She turned the meat quickly and lowered the flame, sobbing all the while.

'Just a minute,' Movita said. 'We don't need no tears in our food. Theresa, take over here. Jen, come with me.'

Jen set the spatula down and followed Movita, still sobbing. She tore a scrap of the crude brown paper towel off the roll and held it to her face.

'Siddown,' Movita ordered.

Jennifer sat.

'You got a choice, Missy. And you gotta make it right now.'

'I don't have any choices,' Jen wailed.

'Shut up. That's just what I'm talkin' about. "*I don't got no choices,*"' Movita mocked. 'You got as many as the rest of us. No. You got more. But what you got that's a problem is feeling sorry for yourself, thinkin' you're some kinda special. Well, let me tell ya' somethin', ya' not. You let those lousy cracker dudes leave ya' with the rap. I think that's a dumber move than anybody else here did. Ya' think ya' educated – hate to tell ya' babe, Maggie in the library is more educated than you. Your education is nothin' compared to the life experiences of these women. So what ya' got left that makes ya' better'n us? Nothin'.'

Jennifer felt the words come down on her like weights. She had nothing left and now she was supposed to be nothing. All she'd lived on all her life was being special. Being special was what got her scholarships and good jobs and rich. So now she was supposed to be nobody special.

It made her feel sick.

25

Maggie Rafferty

*The jury, passing on the prisoners life, may in the sworn
twelve have a thief or two guiltier than him they try.*

Shakespeare

A tragic heroine. That's what I thought of when Jennifer
Spencer walked into the library about a week after she'd
been released from the Special Holding Unit. She looked
ravaged, an Antigone, with perhaps a pinch of Medea under-
neath. In other words, the rage was there too, but buried
under the grief.

I know my literary allusions make me seem both a blue-
stocking and a heartless observer. Rest assured, I never
share them with anyone. Not that there's anyone to tell.
The point is, it's important in this place to keep one's
thoughts to oneself and one's feelings small. Waste none of
them on pity. But there are times when I am sympathetic,
and this was one of those times.

Jennifer Spencer looked pounds thinner, years older, and
hollow eyed, as if she'd glimpsed something horrific. And of

course, she had. She'd been in 'the hole'. I remembered the last time she had come in here, when I'd been reading the JRU information and felt as if I were having a heart attack. She had tried to help me. Now our roles were reversed.

She approached my little table. 'Movita asked me to come and talk to you,' she told me. 'Is this a good time?'

I smiled. She may have faced the horror of prison, but she hadn't yet fathomed the meaninglessness of the word 'time' here. Of all things, boredom is the greatest torture in prison. There is nothing to do for hours on end. Except for the endless daily head counts, lineups, and occasional lockdowns, all excruciating in their tediousness. Not to mention the hours and hours in your 'house' – a cruel joke of a term – and finally the monotony of prison labor. Time is meaningless. 'It's fine,' was all I said.

She lowered her voice. 'She's told me about this JRU thing.'

'I know.' Ever since I had read the report I had not been sleeping well. Or eating well. Or doing anything well, even breathing. I repeatedly called my sons, but I was afraid to speak about it openly (our pay phones are computer recorded and randomly monitored). At any rate, Bryce was in Hong Kong while Tyler was in London for business. They had both promised to visit as soon as they returned.

Jennifer stood there, clearly not comfortable. 'She wants me to help.'

'I know,' I said again.

She was displaying reluctance even to talk about it. 'I'm not sure I should,' she said finally.

'I see,' I said, making it clear by my tone that I didn't see at all. If anyone can spot denial and a resistance to being involved, it's me. After all, I lived denial through thirty years of my marriage. And here at Jennings I'd been totally uninvolved for years. Oh, when I first came to the prison I tried to teach reading and set up child-care, GED, and other classes, but I gave up long ago. Now I could see that Jennifer Spencer had reluctantly accepted being stuck here at Jennings – at least for now – but she wasn't ready to get involved. She certainly wasn't going to start hatching plots with fellow inmates. I totally understood. But unfortunately we needed her. I knew what my role was, and I began to do it. 'You might give it some thought,' I said blandly. 'After all, what else have you to do?'

'It's not that,' Jennifer said, lowering her eyes, 'It's . . . well, you know where I was last week.'

'Yes, I know.' I could see her shame. 'I'm afraid you have the wrong impression of me,' I told her. 'Maybe because I was a school headmistress and I've now become the staid librarian of Jennings.' I paused. 'Sounds like an epic poem, doesn't it? *The Staid Librarian of Jennings*.' She looked at me and smiled, at least a bit. 'Anyway, when I first arrived here, I was down in the hole so often that I was called "The Old Woman Who Lived in the SHU."'

Jennifer looked at me in amazement. 'No! What did you do? And how did you stand it?'

'Oh, I don't know. I was adjusting, I guess. And for me the hole wasn't any worse than above ground. I had a lot of thinking I needed to do.' I looked at her. I believed Jennifer Spencer needed to do some thinking as well. I smiled. 'Not to mention the fact that I was in such a rage at that time it was almost better for me to be alone.'

'God,' Jennifer said. 'I could never stand to go down there again.' Her lip trembled. 'It was horrible. Horrible.' Then she paused. 'Look, I don't expect to be here long. And

I'd like to help, but I never want to be put through that again. And I don't want to spend one more day here than I have to. Not one more day.'

I asked her to sit down. And I smiled at her before I began my lecture. 'They won't put you down there for trying to do a little business deal. Warden Harding is humane. They can't. It's for contraband and violent offenders only.'

'A little business?' Jennifer said. 'What an understatement! And even if it's not violent, working in any way on this JRU thing is a SHU violation. Even the report is contraband.' She paused again. I could see she was a woman used to being in control of herself as well as others – or at least having that illusion. Losing that control had been decimating. 'Look, I'm planning on being good. I want time off for good behavior.'

'That's good behavior in the most passive sense,' I replied. 'The kind of good behavior you're talking about is actually, according to ethicists, the opposite. The worst sin is for good people to stand by and do nothing when they see evil being done.'

I was surprised to see her face redden. Ah, guilt. The working class is rife with it, but I didn't think she would respond so readily. No doubt nuns had educated her. Worse than Jesuits. Of course, she was also still raw from the SHU.

'Even if I help, there's not much I can do,' she protested. 'I mean, I worked in the private sector. I have no government contacts and I'm not sure my lawyer . . .' She paused yet again. 'Well, Hudson, Van Schaank has close contacts with the governor but . . .'

'We don't know how or what we're trying to do yet,' I told her. 'And it isn't all your responsibility. I've already spoken to my sons and once they get back to the U.S. and hear about this they'll be willing to help. You know that they have . . . connections, and power. They may even add an air of respectability to the endeavor.'

'That depends,' Jennifer said.

I was offended. There were those who accused my boys of playing fast and loose but Jennifer Spencer was in no position to throw stones at glass houses. 'Why not? Aren't you being very negative?' I asked, trying not to get upset.

'No. It's just that there's very little we or they can do. Look, I'll ask my contacts to find out all they can about JRU and I'll see if there's anything . . . shady or questionable about them. If we're lucky the CEO, Tarrington, is a declared Satan worshipper and the public will rise up and make it a political hot potato. But that's a long shot.' She turned to the door, as if to leave.

I sighed, the way I used to sigh at my students when I wanted more from them. I can be so manipulative, I thought as she turned around. But it was as much for her good as mine.

'Jennifer – may I call you Jennifer?' She nodded. 'Aren't you being incredibly selfish? Didn't Movita tell you what kind of changes JRU will impose? Doesn't the idea of what they're going to do scare you?'

Before the girl could respond I heard the heavy footsteps of Officer Byrd coming down the hall. 'Shhh,' I whispered, and put my index finger up to my lips. 'He's trouble.' Then I quickly sandwiched the papers in between two boxes of books that had to be reshelved.

'How's the book business today, ladies?' Byrd asked as he stepped into the little room. Neither of us responded to him. 'I think it's time for a little spring cleaning in here don't you?' he asked as he started reaching for a book and then dropped it on the floor. 'Oops,' he said and continued down the wall pulling out books and dropping them on the floor. He often liked to come in and toss part of the library, just for fun. I was used to it by now, but Jennifer froze in horror.

I gave Jennifer the look that meant 'stay in your position'. Karl Byrd had an attitude and arrogance about him to the point of being repulsive. He went around the room disrupting everything from books to magazines to chairs. I eyed Jennifer when he got close to the boxes that hid the JRU papers. He took both hands and caressed the top of the box and looked right at the scared girl but she didn't look away from him. Then he moved his hands away from the box and went to the edges of a table and felt the underside of the wood. Jennifer tried not to show anxiety because, like a dog, Byrd could always smell fear. He ran his hands down two legs of the table and knocked it and its contents onto the floor. 'I guess you ladies have some cleaning up to do in here,' he said with a sneer.

Once he was gone, we both sighed in relief. 'That was a little too close for comfort,' I said.

'He's such a jerk,' Jennifer said. 'And if one thing is going to happen with this transition with JRU it had better be that he's removed from this facility. But none of this can be done single-handedly. It's obvious that the public wants prisons to cost nothing and warehouse monsters. I'm just one person. I can't change that.'

'Look, you won't be doing this all on your own. Responsibility will be divided. And I think the main thing you have to remember is that if JRU gets a hold on this place, gets a hold on *us* . . . well, we'll all wish we were down in the SHU. It's going to be much worse being up here.'

'Listen, I'll ask my sources on the Street about JRU. I'll try to think of anything I can but I . . .' she trailed off, but I thought she was weakening and I pressed on.

'That's all I ask. We can get you reassigned to be my assistant here in the library. And you can use the time to do research. I'll give you whatever help I can,' I volunteered.

'All right,' she sighed, but I felt like dancing. Well, dancing as much as my arthritis would allow. Still, I managed to conceal my elation.

'So, first – if you can stand it – reread that proposal and give me your notes,' Jennifer told me. 'Anything about the prison that is incorrect, unlikely, or unlawful.'

'Already done,' I smiled at her and pulled my notes from inside my copy of *Waiting* – a rather slow-moving but excellent novel by Ha Jin.

'Fine,' she said, and took them, folded them as carefully as a kite and put them in her uniform. 'I'll look for irregularities in the financing or management of JRU, and for unrealistic projections in their business plans.'

'Good,' I said, and watched her leave. I sat there after she was gone, stunned for a moment. I was experiencing a kind of pleasure I hadn't felt in years. It was excitement. And even the tiniest bit of hope. I didn't know what, exactly, I was hoping for, but it felt good.

26

Cher McInnery

I don't want the cheese, I just want to get out of the trap.

Latin American proverb

'Okay. My chicken is served,' Theresa told the crew. For a Yankee the girl knew how to make her chicken. Cher felt her mouth water, but she sat down to dinner with resentment. She knew something was up but wasn't sure what it was. That bothered her. Movita had been busy, and Frances had been delivering a lot of kites along with ice. Cher had heard that the debutante wasn't going to work in the laundry no more. Cher knew Movita was a private person, but when something was on, she let Cher in. Not this time, though.

Cher didn't like to be dependent on no one. In fact, she felt it was best not to get too close to no one. But she had never had a friend like Movita. She had never had no black friend at all, and she had never known a woman who was as on top of things, smart, and resourceful as Movita was. The thing about her was that she was like Cher, but she wasn't like Cher. She was like Cher because Movita was smart, tricky, realistic, and funny as hell. But she wasn't like Cher because she didn't just use her smarts for herself – she was always figuring out a scam or a way to involve or help other people. Of course, the crew came first. Movita tried to keep peace among everyone. Unlike Cher, she was willing to make an extra effort to make things better for someone else. At first Cher had thought she did it to get power over people, or to get something else back. But time and observation had taught her that Movita was also a natural leader. She couldn't help straightening things out for other people. It was her way. Sometimes Cher admired it, and sometimes it was big goddamn pain in her ass.

Like her, Movita was secretive – she was one of the two or three women in the whole damn prison that could keep something to herself. But though Cher had trusted Movita to keep a few secrets of her own, she didn't like it when something was afoot and she was left out. She also didn't like it that it seemed Movita was trusting the debutante with some kind of secret that she was keeping Cher out of.

What do I care, Cher tried to tell herself as she helped herself to the largest piece of the fried chicken. I'm out of here. But she looked over at the debutante and then over at Movita. It irked her. Before the plate was passed on she took another piece of the chicken. What the fuck. Theresa raised her eyebrows but Cher paid no attention.

'Have some coleslaw,' Suki said, passing her the bowl. 'We have plenty of *that*.'

Back in Arkansas, Cher's mama used to say, 'Girlchild, we shoulda spelt your name S-H-A-R-E, 'cuz you are absolutely *obsessed* with that word.' And Mama had been right. As one of nine hungry children in a poor white trash family, Cher learned very early that survival depended on *learning* to share, *doing* your share, and *getting* your share.

Now Cher ignored Suki's hidden admonition. Like Suki knew jack shit about anything. 'The only thing we had plenty of when I was growin' up was work,' Cher told the crew. 'And if you didn't do your share of the work, you didn't get your share of the food. It was just that damn simple.' Everyone had filled their plates and had begun eating. Nobody spoke, so Cher continued. ' 'Ceptin for my baby brother Ellis.' Cher shook her head and took another bite of the chicken. 'Mama spoilt him somethin' awful. She was too damn old by then to have another kid, and little Ellis was so pathetic and weak that she made sure he never had to lift a finger his whole life. And, 'cuz I was the oldest, I was supposed to do his share of the work *and* share my share of the food.' She laughed, but she hadn't laughed then. And nobody laughed now. It pissed her off. She looked over at Jennifer Spencer, so sweet, so damn demure. 'Jesus Christ, I used to think I had two names,' Cher said. 'Alls the time my mama would be shoutin' at me: *Share, Cher! Share, Cher! Share, Cher!* I got damn sick of it then, and I'm damn sick of it now!'

Movita put down her cup hard. 'What'n the hell you jabberin' about?' she wanted to know.

Cher indicated the whole table with her chin. 'They think I didn't share the chicken,' Cher said sulkily.

'Did anybody say that?' Movita asked. 'I didn't hear it. And if you knew what people were thinking, you'd be worried about more serious stuff than that.'

'You know what I always say?' Theresa, the peacemaker, asked. 'Enough is as good as a feast.'

'This *is* a feast,' the debutante said, like she hadn't been eating in four star restaurants her whole damn life.

'Yeah? What did you ever make for dinner but reservations?' Cher asked.

Jennifer stood up. She looked through Cher as if she were invisible, which only pissed Cher off more than ever. 'Thanks, Theresa,' she said. 'Great chicken. Sorry about the coleslaw. It wasn't very good.' She moved toward the cell doors and Cher wished they'd rack the gate and scrunch the skinny bitch. 'I have to make a phone call,' the deb said. 'I'd better go now before the line gets too long.'

'Oh, is that where our little Miss Armani is going?' Cher countered. 'Every time we get done eatin' she's outta here without doin' one damn bit of the cleanup.'

'She helped me make the supper,' Theresa said. 'She made the coleslaw. It's a lot of messy work. And you know the rule: Whoever cooks don't clean up.'

'You call that sharin'?' Cher snarled. 'Nobody ate any of that crap she served up. Coleslaw! Just makes the cleanup all that messier. Can't even get it to flush down the john.' She looked at the bowl, still almost full. It was so vinegary it had made Cher wince. 'Should make her eat it all.'

'She said she's got a phone call to make,' Suki said as she stood to help Cher with the dishes. 'I'm on with you for the cleanup, Cher. I don't mind a little work.'

'I don't mind work either!' Cher snapped back. 'I know how to work and I don't mind doin' my share of the work if everyone else is doin' *her* share of the work. That's all I'm sayin'. You can bet your ass that she's gonna stick around and do cleanup tomorrow night after *I* cook. And I'm gonna make one hell of a mess, too. You can count on that.'

Movita shook her head. 'Girlfriend, you have been

sputterin' and spoutin' about this now for the last fifteen minutes! Don't you got nothin' better to do? Like maybe practice talking about how well you've learned to live with others for your parole speech?'

Cher sat down again. Was that what this was all about? She was shut out because she was leavin'? Was that it? And Mo had picked the debutante to take her place. Cher got a real empty feeling under her breastbone and a pulling at the bottom of her stomach. She didn't like those feelings.

'Fine,' she said. 'I will.' She got up and angrily slammed a kettle down onto the hot plate. Despite her ire, the fact was she liked these women. In all her travels – and Cher had crisscrossed the country more times than the lines on her palm – she'd never met anyone like Movita, and Theresa – for all her wacky optimism and stupid aphorisms – and Spencer – with her smarts – were women Cher would like to keep on knowing. But once paroled she was forbidden to see or speak to any prison inmates. She couldn't even write to the crew without permission from her parole officer. That was cold.

And it was just as cold for the crew to replace her . . . and with Jennifer. Cher felt something unfamiliar, an unpleasant emotion. She was so self-assured, she generally felt so superior to the skanks and hos and marks around her that it was rare that she felt this annoying emotional tic, but she realized with a start that part of her dislike for the debutante was based on jealousy. From the day that girl had arrived in her Armani panties she had seemed an affront to Cher, and if she didn't come right out and say, 'I'm better than any poor white trash like you could ever hope to be,' there was something in her posture and attitude that said it just as plain as speech. And there was no denying that

Movita favored her. Cher was jealous of Jennifer. It wasn't a nice feeling to have, but she supposed there was very little she could do about it. It was a pity that Movita felt that Jennifer was crew material, and it was clear she was planning to replace Cher with the debutante.

It wasn't that Cher blamed Movita – hey, it would be as much as her parole was worth to even jot her a postcard once Cher was out, and she knew she wouldn't think of Jennings or the other women. She could walk right by Theresa on the street and not notice her. But somehow Movita's friendship really mattered. Movita had to take care of herself because she was doin' a long stretch and Cher knew it but somehow seein' herself replaced with the little debutante caused her a pang.

She turned to face Movita. 'And just why are *you* kissin' her uppity white ass?' she spat.

'You ain't go no idea about *what* she's doin'!' Movita spat back. Cher could see that Movita was about to say more, but she stopped abruptly, shut her mouth, and remained silent – avoiding Cher's glare.

Something *was* up; Cher could always tell when a scam or a grift was going down – after all, she'd been grifting for twenty years – and something was definitely going down now. She narrowed her eyes and stared intently at her old friend Movita. The kettle water wasn't heated enough to really clean but she didn't care. She poured the lukewarm water into the plastic dishpan. 'What's going on here, Mo? What ain't you tellin' Cher? Huh?'

'I'm just sayin' we should cut Spencer some slack, that's all,' Movita said quietly, scraping the remains of the chicken bones and most of the coleslaw into the trash. 'That's alls I'm sayin'.'

Cher snorted. No one had ever cut any slack for Cher in her entire life. If there was one thing she had *never* gotten her share of, it was slack. And now she would be damned if some snotty little rich white girl from New York City was going to get all of that, too – especially from Movita, known by all to be tough as hell. It had taken Cher months to get hooked up with Movita. And now the deb was her new best friend?

Cher would never admit to fear anything, and she wasn't *afraid* to get out but . . . Cher let the empty kettle fall to the floor with a clang and headed for the door. 'I'll cut that little bitch somethin', and it won't be any slack,' she hissed. She shoved Suki out of her way. Cher heard Movita say something and follow her out of the cell, but she didn't look back.

The pay telephone was at the far end of the rec room, and Jennifer stood hunched there with her back to the line of women waiting for the phone. She held the telephone receiver to her right ear with her shoulder, and with her left hand she was covering her other ear to cut out some of the noise from the blaring television set. With her right hand she was frantically making notes, stopping now and then to put up her palm to the impatient inmates.

That's all Cher had to see. She crossed the room in less than four strides and without hesitation yanked the receiver from the startled Jennifer and slammed it back into its cradle on the phone. 'What the hell do you think you're doing?' Jennifer asked.

'You need to learn how to share, Missy,' Cher said to Jennifer.

'I wasn't finished and that was a *very* important call,' the deb told her, then reached to pick up the receiver again. But

Cher was having none of that and put her larger and stronger hand hard on top of Jennifer's.

'*I wasn't finished and that was a very important call,*' mocked Cher. She had mastered her impersonation of Jennifer, and her performance earned great guffaws of appreciative laughter from the rest of the women in the rec room. That is, from everyone except Movita, who had witnessed the whole confrontation and now came to the front of the group.

'That's enough, you two,' Movita ordered. 'Spencer's got to finish her call.'

'The hell she does,' Cher shouted. 'What's so damned important that this little bitch gets to hog the phone?'

There were murmurs of assent from the other inmates.

'I have *business* to take care of,' Jennifer shouted in response.

'Business?' Cher spat incredulously, 'What business do *you* have? Anyway,' she taunted, 'I thought *you* weren't going to be here long.'

The rec room was dead silent and all eyes were on the three of them. Cher knew she'd broken the first rule of any crew – no fighting or dissing in front of outsiders, but she felt wild with loneliness, disappointment, and futility. 'Both of you, shut your mouths,' Movita said. She looked hard at Cher. 'Gettin' outta prison isn't always somethin' that's good for a person, you know?' Cher felt herself color. Lord Jesus, she hadn't blushed since she was twelve years old. Movita motioned to the hall. 'Come on over here with me,' she told Cher. Then she turned to the deb and said, 'Get on the end of the line and finish your call.' She looked at the inmates gawking and waiting. 'That all right, girls?' she asked. The women in the line nodded. Jennifer walked to the end and Movita didn't say anything more, except to turn to Linda, the first woman waiting to use the phone, and indicate with a nod of her head that it was her turn at the phone.

Cher followed Movita out into the hallway. 'What in the hell is goin' on here?' Cher demanded the minute they got out of earshot. 'Somethin's up. I can always tell when somethin's up.'

'There ain't nothin' up that concerns you,' Movita said quietly.

'Then why are you dissin' me like that?' Cher asked almost petulantly.

'*You* were dissin' *Spencer* in there,' Movita explained. 'I don't want my crew fightin' with each other. Especially in front of that Jesus-freak group in the rec room. Spencer is *crew* now, Cher. She's one of us, and she was makin' a call I asked her to make, not that it was your bidness. And for a woman who has managed to get her hands on plenty of cash, I'd remind ya' that to diss someone for their financial success might be hypocrisy. It ain't no crime for her to be rich. You just jealous that her scams are bigger than yours.'

Cher went to bed determined to find out just what was going on with Jennifer Spencer. She wanted to know what Jennifer was up to, and she wanted to know what Movita knew about it and why she wouldn't tell her.

The next morning on the way to breakfast Cher managed to mutter a half-assed 'I'm sorry' to the debutante, though that cost her. Cher got her breakfast and parked herself in the seat next to the deb. Theresa was babbling about some new computer program she was learning, and Suki told them about how Gloria finally gave up and started 'dating' Georgette, a stone butch who had been courting her for months. When there was a pause, Cher took the opening. 'So, where do you live in New York?' she asked.

'Tribeca,' Jennifer told her.

'Umm. That's near Wall Street, right?' Cher asked, like some dumb-ass cracker. 'Isn't that where JFK, Jr. lived?'

'Yes.'

'You live on the same street?'

'No, he was on North Moore Street. I'm on Washington.'

'No kiddin'?' Cher said. 'What number? I know someone who lives on Washington Street.'

'I'm two-oh-one.'

'Nah,' Cher said. 'He must have been further uptown.'

Movita joined them then with her usual breakfast – three cups of coffee and a half bowl of sugar. Suki got up and returned with her plate heaped high with something that passed for home fries.

'You know,' Cher said as she picked at her plate, 'I'm really sorry about that boyfriend thing. I've had my own run of bastards. Movita will attest to that.'

Movita, silent as she was most mornings, just raised her head and grunted. 'They ain't worth dog shit but they can make you feel *real* bad.'

Cher looked over at Movita, who seemed oblivious. 'What was your guy's name? Tom Branson?'

'Tom *Branston*,' Jennifer corrected.

'He's a fancy-ass Wall Street dude, right? Loaded and everythin'?' Cher asked, trying not to be too obvious.

'He's an ass, a lawyer, and loaded with shit,' Jennifer answered, and Theresa and Suki giggled.

'You two lived together? He got your crib?'

'No. We were going to get married, though.'

'So who's watchin' your place now? Who's takin' care of your cat and waterin' your plants?' Cher took the opportunity to get on the better side of the deb. 'That call you were on last night, was it to him?'

'No,' Jennifer sniffed in reply. 'But I do need to finish that phone call,' she said.

'You won't be makin' any phone calls till after work,' Cher told her. 'But I won't interrupt you again. Like I said, I'm sorry about that. But what'n the hell's so important about them phone calls anyway?' she asked. Cher wanted Jennifer and Movita to take her into their confidence, but Jennifer made a point of turning her head away.

'What's the guy's name and number?' Movita asked Jennifer. 'Gwen has a meeting and she won't be in till noon. I'll get 'im on the phone and then I'll call down to the laundry and tell 'em that the Warden wants to see ya' in her office, okay?'

When Cher heard that, her forced good humor left her and she couldn't help snorting in disgust. 'You're gonna get your ass in some kind of real jam, Movita honey. And for what? So that this one can talk to her lawyer or something? She won't even tell us what's goin' on.'

Movita dismissed Cher with a wave of her hand, then wrote down the name and telephone number that Jennifer told her. Cher memorized it. When the bell that signaled the end of breakfast rang, there was the usual groan and the women slowly rose to begin their day of work.

Cher began her walk down to Intake but shook her head. What was wrong with Movita? It would be against every regulation in the book for Movita to let Jennifer Spencer use the telephone in the Warden's office.

But Movita shook her head and said, 'I just wanna hear

what she has to say to her lawyer, honey. That's all that this is about.'

Cher worried all day about Movita and the phone call. If she got caught it wouldn't just be time in the SHU, she'd lose her job with the Prez for sure. And Cher couldn't imagine Movita peeling vegetables or delivering ice for the rest of her life. Damnit! Why would she take such a chance for the debutante? Was she in love with her?

None of the women in their crew were lesbians. Neither were a lot of the women who hooked up. Many just did it out of loneliness, or because they were wooed by dykes. Once they left prison they never thought about it again. But there were the stone bulldaggers who were career lesbians. Cher didn't care if people fucked philodendrons, but she couldn't imagine that Movita had gone so nuts that she wanted the deb in that way. So why all of this risk and special treatment? Why even bring her into the crew in the first place? As she processed the candy that came into Intake that day she worried herself over it.

Cher was relieved to see Movita at dinner. Better than in the hole. She waited patiently with the surprise she had figured out, until she had a chance to get the two of them alone in her crib. Cher looked at Movita and then at Jennifer. 'You finally gonna tell me what's goin' on round here?' she asked, but neither woman would answer her question.

'Things might be changing around here real soon,' Movita said as she sat on her bunk. 'I'm not just talking about your parole.'

'Fine,' Cher said, 'don't tell me. I'll find out soon enough.' She walked over to her own bed and sat down.

'But it seems to me that whatever is going on, Miss Armani here needs to use a telephone real bad to make sure it happens. Am I at least right about that much?'

'Yeah,' Jennifer admitted with a nod. 'You're right about that.'

'Did ya' get your call out?' Cher asked Movita.

'Nah. The Warden was in her office all day. There wasn't any time to get away with it,' Movita admitted with disappointment.

'Well, then,' Cher said as she lifted the corner of her mattress, 'I always like to do my share to help.' From beneath the mattress she pulled a cell phone and handed it to Jennifer. 'Here ya' go. Lifted it from a new inmate earlier in this week.'

'What is it?' Movita asked.

'It's a cell phone,' the deb said. 'My God, it's a cell phone!'

'Let me see,' Movita asked. Cher handed it to her. Sometimes she forgot that Movita hadn't been Outside for a long time. 'Where's its base?' Movita asked.

'It don't have a base,' Cher said. 'Whaddaya think, it's a blues band?'

'It just works like this?' Movita asked. 'No base, no electric line, no nothing?'

'It needs a battery and a charger. They get plugged into an outlet,' Spencer said, and looked over at Cher.

'I got 'em,' Cher told her. 'You got 'em now. But you get caught with this, either one of you, and they ship your ass to Iceland.'

'Does it work?' Jennifer said, staring at the cell phone as if it were the Holy Grail.

'Hell yes, it works,' Cher said proudly. 'I called my own

lawyer from it to confirm my parole hearing.' She extended it to Jennifer. 'Consider it a gift – a peace offering from me to you.'

Jennifer turned to Movita and exclaimed, 'Do you know what this means?' Then she turned back to Cher and stammered, 'I don't know what to say. This is – this is just wonderful.'

'Man, if they toss the cell and find it, it won't be wonderful,' Movita said. 'But it's great, Cher.' She looked at her straight in the face for the first time in days. 'Thank you.'

Movita reached out and took Cher's hand. 'Look,' she said. 'I didn't want to trouble ya' with this. You got enough on your mind with your parole and gettin' out. But something real bad is goin' down here and Jennifer has been tryin' to help.'

Cher shrugged. 'What are you talkin' about? The Spanish Inquisition?'

'Maybe worse. The priests left you alone if you were Catholic,' the deb said. 'This will affect everyone.'

Then Movita told Cher about the report she'd copped off the warden, and the plans to privatize, and what that meant. It took them a little while, and Cher listened closely, then shook her head. 'Man,' she said, 'when it comes to scams ya' can't beat rich white men for comin' up with the best. And legal, too. I hope there is reincarnation,' she said, ' 'cause I wanna be a rich, fat-assed white man in my next life.'

27

Jennifer Spencer

*Freedom suppressed and again regained bites with
keener fangs than freedom never endangered.*

Cicero, *De Officiis*

'Spencer,' Officer Mowbry called out in her little girl voice.
'Visitor. Stevenson, Vassallo. Visitors. McInnery, lawyer.' Jen
stood up, glad of any distraction. She knew it was Lenny so
there was no reason to be excited, but it would be interesting to hear what he had learned about JRU.

As Jen walked to the visitor's room along with a cluster of
her fellow inmates, she had a thought that made her hate
herself. For a moment as she looked around it seemed
to her as if she were one of them – she looked like them,
she smelled like them, and the longer she was at Jennings
the more she felt herself slipping lower and lower into
their degradation. She almost felt she was a part of the
prison now.

When she'd agreed to try to help Movita with JRU she'd
immediately been transferred from the laundry job to the

library – leaving poor Suki to fend for herself. She felt guilty but relieved. The thing was, she actually *liked* several of her fellow inmates: Suki, of course, and Movita, and even the laundry supervisor, Flora. She'd even stopped being afraid of Springtime – now she identified with her for trying too hard to get out of this place.

She walked through the security check and into the visitor's room. She didn't bother fluffing her hair – or anything else for that matter – she wasn't worried about her appearance. Instead of her gorgeous Tom, it would only be Lenny. There was the usual noise and chaos in the visitor's room. She looked around for Lenny and saw him waiting. He was average height, a trifle thin and narrow in the shoulders. His suit was gray – she hated gray suits – and wrinkled. Stop it, she said to herself. Sick, sick, sick. It was great of Lenny to show up at all. Remember, Tom is a bastard, not fit to serve food to some of the people here. She smiled to herself at the thought. Flora, walking next to her, saw the smile and smiled back. 'He your man?' she asked, and without waiting for an answer continued. 'Isn't it wonderful?' she asked. 'I *love* visitor's day.'

Jennifer felt thoroughly ashamed of herself for her earlier thoughts. Flora was such a damn sweet woman. She tried hard to be fair with all the women who worked under her in the laundry. And she was a better, cooler manager than some of the men at Hudson, Van Schaank. She certainly had to deal with more troubled employees – although, neurosis for neurosis, the day traders at Hudson, Van Schaank & Michaels could stack up against any inmate here. But as she made her way toward Lenny Benson she admitted to herself that she was a snob. There were, as usual, some children in the crowd, and one voice overpowering the rest sounded like it belonged to one of Theresa's relatives. Her entire extended family seemed to be overly gregarious, and they all cursed more than a commodity trader.

Lenny moved toward her and took a seat at a table between Maria's sister Blanche and Theresa's Aunt Helen. Lenny's modesty was as conspicuous as Tom's pride. He had a large box in front of him wrapped in camouflage-patterned paper. Jennifer had to smile. That was funny. Had he meant it as a joke? she wondered.

'Hi,' she said to him as she took the seat opposite. 'I can't thank you enough for coming.'

'Hey, yes you can,' he answered. 'In fact, you already have. I'm happy to be here.'

She looked around the room at the chaos, tears, and noise, then looked back at him and laughed. What was his private life like if a visit to Jennings Correctional Institution made him happy? But he looked as if he meant it.

'Did you have much luck with the research I asked about?'

'I found out a lot of interesting stuff,' he said. Then he patted at the box in front of him. 'And I brought a lot of interesting stuff. What do you want first?'

'You shouldn't get me gifts. Really,' she told him. 'I have money and I insist on paying you back.'

He waved his hand as if insects flew before his face. 'Forget it,' he said. 'But who is managing your money now? And what about your condo? Who's dealing with the carrying costs and the real estate taxes?'

'I gave Tom power of attorney,' Jennifer admitted. Maybe that hadn't been such a good idea, she thought now. 'I thought he was trustworthy,' she said. 'And he'll keep my canteen fund filled,' she laughed, albeit a bit bitterly. 'I'm only allowed to spend ninety dollars there every two weeks. So it's not a lot of money.'

Lenny just looked at her and was silent.

'I'm anxious to hear about you-know-what. Did you find out much?' Jennifer continued to break the silence.

'Yeah. As much as there was to find.' He picked up his briefcase, a very nerdy one she noticed, not Gucci like Tom's. She looked away, around the room, while he fumbled through the bag.

What she saw amazed her. Flora and Maria, as well as other women she'd seen around – workers from the laundry, inmates from her unit – they all looked so different here! Their faces were transformed by some kind of . . . life, she guessed it was. And even the ones crying, obviously getting bad news about family members or being disappointed, even they looked – well – alive. Jen looked over at Theresa. Even *she* looked happier, if such a thing was possible for a woman on a constant high.

And JRU was planning to curtail visitation? Jennifer felt a surge of anger. She turned back to Lenny. 'So let's cover the situation first. What did you find out?' she asked him. 'Keep your voice down.' She leaned in to him across the table.

'Well,' Lenny began, 'for one thing, JRU is privately held, and pretty closely. It's not easy to get anything on them but . . . well, let's just say I have my sources.' He smiled, and she noticed for the first time that he had a dimple on his left cheek. She wondered why she'd never noticed it, but it could have been because she'd never seen Lenny smile before.

'How big is it?' she asked. 'JRU.'

'Small. It only does about thirty million annually. It's a

start-up. And it's doing nothing in profits. They've gotten these couple of prison contracts all in the last three years.'

Jennifer's eyes brightened. 'That's good, for a start. At least they're not Philip Morris with a fleet of fucking lawyers.'

'Yeah, but news from the other prisons, the couple that they are managing, isn't good. It looks like they're trying to avoid any capital expenditure and milking the facility for profits by cutting costs to the bone.'

'Shit! How much worse can the food get?' she asked. A start-up that wasn't profitable but still going for more of the same. 'So how does this make sense?'

'I did a lot of digging and I think they might be setting themselves up to be acquired by Wackenhut, or something. They, of course, are the "prison as gross industry" super-stars.'

Jennifer's face darkened. 'It *is* a gross industry,' she muttered. 'Who's the CEO? Is it Steve Ross, starting out with parking lots or what?'

'John Tarrington. A senior VP from Wackenhut. Other than him, they're just a bunch of financial guys with *gotz* for industry experience. They're obviously using his contacts to get the contracts, and he's using their expertise to put together the proposals. I got their previous ones, by the way.'

She smiled at him. 'Cool,' she said. 'So what's up?'

'They're not setting it up to go public, and it isn't going to make them risk. I figure they gotta be setting themselves up for acquisition. Their only real assets are those contracts.'

Jen thought about it and nodded. Maybe so. Or the CEO, this Tarrington guy, had a hard-on for someone he'd worked for and wanted to make a point. You never knew with men.

'Whatever it is, they're underfinanced,' Lenny added, then took out some spreadsheets and explained the basics of their financials. They paused. 'Okay,' he said. 'I did as you asked and I haven't bothered you with a single question. But why all this interest?'

'They're going to take over this place.'

'So I heard.'

'How did they get the contract if they're so . . .'

'Hey, since when does the government make sound business decisions? I don't know their political connections. Or their board. But I'll have that information in a couple of days,' he told her. Jen had to admit she was impressed with Mr Benson. 'Jennifer, what are you thinking about?'

'I don't know,' she told him honestly.

'Maybe some . . . interaction with JRU?' he offered.

Jen nodded, then turned her face away and looked again at Flora, Maria, and all the other women. 'This place is awful, but it could be even worse,' she told him. 'I'd like to help stop that.' She leaned even closer to him and lowered her voice further. 'I'm in a bind, though,' she said quickly. 'I don't want to do anything that would be considered "bad behavior" here. I've got to make my stay as short a time as possible.'

'Of course you do,' Lenny said.

They were both silent for a moment.

'I'm sorry,' he told her.

'You were right about Tom,' she said. 'And maybe about everything else.' All at once Jennifer had to struggle to keep from crying.

Lenny reached out and took her arm. 'Don't waste tears on him. He's a yellow rat bastard.'

Jennifer laughed in spite of herself, and felt a little better.

'A yellow rat bastard?' she asked. 'I thought that was a shop in Soho.' At least she could speak. 'I had to go into the SHU last week,' she began, and told him all about what had happened when Tom visited. Lenny listened, his eyes warm with sympathy. After she got to the part about her hands she stopped and looked at him. 'I shouldn't burden you with this. It's all so weird. I'm sorry. I just need to tell somebody.'

'Please,' Lenny said, holding both of his hands out and open. 'Tell me. I'm interested.'

So Jen kept telling him: about the crew, and the trouble with Cher, and especially about Movita and what she'd revealed. As she spoke she looked down and unconsciously wrapped her arms around herself. It wasn't until she was finished that she realized that she was not only hugging herself but also rocking in her chair. She stopped, embarrassed, and looked at Lenny Benson, expecting to see disgust or disapproval. But he was looking at her with such sympathy that she was taken aback.

'Amnesty International officially condemns the U.S. prison system,' he said. 'Did you know that? They list it as the worst in the world. And since 1980 the female inmate population has increased by more than five hundred percent.'

'God!' Jennifer said. 'That is so . . . so . . . terrible. You see, these women' – she moved her eyes to include the other inmates in the room – 'a lot of them never did anything really wrong. They acted in self-defense, or they were in the wrong place at the wrong time. Can you imagine?'

'Hey,' he said. 'I've read up on the subject. How about Rebecca Cross, who was sentenced to twenty years without parole for a first offense? *Possession* of fifty-five dollars' worth of dope.'

'Yeah,' she replied. 'Unbelievable. But only some of them are totally innocent.'

'Like you,' Lenny said.

She shook her head. 'Uh-uh. I'm afraid I wasn't *totally* –'

'Close enough,' Lenny interrupted. 'It's not *you* who should be in prison.' He paused.

'You warned me,' Jennifer admitted. 'I was greedy. And stupid. I was looking for a shortcut.'

'Forget it,' he said, and his expression changed from pensive to efficient. 'Let's get back to JRU. Let me tell you what I think. If you want to influence what they do, we could try to get someone on the board. Or influence people already on it. Do you remember the first Bush administration?'

'It's not something I like to focus on,' Jennifer admitted.

'Well, he followed Reagan, and the Republicans had already had a field day with deregulation. They set all the savings banks free and hotshots bought them up left and right. Then they started giving out loans to their hotshot pals so all the little moms' and pops' and widows' and orphans' savings were lent out to golf-playing Republican scammers like Keating.'

'Oh,' Jennifer said. 'I remember *him*.'

'Yeah. Another yellow rat bastard. Anyway his pals defaulted on the loans, but he'd already been paid off for lending them money and the friggin' bank failed. And then, because of the FDIC, the taxpayers had to bail out the banks.'

'I do remember that now,' she said. 'Wasn't one of the Bush boys involved?'

'Yeah. Silverado. Another big bank that went bust. He'd been put on the board. Not that he knew dick about banking. Anyway, the point is, I think that there's a parallel here. Back then they deregulated savings banks and there was a big opportunity to drain them. Now they privatize prisons and another opportunity exists to collect the fees from the state, pay almost nothing to keep up the infrastructure and take care of the prisoners. They make a few bucks from their labor before selling off quick for a profit or declaring bankruptcy.'

'That's a cheerful scenario,' Jennifer said. 'Hey Lenny, what do you know about the Rafferty boys, Bryce and Tyler?'

'They've dipped their wicks into things no one else would touch,' he said, then blushed. 'Sorry. I didn't mean to be vulgar.'

Jennifer bent her head down so he wouldn't see her smile at that. Everyone on Wall Street swore like sailors – it was a prerequisite. 'The question I want answered about them is if they fuck over their partners as well as investors.'

'I don't know,' he said. 'But it's easy enough to find out. Call me Tuesday. I'll have some info by then. Anyway, why do you ask? You think they might have some influence at JRU?'

'I'm not sure why I'm asking,' Jennifer admitted. 'I don't really have a plan yet. I just want to have . . . options.'

'Well, I wish your option was to forget all of this and get out of here,' Lenny said.

'Tom promised me he's going to really push Howard McBane.'

'I wouldn't trust anything Tom said,' Lenny told her glumly. 'And I'd reconsider that power of attorney. If he goes near your portfolio, I'm going to stop him. I'm telling you that right now.'

'Look. He might not want to marry me, but he's not a thief and he doesn't want me ratting him out, either. And Donald is good for his word.' Lenny looked away. 'I won't be here much longer,' Jennifer told him. 'But it would be terrible to let this happen to the other women. Most of the ones I've met aren't criminals, they're victims.'

Visiting time was almost over, but Lenny wasn't prepared to leave. 'Wait,' he said. 'You have to open the box of stuff I brought. Don't you want to?'

'Are you kidding?' Jen said and smiled. 'I'm the original material girl. I liked stuff before but you can't imagine how we *love* stuff in here.'

'It was all really nicely wrapped,' he said, and sighed, 'but they opened everything. Kinda ruined it.' He held up a bright red bow and a piece of newspaper. It was a page of the *Wall Street Journal*. 'It was black and white and red all over,' he said. 'I figured you'd have fun reading it.'

'Hey. Waste not, want not,' she told him. 'I'll take it. Unusual reading matter here.' She looked into the first opened box. 'Oh God! Floris soaps! How did you know I love them?'

Lenny shrugged, then colored.

Jennifer looked at the other items in the parcel. There was more toothpaste, deodorant, and breath mints. There were Pringles, and onion dip, and Balsen cookies and there was even a box of high fashion chocolates – Richart – that had also been torn apart. 'I'm sorry,' Lenny said. 'They opened it all up.'

'Looking for contraband,' Jen told him and shrugged. She looked down at the tiny, delicate chocolates, each one decorated exquisitely. 'God, they're beautiful! At least they didn't eat any. My crew will go nuts over these.'

'I'll bring you one every week if you like them that much,' Lenny said.

Jen looked at him. Could a man be this nice? Yeah, but only if he was boring, she thought, scanning his face. But the thing was, Lenny – at least the Lenny visiting her and working on this JRU thing – really wasn't boring. He wasn't like the close-mouthed, shut-down, unenthusiastic guy he was at Hudson, Van Schaank & Michaels. How interesting life is, she thought. You never could judge by appearances and maybe all men weren't . . .

'What did you call Tom?' she asked him.

'Tom? I said he's a yellow rat bastard. And he is.'

'Right,' Jen said. Maybe all men weren't yellow rat bastards, she thought, looking at Lenny.

'What's the matter?' he asked. 'You're so quiet.'

'Nothing,' she said. 'I'm fine.' And she went back to opening her box of goodies.

28

Gwen Harding

*Illegal for many years, private companies employing
prisoners directly was again made legal in the mid '70s.*

Prison Activist Resource Center

The intercom buzz brought Gwen out of her reverie. 'The
parole board is waiting for you, Warden,' Miss Ringling's
voice sang through the speaker.

'Thank you, I'll be out in a minute.'

Today was judgment day for Cher McInnery. And Gwen
had nothing but good things to report on the woman. It was
a blessing that someone was going to get out before
Jennings took a dive. Gwen just hoped that Cher didn't cop
an attitude like she had the last time she was up and screw
herself out of the opportunity of being released. Sometimes
it happened, though. The fear of the Outside and the
unknown combined with the smugness of the parole board
members was sometimes too much for the inmates and
they would do whatever was necessary – even get into
trouble – to get to stay in Jennings. But Cher McInnery was

not a career convict. She'd been watching her step for a long time and Gwen thought that she had seen a positive change in her attitude since Movita had taken Spencer in to her crew.

There were a lot of rules in the penal system designed by men for men that didn't work for women. One of the ones that caused Gwen the most profound pain was the enforced parole statute that prohibited ex-inmates from fraternizing with other convicted offenders. Among the male population this made a lot of sense because many young men had come to prison on a first offense, then learned illegal crafts and scams from more experienced prisoners, and then were pulled back into criminal behavior by their prison buddies once they were released. But women – particularly those incarcerated for long periods of time – often made deep and meaningful friendships with other inmates. Prohibiting them from making contact with their prison 'families' Outside always struck Gwen not only as harsh but as counterproductive. For a woman to be cut off from all of her social contacts at a time when she was reentering society and needed all the support she could get seemed ridiculous. It was cruel and unusual punishment to pull someone like Cher out of her crew of 'sisters' and legislate that she could never again communicate with Movita or Theresa or Suki, that she could never see them again or know how they were progressing not only in prison but afterwards when they were out.

So, Gwen pulled the McInnery file from the folder stacks on her desk, walked out of her office, and actually smiled at Movita. 'Change is good for everyone, Movita, it really is,' she said, and went to be Mom, Teacher, and Caring Nurse perhaps for the last time.

After the board meeting Gwen tried not to disclose by her expression the outcome to Movita. She knew that she and Cher were tight, but the word for something so important as parole should come from the board, not through gossip or guesswork. Gwen Harding was so deep in thought that she actually jumped as the intercom buzzer sounded. 'Yes?'

'The JRU people are here to see you,' Movita's voice crackled through the tinny speaker. Was the disturbance static in the system or was it actually Movita's reaction to the group that was on their way to her office?

Gwen knew that Movita Watson wasn't a stupid woman and may well have figured out change was in the air here at Jennings. And on Gwen's night of drunkenness she may have revealed more than she should have, though she couldn't remember. Neither one of the women had ever referred to it.

Gwen pushed the red button on the intercom. 'Send them right in when they get here please, Movita.'

'Yes, ma'am,' the woman's voice responded.

She would miss Movita Watson more than anyone, Gwen thought as she placed her hands on the edge of her desk, pushed her chair backwards, and slowly stood up. She walked over to a small mirror that hung discreetly on the back of her door and looked at the small patch of discoloration that remained on her forehead. At least the visible signs of that incident had all but vanished. Gwen pulled out her makeup and covered the bit of bruise, then freshened her lipstick. She began to pace around her office, waiting for the group to arrive. She couldn't help but wonder how long it would be until she was fired. Perhaps it would be today. She stopped to look out one of the three windows of her office, all of them overlooking the yard. Maybe there would be a transport van in the sally port waiting to take her away once the tour was over and the new JRU representative took her place.

Since the state's response, the JRU staff had been busy as ants at a picnic. There wasn't a corner of the prison they hadn't combed. If anything, Gwen felt more and more apprehensive about the changes coming. Today, she supposed, she was going to hear about them.

As always, it took a while for outsiders to clear security and be brought to her. Gwen's suit was nearly soaked with perspiration by the time there was a knock on the door. She took her seat as Movita popped her head in to announce the arrival of her 'guests'. But there was a strange look on her dark face and she mouthed, 'Only one,' while she raised her index finger into the air. What was going on? Gwen thought. Had JRU canceled the tour and only sent her replacement?

As Movita opened the door wider, Gwen tried to smile as she greeted a tall, thin woman with as hardy a 'good morning' as she could muster. But she shouldn't have bothered. The woman was all business and cut right to the chase after the customary exchange of professional and personal niceties.

'I'm Marlys Johnston and I've come to let you know what we – JRU – expect from you, Warden Harding, during this transition period,' she said even as she slipped into the chair across from her. The woman had a powerful aura. She was even more arrogant and self-confident than Jennifer Spencer had been the first time she stepped into her office, Gwen thought. Perhaps it was because she was older – thirty-six or thirty-eight by the look of her.

Marlys Johnston leaned forward and placed her leather briefcase in the middle of Gwen's desk. It was obvious the woman was well paid because never in all her working years had Gwen been able to afford such a beautiful accessory. The woman's fingertips gleamed in the overhead light as they wrapped around the edges of the case – professional manicure, where the tips of the nails were white and the rest was natural color. If Gwen could have afforded it she would have known what it was called. There was a loud click as the latches of the briefcase flew open and Ms Johnston pulled papers from the suede-lined interior.

'You'll find everything you need in this report,' the Marlys woman said as she handed Gwen a neatly bound report. *Thinking Outside the Box* was printed in bold letters on the cover, along with the JRU logo. Gwen smiled. Somehow the phrase reminded her of Springtime, who was about due for another escape attempt. 'I think reading this will help you to see the potential here at Jennings,' Marlys said with an emotionless smile. 'I think you'll find that the observations that you made in your report to the state will look a little different if seen from another perspective.'

Gwen slowly lowered herself into the chair beside her desk. She looked down at the booklet. She hadn't had much doubt that she had lost the battle. But this news told her she was going to have to surrender. That her complete report submitted to the state, which was supposed to be confidential, had been passed on to JRU was the final nail. It made things very clear that the state was not – had never been – on Gwen's side. And Marlys Johnston was definitely not on Gwen's side, either.

But as the meeting continued it became equally clear that Marlys Johnston had been sent to Jennings neither to ignore Gwen nor to fire her. She had been sent to wear her down or scare her away. 'There is so much underutilized space here,' the consultant kept saying over and over and over again. 'You have both indoor *and* outdoor recreational areas, as well as a visitation center, and both a library *and* an events and programs facility.'

Gwen would've itemized the same spaces as a locker room, a parking lot, a hallway, a virtual closet with some old books, and another closet with a folding table. *An events and programs facility?* Who in the hell was she trying to kid? And a *visitation center?* It was little more than a hallway divided by bulletproof glass. But her objections slid off Ms Johnston. 'Perhaps' – Gwen tried to calm herself so she wouldn't stammer – 'if you saw these spaces. Let me show them to you and you see what you think.'

'I'm quite capable of reading a blueprint, Gwen. May I call you Gwen?'

'We prefer a more formal approach here. I call the inmates "Ms" or "Mrs" and they refer to me as Warden. We expect the same of the COs.'

Marlys Johnston simply raised her brows and said nothing.

'We're concerned that you're at about fifty percent capacity at this time,' Marlys observed as they passed through the cellblock. 'These are four-man cells,' she said, while noting the fact again on her legal pad.

'Yes,' Gwen agreed. 'As I've explained to JRU staff time and time again, they were designed in the dark ages to be four-man cells, but now they are *two-woman* cells.'

Marlys didn't seem to catch the intent of Gwen's reply. She went on to see only what she wanted to see. 'So, Gwen, I'm assuming that all other facilities here at Jennings are equally underutilized.' She continued with her list. 'The kitchen, therefore, was designed to serve twice the number of inmates,' she began, 'and the laundry was designed to do the same. I'm assuming that the health care department would also be more than sufficient for the number of inmates currently housed here. Am I right, Gwen?'

Gwen gritted her teeth. She didn't want this woman to call her 'Gwen'. But she took small, shallow breaths to try to keep her composure and to avoid the possibility of speaking in a stammer. 'Perhaps if the equipment was all updated and we had a medical staff,' Gwen told her. 'Then it might be sufficient.'

'Oh, don't be so negative, Gwen.'

'Miss Johnston,' Gwen said sternly, causing her guest to look up promptly and stop taking notes. 'You and I both know that what you are saying only makes sense on paper. This facility was built over thirty years ago. No doubt with asbestos and then painted with lead paint. All penologists agree that there are and must be differences between prisons for men and those for women. If you read my report, you can't possibly suggest that Jennings could operate with twice the number of inmates.'

'Warden,' Marlys said as kindly as Gwen was stern. 'I'm here to help. I'm here to work with you to make this transition as smooth as possible. I want to work *with* you, Gwen – not against you. We just have to get you to think outside the box, that's all. Okay?'

Gwen wondered what the penalty would be if she slapped Marlys Johnston, but she nodded and tried her best to muster a cooperative-looking smile. She feared that Marlys Johnston was her last chance – small as it was – to get herself heard before more changes were made that would forever destroy everything she had worked all these hard years to build. 'I believe that any transition must be done at a slow pace,' Gwen told the woman. 'A prison population can be volatile.'

'I agree! That's why we'll make the first change small. We'll start with visitation day.' Gwen held her tongue. 'To best structure the work week, the midweek visitation day will be eliminated. As it stands now the inmates have to earn merits to get that day applied to them anyway, so we'll just have them work that day instead.'

Gwen actually gasped. 'But the visits are very important to inmate morale here at Jennings. And some family members work weekends, particularly in lower-level jobs. You can't just . . .'

Marlys Johnston smiled again. 'Yes, we can, Warden. You just have to begin thinking outside the box. And I want you to make the announcement at dinnertime tonight about next Wednesday's visitation. Let the ladies sleep on it.'

'I don't think they're going to sleep after hearing that. And don't you think it's best to give more notice? Some people plan a month or more ahead for visiting.'

'Warden Harding, we need to move forward as quickly as we can so that the facility starts to earn a profit by the second fiscal quarter,' the beastly woman said. 'That will mean cutting costs, cutting staff, and gearing up for productive work – work that industry will pay for.'

'And how will that improve the lives of the inmates? I can't believe . . .'

'If you want to succeed with JRU, Gwen, you're going to have to start thinking more positively.' The woman gathered her papers, closed her fancy briefcase with those fancy painted fingers, and nodded a good-bye to Gwen, who only had the strength to nod back.

Gwen sat at her desk and thought about how badly she needed a drink. She *had* to have a drink. With the JRU International stage set and geared up for 'transitions' she needed a drink. Gwen reached over to her drawer and pulled it open. She looked down at nip bottles she had lined up in rows. She pulled one out and twisted the cap open. She poured the liquid down her throat, replaced the cap back on the glass bottle, and inverted the bottle in the row in the drawer.

It was all psychological. She had to have routine in her life. She couldn't give up everything completely. No cold turkey for her at this time in her life. She had heard that people trying to quit smoking would often have a cigarette handy, hold it, pretend to flick the ashes and place it in the ashtray, even put it in their mouth and try to inhale. But the trick was to *never* light the cigarette. So she improvised with her gin. She bought little glass bottles, filled them with water, and kept them in her drawer. It was a false sense of comfort for her, but she needed comfort now with all the changes going on around her.

Well, she hadn't been fired but she might as well quit. It was going to be a nightmare – hell it was going to be an uproar, a riot – when the inmates found out about visitor's day. Even with all the disappointment that sometimes happened with visitors not showing up or not staying for the full hour, the prisoners worked very hard to earn those days. She didn't want to be the one to have to disappoint these women with the change. They were so sensitive to these sorts of things – not because they were women – but because they were used to a schedule. Jesus, she could remember what a disturbance there had been when the food service took off scrambled eggs and added pancakes. They expected everything to stay as it was. Change was not favored here at all.

Gwen couldn't help but think that she didn't like the changes that were going to have to take place in her life because of JRU. If she left now, she'd have a reduction in her pension or perhaps lose it altogether. And where would she get another job? She chuckled at the thought of seeing herself as a door greeter at Wal-Mart on a part-time basis. Collecting hardly any pay, no insurance coverage, but boy, oh boy, she'd get an employee discount and even more of a break on Tuesdays when it was Seniors Day.

She picked up her cup of coffee and thought of the biblical reference, 'Let this cup pass from my lips.' How true this was. She felt like she was being crucified.

29

Jennifer Spencer

*From jail, it is difficult to prepare an adequate defense
– while on the other hand, a person who can make bail
usually is able to search for a lawyer, round up
witnesses, secure a job, and make a good case for herself
in court.*

Kathryn Watterson, Women in Prison

The only mail that came into Jennings that wasn't
ransacked and examined was the privileged communications from attorneys. When Jennifer received the thick
envelope from Howard McBane, she immediately went to
her bunk and tore it open. There were pages and pages. She
picked up the cover letter and read it.

Dear Miss Spencer,
    *After careful analysis of your case and a reading of the
trial transcripts, we believe that there are no significant
grounds for an appeal. Discussions with your counsel,
Thomas Branston, indicate that he is in agreement.*

    *We could, of course, proceed with the appeal on some
minor grounds, but that is a time-consuming and costly*

undertaking. If, in the face of this advice, you determine to continue, we will represent you, but we first wanted to apprise you of the likely outcome. The firm will also require a sizeable retainer.

As you can see, I have enclosed a detailed estimate, as well as the opinions rendered on your case by several of our senior partners, along with annotated trial transcripts where relevant.

Jennifer looked at the letter with horror. She tried to take a deep breath but the air wouldn't go into her lungs. She read it again to be sure she hadn't made some mistake.

Of course she'd made a mistake, but it hadn't been in reading the damn letter. She'd made a huge mistake in choosing where to place her trust. First, she had been promised by Donald and Tom that she wouldn't be found guilty. Then, when she was, they had guaranteed her a suspended sentence. When she'd been sentenced to prison, they had told her that most likely she would get an immediate pardon, and when that fell through Tom had told her the appeal would take only a matter of weeks. Then Tom had broken up with her, but assured her that Howard would see that the appeal went smoothly. And now she was being informed by Howard that 'there are no significant grounds for an appeal.' How about the fact that it was Donald Michaels, not she, who was guilty?

She turned a page. And the next one made the first seem like good news! It literally took what little breath she had away. It was a request for a $280,000 retainer. Jennifer must have made a noise, because Suki, who had just entered the cell, asked, 'Are you all right?'

Jennifer couldn't answer. She had no air in her lungs and she was sick to her stomach. She moaned a little. God, here she was, thinking she was smarter and better than all the other women in prison, and she was probably the most sophisticated dupe in the joint. She wondered for the first time if perhaps she had been set up from the very beginning to take this fall. Maybe the whole romance with Tom, the engagement, everything, had just been a way to find someone willing to be the victim. She actually felt dizzy and leaned back onto the flat pillow of her bunk. Suki stepped over to her and took her hand. Jen moaned again.

'Are you all right, Jenny?' Suki asked again. 'Should I get Movita?'

Jennifer just shook her head. She wasn't all right, but how could Movita or anyone help? Donald Michaels had been doing questionable IPOs since before the dot-com boom. He and all the rest of Wall Street. But he'd played just a little faster, a little looser, and a lot more visibly than others. He'd always been aware that the SEC and the market self-regulatory agency were tracking him. It occurred to her that it was just possible he had hired her with the idea that a good girl like her, from a Catholic school, might be the perfect one to catch the flak if it ever flew. And she'd thought it had been her rap about Gulbenkian porcelain.

'Jenny? Jenny, you're scaring me,' Suki said.

'I'll be all right,' Jennifer managed to tell her. Then she concentrated on trying to breathe. The brain needed oxygen to think. 'Sit down, Suki,' she told the girl, though she was barely conscious of whether her cellmate was sitting or standing. She had no energy to talk to Suki now. She had to think. 'Leave me be,' she said.

Well, though Howard may have given up on her, Donald

had promised her that they would be responsible for her legal expenses, and she was going to find another firm that felt she had a better shot at an appeal than these puppets at Swithmore, McBane. And they would pay for it, because if they didn't, she would call the SEC on the phone in the rec room and begin to rattle off every secret she knew. And she would hope that the call was monitored, because she would want not only the prison authorities, but the FBI and the IRS to hear about this shit.

She sat up, jumped off the bunk, and turned to Suki.

'Help me,' Jennifer said, and they lifted the bed so she could get to the cell phone secreted in the pipe of the leg.

'Watch out,' she told Suki. 'I have to make a really important phone call.'

Suki just nodded, but her eyes opened wide. Jennifer punched in Tom's cell phone. Despite his caller ID the son-of-a-bitch didn't know this number, so she wouldn't get voicemail. Sure enough, the bastard answered on the first ring.

'Tom Branston,' he said.

'I know who *you* are,' she said. 'You better not hang up when you know who *I* am.'

'Jennifer?' he asked, and she could hear the surprise and dismay in his voice.

She didn't bother with preliminaries. 'Did you see the letter from that creep, Howard McBane?' she asked.

'It's privileged information Jennifer. I haven't seen the letter, but he did communicate with me that . . .'

'Cut the crap, Tom. The first question I have to ask is, was I railroaded from the very beginning? Or was I merely the most convenient dispensable player?'

'Jennifer, I can't really talk to you now . . .'

'Wait a minute! Don't you dare hang up!' Her tone of voice was enough to ensure that he didn't. 'The second question I have to ask is whether you have the phone number of Charles Hainey at the SEC handy, because I'm about to call him and drop a dime on the two of you, as we convicts say.'

'Jennifer, I . . .'

'Listen to me, you liar. If you and Donald don't *immediately* find, and pay, some lawyers who can get me out of here, you're both going to be really, really sorry.'

There was a dead pause, and for a moment she was afraid that they had been disconnected. But then his voice came through as clearly as if he were standing in the cell with her. And his voice wasn't pleasant, but there was an undercurrent of . . . was it fear? she wondered.

'Jennifer, don't do anything crazy. I haven't seen this letter from Howard, but I'll call him right away and I'll get ahold of Donald,' he told her. 'You know we're behind you. But if you're guilty . . .'

'If I'm guilty!' Jennifer screeched. Suki turned around and gestured to her and she lowered her voice. 'Listen,' she said with more intensity than she had ever used in her life. 'I did what you told me to. *Because* you told me to. We all agreed. And if I'm the least little bit guilty, then you and Donald are very, very guilty and in trouble big-time. Maybe you've forgotten I know all about the Fischer offering, and that was before my time. And Sam Sutton told me all the details on the Omnigroup IPO. Not to mention the way Donald bragged about it when he had a few martinis in him.' That ought to put the fear of God into him.

But his voice went cold. 'Jennifer, you're on a cell phone.

This call can be overheard, and it sounds like you're threatening blackmail.' He paused. 'Just because I broke off our engagement is no reason to seek revenge.'

'Revenge? Are you insane?' she asked. 'Don't try to make this some woman-scorned bullshit. Trust me, Tom, this is strictly business.'

His voice was formal. She'd heard it like that when he was about to walk out of a negotiation. 'On behalf of Donald Michaels and Hudson, Van Schaank, I have to tell you that we won't be party to this kind of shakedown,' he told her.

Jennifer actually stared at the mouthpiece of the phone. How crazy was this son-of-a-bitch? And how had she confused him with a decent man?

'You can try and pretend for the record that what went down didn't go down,' she told him now. 'But I need to hear an assurance from you and Donald Michaels, within the next three hours, that Alan Dershowitz or somebody even better has been retained and paid for on my behalf. And if I don't . . .'

'Jennifer, this is a nonproductive conversation at this point. In fact, based on your guilt it may represent a conflict of interest. But I'll try to speak with Howard and Donald. Call me tonight around ten o'clock.'

'I can't call you at ten o'clock,' she virtually spat at him. 'I'm in prison, remember? I'll call you at eight. And you better have some answers by then.'

She hit the end button of the phone, Suki came over, and the two of them got the phone back into its hiding place.

Jennifer could not breathe. She could not speak or move or even swallow the bile that was threatening to choke her. It burned the back of her throat.

'I don't know how much longer I can keep this secret,' Suki said, totally out of the blue, as she rolled over in her bunk.

Jennifer sat up. It felt good to be able to sit upright. Suki had asked to switch bunks since she kept getting up during the night to pee. And the girl never stopped talking about the baby when she was awake. 'You have to be careful about any of this,' Jennifer warned Suki. 'You'll get us all in trouble.'

'How can *you* all get in trouble? It doesn't involve any of *you*,' Suki whined.

Sometimes it was hard to tell if Suki was dumb or just played dumb. 'Like hell it doesn't,' Jen told her. 'We'll all get put in the SHU.'

'Me being pregnant won't do all that,' Suki said.

Jennifer actually laughed out loud. She'd thought, of course, that Suki was referring to the hidden cell phone and all the unusual activity.

'It's not a laughing matter!' Suki said with much more than the usual vehemence. 'The whole thing was a terrible experience. It brought everything back. You know, from when I was twelve and my cousin Travis forced me to do it with him and his friends.'

Jennifer was shocked at hearing this confession. 'I can't imagine Camry being capable of such an aggressive act.'

Suki swung her head out from under the bunk. 'It wasn't Roger. He's the nicest CO in here,' Suki said with anger.

'I just assumed that . . .'

Suki moved her head back into her pillow and talked into the bottom of Jennifer's bunk. 'God! You're crazy. It was Karl Byrd. I hate him.'

Jennifer was stunned – and nauseated. She remembered

the overtures and smirks from Byrd, and wondered how close she had come to being raped. But Suki had never seemed resentful about her pregnancy. She didn't seem to connect the man she hated with the baby she was carrying. For some reason Jennifer remembered a tribe she had read of in her college anthropology course. They had never connected the sexual act with pregnancy. Didn't it bother Suki that the baby she seemed to already love was Karl Byrd's baby as well? Jennifer realized Suki was talking and bent to listen.

'I had just been reassigned to working in the laundry. Byrd worked days then.' Suki stopped for a moment as if to build up the courage to continue. 'We were in the dirty laundry area with Flora when a buzzer went off on one of the washers. He sent Flora to take care of it and he escorted me to the back to get more dirty laundry. There he told me to get a bag.'

Suki stopped again. She must have been starting to cry because Jen could hear her sniffle and see the shadow cast on the floor of her arm going to her face. She was wiping away tears. 'We wore one-piece green dresses before you came here, and when I bent over . . .' She took a deep breath. 'He came at me from behind. He cupped his hand over my mouth and pushed me into the pile of dirty clothes. I didn't know what was happening at first. My face was pushed into the stinking laundry and his hand covered me so I could hardly breathe. He pushed himself on me. He was so heavy, and then I felt his thing – his dick.'

Jennifer jumped off her bunk and bent down to Suki. She felt sick. 'Why didn't you report it? He can't get away with that. You can't just rape someone.'

'Ha. He did. Right then, and he got off twice, Jen. Twice!

The second time I fought him hard. I turned over so we were face-to-face. But he got me by the throat.'

Jennifer felt tears run down her face. 'Oh, Suki. I'm so sorry! The first day I came here, I knew he was no good. But why didn't you say something to Movita or Cher?'

'He told me that he'd hurt me if I told anyone. He said it would be his word against mine and that no one would believe a frightened, lying little whore inmate.' She paused. 'He also told me I was lucky he wasn't a nigger. That's what he said.'

'We've got to do something,' Jennifer insisted. 'It's not right.'

Suki grabbed Jen's arm and squeezed it hard. '*We* will do nothing,' Suki said looking directly into Jennifer's eyes. 'At least I've managed to get far enough along so nobody will try to get me to abort. And even though I got pregnant in a bad experience, I *want* to have this baby. I lost my other to foster care and I'll never get her back. I want to have someone to love, someone that will love me back.' She patted her belly. 'A baby is a new chance, Jenny. And Roger says he'll take care of me – when I'm on the Outside – and he'll be a good daddy to the baby.'

Jennifer sat on the cold concrete floor. She couldn't believe how naïve, and brave, and stupid this woman was. She had been violated in ways that Jennifer had a hard time comprehending, but Suki found the positive in all of it. 'I get it,' she said gently, and added her hand to the girl's belly. 'Mum's the word. No pun intended.'

Jennifer barely ate dinner that night, though Movita's cooking was good. She moved the food around on her plate until Cher asked her, 'You gonna eat that or hang it on your wall?'

She didn't even respond while the chatter went on around her. She was a human stopwatch, counting down the minutes until eight o'clock. She needed to be sure she was first on the line for the phone and she rushed through the washup as quickly as she could. She couldn't take a chance on using the cell phone again, partly because she might be seen by a CO and partly because she was afraid Tom might have caller ID and investigate. Anyway, the cell phone was only for JRU business, not for her personal convenience. Movita asked her a question, but she didn't hear it, and the woman just shook her head, leaving Jennifer to stow the plates in the footlocker. When she was finally done, she rushed down the hall to the rec room.

The noise was already deafening. The television was blaring loudly, and two groups of tough-looking women had taken on sides to cheer on some event. As always, one of the psychotics was ranting, this time at an empty chair. Jennifer moved directly to one of the phones, stooped to make sure she wouldn't block the view of the set, and urgently placed her collect call to Tom's apartment. Her knees were shaking as she waited and rehearsed in her mind the outrage she would unleash upon the betraying Tom. Jennifer could barely hear the operator when she asked, 'We have a collect call from Jennifer Spencer, will you accept the charges?' and she turned and glared at the noisy sports fans, but then she heard Tom's voice. 'Jennifer,' was all that he said. His tone stopped her cold.

'This is the last call I'm going to accept from you,' he said flatly. 'Should you call my home again I will contact the Warden and tell her that you are harassing me. Is that understood?' Jennifer could not speak. 'Is that understood?' Tom repeated.

'Is this Tom Branston?' Jennifer asked weakly. 'Tom, it's Jennifer.' There was silence on the line. 'Tom?'

'I'm sorry, Jennifer,' Tom spoke more quietly. 'But nothing more can be done. We've looked into it and it's clear to everyone involved that you were actively complicit in what was going on at the firm and you got caught. You were a little too ambitious, a little too willing to take shortcuts. There's nothing more I can do about it.'

Jennifer didn't sleep that night but she didn't spend one minute of it crying. She did curse herself for being stupid, for thinking she was smarter than she was, and most of all for trusting men who had made their careers and all their money by taking advantage of the trust of idiots like herself.

But she knew that to continue looking backward would kill her. She told herself that, compared to the other women sleeping in 'houses' all around her, she had been lucky. She had to tell herself that, repeating it like a mantra, or else she might begin to shake so badly she would split down the middle like a log hit by an ax for kindling. She wouldn't split, she wouldn't come apart, she told herself. She thought of Movita's dark eyes and her words of advice when she had come to her in the SHU. 'This place can break you forever. Or it can make you stronger.'

Jennifer had a three-to-five-year sentence. For the first time she tried to imagine what that meant. With good behavior she'd be out in a year and a half. She felt as if she'd already served a lifetime. It was too easy to lose track of time. How would she get through it?

She had always been an optimistic person. She thought it was probably genetic. And she knew how to work hard.

She thought of her condo, the silk rugs, the antique furniture, and the soft, soft Pratesi sheets. The blanket on her bunk, pulled up to her shoulder, was a parody of comfort, but it would have to do. She was lucky, she reminded herself, one of the lucky ones. Unlike Maggie Rafferty, or Movita Watson, she'd be going home, and though she wouldn't mind killing either Tom or Donald, she certainly wouldn't want to pay the price they had. Nor, she realized, did she want to go back to her old job or even that industry – not that she'd be allowed to. Movita and Maggie had been right: She'd been selfish. There had to be more than simply working sixteen hours a day, buying lots of gifts for yourself and taking some splendid vacations sometimes. During that long, long night it became clear to her that dealing with JRU and the situation before her was a responsibility that, for some reason, had been placed in her hands.

She hadn't prayed in a long time. She wasn't sure that she believed in the God the nuns had taught her about, but she still believed in destiny, in fate, or perhaps some higher power that placed people in situations for a reason. As the night wore on she was certain that her fate was connected to these women and their future at Jennings. In this month she already felt closer and more connected to them than she ever had to either her partners or adversaries at HVS – Hudson, Van Schaank.

She tried to find a more comfortable position on the lumpy mattress. It was virtually impossible. She heard a CO go by on patrol. By now she could already distinguish the sound of their steps. It was probably Mowbry, a heavyset, African American woman, who seemed to show a lot of compassion to the prisoners. What this place needed, first and foremost, was a lot more compassion. After that, of

course, it needed about a million other things, from more
library books to inmate classes to a maternal visitation wing
to . . . well, the list was endless.

Jen tossed again and again. She now had no doubt that
she would have to serve her sentence and, for the first time,
she admitted to herself that it was fair that she do so. She
had participated in manipulating and insider trading. Of
course, it was de rigueur. And she, Tom, Donald, virtually
all the men she had worked with at Hudson, Van Schaank,
and the other Wall Street experts at other firms did the
same thing on a daily basis. But that didn't make it right
that she had. More unforgivable was that she'd been so
proud of it.

Yes, that had been her big sin. Being proud that she,
Jennifer Anne Spencer, had been smarter than the other
girls, had figured out a way to get herself out of the life
she'd been assigned and into what looked – on the outside
at least – like a much better one. But her brain was
something she didn't deserve any credit for. It had been an
inherited gift, no different from the pretty blue eyes she
had, or the money that so many of her classmates at
Wharton had inherited and that she had so resented. She
had taken her gift and her energy and she'd squandered it
on Beidermeyer armoires.

Jennifer lay on the thin mattress, the worn and ugly
blanket pulled over her, and decided not to look back. She
had always had a strong will and she would use it now, not
only to help herself but to help others if she could.

Tomorrow she would talk with Maggie and see if she
could reach the Rafferty boys. They were thought of as
outlaws, Wall Street gunslingers who played the very edge
of the line, but she no longer had to worry about her

reputation. There, in the dark, she smiled, if a bit grimly, and began to do what she did so well: try to find the solution to a business problem in front of her. Comforted with the familiarity of it, she fell asleep just as the small strips of sky visible through the high windows were beginning to lighten.

30

Movita Watson

We're not allowed to communicate with the girls after they get out. They can call or write us here, but we can't answer unless they get special permission from their parole officer.

Ms Bonnie Brown, a registered nurse at a state prison.
Kathryn Watterson, *Women in Prison*

The first time I laid eyes on Cher McInnery I thought she was nothin' better than a piece of wild hillbilly white trash. But Cher didn't mind; she never pretended to be anything nor anybody other than who she was. And if I tell you she was smart as a whip, ya' better believe it. Cher was a thief — everythin' she saw was ripe for the pickin'. But she wasn't just a booster; she'd been involved in some complicated scams. She lived without pretense and with both eyes wide open. She was always on the lookout for the next opportunity to take what she needed, and when she got to Jennings, she knew that what she needed was a friend.

So, on the day Cher met me, the thief decided that she would just have to steal my black girl's heart. I wasn't sure I understood how it happened, but until now I was damn glad that it did. She made me laugh, and I could set her off, too. Neither one of us was much of a crier, but if I did have to shed a few tears I would have rather done it in front of Cher than anyone. I knew that Jennings was goin' to be a damn lonely place for me after she was gone.

Those last days before Cher's release were hard on me. I admit it. Cher knew it and she tried not to talk too much about her meetin' before the parole board, her future plans, or any of it in front of me. But it was almost impossible for an inmate not to be excited (and a little nervous) when she was getting out of prison after almost four years. And the others – especially Theresa – couldn't seem to talk about anythin' else.

The evenin' after Cher's parole hearing wasn't easy for me. I wished her well. I'm not a godful type so I didn't pray or nothin' but if I was I would have.

'Well, take a look at Miss McInnery over there,' Theresa crowed when Cher got back to our crib. 'Doesn't she just look like the cat who stole the canary?' Her parole hearin' must have gone well. Cher was not only a great mimic but a really gifted actress – the girl could make a man believe she was a virgin while she was givin' head.

Anyway, real unlike her, Cher said nothin' back to Theresa – except to mumble a halfhearted, 'No way.'

'No way?' Theresa pressed on. 'Cher, you're positively glowing with excitement. I could make a fortune if I could bottle your skin color right now! You look like you're ready to take on the world.' She shot a glance over at me. And again, Cher muttered the same, 'No way.' I could see she didn't want to make no federal case out of it. But Theresa – a woman happiest when beating a dead damn horse – refused to let the subject drop, and after a few more words of enthusiastic encouragement – always followed by Cher's 'no way' – I finally snapped.

'What in the hell is this "no way" shit you keep sayin'?' I demanded.

'Oh, everybody on the Outside says it,' Suki chimed in. 'My sister says that my niece is *always* saying it. You know, "no way" this and "no way" that.'

'Well, it sounds dumb as hell,' I snarled. Sometimes, when I've missed some slang or didn't know they made bite-size Oreos I feel bad. Like the world is passin' me by. Cher just stood up and walked away.

She was tryin' to be kind, but I knew things would never be the same anymore between me and Cher. They couldn't be. Cher was leavin' this place – but I was never gettin' out, and when one of the crew left I always went through a low time. But it would be really hard to lose Cher.

She got her parole and we celebrated, but it was still a bittersweet supper that we all shared on Cher's last night. Theresa tried to make jokes about it bein' the Last Supper, but the laughs were forced and the smiles were pretty sad. Cher would be gone in the mornin'. Her time was up. No one could think of anythin' more to say that would make sense of the situation. How could Cher be anythin' 'cept happy at the thought of gettin' out of prison? But how could any of us be anythin' 'cept envious or real damn sad at the thought of losing a friend? Our conflict of emotions couldn't be put into words.

Over dinner I studied Cher's face. How did she feel knowin' it was her last night on a lumpy mattress, her last night of starin' up at bedsprings? How would it feel to me? I couldn't imagine it. Her face, angular and no longer young but not yet middle-aged, showed nothin'.

I hoped she had changed, but I doubted it. She might have been punished in Jennings but she sure hadn't been rehabilitated. If anythin', it seemed like Cher was only tougher and hungrier for more thievery. No one said it, but in their hearts I think all the crew suspected – maybe even hoped – that Cher would be back before long.

'So, what exactly are your plans, Cher?' Jennifer asked. The two of them had become much more friendly since the cell phone incident. Cher had spent hours in their house, rubbin' Suki's swollen feet and talkin' to Jenny about her business, Wall Street, and all kinds of shit. Now Jen asked, 'Will you be staying with your family?'

Cher shook her head. 'Do you have any kind of job lined up or anything like that? It seems like after this it might be kind of hard to adjust again.'

'Don't worry about me, Jenny,' Cher said with her smile. 'I have plans.'

'Such as?' Jennifer asked.

'Well, I thought maybe I might become a stock broker like you,' Cher replied. 'Seems to me that you and your kind have figured out a legal way to steal. You just dress better while you're doing it, that's all.'

Jennifer's laughter was uneasy. Then she shrugged. 'I don't think felons can become registered brokers. But if you need a recommendation, just let me know.'

I watched Cher look directly into Jennifer's eyes. I knew she was sensitive about havin' been busted – it hurt her pride. In all her years of stealin' she'd been busted but never convicted before. With a cold calm she said, 'Thank you Jennifer, but you've already helped me more than you can know.'

I should have put two and two together and seen what

was comin' then, but I didn't. The uneasy silence that followed Cher's remark was of course, broken by Theresa.
'Maybe we should have a toast,' she suggested as she refilled
their glasses with grape juice. When everyone was ready all
eyes turned to me, like I was some kind of toastmaster.

'You know,' I began after some thought, 'I haven't seen
my babies now in quite a while. And it breaks my heart to
think about how much they must've grown since I last saw
'em.' I stopped and closed my eyes tightly for a moment
before continuin' with the toast. 'A mama is supposed to
want her babies to grow *up*, but there's not a mama I know
that wants her babies to grow *away* from her. But babies
gotta go out on their own. And so does Cher, I guess.'

'You calling me a baby, Movita?' Cher asked in mock
protest.

I got over my mood. 'You know what I'm callin' you
honey,' I shot back. 'I got this crew together so we could
take care of each other in this place. And we have one of us
is leavin' and it ain't so easy to see her go. I'll worry about
ya', girl. Who'll cover your back?'

Just then Suki screeched. 'Oooh! The baby's moving!'

It was a mood changer for sure whenever Suki shared the
baby's activity. I went over to her and put my hand on her
belly. The baby kicked again. 'He's gonna be a football
player with a kick like that,' I told her.

'It's gonna be a girl,' Suki said matter-of-factly.

'Now, just how do you know that?' Theresa asked.

'My sister Louisa says that when you carry in the front
it's a girl, when you carry in the back it's a boy,' Suki said.

Jennifer came over to Suki. 'Can I?' she asked, indicating
her belly.

'Sure, everybody else does. Heck, I should start charging

for the feel. What do you think it's worth? A bag of Fritos from the canteen?' Suki asked.

I went back to my seat and watched Jennifer with Suki. She seemed a little bit scared of the whole thing and, when the baby kicked, Jennifer actually jumped back, startled. I had to chuckle to myself. I had to admit it was kinda weird to know there was a baby in Suki's still relatively flat stomach. I wished I had been able to conceal my belly durin' my pregnancies. But I gained fifty pounds. I started to get lonely for my girls so I had to start talkin' again. 'So what kind of names do you have picked out?' I asked Suki.

'I like Allison,' Suki said.

'How about Juanita?' I suggested.

'Oh Jesus,' Cher said in mock panic, 'don't listen to a black woman when it comes to naming a baby!'

'What in the hell is that supposed to mean?' I asked her.

'Oh, please!' Cher said, 'if she listens to you that baby will end up with some kind of name like Metamucil or Mylanta.'

'Is Stephanie, Bethany, Tiffany, or Brittany any better?' I asked, and made her laugh. 'You're gonna need Mylanta if you don't shut your dumb honky mouth,' I threatened good-naturedly.

They were all laughin' so hard that no one noticed as the Warden stepped into the cell and gently put a hand on Cher's shoulder. 'Sounds as if you're enjoying yourselves,' she said.

Cher pulled her shoulder away and said, 'We're just trying to make the most of my last night.'

'I just came by to wish you well, Cher,' the Warden said. 'And to see how you ladies were doing. I guess it's going to be rather different not having Cher around, isn't it?' She looked around the room but made eye contact with me.

No one said anything. So I stood up. 'Thanks for comin' by, Warden,' I said.

The warden nodded at me. 'Well, I'll leave you to enjoy each other's company,' she said, and she turned and walked down the hallway.

Once she was gone, all the women fell back in their seats and bunks and let out a simultaneous sigh. 'Whoooeee!' Cher exclaimed. 'That was a close one. You girls better be careful with her; ya' never know when she's gonna pop in. As for me, I'm gonna be gone.'

I turned and looked first at Cher, then at each of the others. The pain in my eyes was almost more than they could bear, but not one of them looked away. 'I'm gonna die in this place,' I said simply. 'I'm never gettin' out of here. Never.'

'But . . .' Cher tried to speak.

'Shut up, girl,' I said, raising my hand. 'Shut up and listen, and make sure you don't make the same mistake I made. You hear me? Don't you trust no man when ya' get outta here. They set ya' up and then they let ya' down. I was dumb enough to trust my Earl. I let him keep his drugs at my place 'cause he told me it was just petty dealin'. But when the cops showed up and arrested me right in front of my babies, Earl was nowhere to be found.' I shrugged. 'When the police released me for turnin' Earl in, he hurt me. He hurt me real bad. But all of the reasons and all that shit don't mean a damn thing anymore. I killed him. And now I'm gonna live the rest of my days in here.' I walked over to Cher and took her hands. 'Much as I love ya', girl, I don't want ya' comin' back here, ya' understand? When ya' leave here tomorrow, I don't want to ever see your face again. I just love ya' too much.'

Cher only nodded. She understood all too well.

'We're gonna miss you, Cher,' Theresa said with un-characteristic brevity and no Hallmark bullshit.

'I'm gonna miss all the stuff you steal,' Suki added. We laughed.

'Don't worry,' she told Suki. 'The very first thing I'm gonna boost is a layette for the baby.' We all laughed again. 'And I might just miss all of you, too,' Cher admitted. 'But I'll come back on visitor's day. Wait'll you see me then. I'm gonna get me a face-lift and a nip and a tuck . . .'

'How are ya' gonna steal a face-lift?' I asked. Of course she couldn't come to visit. But Jennifer raised her glass and the others followed. She said, 'Here's to our new and improved, soon-to-be-free Miss Cher McInnery.'

'Hear! Hear!' the others chimed in.

I couldn't really tell what Jennifer was thinkin'. It wasn't like her and Cher ever got along real well, though since the phone thing they'd been chummy. I'm sayin' they respected each other – but they weren't tight. Oh, she was jokin' and laughin' with the rest of us – but I couldn't tell whether she was happy for Cher – or happy to see Cher go. And then that girl did the nicest damned thing. 'I've brought something very special to the party,' she said with a smile, and she pulled out the fanciest box of candy I had ever seen. 'It's Richart Chocolat,' she said – in French! 'Lenny brought them for me.'

The crew couldn't get over these things – each one no bigger than the size of a sugar cube but all decorated up like a work of art. Some had dots – some had squiggles – some were striped. Each one a tiny little masterpiece. Who takes the time to paint on a piece of candy? And what does it cost? 'Cher goes first,' Jennifer said.

I think Cher liked that. She reached into the box, fished out a deep dark cube. 'It's almost too pretty to eat.'

She was about to put it in her mouth when Theresa, who was looking at the card or such that came with the chocolate, let out a screech. 'Stop!' she shouted. 'You're not eating it right.'

'I'm not what?' Cher asked.

'There's this little book here with the candy,' Theresa explained. 'And right here there's a whole page on "tasting technique".'

'You mean I can't just eat it?'

'Girl, I been eatin' chocolate all my life and it seems just fine. Never got arrested for it,' I said.

'No. If something's worth doing, let's do it right,' Theresa said. 'Everybody get a chocolate.'

We did. She began to read. 'Now, "To really taste the base and primary flavor notes, wait a few seconds after you place a piece of chocolate into your mouth. To release the secondary flavors, expand the chocolate's surface area by chewing five to ten times. Let the chocolate melt slowly by pushing it gently against the roof of your mouth. Make note of the flavor, the texture and the way the chocolate lingers on the tongue."' Theresa read.

We tried to do it just like the book said, but I was laughin' so damn hard I nearly choked. Suki drooled some chocolate down her chin. Jennifer shook her head and just walked out.

Cher took another piece.

'Wait,' Theresa commanded. 'Is that a plain chocolate or a filled chocolate?' she asked.

'It's a good chocolate,' Cher said.

'It's a filled one and there's a different way to eat them,' Theresa said.

'Get the fuck outta here,' Cher said and grabbed the little booklet. She looked it over. 'Holy shit,' she said. 'It's true. Look at this. They tell you to chew the filled chocolate only three to five times!' She then read aloud from the book. '"New flavors continue to appear as the two melt in your mouth. Finally, make note of how long the flavor lingers on the tongue."'

'Are they talkin' about eatin' candy or givin' a blow job?' I asked.

'Screw it,' Theresa finally gave in. 'Let's just eat the damn things. Besides, what kinda world is this?' Theresa asked. 'They got pages and pages on what wines and what teas you can mix with this stuff. Who had the time to think this shit up?'

Everyone laughed but Cher. 'That's the world I'd like to live in,' Cher said.

You ain't allowed to see an inmate off. I don't know why they would think there's a security risk. Cher wasn't gonna try and make a break for it – she was free as a bird. No one else would, because even Springtime with all of her botched escapes wasn't dumb or crazy enough to try to escape out the front entrance of Jennings while the officers and the guns were right there. I didn't expect to see Cher again but The Woman, tryin' to be nice, I think, invited me to join the escort party to take Cher out.

Fact was, I didn't want to. Night before I had had a few bad readings after the good-bye party and in the mornin' I didn't even look in Cher's direction before I went up to the office. What's gone is gone, and another ten minutes with Cher didn't seem like no favor, since both she and I knew that we would never see each other again. Livin' Inside ya' gotta learn to cut your losses and let go. I had been in the process of lettin' go for weeks and this wasn't gonna be nothin' but painful. Still, I knew I couldn't explain it to the Warden, so I got up and went with her.

I know it was sorta an honor to be invited. They don't let no convicts into the group and I suppose – since I was never gonna see it any other way – it was interestin' to check out the release procedures. But the fact is, I could hardly look at Cher and she could hardly look at me. The two women officers were quiet in front of the Warden, and although Gwen was present it couldn't make up for the awkwardness between me and Cher. I watched as she traded her uniform for the clothes she had worn in. She looked real good in them, too. She got a bagful of possessions, the cash from her canteen fund and the money the state gives you to start a new life – a pathetic amount that wouldn't pay for a bus ticket past Pennsylvania. There was a lot of paperwork – the stuff I saw afterwards and often had to file and put away, and Cher was busy signin' her name on a lot of sheets and copies.

I kept my head down and my eyes on the floor durin' most of it. Fact was, I was jealous that she was goin'. I was sad to see her leave. I was happy for her, and I was generally miserable. Finally we got to the exit and The Woman gave her some little talk about somethin' and Cher, bein' Cher, cracked wise. I don't remember what she said but I remember what happened next. 'Well,' Gwen Harding said, 'I guess you two will want to say good-bye.' I guess she expected a warm prison scene, somethin' where the two of us hugged and cried on each other's shoulders or somethin' like that. But I had already been in enough pain and Cher was too eager to go to be bothered with that.

Cher and I stood there. I looked up from the floor. Somethin' was expected so I put my hand out. 'Good-bye,' I said, and Cher took my cold hand in her cool one.

'Good-bye,' she answered. She turned around and I looked at her back, dressed in some real nice jacket. I figured that would be the last time I'd ever see her again, and I turned around and headed back into Jennings.

31

Maggie Rafferty

Murderers – the people we fear the most – make up a minority of the prison population, and most of them have killed a mate, not a stranger. They represent no danger to society.

Kathryn Watterson, *Women in Prison*

For a murderess serving a life sentence, I'm lucky. I'm also well aware of the humor of that statement, but it doesn't make it any less true. I have a room to myself, a constant flow of books from the Outside, two loving sons who try to make my days as interesting as possible and visit me often. I'm also lucky in having an understanding warden who doesn't go out of her way to 'bust my chops' – as they quaintly put it here at Jennings. So when I poured boiling water into my tea cup and bowl of McCann's oatmeal as I did each morning rather than eating in the mess hall, I also opened the pages of the *New York Times*. One of the small pleasures of imprisonment has been having enough time not only to read the *New York Times* daily from cover to cover, but also to read the *New Yorker* each week before the next one comes.

When my oatmeal was ready and the tea steeped, I had a spoonful of one and a sip of the other and then continued to thumb through the *Times*. When I reached the business section I paused and nearly spilled my tea. I looked down at a picture of Tom Branston and Donald Michaels. They were standing next to – and *smiling* with – the investigator who had charged and arrested Jennifer Spencer for investment fraud. The headline over the photo read: FURTHER INVESTI-GATIONS INTO HUDSON VAN SCHAANK & MICHAELS CALLED OFF. The caption below the photo quoted Branston: 'Hudson Van Schaank gave full cooperation throughout the investigation, and the weight of evidence now convinces me that Jennifer Spencer – and she alone – was the "bad seed" at our firm.'

Bad seed, indeed! Was there no end to the perfidy of men? It was then that Frances came to the cell door to deliver ice, and this time it wasn't just the frozen H_2O I received but also a kite. Frances, as always, was careful to fill the cooler to the very top. I thanked her and waited until she was gone to open the note. *Meet me and the deb during recreation at* 2:30. It wasn't signed – kites are contraband and it would be stupid to sign one – but I knew Movita's handwriting and who 'the deb' was.

Recreation always struck me as a particularly sad word for the ninety minutes that we were allowed outside the walls of Jennings every day. In effect, though we were out-side we were still within the walls because the three wings of the prison created a U-shape and the open part of the 'U' was blocked by double fencing. Still, it was a chance to see the sky. I have never understood how many of the women could bear to go on without any view of the sky at all or why the prison architects consciously decided to create prison cells – and I'm not talking about the ones in the SHU – that had no windows at all. Oddly, at least to me, because they were in a newer part of the building they were considered very desirable by many women, but I would never give up my window, small and too highly placed as it was. Recreation for me was the time I tried to do what the Buddhists and contemplative nuns call walking meditation. I usually started by keeping my feet moving around the perimeter of the yard and slowly closing in. I took a breath with every other step and if I was lucky – which I admit has been rare in my life – I could complete a constantly shrinking square until I ended my ninety minutes in the very center of the recreation yard. But more often than not, arguments, interruptions, distractions, or athletics prevented me from my pilgrimage. Still, I looked forward to the time and the challenge. I wasn't really pleased to think of spending it talking, but I knew this was, of course, important.

The weather was what I used to call gray and drizzly but now I thought of as 'soft'. Somehow the light and the dampness were kinder than the sunshine against the brick and I, like all the other inmates, needed as much kindness as I could get. But I took it as a good sign and although I saw Movita from the moment I got out to the recreation area I made sure that I began my walk as usual.

Movita hadn't been herself lately. Of course it was particularly difficult on us lifers when an inmate 'graduated', since we never would. And it was particularly cruel that they were not allowed to communicate with us or us with them. But as a lifer I had learned to let changes like this flow over and through me. It was unusual that Movita had gotten close enough to Cher that her leaving upset her. This is one of the lessons prison teaches: not to care too much about anyone.

At any rate, Movita was moping and I did not join her. It wasn't my way. Inmates, particularly female ones, are attuned to *any* change in the pattern of the day, and this was not a meeting we needed to have attention drawn to. Still, it wasn't unusual for me to be interrupted a dozen or more times when I was doing my walk.

Jennifer Spencer joined us shortly after Movita and I met and we decided to keep walking, although not in the deliberate way I usually did. I liked Jennifer Spencer. I admired her spirit and I was amused by the personal naïveté that I occasionally glimpsed behind the mask of a sophisticated and shrewd businesswoman. I felt that I understood Jennifer Spencer – her dreams, her determination, her now bitter disillusionment with a man she thought she loved. I certainly respected her business acumen. 'Okay,' she said to both of us now, and she spoke with complete authority. 'Based on what I know, I think we have a situation here.'

'Well, we all know it's a situation,' Movita said darkly.

'I misspoke,' Jennifer said. 'I meant to say we have an opportunity.' She began to explain the financial status of JRU. How the company was underfinanced and looked like a candidate for takeover. 'I've been thinking,' she said, 'better than trying to influence the board, or take one of those paths with an uncertain outcome, like trying to buy an influential minority of private stock, I think we should buy the company.'

Movita shook her head. 'This is not the time for jokes.'

But I knew Spencer wasn't joking. 'How much would it take?' I asked, with the first feeling of hope I'd had since the day I read the report.

'That's hard to say. But they're very underfinanced. The other two prison contracts they have haven't yet turned the corner and become profitable. I'm not sure whether either a CCA or a Wackenhut would step in at this point. And my information leads me to believe that they're not going to have much more capital.'

'What would it take?' I asked her again.

'I don't know, but I think it's time to meet with your sons.'

Movita looked at the two of us. 'You bitches are crazy,' she said. 'Or else you're richer than I ever thought, and bigger thieves than Cher McInnery on her best day. How you goin' to buy a big company like that?'

'I don't know,' Jennifer told her. 'I don't know if we can do it, but sometimes a leveraged buyout works. That's what it's called. You just need to offer some of the private owners more money for their share of the company than they think they'll get any other way. And if they're greedy or they've lost confidence in the business, they say yes and there we are.'

'What do you mean, "we", white girl?' Movita asked. And I actually laughed out loud. 'Then can you open all the doors and let us all out?'

'Look, you know perfectly well that JRU can't do that. You know they can't change our sentences, affect our parole, or give us extra prison time. They are only going to administer the facility for the state. But if we were doing the administration . . .'

'The changes we could make! We could institute classes again. We could create a wing for the really deranged inmates. We could have more exercise time, better work details, a better library,' I said.

'Hold on, hold on,' Jennifer Spencer said. 'We can't lose money or throw it away. We would have to come up with a way to make reform pay. But maybe we could do that. Still, we're getting ahead of ourselves.' Jennifer turned to me. 'Could you ask your sons to come up here for a meeting?'

'Of course,' I told her. 'And let the games begin.'

Both of my boys are good-looking. Bryce is thirty-five and divorced. Tyler is thirty-nine and he's never been married. They have all of my brains, their father's charm, and more than a little of his larceny, but they have managed to direct it into an enterprise where brains, charm, and larceny – with the latter kept within limits – create a healthy profit. Both of them are rich in their own right, aside from the trusts they inherited from my parents and the not inconsiderable sum I will leave them.

Yet, I have always felt nothing but sorrow for the women they have become involved with, beauties with brains whom they seduce and inevitably abandon. I have, however, stopped blaming myself and have to believe it's either genetic or learned behavior from their father. That was only one of the reasons why I felt most uncomfortable when Bryce and Tyler came to Jennings for the visit and, though they sat across from me, kept their eyes on Jennifer Spencer. She, too, had a visitor, a nonentity named Leonard Benson whom I had to admit, after a little while, did impress me with his understanding of the situation. But when it came to first impressions Jennifer was making a large one on both of my boys. And it seemed to me she was quite taken with Bryce. As usual, that only served to incite Tyler's greater interest.

Needless to say, from the Jennings Correctional Officers'

point of view the meeting was not supposed to be a meeting but coincidental simultaneous visits. In the mayhem of the visitor's room – and with the invisible help of Movita – we were assigned to adjoining tables. It wasn't difficult for the five of us to talk without attracting too much attention.

I had already gotten the JRU proposal and its acceptance to my boys. They were appropriately outraged and worried for me but eager to listen to Jennifer and – somewhat less so – Lenny Benson. When they had finished Bryce began. 'It's inspired,' he said. 'It gives a whole new meaning to the prison term hostile takeover.'

'Yeah. Now it doesn't mean Attica,' Tyler laughed.

'You know, if what you've told us is reliable,' Bryce said to Lenny, 'I don't think it would take much to leverage a buyout.' He turned to his brother. 'Don't you know that schmuck Tarrington, CEO?'

'Yeah. Went to Yale with him. Dumber than Dubya and a lot more greedy,' Tyler said. 'We could make him an offer. And I think our firm could throw seven or eight million behind this.' He turned to me. 'Things went well in Hong Kong despite that sucker Murdoch.' The boys don't curse in my presence, even though everyone else here cusses at the drop of a hatpin, much less a hat.

Jennifer opened her eyes wide. 'You'd invest that much?' she asked. She turned to Lenny. 'Would that be enough?' she asked.

'Marginal,' Lenny told her. 'We'd get a large minority position but not necessarily control.'

Bryce looked a little crestfallen.

'Sell my damn house and put my money into this,' I directed them.

'Sell your house?' Tyler asked, as shocked as if I'd just yelled 'motherfucker' at the top of my lungs.

'But you've always wanted to hold on to the house,' Bryce said. 'Always.'

'Until now,' I told him.

'Do you know how much that "damn house" is worth?' Tyler asked me. I replied to this question with a smile and a shrug.

'In for a penny – in for a pound,' I told them. It was the most liberating moment I had known in many years. I had clung to the idea of the house – my adult home and garden – for many years. In my head I redid the perennial beds, thought about painting the hallway a light yellow instead of its current blue, and sometimes looked at catalogues, thinking of what I could buy to make the house more comfortable, more attractive, more homey. The problem was it wasn't my home and it never would be again. I realized I could play the same mental games without owning the place. And my life was here and its quality was far more important.

'That may be as much as ten million dollars,' Bryce said. 'Real estate in Greenwich had skyrocketed,' he reminded me. 'And they're not making any more waterfront land there.'

'Yes, I know,' I said with a faraway look in my eye. 'I can't imagine why anyone would pay ten million dollars to live in such a monstrously huge house in such a miserably petty place as Greenwich.' I laughed. 'I don't think it was the infidelity that made me shoot your father, I think it was that place.' I stopped and thought about what I had just said. 'We should've sold it years ago,' I told the boys. 'It's not where you boys grew up. I have no good memories of the place.' I was lost in the past when I suddenly brightened and turned to Jennifer. 'What do you think you could get for your apartment, if you sold it?' I asked.

Jennifer thought about it for a minute. 'I imagine it'll bring a little over four.'

'Four thousand! Is that all?' I asked.

She laughed. 'No, Maggie – I meant four *hundred* thousand. Maybe even five.'

'But I thought it was a loft.'

'It's a very big one bedroom,' she smiled, 'but I wasn't up to the million-dollar level. But now the market is such that you get four million for real lofts – whole floors – in old factory buildings.'

I shook my head and had to laugh. 'Well, I guess if someone is willing to pay ten to live in Greenwich they'd be willing to pay four to live in a factory.' I stopped laughing, turned quite serious, and looked around. 'You know, if we actually do end up owning this place,' I said, 'perhaps we should turn it into condominiums.' I stopped again and waited until they all realized I was joking and laughed.

'Hey, if we're going to put out that much, let's really do something with JRU once we own it,' Tyler said.

'Well, of course we will,' I told them. 'Isn't that the point? We'll make this a far better facility. We'll actually train and rehabilitate those who are willing and capable.'

'That wasn't exactly what I was talking about, Mom,' Tyler said. 'I meant make some money with it.'

'Are you certain you should risk everything you own on this scheme?' I asked Jennifer.

'You are,' Jennifer countered. 'Anyway, I might not have to sell it, yet.'

That was true. 'But I'll never leave here, Jennifer. You,

on the other hand, will need a place to go to. I'm never going back to that house anyway,' I said. 'And if selling it can make life in here a little bit better – not only for myself but for everyone else – well, I really have nothing to lose, except the money.'

'We'll call it the Jennings Estate for the Criminally Rich,' Tyler said.

'Yeah. Milken, Boesky, Trump, maybe Leona Helmsley,' Bryce said.

'Great. The campaign can be, "You don't have to be a felon to live like one."' Jennifer smiled.

'It would definitely be a gated community,' Lenny contributed, totally straight-faced.

'One of the biggest concerns I have is how I am supposed to communicate with you. I mean, it's not as if you're my lawyers and can show up every day,' Jennifer inquired 'And they monitor the telephone calls from the pay phones.'

'We can set you up with a Palm Pilot with a communications option. Get you the newest and smallest laptop or perhaps a cell phone that can be linked to the Internet. But then our problem is getting them to you,' Bryce said.

'None of this is without risk,' Jennifer told them. 'But it can be done, can't it, Maggie?'

'Sure, if we're careful. We'll ask Movita. She'll figure out a way and we'll let you know what to do,' I told my boys.

I was worried not for my sons' investment firm, but for Jennifer Spencer. I saw the look in Bryce's eyes as Jennifer and that accountant shared their plot of prison take-over and reform. Bryce was a dreamer – a trait that he had inherited from his father. But Bryce was a ruthless and manipulative dreamer – traits that had gotten his father a bullet between the eyes. I hoped that I wasn't watching anything starting here, and that Jennifer Spencer would not someday want to murder my son, but it seemed to me that the chemistry between them as they concocted this scheme in the hour of a prison visitation could lead to nothing but trouble.

During my time in the prison library, I had listened to some pretty bizarre plans as inmates desperately tried to research new ways to beat the system. For myself, I harbored no hopes of beating the system. I had stopped the boys from their constant attempts at appeals, throwing good money after bad. I was in prison for life, and, as the old adage put it, 'If you can't beat 'em – join 'em.' Experience had taught me that 'joining 'em' was a whole lot better than 'killing 'em'.

As Jennifer Spencer and 'Son Number Two' enthusiastically spun their web of intrigue and revenge, I couldn't help but wonder how different my life might have been had I been born into this new generation. Up until now, it had never occurred to me that instead of 'join 'em' or 'kill 'em', 'buy 'em' might actually be a delightful way to beat your enemies at their own game. Seeing the glint in Jennifer Spencer's eyes made me feel young again.

32

Jennifer Spencer

The narrower the cage, the sweeter the liberty.

German proverb

On the nights when Byrd wasn't on duty after lights-out Movita would work her charms on the officer filling in so that Jen and Movita could meet Theresa and hunker down in her house to go online with the slim, sexy laptop. Jen would hand over the memos, letters, and emails she had drafted during the day in the library, and Movita, who could type over a hundred words a minute, would get online and knock them out.

Bryce and Tyler did most of the negotiating with Tarrington for his share of the JRU stock and its options. In the meantime, Lenny Benson set up not one, but two significant loans for the financially strapped firm, but made sure that the small print gave the lenders not just veto power over financial decisions but also the ability to vote for board members. Bryce and Tyler became board members the moment the loans were delivered.

Both processes were fast and fairly simple; after all, Jen explained to Movita, it didn't take much to get people to accept an offer of free money. The next bit would be trickier. Normally they would not have needed a majority of shares to own a controlling interest in the company, but in this case more than forty percent of the issued stock belonged to Tarrington, who would take any questioning of his power badly. 'We don't want to have to buy all sixty-two percent of the remaining friggin' stock. And by the way, you've got great eyes.' Bryce emailed her. Movita read the message too and just gave her a look. 'We've named ourselves to the board, and with what Benson and you can manage to dig up we can probably unseat Tarrington, but that doesn't mean we want to spend more money than we have to control this fucker. Any thoughts?'

'What the hell are they talking about?' Movita asked.

'It's simple,' Jen told her. 'You can sometimes control a very big company with a fairly small percentage of their stock if you can get other large stockholders to vote with you. If you know the holdings are really widely dispersed among a lot of small stockholders, then unless Tarrington can get 'em all to vote with him, you can also get control.'

'Okay. I got that,' Movita nodded. They were crouched in the corner beside the commode, over which Theresa had placed a cloth and a puzzle box so they could use it as a workstation. Tonight they were lucky because Officer Mowbry was patrolling the unit until midnight and she was too big and lazy to walk much. But even so, once in a while she walked past the cell and then Theresa signaled them. They had to be prepared to get into her bunk while Jen plastered herself under Theresa's bunk as close up against the wall as possible. They crawled back together and Movita asked what else could be done.

'Well,' Jen explained, 'the only other option I know of is buying more of the privately held shares. Or setting the place on fire.'

'What would that do?' Theresa asked. 'Get insurance money?'

'I was only joking,' Jen whispered. 'I was trying to dramatize how important it was to get controlling interest of the stock. I could still sell my condo,' she murmured. 'Lenny tells me it would raise about half a million dollars after I paid off the broker and the mortgage.'

'Girl, ya' got a half a million dollar crib?'

Jen tried not to smile. In Tribeca a half a million dollars bought a one-bedroom apartment, but there was a limit to the economic lessons she was going to teach tonight.

'You gotta keep your home,' Theresa said firmly. 'You're young and you're not going to be here forever.'

'There has to be some other way,' Movita said.

'There sure does,' Jen sighed. 'Because half a million dollars wouldn't do much to get us controlling interest.'

Movita shook her head. 'Those JRU men aren't just mean bastards,' she said. 'They're rich mean bastards.'

'Honey,' Jen told her. 'Now you're startin' to understand Wall Street.' She answered Bryce's email, resisted flirting with him electronically, and sent another message to Lenny. By then it was almost midnight and Officer Mowbry was going off shift. Jennifer slipped off to her own cell.

It was the next morning that Jennifer came up with the plan. She was so excited that she had to tell Maggie. That wasn't enough, though. She took the chance and punched in Warden Harding's phone number into the cell phone. She was lucky that Movita and not Miss Ringling answered the phone. 'I got it, girl,' Jen told Movita.

'I knew ya' would,' Mo said calmly, but Jen knew her well enough now to read the pleasure in her voice. 'The Warden is in a meeting right now. Can I take a message?'

'We're going to take them public.'

'And that would mean . . .' Movita said.

'We offer Tarrington and the rest of his crew a minority position in a company that gets publicly traded.'

'And that would mean?' Movita said again.

'We tempt them with the idea of getting paid out when we raise a lot of money for them to take them public. They'll have a smaller percentage of the total stock but the stock will be traded on Wall Street and because their holdings are publicly traded they can cash out whenever they want to,' Jennifer explained.

'And that would benefit the situation because . . .' Movita inquired.

'Because then we'd control them!' Jen said, and she actually giggled.

'You white girls got a strange sense of humor,' Movita said, her voice lowered, and then she chuckled. 'I'll tell the Warden, as soon as she's out of her meetin'.'

Jen hung up and went over the whole plan again with Maggie, then phoned Lenny and presented it to him. 'Do you think you can you put together halfway decent financials for an IPO?' she asked him.

'Sure,' he told her. 'As long as you save a bunk for me in your cell.'

Jen smiled. 'I think for that you go to Allenwood,' she told him.

'Yeah, I hear it's a real country club,' he cracked. That made her laugh out loud and Maggie raised her eyebrows and looked over at her. They had to be as circumspect as possible because the door to the library had to be kept open and an officer was always merely steps away.

Jen had to make all of her calls from the corner of the library by the window to keep the static down. The cell phone got the best signal there but it meant that she could be seen from the doorway and Maggie had to spend her time watching out for the authorities. Worse yet, now Jen was working on the laptop – running spreadsheets and projections based on a set of givens that were so far from given that they were more like fairy tales. But she had to start somewhere. Working on the laptop was even more dangerous than using the cell phone and when she used it Maggie actually had to stand in the doorway, her arms crossed, pretending to be doing something while she kept an eye out for an officer. 'It's my punishment,' she had said. 'For being the authority in so many classrooms for so many years. Now I'm chickie. Do they still call the lookout that?'

'I don't think so,' Jen admitted.

Maggie sighed. 'I think it would have been more fun to spend my life misbehaving.'

Keeping her back to the door and being far enough back from the library window so she couldn't be seen from the yard, Jen worked on convincing Lenny. 'Look,' she said, 'we don't have to promise them anything financially in the IPO. We break it out, separate from the other JRU holdings. Prisons right now are a glamor stock. It's a growth industry in an uncertain economy.'

'Well, *there's* a stunning indictment of the American Way if I ever heard one,' Lenny told her.

She looked down at the spreadsheet she was running. 'The point is, we'll get buyers. Then Tarrington and his boys will get some money to further dilute their holdings, and for our services we retain the lion's share.'

'The lion's share, Jennifer, means everything,' Lenny told her. 'Most people get that wrong and they think it means the majority. But the lion takes all.'

'Well, there wouldn't be anything wrong with that, either,' Jen said. She paused. 'Please, Lenny. Do you think that you can do it?'

'Maybe,' he admitted.

'Can you get an accounting firm to rubber-stamp it?'

'You know the answer to that.'

Simultaneously they said, 'For the right price.'

'Do you want me to try to get HVS to underwrite it?' Lenny asked.

Jennifer thought about how poorly he was regarded at HVS as a rainmaker. She doubted they'd pick up any deal Lenny Benson brought in. Plus, she didn't want any of those sons-of-bitches to have any idea what she was doing. 'Nah,' she told him. 'I think we can do better. You think the Rafferty boys would place it?'

'Those pirates? They'd mutiny if you brought in anyone else. Anyway, if we actually do take JRU public we'll want to use every greedy bastard there when the IPO's floated to buy the thing and hype it.'

'The point is, Lenny, could you use Hudson, Van Schaank cards, stationery, and letterhead now to make them think that HVS is interested? Then we can switch later once they've taken the bait.'

'Ah, the old bait and switch,' Lenny said.

You have lovely eyes. The phrase from Bryce's email – for

no reason she could think of – came into her head again. She put it out. 'Well, we've got the HVS bait,' she said.

'It won't just be bait, Jennifer, it'll be money.'

'Yeah, but it won't have to be so much. Not if they think there's a shot of a public offering. They'll dilute themselves. Then, once we are in an ownership position . . .'

'Look, I don't want to rain on your parade but I'm just pointing out they may not want to dilute their stock if they think there's going to be a public offering. It depends on how greedy they are.'

She paused. He was smart and he was right. 'Okay,' she said. 'Then we make it a two-step waltz. First we give them some money infusion for some stock. Not just the loans. Then we tempt them with a possible offering or an acquisition and dilute them further.'

Before she could hear his response, Maggie hissed at her. 'Byrd,' she said, and Jennifer hung up, just like that, stashed the phone behind the books on the self-help shelf (after all, they were helping themselves), closed the iBook and crossed the room to the pile of books waiting to be put back alphabetically. It was a good thing, Jennifer thought, that in all her years in prison Maggie had never been caught with contraband.

Movita handed the kite to Jen at dinner. She opened it and read it. 'Could you join me this evening in my cell. Maggie.' Jen looked over at Movita, who nodded and Jen nodded back.

It was an odd thing, but everybody knew not to visit Maggie, at least not in her house. Unlike everyone else in Jennings she neither ate in the cafeteria nor with a group. She could always be approached in the library on any prison business, somehow the unwritten rule 'not in my cell' totally applied.

Jennifer and Movita were walking down the hallway with an escort to get from one unit to another, but with Movita's connections, the officer only went as far as the metal door that closed her wing off from Maggie's. Once the door closed behind her, Jennifer proceeded down the corridor. She felt as if she were on her way to see the headmistress of her school. Then she chuckled. Actually, she was going to see the headmistress. When she approached Maggie's house door, she knocked softly on the metal door frame.

'Hello,' Maggie said, and Jennifer followed Movita in.

As far as Jennifer knew, Maggie was the only inmate at Jennings who had a private cell. Sometimes others, for a time, didn't have to share when inmates were released or reassigned, but nobody ever seemed to be assigned to Maggie's cell. Looking around, Jennifer was amazed. She had never seen such order or cleanliness. The woman must scrub the place with a toothbrush, she thought. She noticed that the blanket on her bunk was pulled very tight – military style. Her magazines were stacked neatly by date on the floor near the head of her bed. All of her hygiene products were lined up along the ledge of her high windowsill. But the one thing that wasn't visible for inspection was the fact that Margaret Rafferty had privacy, and that was what Jennifer craved most of the time.

Maggie sat down on the chair and gestured toward the bunk. 'Have a seat,' she said. And then took out a plate – a real plate with a line of gold around the edge and twining leaves and flowers on it. Jennifer realized she hadn't seen china or a real cup or bowl in months.

She took the plate from Maggie's hand. On it were small

wedges of cheese, each one centered on a Ritz cracker and topped with a pimento-stuffed olive. There were also a few thin stalks of celery, with a white strip of what looked like cream cheese on it. Was it possible? It made Jennifer think of Sunday afternoons at her grandmother's.

Movita took an hors d'oeuvre, as if having canapés at six o'clock was the norm at Jennings. Following her lead, Jennifer picked up a celery stalk. Meanwhile Maggie took out three perfect martini glasses. Just the sight of them gave Jennifer a stab. Of course, they were totally contraband, but they made Jennifer long for the days that she hung out in bars and drank Cosmopolitans until she was pie-eyed. She knew better than to ask how Maggie managed to keep them hidden from random cell searches.

Maggie cleared her throat. 'Movita,' she said, and inclined her head toward Mo. 'Jennifer.' Jen felt the woman's eyes on her. 'I know that you are both very bright and very motivated. I certainly don't think I underestimated you, yet working together I feel as if in the past I didn't know the full breadth of your abilities.' She paused for a moment and, to Jen's astonishment, she took out a martini shaker. 'Blocking the dreadful JRU takeover is going to take a lot of work, could fail, and may very well cause us enormous problems.' She looked from Jen to Movita. 'This afternoon I realized just how much was involved and how much is at stake. The question I want to put to you is whether or not you want to pursue this, balls to the wall, no matter what?'

Movita reached for another cracker and then crossed one long leg over the other. 'I don't see that we have much choice,' Movita said. 'If we don't do nothin' life here will be unbearable. If we try and fail or if we try and succeed at least we know we tried.' Movita smiled. 'Am I startin' to sound like Theresa?' she asked.

Jen shook her head. 'I know what you mean. I guess I am the one among us with the most to lose since I don't have to do as much time as you do,' she told them. 'But the truth is that I have a lot at stake as well. Because I may die or go crazy if I continue this way.' She looked down. Everyone was silent for a moment.

'Well then,' Maggie said, and her voice was so cheerful that Jen managed to look at her and see that she was pouring the martini glasses full. 'Onion or olive?' she asked. And to Jen's complete amazement she had both.

'Onion,' Jen breathed and was rewarded with a perfect martini, two pearls lying side by side in the V at the top of the stem. Jen was smart enough in prison ways not to ask how, why, or how often Maggie managed to put together a treat like this. She just grinned and nodded to Movita, who grinned back at her.

'So,' Maggie said. 'We're going to do this thing.'

'Absolutely,' said Movita.

'Absolutely,' Jennifer echoed. And the three of them drained their glasses.

33

Gwen Harding

Better starve free than be a fat slave.

Aesop, 'The Dog and the Wolf,' *Fables*

When Movita Watson asked Gwen Harding to see Jennifer
Spencer, the Warden just shrugged. She had been living
with nothing but complaints, problems, and pressure for
weeks and weeks now. Not to mention her own fear and
despair. She felt what she imagined a nun who had served
in a convent for years and lost her vocation must feel –
empty, futile, and afraid.

But despite that she hadn't had a drink. And she supposed part of her emptiness came from the lack of gin that
had filled her bloodstream and her life for so long.

Seeing Jennifer Spencer was no worse or better than the
other tasks she had to do, though she wondered at it. It
seemed to her that Jennifer Spencer had settled down and
settled in. While she wouldn't look forward to a meeting
with her, she nodded. Her days at Jennings were numbered

and she didn't know if she would then be transferred by the state to some prison elsewhere, whether she'd be offered early retirement, or whether she'd quit. She felt as if leaving would be a betrayal of the women she had tried, so ineffectively, to protect and assist. But it was clear to her that all of this was out of her hands now and far too difficult and complex for the likes of her to grapple with.

She had already brought a couple of cardboard cartons into her office. There would also be a lot of things to be fed into the shredder, but she could wait on that until just before the ax fell. Bit by bit she was packing the personal mementos and the relics from her years at the prison. There were the gratifying thank-you letters from inmates who had moved on and were succeeding in a life Outside. There were the sadder but just as meaningful notes from women who had gone on to other prisons and wrote for advice or help. She had the meaningless awards that she had won both from the community and the state. They were empty of any feeling of achievement now but she supposed she'd take them. She was trying to do the packing discreetly, but she knew that Miss Ringling, Movita – and probably every inmate in Jennings – knew what was up, though she was almost certain Movita hadn't said a word. Still, when there was the knock on the door Gwen put the box, along with two others, under her desk.

'Come in,' Gwen said, and Jennifer Spencer entered the office. This time she stood and waited to be asked to sit down. Gwen thought of Marlys Johnston of JRU and her arrogant behavior and grimaced. When Gwen made a move indicating that Spencer could take a seat, Spencer – appropriately – sat across from the desk rather than next to it. Yes, Gwen thought, the girl had changed and perhaps for the better although Gwen no longer knew what 'better' and 'worse' meant.

'Warden Harding,' Spencer said. 'I have some news for you.'

Gwen felt her eyebrows raising. Perhaps she'd been premature in thinking that this girl had gained some humility. Gwen, as she often did, sat silent and waited.

'Maybe I should begin by saying I've known about the JRU takeover for some time,' Spencer said.

Gwen wasn't surprised. Between the visits the JRU staff had made, the communications with the state, and the contacts this girl had in business, it was inevitable that people, inmates included, would know about the change. 'Yes,' she said.

'Well,' Spencer continued, 'there's been a recent change in management at JRU and I think that will affect what goes on here.'

'Really?' Gwen asked. 'In what way?' She wasn't sure if she should tell the girl to shut up and get back to the library, or listen. She had to admit she was curious, but she wondered if Spencer thought she could trade information for favors. Wasn't that kind of insider stuff the very act that had landed her here in the first place? Perhaps the library wasn't enough of an upgrade and she was hoping for a job in the office here. For all Gwen knew, the girl wanted Movita's job; maybe she felt she could help JRU. Gwen stopped herself. Perhaps of everything having to do with the inmates, Gwen Harding felt worst about having to leave Movita in the hands of these profit mongers. No doubt she'd be useful to them initially, but Gwen didn't want to think about where she might end up longer-term. Well, Gwen shrugged and figured she had nothing to lose in talking with Spencer, though she wasn't making any deals. Somehow she still didn't seem the kind of girl who would step on others, although her crime indicated that her values might be less than correct. 'What kind of changes?' she asked. 'Although JRU doesn't inform me of everything, I'm sure that I'll be told anything important.'

'Well, JRU doesn't actually know this yet,' Spencer told her.

Was this some gossip from Wall Street? 'Yes, Spencer. What is it?' Gwen snapped, her voice showing her impatience. 'I have a lot of work this morning.'

'The fact is, JRU has been acquired.'

'Acquired?' Gwen repeated. 'Acquired by another firm?' God, Wackenhut or CCA had eaten up JRU.

'Not exactly,' Spencer said. 'They've been bought out by another management group.'

'I see,' Harding said. 'And when did this happen?'

'Just in the last two days. Some of the staff there might not even know about it.'

Gwen thought of Marlys Johnston and a small smile came to her lips. Did she know? Perhaps Gwen herself could call Ms Johnston and give her the tips. She couldn't help think how lovely it would be if this change affected that woman in a negative way. Live by the sword, die by the sword, she thought. But, life being what it was, no doubt this would only benefit the Marlys Johnstons of the world. She'd probably wind up as president. 'How do you know this information?' Gwen asked Spencer. The girl looked down at her lap for a moment.

'Well,' she said, 'I acquired it.'

Had Inmate 71036 gone mad? She had come into this office months ago with a chip on her shoulder and an air of arrogance to boot and here she was saying she'd 'acquired' Jennings? Gwen knew Spencer was smart in business but just how in the hell did she expect her to believe that she had done a quiet takeover of her facility? That would mean that *she* now worked for *her*. Unbelievable! 'What?' Gwen asked, reduced to single syllables to avoid stammering more than ever.

'Not me personally,' Spencer told her calmly. 'A group of investors. But I have been, well, the point man, I guess.'

Gwen stared at her. It still wasn't safe for her to speak. She thought that one of the two of them had gone mad, probably her. Was Spencer delusional? It was possible, but it was equally possible that Gwen herself was hallucinating. And if she wasn't, she'd not only completely under-estimated this girl, but also totally failed to supervise her. 'Run this by me again,' she demanded, not knowing what to hope for.

'A group of investors have bought JRU. And I kind of led the acquisition.'

'From here?' Gwen asked. 'You managed a Wall Street acquisition from within Jennings?'

Jennifer nodded. 'And I know it doesn't change our relationship as inmate and warden,' she added. 'But for the time being, until we can find the proper management, I will serve as de facto chief of operations.'

Gwen began to laugh. Once she started it was very hard for her to stop. In fact, it wasn't until she saw the alarm on Spencer's face that she came back to herself. 'Surely, if this is true,' she said, 'you see the bizarre implications of this.' This couldn't be happening, Gwen thought. This woman might be good, but she wasn't that good. And how had she done it alone? Gwen herself had set up the connection between Movita and Jennifer, and she also knew that Spencer had been getting chummy with Maggie. That was understandable; eventually most of the girls ended up going to her for comfort, advice, or just to be around someone who was more cultured and mature than most of the other inmates. But surely those two women, and little Suki Conrad or big-mouthed Theresa LaBianco were a poor and puny team for a caper like this. Gwen took a deep breath to manage her speech. 'I hope you don't think for a minute that you're going to be acting in a warden capacity. That just isn't going to happen. You may be able to fire me but the state charter makes it clear that the prison will continue to be run by penologists.'

Jennifer nodded again. 'I can promise you I didn't choose this,' she said. 'It kind of chose me.'

Gwen bent down, took out one of the boxes from under her feet and put it on top of the desk. 'Well, regardless of the truth of this, in the words of the late Richard Nixon: "You won't have me to push around anymore." I'll be resigning. I was going to do it anyway.'

Jennifer Spencer opened her eyes very, very wide. 'Oh, no,' she said. 'You can't do that. No, you can't do that at all. You can't leave, I'm going to need your help. Together we can make a change.'

'I can leave and I will,' Gwen assured her. 'You may already be my "de facto chief of operations", but even if you are, you can't stop an employee from resigning.'

'No,' Spencer said, 'not unless she's a prisoner, working for JRU. Then no matter what job she's been assigned to, she can't quit, she doesn't get vacations, and she'll barely be paid.'

Gwen stopped putting things into the box. 'I gave

you credit for being smart,' Gwen said. 'But maybe not enough credit. Is what you're saying true?'

'Oh, yes,' Jennifer assured her. 'In fact, I thought we might start simply by going over the list of JRU personnel you'd like to see fired.'

Gwen actually laughed again. 'You're serious,' she said.

'Oh, yes,' Jennifer told her again. 'I'm not sure I want this job but now that I have it, I'm going to do it.'

Gwen sat there for what seemed like a very long moment. 'Let this cup pass from my lips,' she murmured.

Jennifer heard her. 'Yes,' she said. 'That's sort of it.'

The girl didn't know that Gwen had been talking to herself. Gwen thought about all of the nonsense she'd been hearing in meetings about 'higher power' and the like. This was not going to make her a believer but it certainly looked like a Hand was involved. Then she narrowed her eyes. 'Is this some kind of Wall Street scam to get you out of here sooner?' she asked. 'Because it will not work. I don't care if you are the chairman of the company, it won't get you one day less for your sentence.'

'I know that,' Jennifer said. 'There's no reason for you to believe me, but I actually *am* thinking of others.'

And, for the first time in a long while, Gwen believed in the possibility of the redemptive power of Jennings. She looked at Jennifer Spencer as if for the first time. This woman might believe she, as warden, would be resentful or punitive, but all Gwen Harding felt was gratitude. Jennifer Spencer had taken her talent, intelligence, and experience and used them all, along with her financial contacts and God knows what else, to do good. The very end of the morning sunlight flickered in through the window and Gwen, who was not a fanciful woman, could almost swear that the light reflecting on the corner walls behind Spencer looked like the dancing of angels' wings.

Gwen extended her hand and, after a moment's pause, Jennifer took it. 'Congratulations,' Gwen said. 'I'm very pleased and proud of you.' She thought she saw another flicker, this time one of pleasure, in Jennifer Spencer's eyes. Gwen smiled. She thought of the changes they could begin to institute and began to get truly excited, but then felt that, after the surprise she'd been handed, Jennifer should be punished. She gave her best stern look to Spencer.

'I realize, of course, that you must have broken a great many rules to manage to do this from inside our institution,' she said. 'Your position of ownership doesn't change that fact.' Then she raised her hand and shook a finger at Jennifer. Using her best schoolmarm voice she told her, 'This is going on your permanent record, Missy.'

After a moment they both began to laugh. When their hilarity calmed, Gwen thanked Jennifer Spencer with all sincerity. 'You've saved a lot of women a lot of pain,' Gwen told her.

'Well, I'd like to save a lot more women a lot more pain and there's one way we can do that immediately,' Jennifer said.

'Good afternoon, Officer Byrd,' Gwen Harding said as the CO walked into her office. He looked around and Gwen glimpsed the panic that he quickly covered when he saw Jennifer, Suki Conrad, and Theresa LaBianco sitting in her office.

'Yes, Warden?' he asked, his voice deep and fairly strong. It didn't sound like the voice of a rapist, but then whose did?

'Officer Byrd, I'd like to introduce you to the new owner of Jennings, Miss Jennifer Spencer. Minority shareholders include Suki Conrad and Theresa LaBianco.' Byrd just nodded silently. It was obvious that he was trying to think fast, but was simultaneously confused by the lay of the land.

'New owners?' he asked. And Warden Gwen Harding hoped she heard a tremble in his voice.

'Yes,' she told him. 'The prison is no longer a state agency. It's been sold. The point is, you are no longer working for the state, nor are you union protected. And Miss Spencer, the new chairman of JRU International, has something to share with you.'

'Yes?' he asked, turning his head.

'Miss Spencer would like to read you something from the *New York Times.*'

'That's right,' Jennifer said, and took out a piece that she held before her.

Amnesty International documented custodial sexual misconduct toward female prisoners in forty-eight states. This may not be surprising given that the number of women in prisons and jails has tripled in the last fifteen years and that at least forty percent of those guarding women are men. But until two years ago, sexual abuse of prisoners by correctional officials was not even a criminal offense in fourteen states. Today, thanks to the efforts of Amnesty and other groups, only five states remain without such laws. What remains is to enforce them.
Curt Goering, Deputy Executive Director
of Amnesty International USA 4/15/01

Gwen could see Byrd lose all his color. Good, Goddamnit. She had to stop feeling sorry for everyone. 'Unfortunately,' Jennifer said, 'we are in one of the states where you can't be tried for the rape of Suki Conrad or the other victims that were documented, or for sexual harassment of myself, Theresa LaBianco, Flora Cravets, Pearl Mendoza, Sally Waterman, and probably a minimum of two dozen more.'

'What?' the lunkhead began. 'What do you mean?'

'Please don't insult us,' Jennifer said. 'You know perfectly well what we mean.'

The warden stood up. 'What I'd like to see is you carried off in handcuffs, ready to spend some time being raped by men in a different facility.' She sighed. 'Since that's not possible, we have only two words for you.'

For a moment the women looked at each other, as if an obscenity might be said. But real power was so much better than words, no matter how obscene.

'You're fired,' Jennifer Spencer told him.

Book III

Book III

34

Jennifer Spencer

It is the nature of desire not to be satisfied, and most men live only for the gratification of it. The beginning of reform is not so much to equalize property as to train the noble sort of natures not to desire more, and to prevent the lower from getting more.

Aristotle

As Jennifer stared at the pages of notes spread before her on the library table she felt as if she were back in Catholic school and some nun had just handed her an impossible word problem: If it takes ten men nine hours to dig a fifty foot long ditch four foot deep by two and a half feet wide, how long would it take one female with the help of several friends to turn around the attitude, facility, and costs in a women's prison? Actually, it was more of an essay test: You own a correctional facility for women. In one thousand words, explain how you would a. make it humane, b. make it effective, and c. make it profitable. (Neatness counts.)

Jennifer didn't know where to begin.

Back in school Jennifer had always known what the nuns wanted to hear; she knew how to give a snow job to a nun. But this was different. This assignment hadn't come from a nun or Donald Michaels. This wasn't a snow job or a blow job. For the first time in her life she wasn't doing intellectual exercises or selling an idea and running. She had never in her life been responsible for the daily management of anything – not even an apartment. It was a challenge that Jennifer had willingly taken on herself, but it was going to take a lot more than one thousand words to make Jennings a. humane, b. effective, and c. profitable. It was going to take thought, planning, training, and money – lots and lots of money. So where should she begin?

She had been sitting and stewing over the paper before her for two days. Then, all at once Jennifer smiled. The lyrics to 'Do-Re-Mi' suddenly popped into her head. *The Sound of Music* had been her favorite movie when she was a kid, and she remembered Sister Maria's suggestion that the beginning was a very good place to start. 'Nuns!' Jennifer thought, shaking her head. 'They always have all the answers.' She chuckled as it occurred to her that she might have to become a nun herself after all this was over. Convents were one of the few employers she could think of that welcomed ex-cons.

Jennifer knew how she'd begin, but turned to her computer and clicked on her email account for new messages. One of the perks of being the new official assistant librarian was having an official phone line installed for her use in the library, plus a DSL line for fast Internet access. Gwen Harding had suggested the change in Jennifer's position, acknowledging that Jennifer needed a private place to work from and communicate with the people at JRU, but that a private office could look dangerously like favoritism and bring down a lot of anger and jealousy from other inmates. Jennifer knew she could trust Maggie, Movita, Theresa, and

Suki to keep quiet about the recent turn of events at Jennings, but beyond the crew it could be dicey. Now Jennifer opened her email account, and a new email message from Bryce popped up marked 'URGENT – OPEN IMMEDIATELY!!' Her stomach sank. Something must be wrong. Feeling sick, she clicked on the message.

> *Yo, Jen! Just joking! I just wanted to get your blood pumping a little, I know you don't get enough stimulation in there. Actually, everything's fine. Everything's going really smoothly on my end. Don't worry about a thing.*

Easy enough for him to say, Jennifer thought. But she breathed a sigh of relief that he was just joking around.

Then she read the rest of the message and felt a blush bloom on her face.

> *But seriously, urgently, I do wish I could see you face-to-face again soon. Visitor's day just seems way too far off when you really get along with a person, you know? I was very impressed with all your ideas last Tuesday, not to mention your other . . . assets.*
>
> *Anyway back to business . . . Listen, we're going to make this thing work. Trust me, and have a productive day!*
>
> *Bryce*

She read the message again with mixed feelings. She hated when guys said 'trust me'. It almost invariably meant the opposite. But she thought he was sincere, at least about the business end of the deal. Regarding the other stuff, she

331

wasn't sure. He's just a typical financial prankster, Jennifer thought. They littered Wall Street. Deep down, though, she was flattered by his attention. He was good-looking and smart and self-assured and it was nice to have a little flirtation with a man, even if it was only over the Internet. She was pretty starved for male attention here in an all-women's prison. You couldn't really count the male officers as men – most of them were no better than dirt under your shoe. She laughed to herself as she read over Bryce's email again. But she promised herself to try to keep all her communications with him strictly business.

She shot him off a note saying that things were going well on her end, and mentioning the fact that she was currently working on plans for a Proposed Profit Center at Jennings, and organizational and management tactics.

'Have you come across something humorous?' asked Maggie when she heard Jennifer laugh.

Jennifer laughed again as she looked up at Maggie, reflecting that it was odd that she was here in prison with Bryce's mother. Wanting to cover the real cause of her laughter, she said, 'It just seems so surreal.'

Maggie nodded. 'I imagine so. It probably also seems impossible.'

'Let's just say extremely, very, extraordinarily, unimaginably, overwhelmingly difficult.'

'Well, as long as you have a positive attitude,' Maggie said. 'Let's see what you've come up with so far.' She walked over to Jennifer's table and looked at the plethora of lists, charts, and proposed reorganizational plans that Jennifer had made. 'What's your main objective?'

'To make this place a little better for the women who live here,' Jennifer said matter-of-factly.

'And what do we need to make it better?' Maggie pressed on.

Jennifer shuffled the papers until she found the one on which she had already itemized a response to Maggie's question. 'First,' she began, 'better living conditions – especially better meals, increased privacy, improved relations with the staff, and different uniforms.' She looked to Maggie for a confirming nod and smiled when she got it. 'Secondly, improved health care – I was going to itemize here, but basically we need health care of all kinds.'

'I agree,' Maggie said.

'And finally, better educational programs for basic skills like reading and math, GEDs, life skills, mothering. And more substance abuse and twelve-step programs. Then job training,' Jennifer lowered the page and looked at Maggie.

'But there's something they need first. Self-respect and discipline.'

'Hey, I went to a psychiatrist all through college and graduate school and I'm not sure I go there,' Jennifer joked.

'Well, I realize that we can't change people from the cellular level on up. But we can improve their clothes, address them by name, insist on timeliness and courtesy, increase their privileges if they deliver and learn the rules and the problems they incur from breaking them.'

'Spoken like a true headmistress,' Jennifer said.

'We also have to create a wing for the women who disturb the peace. The ones who are mentally ill and habitually scream all night and disturb everyone's sleep, the ones who go off at the slightest provocation, the ones who harangue guards endlessly. Nights of sleep uninterrupted by screaming would do a world of good for everyone, and it wouldn't cost anything.'

'We also need a better orientation for the candy when they first get here,' Jennifer said.

'Yes. And we need better training for the COs so they are more consistent. And we have to weed out the corrupt ones and the abusers.'

'That would do a lot for morale,' Jennifer agreed.

'So would some physical changes: a real gym for wet days.'

'Now you're starting to talk money,' Jennifer commented.

'And where is the money going to come from?' Maggie asked.

'We have to earn it,' Jennifer said with a sigh, and in anticipation of Maggie's next question, she shuffled the papers once again and produced the chart entitled *Proposed Profit Center for Jennings*.

Maggie studied the chart for a moment. Then she said, 'This is a wonderful start, Jennifer. Income-producing businesses.'

'I'm not sure I can make it work,' Jennifer admitted.

'It *has* to work,' Maggie told her.

Jennifer nodded. 'Without money, nothing can happen here.'

'But if this plan is going to work, you're going to need as much of the full and – I might add – *enthusiastic* cooperation of the women here as possible.' Maggie sat down next to Jennifer at the paper-strewn table. 'Do you have a plan for that?' she asked.

'Not really,' Jennifer admitted. 'We have to improve the general attitude around here, but the only ways I can think of to do that are the things that cost the most money, and since we don't have the money we can't improve the attitude, and if we can't improve the attitude we can't raise any money, and – well . . .' She stopped with a helpless shrug of her shoulders.

'It's a bit of a chicken-and-egg kind of problem, isn't it?' Maggie observed.

Jennifer nodded as she shuffled the papers yet again until she found the *Inmate Handbook* that she had been given on the day of her incarceration. 'I've been looking through this,' she said. 'I thought maybe we could change some of the rules and that would improve morale.' She opened the manual and went on. 'Like this one,' she said, pointing to a page. She read, '"Each inmate is allowed only six photographs on the cell wall." Why can't we have eight, or ten, or as many as we want?' She closed the manual and questioned Maggie: 'Don't you think if we changed some of those stupid rules it might make everyone feel a little better?'

'For a while, perhaps,' Maggie said sadly. 'But women without any pictures will be jealous. And because some of these women need to push authority, eventually, Jennifer, some women would have hundreds of pictures and cover other inmates' walls and then there would be trouble.'

'Oh,' Jennifer said dismissively, 'what trouble can there be in pictures?'

Maggie reached across the table and picked up the manual. 'I've been here a long time, Jennifer,' she began. 'And I have come to understand that there is not one rule in this manual that is either arbitrary or nonessential. Each and every rule has been made in response to a problem – *the* problem. We can each have only six pictures, because that way no one has more pictures than anyone else does. We must all wear uniforms, because that way no one will be better dressed than anyone else. Do you understand what I am saying – do you know what the problem is?'

Jennifer shook her head.

'Inequality,' Maggie said simply. 'Some *have* and some *have not*. It's the root of every conflict and crime in the world's history. And in here, every effort is made to eliminate inequality. We're all in the same mess, eating the same slop, and wearing the same hideous uniform. It's what keeps us from killing each other.'

Jennifer considered what Maggie had said and then observed, 'It sounds like communism, and communism isn't exactly the plan I had in mind for making money. Look what happened to Russia.'

Maggie laughed. 'You're getting way too far ahead of yourself, dear,' she said. 'Start with the basics: food, shelter, and clothing. Make the meals a little tastier, make the place a bit more hospitable, and maybe make the uniforms slightly less hideous. Give more, but not unlimited choices. Start with those things and then see what happens next.'

'Do – Re – Mi,' Jennifer sang in response.

'That's right.' Maggie smiled. 'Food – Shelter – Clothing. But we've got to really think about how we're going to change these women's attitudes. Most of them have been so used to being ordered around and having so few choices to make – even before they ended up in prison – that they probably don't really know how to make responsible decisions for themselves. And that's going to be a big problem when you're trying to change the atmosphere around here and turn these women into productive, self-motivated people,' Maggie continued.

Jennifer nodded. 'It's true. I always thought I got to where I am because of my own hard work, but I forget how many advantages I had. Even the nuns, who I hated, gave me a better education than I would have gotten elsewhere. But until I got to Jennings I didn't know I was privileged.'

Maggie nodded. 'Some of these women have never had anything and they're just too cynical to believe that they'll ever get anything. They were never taught anything so they think they can't learn anything. When they do get a shot at a meal, or clothes, or money, or love, they grab. And grab. They cram it in. So we must move with moderation. It's like giving food to somebody who's starving: You have to be careful not to give them too much or they'll vomit. We have to make these changes very gradually, so that nobody gets sick.'

'Point taken,' Jennifer said. She really admired Maggie as a woman and an educator. She wondered what kind of a mother she'd been to Bryce. 'Ideally,' Maggie continued, 'if we can inspire inmates to be a productive part of the changing process instead of just empty vessels taking handouts, then there's a chance we might make them "good citizens" of Jennings. And if they learn how to be "good citizens" here, then they might be able to become "good citizens" of their communities Outside when they're released.'

'Hear, hear! You're really on a roll today, Maggie,' Jennifer teased her, but she was impressed.

'Oh, stop it.' Maggie looked away. 'I guess I'd gotten cynical myself, but now, since this miracle, I'm getting rather enthusiastic at the possibility of improvements. But I'm going to get back to work now, as should you, or none of this is going to become a reality.' Maggie smiled, and wandered back to her shelves to reorganize a newly arrived carton of books.

Jennifer turned back to her computer. She was surprised

to find another new email from Bryce. Already? She clicked it open.

> *It's the sunniest day here. I walked to work and it almost broke my heart when I thought of how you and my mother probably aren't getting any sun in that dungeon of yours. I wish I could email you some. Because every email from you is like a beam of sunlight in my day.*
>
> *Bryce*

He's really laying it on thick, Jennifer thought. She didn't know how to respond to this email or if she even should. Instead, she decided to send Lenny an email, and thought it would be funny to use Bryce's little 'URGENT' trick on him. She started typing up the message.

URGENT – PRISON RIOT!

> *The positive changes here have already become too much for the inmates and now they're holding me hostage in the library . . . Just kidding! Lenny, I wanted to get your attention right away. I feel like we haven't talked for ages. I'm trying to put together plans on how to make this place profitable, and I just wanted to write and tell you how much I appreciate all that you've done for me. And your visits . . .*

Jennifer stopped typing, trying to think of what to say. Then it came to her.

> *. . . are like sunshine. Thanks.*

35

Gwen Harding

Of a good beginning cometh a good end.

John Heywood

'Let go and let God,' Gwen said to the reflection in the small mirror that hung in her office. It was one of the slogans they repeated endlessly at the AA meetings she continued to attend. She was still afraid that, despite the rule of anonymity, she'd be seen by a CO or a correctional staff's relative or even an ex-inmate who had stayed in the area. It shouldn't, of course, matter to her, with anonymity being such a rule, but she couldn't imagine bumping into Miss Ringling and not having word get out all over the prison. On the other hand, she could always raise her eyebrows, look Miss Ringling – or whomever – in the eye and ask, 'And what are *you* doing here?' She wasn't sure she'd have the balls, but that idea gave her the confidence to walk into the church basement door each time she attended.

She needed a different kind of confidence this morning.

Today was the dawning of a new beginning at Jennings. She had gotten over her surprise – no, shock – at Jennifer Spencer's disclosure and she'd even come to appreciate what the girl had done. They had agreed to work together to save Jennings and its inmates. And they had also decided it was best to keep Jennifer's unusual situation quiet. She could keep working in the library and the changes they planned could be implemented by Gwen and her staff.

She hoped that the announcement she had to make at breakfast would go well. If it didn't, she'd have egg on her face – literally. Most people didn't like change. Oddly enough, it was the people with the least to lose who were most often resistant to something in which they might, in the long term, gain. Between Jennifer Spencer, Movita Watson, Maggie Rafferty, and the new consultant they had brought in, they had a formidable team and had already begun to make significant changes. But, she reminded herself again that people did not like changes, even for the better.

Gwen tugged on the front of her pant legs to help reduce the creases from where she had been sitting in her chair. They had all decided to make the wake-up time more pleasant. Instead of the heart-stopping, dream-shattering clang of the wake-up bell, today the pleasant sound of the Cat Stevens song 'Morning Has Broken' was softly wafting throughout the halls and cellblocks. Of course, it was possible that some people might not like the old hymn, but since the man had converted to Islam they couldn't be accused of being insensitive and Theresa LaBianco had put together a multicultural morning mix for the future including the Beatles' 'Good Day, Sunshine,' the show tune 'Oh, What a Beautiful Morning,' and some hip-hop boy singing about how good it felt to wake up. Gwen suspected it meant waking up after almost overdosing but she listened to the lyrics and approved the song.

Gwen cleared her throat. She had worked with Spencer and Maggie Rafferty on the announcement about JRU. She had practiced it until she had it memorized, but she was still afraid she might begin to stammer. She took another deep breath. 'Good morning, ladies,' the Warden announced over the speaker system. 'Today is Thursday. Please be advised that breakfast will be served in the cafeteria in just fifteen minutes. And an announcement will be made. Please attend. Thank you.' Then, without the usual blast from the bullhorn, the cell doors slid open and the music continued. Gwen took fifteen minutes and spent it walking up and down the halls. Women were actually smiling. People seemed to be moving to the cafeteria in a more quiet and orderly way. Gwen herself smiled. Why hadn't she thought of this? What an improvement. It hadn't cost a dime to do, but the effect was priceless!

Gwen, no longer reporting to the state, had fired Ben Norton and they had replaced the head of food services. For the last few mornings she had eaten her own breakfast there and had made certain that all of the breakfast foods were hot and looked recognizable. No more would her girls be seeing blobs of gray oatmeal, no more rubbery squares of Jell-O. There was more fresh fruit, and they had added healthy cereals with skim milk. Breakfast was actually a more pleasant meal now and it was cheaper per person because there was less spoilage.

Today the Warden stood at the front of the breakfast line and handed out trays with plastic utensils wrapped in paper napkins. She greeted each woman with a hardy good morning. She could see from the expressions on their faces that they couldn't decide if they should go along with her or fear the calm before the storm.

The line did not move quickly. The inmates weren't used to having so many choices, and breakfast had always been such a horrendous meal that many of them stood frozen, without making a choice. 'Scrambled or boiled?' – 'Hash-browns or home fries?' – 'Bacon or sausage?' – 'Orange or cranberry juice?' – 'Coffee or tea?'

The inmates were nearly speechless as they were confronted with each new choice. And unlike Ben's staff, the new food-service personnel seemed positively delighted to be able to offer the choices. There were smiles and pleasantries exchanged, and the warden was pleased to notice that the food was served with greater pride and accepted with less belligerence.

It took longer than usual for people to get their meals and take their seats. Then Gwen gave them some time to luxuriate in the unexpected quality of the food in front of them. When she could put it off no longer, the Warden stepped to the front of the room and asked them all for their attention. She greeted them with the same tone that she had used on the public address system. 'You have probably noted some changes,' Gwen began. Some inmates laughed, a few clapped and cheered. 'We hope you approve,' Gwen said. 'There has been a change here at Jennings. It is called "privatization". This means that the state has asked a company, in our case one called JRU, to manage the prison. It doesn't mean I stop being warden but it does mean that there will be other changes. We hope all of them will improve our lives here.' She could smell the suspicion in the air, and throughout the room rumblings were heard as

Gwen continued to explain the 'changes in management and changes in attitude'. Nobody liked change and to these women any change in their blighted lives had meant a change for the worse. She needed a way to tell them that change could be a positive thing or else she, Movita, and Jennifer might be saddled with a mutiny. Every warden lived in fear of a hostage situation, and if the new owners of the prison were actually a part of the prison population it would not make things easy.

But luck and a deeper problem that she had known about now served her well. 'I would like to announce,' she said, 'that as one of the first changes Officer Byrd has been fired.'

There was a moment of silence, maybe two. And then the population broke out into such cheering and table banging and whooping and clapping as Gwen had never heard. Applause was a powerful thing. Gwen met it and felt it hit her face and belly and move past her. But the wave of approval kept coming. Every woman was on her feet, stamping them and, as people said today, 'putting their hands together'. Gwen was shocked by their reaction and by how clearly Byrd had been universally despised. She put aside her shame at not having known it herself and instead focused on her delight at seeing all of the women united in a single feeling. She tried several times to speak but the applause and hooting continued. At last, she got them to sit down. 'I hope *all* of the changes will meet with that kind of approval,' she said.

She was pleased that she wasn't stammering and she got through the rest of the announcement. She did not ask if there were any questions, because there were so many that she couldn't answer that she herself was reeling.

'I don't like this,' Springtime said to Movita. 'I don't like this at all.' But as Rodgers and Hammerstein was followed with the Fifth Dimension's 'Age of Aquarius' on the PA system, many of the women started to smile and laugh and even to dance a little in their seats as they ate their breakfast.

'What in the hell is going on here?' Theresa nervously wanted to know.

'I think it's kind of nice,' Jennifer said encouragingly.

'I think it's damn weird,' Springtime countered. Springtime suddenly leapt up from her table and ran toward the Warden. Quickly the officers tried to intervene, but Springtime managed to elude their grasp. Gwen was nearly paralyzed with fear as she watched helplessly with the other silent inmates. But Springtime did not attack her; she only whispered in her ear. Then, the Warden nodded and indicated that two officers should take Springtime from the room. 'Please continue with your breakfast, ladies,' the Warden instructed.

As the women ate, the Warden explained how new programs were going to be implemented, that health care staff would be on duty three days a week, that visitation would be expanded to include Mondays and Sundays. That church services would be able to be attended with visitors and that a play area was going to be added for the inmates to interact with their children in.

Someone started to tap her tray with the plastic utensils and was soon joined in by the rest of the population. Gwen couldn't suppress her happiness. She smiled and nodded to the group. Here she was mother, teacher, nurse, and bearer of good news.

Gwen Harding put her hands up in the air gesturing for

quiet. 'We have one more little surprise,' she explained. And as she spoke, a beaming Springtime entered the cafeteria carrying a tray. On it were plastic cups filled with the marigolds taken from the sign that Springtime tended in front of the prison. The musical tape was playing 'Good Morning, Starshine,' as Springtime placed her small floral offerings in the center of each table.

36

Movita Watson

*You get privileges, you get to wear one of them print
blouses instead of the T-shirt uniform. We mostly all
want 'em. When someone new is down, one of us say
'Don't worry. Some day your prints will come.'*

Kristen S., interviewed by Olivia Goldsmith
(anonymity requested)

Ain't nobody don't got a secret wish, 'bout what they mighta
been, or woulda really liked to do. Mine, and I'm sure nobody in the world knows it, 'cept maybe my baby Jamorah,
was always to be a fashion designer. Funny, I can hear
people actually laughin' at me in my head every time I even
think it. But anyway, even though it's harder to believe than
a good time at Jennings, I'm actually doin' it! Designin'
fashions! For some reason, doin' new uniforms was the job
that got given to me. I didn't ask for it, 'cause I got this
superstition that whatever I really want, and especially what
I ask for, I ain't gonna get. I know I got the job I wanted in
the Warden's office, but that's all the more reason to know
I couldn't have another good thing happen to me. The
chance of *two* good things happenin' to a black woman
inmate like me is slimmer than Jada Pinkett's thighs. But

346

somehow it happened anyway. The Lord moves in mysterious ways, I guess.

Warden Harding and Jennifer asked me if I wanted to do it. I said, 'Are you kiddin' me?' And there I am sittin' with paper and crayons. (They still didn't let us use pencils on account a their weapon possibilities.) It took me all of two minutes to start drawin'. Man, I know every woman in the joint is gonna have a preference, a problem, a beef. I don't expect no gratitude. It's the doin' of the job itself. I got a million ideas.

The first thing I'm thinkin' to change is the material these jumpsuits we gotta wear are made out of. It's some kinda polyester junk that chafes like crazy. By the time it gets soft it pills and there are these ugly little gray balls all over. The seams feel like rope and if you got a active job the seams hurt at the knees and elbows and under the arms and the crotch. I've decided to make the new uniforms out of some kinda cotton that ain't so stiff and weird. Jennifer gave me a budget per piece, and Miss Ringling, believe it or not, was assigned to help me bid on some fabrics from our previous suppliers. But when I showed Jen the prices she laughed. 'That's the seven-hundred-dollar toilet seat,' she said. 'You remember they sold a toilet seat to the government for seven hundred dollars. I think hammers were four hundred.' She shook her head. 'I can get this in New York from an Indian fabric dealer on West Thirty-eighth Street for three dollars a yard. Why don't I have him send some samples? He'd be thrilled for the business.'

Boy, when those samples came it felt like Christmas. It wasn't just the cotton. Ravi had also enclosed some Thai silks and they came in ten thousand colors, one more beautiful than the other. And, girl, they were cheap. So I got the idea that we would make curtains for the cafeteria out of the sky-blue fabric and do the same thing in the visitor's room with a bright pink. And then I thought that if the stuff washed good – and we tried it and it did – we could sell some of the other colors in the canteen and that women could make bedspreads and curtains out of it. Just havin' somethin' pretty to spend their money on would be a real lift. Plus, the raw silk came in about thirty colors, so even if every cell was the same, it could be different because the colors were so different. Of course, I had to discuss it with the Warden, Jennifer, and Maggie, but they were all for it. Then I got me an even better idea: Why not make up T-shirts and sashes and neckerchiefs out of some of the colored silk? It would mean that women could do all kinds of shit – be in uniform but also be individual.

Then I started thinkin', why a jumpsuit at all? What are we, Oompa Loompas? Why not pants and shirts like everybody else in the world wears? I didn't think separate pieces got weapon possibilities. I checked with the warden and she said it was okay.

So I'm really cookin', drawin' away, and Theresa comes into the Warden's office. Just what I needed. I'm sure she thinks she'd be better than me at this. I don't think so. 'What are you doing?' she asked, in a tone which said she knew damn well what I was doin'.

'I'm designin' new uniforms for us. New clothes, Theresa,' I said. 'And ya' gotta try and not hold it against me.'

'I don't hold it against you,' she said. 'You don't mind hearing my opinion, though, do you?'

'I guess not, but I just started, you know. I'm thinkin' about what they should be made out of.'

'Clothes make the woman. They have to be neat and

flattering. And not wrinkle. So they have to be permanent press.'

'Hell, no!' I said, beginning to draw again. 'I'm so sick of this synthetic garbage. I say cotton all the way. It looks natural wrinkled. And puttin' it on fresh in the mornin' feels good. If I ever get outta here my kids are gonna wear nothin' but cotton.'

She looked down at my drawin'. 'Not bad,' she said. 'But slim down the pant leg. You've got the legs too wide. It's not flattering. Not everyone's as tall as you are. And put some darts in the top so that they have some shape. If a woman looks good, she feels good.'

'No fuckin' darts,' I answered. 'How's somebody like Renee or Mavis from Unit B gonna wear somethin' with darts?' Renee and Mavis are both at least two hundred fifty pounds. They bulk up so their bellies blend with their breasts and they wind up with no shape whatsoever.

Theresa shrugged and made a disapproving noise.

'Hey,' I said. 'We ain't gonna be goin' for job interviews, you know, Theresa. We're just gonna be hangin' out here as usual, and we want to be comfortable.'

'Maybe we could have different outfits for visitor's day.'

'I doubt it,' I said. 'There's a budget issue, ya' know.'

Theresa made a face of givin' up and walked out of the office. That made me feel good.

Anyway, it took me three days to design a bunch of pieces. I did long pants, Bermuda shorts for the summer, two different styles of shirts – one sleeveless and one sleeved – a skirt for visitor's day or Christmas or that kinda thing, some T-shirts and a couple of jacket styles for when it's cold out and we need some warmth. The only thing still to decide was the colors. I thought I'd get the opinions of some of the others about that. It proved very interestin', besides bein' a big pain in the ass. The crew talked about it over dinner.

'Can they be light blue?' Suki asked. 'Please?'

'They're already light blue, girl,' I said to her. 'Whaddaya mean?'

'They're not light blue, they're gray.'

We laughed, even though it wasn't funny. They had started out some kinda gray-blue, but now they were gray. Suki was right.

'Light blue's too light,' Theresa said. 'We need a color that won't show the dirt.'

'Or be so boring,' Theresa said. 'How about prints? Animal prints. Leopard or tiger or something like that. Safari.'

I nearly spat out my food laughin', picturin' Jennings crawlin' with animal prints. 'That's wild, Theresa,' I said. 'But I don't know if we could stand lookin' at it.'

'Well, then, how about black? Black is always cool,' Jennifer chimed in as she entered the cell.

'Black is a depressing color. We need to find out what colors of the spectrum are psychologically uplifting. Like red or orange, or coral maybe. Maybe the library has some books on color,' Suki said.

I shook my head picturin' a sea of coral-colored inmates. God. Some people ain't got no vision.

Jennifer came up with the practical suggestion of khaki, which I thought was too dreary. Then someone, namely me, suggested dark blue denim. Everybody was shocked that they hadn't thought of it. 'It's 'cause I'm a fashion designer,' I said, teasin' 'em. 'It ain't by accident I get ideas.'

Jennifer Spencer sweet-talked the Paragon Uniform

company in Yonkers to do up some samples for us, tellin' 'em they'd get a big order if they did. In the interest of a little variety I decided to have 'em do some pieces up in black denim and some of the shirts in a lightweight khaki. I often realize later that an idea is good and then I'm not afraid to do it, even though someone else thought of it. But we didn't order no animal prints.

Then we had a most amazin' event at Jennings, no doubt at all the first time anything like it happened. We had an honest-to-goodness fashion show!

At first everyone wanted to be a model and Warden Harding thought we were gonna have fights or at least a very bad scene. But funny thing was, as the day and the actual doin' it got closer, most all of 'em that wanted to turned chicken and backed out and we didn't have enough. Suki's belly was slightly rounded now, but she wanted to be in and we let her. Why the hell not?

The occasion itself had to be the most fun we ever had at Jennings. We moved the tables in the cafeteria together lengthwise to make a catwalk – this was Theresa's idea. Then we set up the chairs in rows on each side and put fashion pictures from magazines on the walls. I had the new curtains for the windows and they were beautiful – yards and yards of the most gorgeous sky-blue silk. The day before we hung 'em Warden Harding authorized repaintin' the cafeteria and instead of that dirty old color we got it a clean pearly white and my curtains made it look like a kinda heaven. I mean, you were still in the joint but it looked like the nicest joint ya' ever saw. Cher woulda been shocked, and then she'd probably try to cut off a piece of the curtain to turn into a skirt. I had to laugh. Maybe it was just as well she wasn't here.

I stood at one end of the catwalk and I gotta say I was real nervous as all the inmates filed in and took their seats. There was a little printed brochure on each chair and they all started reading it right away. It had an allowance for each inmate and little drawings of the different tops, pants, jackets, and accessories. I'm not a shy person, but that was a tough crowd and I was a little worried about the dykes. I'm not afraid of speakin' my mind but that's different from speakin' in public. So the models were ready – we used Flora and Frances and Theresa. Cher woulda been great to go down the catwalk but we got a tall, thin new girl named Lorrie instead. Jennifer wouldn't do it, even though I begged her. And Maggie just laughed, even though I told her we needed someone to represent senior convicts. In the end I had seven women. And I made sure that their outfits fit and that they were scheduled so they had time to make changes in between each appearance. Maggie and Suki were in charge backstage.

So, once the cafeteria was full and the COs were leanin' against the wall with their arms crossed, the warden introduced me. I started talkin', well, readin' from my cards 'cause I was too damn nervous to even look up. Old Gwen had explained that this was the new choice of uniforms and that everybody would get seven pieces – after that they could buy 'em. No one could have more than twelve. But the first seven came to you as a gift. So then out steps Frances and I say, 'Ladies and bulldaggers, presentin' Prison Blues.' And the music comes up loud and those girls began to strut just like they were real models and for a couple of minutes, well seconds really, nobody in the audience does nothing 'cause it was all so different from what we was used to. And then the place went crazy – but in a good way.

Theresa and Flora and Lorrie and all those model girls came out in my clothes and the women started to whoop and cheer. The dykes were whistlin' and the music kept playin' and for a minute I thought we was going to have a riot – not the good kind – but it was just everybody's enthusiasm and they were clappin' for my things. Then they started arguin' with each other about which would be better to have and I could hardly believe it. But I kept on talkin' and I explained that we were settin' up a production sewin' unit and that anybody who was workin' for a higher-level pay scale could apply. And we'd be makin' these uniforms and other stuff as well. And by the time the whole show was over I looked up from my cards and it wasn't just everybody in the audience clappin' but it was also Jennifer and the Warden and Maggie and every single one of the COs.

I never felt so proud of myself in my whole life.

37

Jennifer Spencer

Through all the drama –
whether damned or not –
Love gilds the scene,
and women guide the plot.

Richard Brinsley Sheridan

There weren't enough hours in the day. Jen felt pumped, the way she used to feel during high-stakes negotiations at Hudson, Van Schaank. But now it wasn't indirect. She would receive benefits from what she was doing that would daily influence her quality of life and that of others. When the music came on for wake-up, the lassitude and depression she had faced each morning since her arrival had gone. She hopped out of bed, full of new plans and new tasks.

It seemed as if the IPO package she and Lenny had worked so long and hard on might be acceptable, but it presented Jen with another financial issue. She needed, of course, for the IPO to go smoothly and for people to buy up the stock. She also needed some money with which to buy as much stock as she could and to help in making the offering look as good as possible.

That day at the library she got on the phone and called Peter Grant, one of the dumbest brokers she knew, and the one with the biggest mouth. Donald had used Peter when he wanted word circulated out on the Street. 'Peter?' she asked when he picked up the phone. 'It's Jennifer. Jennifer Spencer.'

'Hey! Great to hear from you!' He lowered his voice a decibel or two. 'Sorry about that trouble you were in. Glad it's over.'

'Yeah,' she said. She shook her head. He probably assumed she was out of prison. It was hard to remember that you were not the center of everybody else's life and interest. 'I took the fall for Donald but I'm getting repaid big time now.'

'I figured it was something like that,' Peter said, voice booming. 'Good for you!'

'Yeah,' she agreed. 'It's not like a grand larceny conviction stops you from getting invited out.'

He laughed, a real *har-har-har*. 'Actually, it's more of a social asset,' he told her. 'You know what they say: The unindicted are uninvited.'

What a jerk! 'Well,' she said, 'my social life *has* been looking up since I got out.' Why not let him continue with his assumption. She lowered her voice conspiratorially. 'Listen, Peter, I'd like an account. I'm going to do a lot of . . . well, just between you and me, a lot of things Donald's told me to, but I know I can count on you for absolute discretion.'

'Absolutely.'

Absolutely the opposite, she thought. That's why I'm calling you, you schmuck. Then his stupidity and greed gave her another idea. 'Could we put it in his name?' she asked. 'I'll get it in writing or put him on the phone if you like.' She held her breath.

'Hey, I'd be honored,' Peter said. He paused and she thought that perhaps she'd gone too far and the jig was up. Then he continued. 'You know, he opened one before. Remember? It's been inactive for a long time. I've been very disappointed about that.'

It had been inactive because Donald had only used Peter Grant's account when he wanted every dumb bastard to jump on something. You couldn't keep an account like that going for long because the SEC monitored big gains and would be on his back. But it was a great bit of luck that he had never closed the account. Jennifer thought as quickly as she could and smiled.

Peter was the kind of guy who would watch every trade Donald made and would jump on any wagon, no matter how rickety. 'Great,' she said. 'Let's just use that one. Send all the info to my new email address and you'll be hearing from me. We'll make a small initial deposit, and then probably work on profits from then on.'

Peter laughed again, his stupid *har-har-har*. 'Hey, Donald's credit is always good with me.'

Yeah, she thought, you and every other greedy bastard on the Street. 'Trades may come from other email addresses, phones, or faxes,' she told him. 'You know how it is.'

'Yeah,' he said. But he didn't know anything.

'But let's for security's sake use a code word to insure authenticity.' She thought for a moment. Then she said, 'Could you hold? I just want to ask Donald,' she said.

'Sure,' Peter said. 'Tell Don hello for me.'

A, Donald didn't know Peter Grant from a Chinese wok and B, anyone who knew him knew he *hated* to be called

Don. Jennifer put Peter on hold and tried to think of a code word that only Donald and his closest associates might use. SOB? YELLOW RAT BASTARD? She thought of Lenny and smiled. Then it came to her. Oh, it was so great! Yes! She got back on the line. 'Peter, I've got it. It's Grendel,' she told him and spelled it for the ignoramus. She doubted that he knew Grendel was the monster in *Beowulf*. Or that it was the name of Donald's female bull mastiff. 'Oh, and he says hi,' she lied.

'Great!' Peter said. 'Tell him we ought to get together sometime for a round of golf.'

'I'll tell him,' she said. The guy must have been named Peter because his mother knew he was going to grow up to be a dickhead. Donald hated golf, and an invitation like that from a guy like Peter would be enough for him to sic lawyers on the dumb bastard. Lucky for Peter Grant this interaction with Donald Michaels was all imaginary or he might wind up in trouble. Well, with any luck, he'd wind up in trouble anyway.

'Great!' Peter told her.

'He says he'll call you. Well, gotta go. Thanks for your help.' She paused, just for a moment. 'Oh, and Peter?'

'Yes?'

'I may ask that some of the ... profits,' she giggled, sounding as close to a foolish, guilty girl as she could. 'Well, some of the profits – not much, but some – we might want distributed in cash.'

'Hey,' he said, 'under ten thousand dollars and we'll give you a cashier's check. If you want I'll run down to the bank and cash it for you. In pennies, nickels and dimes if you want.'

'What a guy,' she said. And at least that line was true.

'Gotta go,' she told him again. She took the concealed laptop from under the table top, opened it up, and went online. She picked several dozen penny stocks, did a Google search and selected the handful that looked like there was some way to sex them up. She put in a buy order and then she began the ancient process known in the trade as 'pump-and-dump'. She visited chat rooms and Web sites, and sent out emails to brokers and mutual fund managers, all touting the stock. Needless to say, she used different screen names, different writing styles, and gave Movita several dozen similar messages to post from her workstation. When Miss Ringling was out to lunch they signed on and sent another few dozen messages from there. Then she called Bryce.

'Hey, gorgeous,' he said when he picked up the phone. 'Can I send my car for you?'

'If only,' she said. 'No, right now I'm in a little money-raising compulsion. No time for a ride.'

'Hey,' Bryce said. 'Those rides are the best of all.' And Jennifer was sure he believed that to be true. 'What can I do for you?' he asked.

'I'm buying ten thousand shares of a company called Rivdek.'

'What is it?' he asked.

'What do you care?' she answered. 'It's a vehicle right now. Since I can't use your car. Anyway, I need you to buy some too.'

'Sure,' he told her. 'How many ya' want?'

'Well, right now it's priced at a dollar nine,' she said. 'I'd like you to buy up to thirty thousand shares, but not if the price goes higher than a dollar twenty.'

She heard the smile in his voice. 'I see,' he said. 'And

you will let me know when I'm supposed to unload these suckers.'

'I certainly will,' she promised him.

'And you will also let me know whether you think I'm a manly man,' he added.

He was a ridiculous flirt. He could dish it out but she wondered if he could take it. 'I thought I already told you that,' she said.

'Did you?' he asked.

'Uh huh,' she said, 'but only in body language. Perhaps you don't read body language.'

'I not only read it, I speak it fluently.'

Set and match, she thought. 'Well, I look forward to a more complete conversation at some other time,' she said. 'Gotta go.' Bryce was fun to flirt with, but between the two brothers she thought Tyler had a little more depth. Not that that mattered. She had missed flirting, being looked at like she was attractive. God, it must be hard for women who spent the best decades of their life in prison. She had forgotten how nice it was to communicate with attractive men. She didn't wonder that some of the women inmates would do almost anything to get a male CO's attention.

She dialed a number on the cell phone. 'Lenny Benson, please.'

'Accounting.' His voice sounded stern.

'It's me, Jennifer. I need your help transferring money so I can buy some Rivdek stock,' she told him.

'Hi, there.' She could hear his voice soften. 'Before I do that, have you gotten the power of attorney back from Tom?'

'He should have all the papers by now and everything should be transferred.'

'Well, just in case they're not in place, I'll bring the papers up for you to sign,' Lenny said, and she thought she heard a bit of excitement in his voice. 'And since it's of a business nature I shouldn't have to wait for visitor's day.'

'But I've already signed them.'

'Well, it's just an excuse to come see you,' Lenny said quickly as if she wasn't supposed to hear it.

What was going on? First Bryce, now Lenny. Was there a certain thrill to hitting on a woman who's incarcerated? She had to get him back to business. 'Look, I want you to do whatever you need to do to get the stock purchased and I want you to hype the hell out of Rivdek.'

'Okay, and if I have to I'll float you a loan,' he assured her.

'Thanks, Lenny. Well, I gotta go.' She pushed the red button on the cell phone and went back to the laptop.

She bought a little over ten thousand shares of Rivdek and watched the quotations. Her purchase at a dollar ten was fine but when you added all of her touting and then Bryce's purchase the stock rose to a dollar eighteen. Then a dollar twenty-seven. She'd already made twenty-five percent additional but it wasn't enough, so she sent out more messages of congratulations to many of the Web sites and chat rooms until, by closing, the stock was up to two ten. She put a call in to Bryce. 'Sell,' she said. And she did, too.

She doubled *her* money that day, and then did it again the following day. She'd always had nothing but contempt for day traders but she could see the compulsive pleasure one could take in the game. If everyone in the prison were given an account with Peter Grant, she thought, there would be no more acting out. They'd all be busy buying and selling stocks. Of course, like all outsiders, they'd eventually get burned. But even that would give them something to think about.

That night, over a dinner of tortellini and 'gravy', Jennifer didn't have the energy to talk much, but she felt as if she'd had a really good day.

38

Cher McInnery

The hardest thing to face getting out is the decisions.
For months, for years, you haven't been able to decide
anything for yourself. Then all of a sudden, you're
supposed to be able to decide everything, make every
kind of decision. It's just too much.

Emma Green, parolee from the state prison for women in
Lansing, Kansas. Kathryn Watterson, *Women in Prison*

Cher wriggled her toes with pleasure in the thick pile of the
silk Kirman. She loved watching her flat-screen TV in her
new Tribeca loft.

On the day she was released from Jennings, Cher regretted that she had to be somewhat selective in what she
actually took with her. It broke her heart to leave so much
of her hard-earned bounty behind, but she had no intention
of leaving those items that belonged to Jennifer Spencer.
She took them all, and when her processing was finished,
Cher McInnery walked out of the Jennings Correctional
Facility a free and well-dressed woman. She had served
close to four years for grand larceny, and she couldn't wait
to get started again. Except this time there would be no
petty coins, no boosting from stores, no grifting. After all,
Jennifer Spencer's Armani suit was a perfect fit, and there

was no reason to think that everything else in her closet wasn't going to fit Cher as well. She was grateful to Jennifer for opening her eyes to a larger world, one where stealing and manipulation was a respectable way of life.

It had always seemed dead wrong to Cher that everyone else had more than she had, and stealing was the only way she knew to settle the score. She only had one rule when it came to thievery: Never steal from no one that's poorer than you. And besides, it was a lot easier to steal from people who had more than they needed.

They got sloppy and did stupid things. They took their house keys to prison. It didn't take a rocket scientist to find the doors that those keys unlocked. When she first got to Jennifer's address, Cher was somewhat surprised to see that Jennifer's place was in an old meatpacking plant or something, but once she got inside she knew that she had struck gold. The views out the window from the huge living room looked south all the way down the Hudson River. Cher could even glimpse the Statue of Liberty in the distance – a good omen for her for the beginning of her new freedom.

She left prison with over thirty-eight hundred dollars that she had managed, bit by bit, to accumulate by acquiring and selling things on the black market. She was shocked to see how quickly money went here. She couldn't get into a taxi or eat a slice of pizza without breaking a ten dollar bill. And Cher didn't like to live tight and have to watch her pennies. She preferred to make lots of Benjamin Franklins rather than watching every George Washington. But Cher had plans. She had learned something in prison and it wasn't any crap about reforming. She had learned that she'd been thinking on too small a scale – that what she had considered success was penny ante. Prison had opened her vistas. Just like this view down to the New York Harbor did. And both were courtesy of Jennifer Spencer. She had to be grateful to the girl, and she was, in her own way.

Cher went to her purse – well, it had once been Jennifer Spencer's purse but it was her purse now – and took out the phone numbers she had hidden there beneath the tiny slit she had made in the lining. She was finished with the short con or even the big con. Blowing off the mark had become more and more difficult and they were more and more likely to bleat – go to the police. In the old days, marks were too embarrassed after getting conned to do anything about it. That was the whole point. Cher didn't plan to spend any more time Inside ever again.

She looked down at the phone number in her hand. JoJo ran a boiler room and a bucket shop here in New York. Cher had no interest in sitting all day, trying to make scores over the telephone, talking old ladies in Des Moines out of their savings, but the bucket shop might work. That was, if JoJo gave her a chance. His brother was a pickpocket with a whiz mob that sometimes worked New York, but JoJo looked down on him. She didn't want to try to talk herself into a job with him over the phone – she doubted if that would work, even with her refined tone of voice. But if she could find out where he was, go in for a meeting, or get him to take a walk, she was certain, dead certain, that she could move up.

But enough daydreaming. Cher had luxuriated in the pleasures of her new digs long enough. It was time to get to work. There was a whole lot she needed to get done before sunset. She clicked off the TV with the remote control and headed for the kitchen. It was a damned nice layout, but it didn't look as if the debutante had ever prepared a meal here in her life. Cher thought back to the crap Jennifer had served up at Jennings. Hadn't her mama taught her how to cook? The only useful thing Cher found in that kitchen was the drawer stuffed full of menus from places that delivered. She remembered Theresa's favorite joke: 'What does a debutante make for dinner? – Reservations!' Hell, this girl didn't even do that, she made phone calls. Well, if that's the way they did things in Tribeca, that's the way Cher would do it, too.

She decided she'd get a delivery from Balthazar. She was crazy for sticky buns, and she wanted to see what a sticky bun that cost five bucks tasted like. It was an extravagance that she couldn't really afford, but she'd worry about that later. As soon as she was working with JoJo she'd eat three five-dollar sticky buns a day if she wanted to. She dialed the number on the menu and was surprised when the voice on the other end answered with, 'Good morning, Miss Spencer. How may I help you?'

A lot had changed in the five years Cher had been at Jennings. Every damn place in America had new telephone systems that let them know who was calling before they even asked and a computer record right there with everything they needed to know about you. But Cher didn't miss a beat. 'I'd like to order breakfast,' she said casually.

'Would that be your usual order?' was the next question.

Cher thought, why not? 'Sure,' she said. 'Send over the usual.' Her stomach knotted at the thought of how much she was spending, but she was curious to know just what 'the usual' was for someone like Jennifer Spencer.

'And we'll just put that on your American Express as usual, right?' asked the order taker.

When Cher heard that, the knot in her stomach instantly untied and she was suddenly hungrier than she had ever been before in her life. 'You bet,' she said. 'Just put it on the American Express.'

'Very good, Miss Spencer. Your breakfast will be there in ten minutes.'

It was better than very good, thought Cher, this was damn good. With breakfast on its way, Cher picked up the phone to make another very necessary call. She flipped through Jennifer's address file until she found 'Branston, Tom,' and she dialed the number. She felt a deep sexual itch that just needed to be scratched. Tom Branston was a very handsome man – maybe a bit of a slimebag, but one in very nice packaging. Cher had always been attracted to those Wall Street types in their fancy suits. Now she had one of her own.

'Good morning, Tommy,' she cooed when she heard him answer. 'I'm all settled in.'

The first thing Cher had done after she got to New York City was to look up Jennifer's old beau. From what she had heard from the debutante, this guy was a bit of a dim bulb who thought primarily with his crotch. Cher had known plenty of guys like him. You had only to stroke the ego – and nothing else – to get what you wanted. Branston was no exception, and Cher played him like a cheap piano. When he heard that Cher was just released from Jennings, he was more than anxious to meet with her. Of course, Cher intimated that the deb had told her more than old Tom wanted anyone to know, and fearing blackmail, he willingly agreed to meet for a drink. That's when Cher surprised him with an easy way out. She had faked a letter from Jennifer asking for Tom's help in securing a 'sublet' on the apartment for Cher. 'She wants me to look after her belongings,' Cher assured the initially dubious attorney. When she showed him that she had Jennifer's keys, he believed her. Tom cleared Cher's way with the co-op board, and she moved in.

'I just wanted to say thank you,' Cher told Tom over the phone. 'Maybe I can do that personally sometime, huh?' she teased. She imagined that Mr Branston, like every other healthy young stud in the world, woke up ready for action. She would've been happy to help out with a little phone sex, but breakfast had arrived and Tom would have to finish up on his own. She bid him 'bye bye' and hung up. Always leave 'em asking for more, Cher thought. She smiled as she thought about how she might eventually pluck that chicken naked.

It seemed Jennifer Spencer shared Cher's taste for sticky buns. The 'usual' suited Cher just fine – as did everything she found in the closet. It was like dying and going to fashion boutique heaven to pick out an outfit from the debutante's closet. Cher tried on every damn suit in the wardrobe, but finally settled on the Prada. The others would have to wait. There'd be plenty of time to play dress-up just as soon as she got set up in the bucket shop. Cher was ready for business – looking good, feeling good, and ready to bite into the Big Apple – right down to the core.

It was good to walk the streets of New York City again. It always inspired Cher to feel the pace and the pressures of the pavement. But damn, the shops were distracting. With Jennifer's Gucci purse slung over her shoulder, Cher could just hear those credit cards calling out to her: *Use me – charge it – buy it – have it.* What the hell, Cher thought, and she succumbed to temptation and strolled into Agnes B. for a new outfit of her own. One thing that hadn't changed while Cher was gone was just how snotty the sales clerks could be at these fancy clothing stores. But now Cher was wearing Prada and that seemed to make all the difference in the world. She just started tossing stuff on the counter like she knew what she was doing. And little Isabelle the store clerk couldn't ring it up fast enough.

'You do deliver, don't you?' Cher asked, haughty as hell.

'Oh, yes,' Isabelle assured her.

Cher flipped out Jennifer's American Express and tried to act casual as she waited for the reassuring 'bleep' of approval from the credit card terminal. It sounded, and Cher started breathing again. She gave the address for the delivery and was about to be on her way, when she heard a voice behind her exclaim, 'Miss Spencer? Miss Spencer?' Cher froze, then turned very slowly. An older woman had appeared from the back office and was staring at her intently.

'Yes?' Cher asked.

'Is that you, Miss Spencer?' the woman asked. 'Have you done something different with your hair?'

'Dyed it,' Cher said quickly.

The woman squinted slightly and tilted her head as she considered Cher's answer. 'I like it,' she said finally. 'It changes your whole look.'

'Thank you,' Cher said with a smile.

'Anyway, I'll let you go now,' the woman said. 'I just wanted to say hello and to welcome you back. I'm glad you didn't forget us. We look forward to seeing you again soon, I hope?'

'Oh, yes,' Cher said as she turned and left the shop. Her heart was racing. She'd have to be more careful in the future. Tribeca was a small pond where Jennifer Spencer had been a very big-spending fish. From now on, Cher would do her shopping uptown.

39

Jennifer Spencer

Opportunity makes the thief.

English proverb

'I can't believe this shit,' Jennifer snarled to anyone who might be listening in the rec room. She waved around the letter that she was holding in her hand. 'I got this notice from my co-op board saying that I'm in violation of my contract with them because,' and she started reading directly from the letter:

> *In your absence, you have illegally subleased the unit to a third party which is in direct violation of building by-laws. When sublets are approved – which is done on a case by case basis – the lettor must be present.*

'I don't know what in the hell they're talking about,' Jennifer said aloud. 'I haven't sublet my apartment. I don't know what in the hell is going on, but I'm afraid Tom Branston has screwed me over once again!'

'Rich girls' problems,' Movita said.

Jennifer stalked over to the pay phone. She dialed Lenny's number. He helped fix everything. What would she do without him? 'Do you know what's going on with my loft?' she asked when Lenny picked up.

'Not a clue. Are you behind in maintenance? I've been sending it on the first of the month.'

'No. Nothing that simple. The co-op board is threatening to take me to court because of my illegal sublet. What sublet?'

'It must be a mistake.'

'I hope so. I don't need to be convicted again for crimes I didn't commit. What in the hell is happening out there, Lenny?'

She waited for him to castigate her for ever giving Tom Branston power of attorney. As Jennifer's accountant, Lenny had never been comfortable with the arrangement. As her . . . friend, she knew he resented Tom every moment of every day.

'I'll look into it, Jennifer,' he assured her. 'I'll talk to Tom and I'll talk to the people on your building's board. I'm sure that it's just a misunderstanding, or a paperwork screwup, okay?'

'But they say someone's living there!' Jennifer insisted.

'It's probably me they're talking about.' Lenny reminded her that during the secretive days of the holding company's formation and the subsequent buyout of JRU he had occasionally used her loft as his headquarters for the clandestine operation. 'Someone probably saw me coming and going and just thought I was living there, that's all. I'll straighten it all out. Stop worrying.'

Jennifer wanted to stop worrying about her place, just

like she wanted to stop worrying about her prison, but she couldn't shake the fear that whatever was happening on the Outside was somehow a direct threat to what she was trying to achieve at Jennings.

Those fears were realized when Lenny arrived at Jennings just two days later to report to Jennifer on what he had discovered. They sat together at a table in the visiting room and he started to explain.

'Look, you're sure Tom's name isn't on your co-op? He doesn't own shares, does he?'

'Absolutely not!' she told him.

'Well, he's living there. Or he's using it, a lot.'

'What? How do you know?'

'I followed him two nights ago. He didn't see me,' Lenny assured her. 'I snuck over to the newsstand and watched him from behind a magazine.' The mild-mannered accountant was almost panting with the intrigue of his adventure. Actually, Jennifer thought, he would have made a good John le Carré spy. 'At first, I just figured that maybe Tom was using your loft,' he said. 'After all, you two were engaged and he obviously still has a key. But then I thought, "Why would Tom start living here now? He has his own place."'

'Lenny, please,' Jennifer begged, 'just tell me what you found.'

Lenny was a little crestfallen that Jennifer did not find his tale of sleuthing as intriguing as he did, but he picked up the pace and continued. He told Jennifer how he had waited until he was certain Tom was gone, then he took his key and set off on his own expedition to uncover the truth. Before the elevator had even reached Jennifer's floor, Lenny could hear the blare of music that emanated from the loft. 'The thought of actually finding someone living there was pretty scary,' he told Jennifer. 'So I stayed in the elevator for some time, peering at your door through the wooden slats. And just when I mustered the courage to go in, the door to the apartment flew open and some woman came out with a bag of garbage!'

'Who was it?' Jennifer demanded to know.

'I don't know,' Lenny said, 'but she was obviously living there.'

'So what happened?' Jennifer asked.

Lenny took a deep breath, stared intently into Jennifer's eyes, and continued. 'I'm not sure you want to know,' he said sadly. But Jennifer *did* want to know, and from what Lenny told her, it soon became clear that Tom Branston was using Jennifer's loft to keep another woman.

'I can't believe it!' Jennifer said. She didn't want Lenny to think she still had feelings for Tom – she did, but they were all angry ones – but jealousy did flare up. She was holed up in this . . . this *convent* while he . . .

'How does a guy like Tom Branston sleep at night?' Lenny asked. 'Do you know how lucky you are to be rid of that guy?'

'Was she wearing my diamond?' Jennifer asked him.

Lenny stared at Jennifer for a moment. 'After everything I just told you, is that all you can think about?'

'Was she wearing my diamond or not, Lenny?' Jennifer insisted.

'I don't know,' Lenny answered in exasperation. 'I doubt it. I think she's just a . . .' Lenny hesitated.

'A what?' Jennifer wanted to know, but Lenny said nothing. Neither spoke for a moment, then Jennifer asked hesitantly, 'Is she pretty?'

Lenny couldn't take it anymore. 'She's a whore,

Jennifer!' he almost shouted. 'Whores are not pretty, and they don't get diamond rings.'

Jennifer couldn't sleep that night. She didn't want to disturb Suki, so she got up from her bunk and walked out into the dayroom. It had been one of her life's sweetest victories when the battle was finally won that allowed the inmates to leave their cells at night and spend their sleepless hours in the rec room if they chose, playing cards or doing jigsaw puzzles. You could always find someone to talk with, no matter what hour of the night it was. Most people had troubles worse than hers. Jennifer was glad of that tonight when she walked in and saw Movita there.

'You can't sleep either?' Movita asked when she saw her.

Jennifer shook her head and sat down across from her at the table.

'What's the problem?' Movita wondered.

Jennifer shrugged. How could she explain to Movita that she feared her eventual release from prison? How could she tell a woman who was serving a life sentence in prison that she was worried about a luxurious loft, her ex-engagement ring and her ex-fiancé. She didn't want to tell Movita that that was the reason she couldn't sleep, because she was ashamed. She was ashamed of the art, and the rugs, and the antiques. She was ashamed of the Biedermeier armoire filled with designer clothes. She was ashamed that her life had added up to nothing but a lot of stuff, and now that the stuff might be gone, she was ashamed that she might not know what to do without it. 'I'm just not sleepy,' Jennifer finally said in answer to Movita's question.

Movita nodded, as if to say that she too would rather not talk about the real causes of her insomnia. But Jen knew her daughters' names, and that Mo's pain was too deep to probe. So, after an hour or two of small talk and prison gossip, they were both tired and relaxed enough for sleep. Jennifer crept quietly back into her cell, careful not to wake the snoring Suki.

To keep peace among the inmates who were complaining about Jennifer working in the library, the Warden had her start to divide her time between there and the laundry. So her work detail for today was in the sweat pit of the Jennings laundry. She staggered quickly across the laundry room floor under a bundle of sheets almost as big as she was, because if she didn't get everything into the machines fast, Suki would be picking up laundry and Jennifer got sympathy pains in her own abdomen just thinking about it. Suki was nearly nine months pregnant, and Jennifer had nightmares worrying about the silly girl. Suki would bend over and pick up laundry as if it were perfectly okay to do.

'Just sit down!' Jennifer said to Suki now as Suki wandered dangerously near to the piles of whites. 'Don't you understand that it's easier for me to do it than to watch you do it? Please! They've still got lousy health care here and if you're premature it'll be a terrible thing!'

'I'm fine,' Suki answered. 'My sister was working on the day her first baby was born. And she was a telephone lineman.'

'A lineman had a baby? Was she up a pole?'

Suki shook her head, as if Jen were serious. 'Uh-uh. But she had it in the truck. And fast.'

'Really?' Jennifer asked.

Suki nodded, bent down, and picked up some towels.

'Towels are too heavy! Leave those!' Jennifer said, walking up to her and taking them out of her hands. 'Sit.'

'I can't just sit,' Suki said, looking down at her belly as she pulled the material of her jumpsuit tight across her abdomen to reveal her bulge. When she held her baggy suit against it you could see. It was stupendous.

Jennifer increased her pace, sorting and carrying laundry faster than she ever thought she could. But then, a couple of minutes later, out of the corner of her eye, she saw that Suki had, in fact, sat down.

'Are you okay, Suki?' she asked, turning to her. Suki didn't answer at once, and it seemed to Jennifer that she had a strange look on her face. 'Suki?' she repeated. 'Are you in pain? Are you having contractions?'

'No,' Suki answered. 'I'm just getting . . . feelings.'

'Feelings?'

'Yeah.' Suki was sweating, tiny beads coating her upper lip and nose.

Jennifer stared down at her for a minute, made sure she was all right and then went back to work, but now she looked over at Suki every minute or so. 'Are you okay?' she asked again. 'You don't look so good.'

'I think I might be sick,' Suki said. 'I feel a little sick.'

Jennifer dropped the sheets she'd just folded on a table and went over to help Suki up. 'C'mon, Suki,' she said. 'We better go to the infirmary. You can't be too careful about these things.'

'No, actually I feel much better now,' Suki said. 'I think it was just gas.'

'Are you sure you're not getting contractions?' Jennifer asked her.

Suki seemed to think about it. 'No,' she said, 'this is not

what I read about in the book. And it's over already.' She looked up at Jennifer and shrugged. 'False alarm,' she said.

Jennifer looked at her. She couldn't very well force the girl to go to the infirmary, so she just went back to work, sorting, hefting laundry in and out of the machines, folding, and all the while watching Suki. An hour later, work duty was over and it was nearly time for dinner. Suki slowly walked back to the cells with Jennifer. She would stop every now and then to remark on something. Jen thought it was to rest as well, but Suki said she felt absolutely fine. Jennifer guessed that it had been false labor. The fact that Suki ate very little dinner didn't mean anything either. Suki hadn't had a consistent appetite since early on in her pregnancy.

So it came as a total surprise when, just after lights-out, Suki sat bolt upright in her bunk and announced that the baby would be coming soon.

'Oh my God! What do you mean, Suki?' Jennifer cried. She was very alarmed, and frightened for the girl. 'I thought you weren't even having contractions!'

'I guess they must have been what I was having all day. But now they're getting closer together and worse. They're getting really bad, Jen. I think you're gonna have to help me.'

Jennifer jumped out of her bed and sat down next to Suki. She took her hand and told her to just keep on breathing calmly and deeply.

'I'll call a CO,' she said. 'They'll get an ambulance.'

'No. No, please,' Suki begged in a whisper. 'Don't tell. And don't be mad at me.'

'I'm not mad at you, Suki,' she said, 'but will you please tell me why you kept this a secret? What were you thinking of?'

'Oh God, Jenny,' Suki said, beginning to cry. 'I just

couldn't stand to be in handcuffs and . . . and . . . have my legs shackled to the table. I just couldn't stand it.' She gripped Jennifer's hand tightly. 'I'm not afraid to have the baby, but I'm afraid to let them take me away. I could have the baby here, Jen, before anybody comes. Please help me. I don't want to have my baby in cuffs. Please.'

'God, Suki!' Jennifer said. The strength and weakness of each woman overwhelmed her. 'You pretended all day?'

Jennifer felt Suki nod in the darkness. 'Ohhh,' she groaned. 'I want Roger.'

Jen called for an officer. It was Officer Ryan, thank God. She thought the white-haired older man would at least try to help them. 'We have a situation,' Jen said to him. 'Suki's going to have her baby.'

'Oh my God!' Ryan whispered. 'Infirmary's closed. Locked up. What do ya' wanna do?'

'I think you should call the Warden and tell her,' Jennifer said. 'She'll know what to do.'

Suki was making groaning noises now and Jennifer went back and sat with her. Ryan called the Warden and then brought the phone to Jennifer.

'I'm breakin' the rules and lettin' you talk on my phone,' he said. 'Don't you ever tell anybody I did it.'

Jennifer almost laughed aloud. She could lend him *her* cell, but instead she just took the phone.

'Suki Conrad is in labor?' the Warden asked.

'What should I do?' Jen asked back.

'I think you should take her down to the infirmary,' the Warden said. 'I'll tell Ryan to get Movita and Theresa to help you, and I'll pick up my friend Lucille and come right over.'

'Who's Lucille?'

'She's a doctor. Not an OB-GYN but a good internist.'

'Good. Thank God.' Jennifer handed the phone back to Ryan and went back to Suki. 'C'mon, girl,' she said, 'we're going to go for a walk.'

Officer Ryan turned on the auxiliary lights and unlocked their door. He spoke to another officer on his walkie-talkie and told him to bring Movita and Theresa to the infirmary. Then the three began to walk. Suki was fine between contractions, but they were coming every minute or so and she'd have to stop and bend over with each one.

'I wish we could ride,' Jennifer said. 'This is such a long walk for her.'

Officer Ryan shrugged. 'It ain't a bad thing to walk at this time,' he said. 'Gets things movin'. Did it with my wife for all three of our kids.'

Jennifer didn't say it, but she thought things were moving plenty fast enough already, and she was right. They didn't make it to the infirmary. Suki started to scream that the baby was coming right then. Jen nearly passed out, but Suki was wrong. Before she could drop to the floor and lie down on her side, her water broke and gushed all over the floor. Fortunately, Movita and Theresa came down the corridor just then and neither one seemed rattled. Officer Ryan went with Theresa and Jennifer to get the things that Movita, who was already down on the floor with Suki, said they would need.

'Pillows and blankets,' she said, picking Suki's upper body off the floor and cradling her in her arms. 'A good pair of scissors and antiseptic, and one a them aspirators to clear the baby's nose out. You know what I mean? And then we're gonna need some warm water and little blankets. I don't know where we're gonna get those.'

Jen assured her that they'd get everything Mo wanted, but she was praying all the while that the Warden would come with the doctor, because she was sure that there wouldn't be any of what Movita needed in the closet. Suki was moaning and making another noise that didn't sound good.

'Breathe, girl, breathe,' Movita said. She looked up at Jen. 'Go with that CO and look in the infirmary for the necessary supplies.'

There was a blanket and there was a pillow, but nothing else. They went into the infirmary itself next and found another pillow. They saw a pair of scissors and antiseptic in a glass-doored cabinet, but Officer Ryan didn't have the key to it. Jennifer was about to beg him to break the glass when she heard talk coming from the corridor.

'Listen! Maybe the doctor's here!' Jennifer cried, but it was Roger Camry, with Officer Mowbry dogtrotting along.

'Where is she?' Camry asked, and Jen pointed. They all ran together.

By the time they got back to the birth scene, Suki had Movita and another woman – the doctor, Jen realized – caring for her, and the Warden was sitting next to her on the floor holding her hand. After that it was just a matter of time. 'Roger! Roger!' Suki cried, and he took her hand. Officer Ryan left and a kind of peace descended. Lucille was calm and efficient and had everything under control. She and Movita were working like partners, both telling Suki when to push and when to let up. Suki looked up at Roger Camry and Jen saw the Warden look at them both. Suki was grunting loudly with each push and collapsing with fatigue in between. But with each push Jennifer could see the patch of baby's head get a little bigger, and she was mesmerized. So was Theresa, who stood next to Jen. When the little head finally popped out, accompanied by a yelp from the mother, Jennifer let out a cry herself. It was a sight she would never forget, the birth on the floor of the prison unit of Suki's innocent, seven-pound-six-ounce baby girl.

40

Jennifer Spencer

> When one has been threatened with a great injustice,
> one accepts a smaller as a favour.
>
> Jane Welsh Carlyle

Jennifer felt as nervous as if she were giving birth. It wasn't as if she hadn't done an Initial Public Offering before, but somehow, even when it had been at the beginning of her career and it mattered a lot, it hadn't felt as important as this. If they could raise money, improve the prison's infrastructure, and generate a little profitability, it would be what Martha Stewart called a 'good thing'. Jennifer wasn't sure that she wanted to grow JRU until it was a behemoth like Wackenhut, running a couple scores of prisons, but the choice in America was grow or perish and she supposed this was the lesser of the two evils.

The Rafferty boys had put together a syndicate but against her better judgment she had allowed them, rather than the investment group of Tucker Anthony, to be the lead managers. She hoped that they hadn't been too aggressive in setting the price per share at somewhere between five and eight dollars. She thought about the classic job that had been done when Yahoo! went public and had been so undervalued because older analysts hadn't seen the technical revolution that was about to bite them in the ass. The lead manager had low-balled it and when Yahoo! came to market the price was so low and demand was so great that it had risen four hundred percent and gained tremendous publicity. She didn't need that, but last night Bryce and Tyler had set the price at eight dollars a share and this morning they were calling the sales people in the syndicate, allocating the shares among them before the market opened and hoping that the demand would be greater than the allocations. Since the tech market had cooled, pharmaceuticals were at an all-time high, and prisons were – unfortunately – a growth industry. Jennifer was hoping there would be a demand that exceeded the available stock.

Bryce had promised to allocate plenty of shares to Lenny, but Jennifer wanted to be sure that the risk was limited and that no other salesmen at Hudson, Van Schaank would get access. She took a deep breath. It was 9:25. The allocations were being made in New York right now, and when the offering took place this morning she would see how they fared.

Because she couldn't bear to sit still, she got up from her desk and paced around the newly expanded library. It was great to see the orderly rows of books, the reading tables, the encyclopedia, and the law books in the reference section, as well as the two computer workstations that gave the library users access to library databases. In the alcove there were five women, their heads bowed over books as if they were in prayer, learning to read. Maggie, strict but patient, was quietly teaching them, while other women sat at tables, reading for pleasure or taking notes. This is worthwhile, Jennifer thought. I've made a change, and it's worthwhile.

The problem with the success was that she had less privacy. Although as assistant librarian she was granted the privilege of a desk in the corner with her back to the rest of the library, she couldn't make phone calls easily and she certainly couldn't receive them on the cell phone. Inmates were nothing if not observant, and any infraction, any special treatment was immediately spotted, commented on, reported, or envied – sometimes all of the above. Jennifer did not want to improve the prison at the cost of her own safety.

She decided it was best to go up to the Warden's office. There she had Miss Ringling to contend with, but she could talk with Movita and go online. What she wanted to do was go into the rec room and put the television on to watch CNBC and follow the quotations, but she didn't think that the women addicted to *Live with Regis and Kelly* or *Ricki Lake* would allow it, never mind trying to get the use of the TV during the soaps. She smiled at the very thought. There were two factions – the CBS addicts, who watched *The Bold and the Beautiful*, *The Young and the Restless*, and *As the World Turns*, seemed to be winning the war against the ABC addicts who watched *All My Children*, *One Life to Live*, and *General Hospital*. At least that's what she thought. She didn't even know what was on NBC because Jennifer hadn't been home to watch television in the afternoon since grammar school, when she had flirted briefly with Luke and Laura on *General Hospital* but could never stay sincerely interested.

Now she had to ask Maggie to telephone the Warden's

office and send her on some kind of trumped-up mission. She hated to interrupt Maggie during a class but motioned her aside. 'Restless, huh?' Maggie asked her.

'Shouldn't you be?' she asked. 'Your whole fortune is riding on this. If the offering is successful you can sell off your holdings in JRU and recoup some of your investment.'

Maggie looked around the room. 'I've already recouped my investment,' she said, smiling at the books, the library, and the women busy at the tables. She gave Jennifer a copy of *Corrections Officer Monthly* and said, with a voice slightly raised, 'Would you take this up to the Warden's office? They requested it.'

Jennifer walked down the hall toward the center of the prison. She passed the section of the old kitchen facility that now housed the sewing room. They had only been able to buy fourteen professional sewing machines, but they already had two teachers and the new uniforms were being cut and sewn. Beyond the kitchen and the cafeteria was the canteen, which was already stocking a wider and healthier selection of foods, including protein bars, more fresh fruits and a selection of half a dozen frozen vegetables. Outside the canteen, on a wall at least twenty feet long, photographs from the fashion show and the actual garments were pinned up along with a box where order forms could be placed. Jennifer sighed. It was very little but already the prison felt like a different place. Not all but perhaps half of the women were clambering for job assignments so they could earn more and buy more.

Movita and Warden Harding had already begun to put together a list of the deranged or extremely difficult inmates. They would be reassigned, all together, to a new wing where, Jennifer knew, bedlam would reign, but everyone else would get a sounder sleep and have an easier day, including the COs. Warden Harding was looking for COs with psychiatric hospital backgrounds to staff the new disturbed wing.

Jennifer got to the Warden's office, passed Miss Ringling's desk, and walked straight to Movita. 'Have you seen yet?' Movita asked.

'Seen what?' Jennifer had no idea what Movita was talking about.

'The offering,' Movita told her. 'It opened at eight and a quarter. And it's already up to ten and a half,' Movita said, sounding as if she'd been selling in a boiler room for the last ten years.

'You've got to be kidding,' Jennifer said, really stunned. My God, she thought. How much money would that raise for the prison?

She pushed Movita on the shoulder and tried to share her seat. 'I don't have it online,' Movita said. 'I got a call from one of my friends.'

Jennifer stared at her. 'You have friends at the market?' she asked.

'Hey, girlfriend, you don't know everything about me.'

Just then Warden Harding put her head out the door. 'Miss Watson, Miss Spencer, would you join me in the office for a moment?' she asked.

Jen and Movita followed her in and she closed the door behind them. She had a small television sitting on her windowsill tuned to CNBC. Without even thinking about it, Jennifer sat down on the floor. She was mesmerized by the numbers flashing across the bottom of the screen. She was looking for JUI, the initials that had been assigned to the company (apparently there was something else that was

JRU). It took a while, but eventually it showed up and it was at fourteen and an eighth. Jennifer actually half rose from her lotus position and screamed. This was a good sign, a really good sign. 'What's up?' Movita asked, Warden Harding right behind her.

'We're in the action,' Jennifer said. 'It looks good. We're up to fourteen.' She looked at the time. 'And it's only ten ten. Of course, anything could happen, it could have been a burst of enthusiasm early in the day that'll be followed by a crash. It could be a plateau, but even then . . .'

'You mean we've doubled our money?' Gwen Harding asked.

Jennifer smiled at her as if she were a simpleton. 'Well, you would have doubled it if you had had it in the market on this stock in the first place.'

'But I do,' Gwen Harding said.

'Oh, no!' Jennifer moaned. 'I can't take any more pressure. Don't tell me you invested personal money. This is a business. We always do it with other people's money.'

'Well, I'm another person,' Gwen said. 'And I don't believe I'm alone. As far as I know there are quite a few people here who have invested.'

'Who?' Jennifer asked, but then was distracted by hearing something mentioned on CNBC.

'One IPO that seems to be on the move today is JRU. And here to discuss it is Chris Olsen, of the investment firm of Tucker Anthony.'

An attractive woman with short platinum hair nodded at the camera. 'This is an interesting public offering, Bob,' she said. 'We were hoping for an allocation of five thousand shares but while we feel good about it and we have additional demand, we didn't get any allocation at all at the seven-dollar opening price. I think the investment bankers may have been a little too conservative on this one. JRU is a new firm but it has three lucrative prison management contracts and when you look at their major competitors, the giants Wackenhut and CCA, JRU looks like a David to their Goliath. It's a feisty young company, they have some good staff and I'm expecting demand to continue. I think our clients might be willing to buy it at as much as twenty dollars a share.'

'Oh, my good Lord!' Movita cried. 'They talking about the stock tripling?'

Jennifer's heart was thumping in her chest but she tried to keep calm for the sake of the others. 'Hey, it's only ten thirty. It could drop to three bucks by nightfall.' She looked at the television. 'Although this certainly didn't hurt,' she said. She looked at the two women. 'May I remind you that I am here in part because of dealing in so-called "insider information". I hope you haven't made me guilty of that again.'

'Hey, I'm not goin' to drop a dime on you,' Movita said. 'How 'bout you, Warden?'

Warden Harding just laughed and Jen couldn't tell if it was over the mild joke or the fact that the woman had just made a few thousand dollars.

It was time for a head count just before lunch and they made their way back to their hallway. After the cafeteria, Jennifer and Movita went back to the library to tell Maggie the news, but Maggie was already in the know. 'Bryce and Tyler called the Warden and she relayed the information to me. Isn't it just grand, girls? You know, it's up to twenty-four and a quarter,' Maggie told them.

Jennifer opened her eyes wide. 'Your sons have been . . .'

Maggie smiled a full, slow grin. 'Are you trying to tell me I'm not the only criminal in my family?' she asked.

Jennifer couldn't help it – she went back to the Warden's office and spent the rest of the afternoon alternating between the telephone, the television, and Movita's online service while she watched the stock climb and climb. By the end of business that day it was at thirty-seven and she made sure that she called everyone she knew to tell them to get out.

'Hey,' Bryce said when she spoke with him. 'We've only just begun.'

'Please, Bryce,' Jennifer told him. 'Just get out. Let it cool off.'

'Not on your life,' Bryce told her.

41

Maggie Rafferty

Time discovers truth.

Lucius Annaeus Seneca

America's insatiable hunger for novelty is a constant source of bewilderment to me. I, who have never hula hooped, visited any Disney Kingdom, eaten buffet in Branson, Missouri, or petted a rock (domesticated or wild), find it inconceivable that there are those who have not only done these things, but who have willingly parted with generous sums of their cash in order to do so. As Mr Barnum would say, well, we all know his theory on the frequency of patsy births.

That great showman's maxim was never so gloriously affirmed as it was at the Jennings Correctional Facility for Women. With suckers proliferating nationwide at a rate of one per minute, it only stood to reason that whoever came up with the next 'new thing' to satisfy their infantile oral cravings would become very rich indeed. And what better way to satisfy a sucker than with a lollipop? That is how 'Prison Pops' came to take America by storm – and for an even 'buck a pop'. It was a glorious thing to behold.

Ice was long the rarest of commodities here at Jennings. In the pre-privatization days, residents here were forced to rely on primitive methods of refrigeration to keep any precious food provisions from spoiling in the prison cells. One's weekly allocation of ice was used for this purpose, and rarely did it last long enough to do the job adequately.

A greedy but ingenious woman in Unit B by the name of Sally Waterman had come up years ago with a marvelous confection that came to be known as 'Prison Pops'.

It was a really rather simple recipe that required only coloring, gelatin, enough caramelized sugar to rot the teeth of an entire kindergarten class, and a secret flavoring that Sally wouldn't disclose. Richer than a Tootsie Pop and a Sugar Daddy put together. Prison Pops were the new taste treat that the suckers in America longed for. Initially we produced only small batches of the pops during the new professional cooking classes that had been instituted as part of the training courses. Lacking proper sticks, the sweet and icy delight was served in bowls and eaten with a spork. It was actually Suki Conrad who suggested that the pop be frozen right onto the spork, and old Springtime who observed, 'These are good enough to sell in a store Outside.'

Well, that's all Theresa LaBianco had to hear. Given the new technologies of the computer and the Internet, it wasn't long before that business-mad mind had developed a telephone sales plan, an outline for a mail-order catalogue, and a Web site. Jennifer Spencer got behind it and made a presentation (including a taste test) to my boys. Well, Bryce had always had a real sweet tooth. Soon we were, as they say, in business. I don't really want to speculate as to why Internet users might be searching for Web sites with the name 'Prison Chic Candies', but it seemed to be an immediately popular site. We had thousands of 'hits' within just hours, and hundreds of orders within days. Theresa trained a staff of nearly twenty women to handle the orders. Jennifer bought the equipment to mix and make and wrap the stuff in big batches. It was nothing short of amazing. Dear old Gwendolyn Harding was delighted to see that this burgeoning new enterprise was equipped with everything it needed for success. It was a rare occasion that you didn't see the Warden with a pop in her mouth.

At first the demand was nearly overwhelming, but Theresa managed to turn our inability to meet the orders into a brilliant marketing ploy. 'PPs' became as rare as those homely stuffed dolls once were at Christmas, and shops like Neiman Marcus, Gump's, and the like clambered for them. They weren't to be found in supermarkets or candy stores but only via the exclusive shops, our catalogue, or the Prison Chic Web site. As I say, it is our nation's insatiable hunger for novelty. You just can't underestimate gullibility.

Anyway, when Prison Pops were unexpectedly 'picked' by *People* magazine in their 'Picks and Pans' column, the visionary Miss LaBianco was ready to take Prison Chic Candies to a whole new level of operation. Sally was testing recipes for new flavors while the Web site was constantly updated with 'Sweet Thoughts from the Prison Chics'. It was originally thought that I might be of some help with this project, but it soon became apparent that this particular old prison 'chic' did not possess the verbal skills that Web-browsers were surfing for. You might say that I laid an egg. However, as the new products emerged from Sally's lab, my tongue was loosened by their sweetness, and it was I who dubbed her pistachio fudge nut brownies 'Prison Bars'. They were an immediate success. It was also I who named the hard confectionary division 'Jailhouse Rock Candies'. They became big holiday sellers. I even tried my hand at advertising copy, but it seems that I'm far too verbose for the succinct and 'punchy' requirements of that particular medium. Well, we all do what we can.

This unexpected revenue stream provided not only cash flow, jobs, and training but also secured for JRU the kind of publicity on Wall Street that you simply cannot buy. The stock skyrocketed as everyone wanted to cash in on the phenomenon that was called 'the next Ben & Jerry's' in *Barron's* and 'a sweet deal' in *Forbes*. Meanwhile every inmate in the joint came up with some family recipe or secret ingredient that could be the next big thing. Several of them are actually in development, and two look promising. As if all of this wasn't enough success for Jennifer Spencer, it wasn't long before our cottage industry captured the attention of several food-manufacturing giants across the nation, and Miss Spencer and my sons are currently in negotiations for a buyout. Tyler and Bryce were both instrumental in securing billions for a similar operation that was begun by two hippies in Vermont. They are working on this as I write. In the meantime, I understand Frances, the ice queen, is concocting her own version of a marshmallow-based puff that will be ready for Halloween. I've been conducting focus groups to determine a name, but thus far we have not decided between 'Gallows Ghosts' or 'Dungeon Devils'. The girls in copy are anxious for us to make up our minds in order that they can develop the verbiage for the

Web site. Then, of course, the packaging must be designed.

As they once said back in the seventies, 'We've come a long way, baby.'

I do wish I could write a punchy line like that.

42

Jennifer Spencer

*A business with an income at its heels furnishes always
oil for its own wheels.*

William Cowper

Jennifer thought that Movita was a hoot. She had never seen
anybody become as totally obsessed with anything as Movita
had become with fashion. She begged Maggie to use library
funds to subscribe to every fashion magazine and though
Maggie refused her most of them, Movita did prevail with W
and *Women's Wear Daily*. She spent her own money on
Vogue, *Bazaar* and even more arcane ones. She pored over
them night and day and was always sketching improvements
and additions to her line of prison wear. Only Theresa had
the patience to look and listen to her constant stream of
fashion talk, and even she eventually grew tired of it. But no
matter how long Mo worked on a shift in the sewing room
she always came back excited and filled with new ideas.
Jennifer felt just a little bit as if she'd unleashed a monster.

She was also worried about the financial realities of

running the prison. Although the IPO had raised money that could be used for capital improvements or the actual budget, there didn't seem to be a lot of income re-creation possibilities. Prison Pops and Bars were selling strong and the new catalogue they were producing would probably increase sales, although right now it was just cost. But Jennifer knew she couldn't count on the candy to support all of them. It wasn't as if they were a tiny convent and baking bread would do the job. In its original proposal that won the bid, it was clear that JRU had planned to take a loss simply to build a presence. Unless she wanted to be taken over by one of the larger prison management firms – which she definitively did not – Jennifer couldn't see a way to make their projection and she knew what that would do to the company's financial rating. Wall Street analysts went nuts when there was any surprise. They weren't even thrilled with surprise profits. Well, okay, they were thrilled with surprise profits but they went nuts buying stock as if it was the first offering of Bell Telephone.

Movita was trying to talk Jennifer into doing a mail-order catalogue of casual clothes, but Jennifer felt it was far too risky and that the catalogue business was probably saturated. After dinner that evening she actually missed Cher, who, if she had still been there, could have probably come up with some thieving scheme that might actually work. Just then Theresa, who was thumbing through one of Mo's magazines, interrupted her thoughts with an expletive that she rarely used.

'Holy shit!' Theresa said. 'I don't believe this and I'm seeing it with my own eyes. Did you see this, Movita?' she asked.

'Oh, yeah,' Movita said. 'Isn't that a scam and a half.'

'What's that?' Jen wanted to know.

'It's this company, a French one called Imitation of Christ,' Theresa said, the outrage in her voice apparent.

'A charity?' Jennifer asked.

'No, a fashion company,' Theresa said.

'Well, it does make a statement,' Movita said.

'Like what?' Theresa said. 'That French people are fuckin' nuts? It says here that they buy old clothes from the Salvation Army and other shelters and thrift shops and then they tear them up or draw on them or add different buttons and sell it as high fashion.'

'Well, it is high fashion,' Movita said. 'First of all they're French and they have good taste and secondly they don't pick just anythin' from the thrift shop. And it's what they do with it that makes all the difference.'

'Let me see,' Suki said, shifting the weight of baby Christina from one hip to the other, then bending down to take a look at the magazine. 'God, that stuff is ridiculous. And the prices. Holy . . .'

'Let me see that,' Jennifer demanded. She took the magazine from Suki. It all seemed to be true, hard as it was to believe. Well, two years ago she might have been convinced that homeless chic was a look. She speed-read the article looking for the names of the American distributors and retailers who sold the garbage. She shook her head and wrote the names down.

'You gonna buy some?' Suki asked and moved the baby to a cradle position in her arms.

Jennifer didn't even deign to answer her.

The next day Jennifer got on the phone as quickly as she could. Her French was lousy – she hadn't used it since college – but she managed to get in touch with Imitation of

Christ, and through them with another firm that was larger and less avant-garde. She spoke to a Pierre Duchamps who, luckily for her, spoke English and was a big fan of *Con Air*. 'I love zee cinema of Jerry Bruckheimer,' he said. 'We can get zese real prison clothes? But for women? *C'est fantastique. Merveilleux.* Can you fax me zee choices? You have many sizes, many styles?'

Jennifer looked up into the air at the library ceiling over her head and wasn't sure if she was thanking God or giving up. The world Outside was sometimes so very, very weird. 'Sure,' she said. 'I'll fax them to you.'

'But with prices you must also tell me if it is exclusive for Duchamps Couture. We will pay more but it must be exclusive to us. *Comprenez-vous?*'

'*Oui, je comprends.*'

Jennifer made almost four hundred and sixty thousand dollars from the uniforms and realized that after it caught on in Paris there was a good chance it would move to London and New York. And, she thought, she had an endless supply of used ugly prison gear because the candy were still being issued jumpsuits until they settled in. When she and Warden Harding discussed it, neither one of them could keep back their laughter. But conservative projections indicated that they could expect to make close to a million dollars in pure profits as long as the trend lasted.

In the meantime, virtually every prisoner was bringing in recipes from their grandmothers, their great aunts, their mothers' sisters' cousins who had candy recipes that couldn't be beat. After dinner in the cafeteria on Thursdays and Sundays they had tastings as a kind of rough market research. Though Jennifer noticed there was definitely a tendency to go for milk chocolate instead of the more expensive – and delicious – dark chocolate that she preferred. She figured it was a class thing. Two winners that they added to the collection were hard candies that were beautiful to look at and stored well. That was important, because while they valued freshness, it was impossible to guarantee at what temperature and for how long things would be stored while they were being shipped.

At Jen's insistence, Maggie had begun joining them at dinner and once Maggie had even cooked, making coq au vin. 'I don't think anybody makes this anymore,' she admitted to all of them. 'But in my day it was the classy dish, sort of like my mother's chicken à la king.' Everybody ate the chicken happily, simply because it was something different. 'I had to cheat, of course, with the wine,' she said. 'I suppose you can't call it coq au vin when you're using flat grape soda.' She lowered her voice. 'But I did add a little alcohol. Bryce smuggled it in to me. He injected some vodka into oranges that he brought me.'

'Man,' Movita told her. 'You lucky with your sons but you stupid with your cookin'. I would have rather just sucked that orange instead of eatin' this chicken.'

Maggie smiled. 'Believe me, Miss Watson, I had already sucked several of them.'

'You bad,' Movita said. 'And smart. Tell your boys to bring me a few dozen oranges next time.'

Maggie laughed. Jen smiled as everyone else at the table began clambering for the liquor-laced fruit. 'Bryce is coming up on visiting day,' she admitted. 'But it's to talk business with Jennifer.' She looked across the makeshift table at Jen. 'Apparently, our little JRU is doing very well,' she said. 'It looks as if my ship has come in.'

'What does that mean?' Suki asked, holding little Christina to her breast.

'It means we all made money,' Theresa explained.

Jen smiled at her naïveté. 'No, it means that JRU made money for its stockholders. You only make money if you own stock and get a dividend or if you own stock, its value rises, and you sell it.'

Theresa smiled a big smile and said, 'I do own stock and the value has increased and I may sell it.'

'You own stock in JRU?' Jennifer asked.

But before Theresa could answer Movita began bobbing her head. 'I own stock,' she said. 'You think I'm gonna let the two smartest financial women I ever met get into a new venture without me takin' some of the ride?'

'Are you serious?' Jen asked.

'Um-hum,' Movita told her.

'Where did you get the money?' Jennifer asked. 'You've been in here for quite a while. How did you . . .'

'I've got some money on the Outside. I got my ways,' Movita said. 'There are quite a few of us that got on board.'

'But you weren't supposed to say or do anything with this, Mo, it was too much of a risk. You could have lost everything.'

'Yeah, well, considerin' we're in here it doesn't really much matter if we win or lose, now, does it? Besides, we didn't lose – we came out rich as we ever been.'

Jennifer sat herself down on the bunk in total shock.

43

Movita Watson

A deer with a chain of gold, if she escape, will run to the forest to eat grass.

Malay proverb

A couple of weeks before my kids were gonna be comin' to see me, I sent off to a toy store catalogue and got 'em all presents. I got a dall for Kiama, a chapstick for Talitha, and an art set for Jamorah.

Of all the things that Jennifer Spencer has done since she got started improvin' conditions at Jennings, helpin' kids come to see their mothers on visitin' day is the best of all. By far, I think, and I'm not alone in this. I hadn't seen my kids in four years and you can bet I could hardly stand the wait once I knew I was gonna see them. We had been writin' to each other all the time and I talked with 'em on the phone but of course none of that's the same as bein' actually with them. I couldn't sleep for the excitement and got myself so worn down that I was cryin' about the slightest thing.

'Can you please stop?' the candy who had been assigned

as my new cellmate said to me, puttin' her face over the side of the bunk. 'I can't sleep.'

'I would if I could,' I answered her. 'I just can't.'

She put her pillow over her head and I buried my face in mine. I don't know why I was cryin' so much, but I guess it was just because it was such a terrible thing, me bein' separated from them for so long.

The day finally came. I got dressed in a pair of denim pants and a white shirt and a jacket. I had stopped cryin' and now I couldn't stop smilin'. The presents were wrapped up and sittin' on my bunk.

I went to the cafeteria but I couldn't eat lunch. I was so nervous. Then, finally, it was almost one o'clock. I took the toys and the wrappin' and went to the visitor's room. People were already comin' in, but I had time to quickly put the paper back on, lookin' up at the door constantly. Then I saw 'em.

I don't suppose there's any better sight than your kids after you haven't seen 'em in a long time. I was so amazed at the looks of 'em that I couldn't even speak. I just stared, smilin' and even laughin'. They were smilin' too, except for Kiama who's six and hardly knows me. She came walkin' over, real serious.

'My babies,' I cried, holdin' my arms open big enough for all three.

'Mama!' Jamorah said, and then Talitha after her. 'Mama! Mama!'

I scooped 'em all together in my arms and we was kissin' and huggin' and cryin' and laughin'. I couldn't get over how beautiful they were. It made me sad that they weren't dressed nice enough, but they were so beautiful! They were pictures of health to me.

'I got somethin' for each a you,' I said, after we'd calmed down.

'What, Mama?' the two older girls asked together. Kiama looked at me, still wonderin' who the heck I was.

'First Kiama's,' I said, ''cause she's the youngest.' I handed her the dall and helped her open the package. Her fingers were still so small and soft! When she saw the dall she took it and hugged it and finally smiled at me. I was gonna cry again if I didn't turn my attention to the others.

They opened their gifts then and were so pleased with 'em. I never felt better in my life, havin' 'em there with me and happy. I took Kiama up on my lap and put my arm around Jamorah.

'How are you all, my sweet little girls? Tell Mama all about everything.'

Well things just started spoutin' outta them, things about school and their friends and their rooms at home.

Kiama sat pattin' her lil' dally and then she started to talk, too. 'Will you come home with us, Mama?' she asked.

Jamorah got a sad look on her face and Talitha started appylin' the chapstick to her lips.

'Mama can't go with you now,' I said to her. 'Mama's got to stay here for a while more.'

'But you know somethin'?' I continued. 'There's cookies and juice over there that we ain't even had. Let's go and get some.'

So we walked over to the refreshment table where Jen was pourin' juice for everybody. 'What beautiful children you have, Movita,' she said, smilin' at them.

'Thank you,' I said, and introduced them. I was so immensely proud of them at that moment. They were fine, well-behaved children. I could see Jen was impressed and I felt like I had done at least somethin' good in my life.

The end of our visit came way too soon. When the ten minute warning came, I felt so bad all of a sudden I didn't think I'd be able to stand it when they left. I was afraid I'd scream and sob and had to think of some way not to. Maybe Jen would help me, I thought, and took my kids back that way to say good-bye – under the pretext of gettin' some more cookies.

Then I told 'em all that I loved 'em and that I had each one's picture up in my room and that I prayed for 'em every day. I said they could come again to see me soon. When I actually had to watch their little backs walkin' out, leavin' me, I took hold of Jennifer's hand. She seemed to understand and put her arm around my back. I started cryin' the minute I couldn't see 'em no more, and I cried nearly the whole rest of the day, except for when I was feelin' good, thinkin' of 'em playin' with their presents.

44

Maggie Rafferty

'Association' is one of the most noxious of restrictions placed on people released on parole. 'Association' means that the parolee is not allowed to communicate with any person who also has a prison record . . . [T]hey are not able to associate with any of their old friends and buddies.

Kathryn Watterson, *Women in Prison*

Working with Jennifer Spencer was a great pleasure. And she brought other pleasures into my life. I must admit that I had cut myself off from people and my feelings, and that for me it was a more comfortable way to live. But Jennifer, with her intelligence, her enthusiasm, her optimism, and her can-do attitude, revitalized me. Perhaps she reminded me, just a little bit, of myself at her age. As problems were hurled at her daily she responded with solutions. Once she had a mission she was busy, optimistic, and good company.

And Jennifer Spencer did a lot more than improve my quality of life. She improved the quality of life for everybody at Jennings and she brought people together. After years of keeping to myself, she forced me to deal with Warden Harding and I found that I had been a snob and that I had not given her enough credit for her intelligence and imagination. She had been hog-tied by the system but she had never lost her compassion. Jennifer also forced me to interact with her crew. Movita Watson, Theresa LaBianco, Suki Conrad and her adorable baby. We had so many meetings that it was easiest to meet over dinner. I found myself enjoying their company, even that of the platitude-spouting Miss LaBianco. And the baby! Neither one of my boys has made me a grandmother but little Christina brought out all my grandmotherly feelings. Despite my arthritis I even began crocheting again.

As I sat in the library crocheting, I would sometimes be overwhelmed with sadness. The problem of feeling pleasure again is the fact that it also brings pain along with it. It is impossible to catalogue the myriad soul-numbing cruelties that are visited upon us as we serve our time in prison. It is impossible, and it is of no value to try. We need not be reminded of these degradations, for we submit to them daily.

There is, however, a particularly cruel regulation that tears at our hearts only on occasion. And even under new management this rule couldn't be changed. That is when a beloved friend – or as they say 'crewmate' – is released from incarceration. From the moment she passes beyond these bars, the law prohibits any further communication between that woman and the friends that she leaves behind. After five, ten, or perhaps twenty years of friendship – of living together, laughing and crying together, comforting and nursing one another, and growing together as sisters and friends – it is all brought to an abrupt end. No letters, no phone calls, no visits – nothing. We dare not even mourn, for we know our friend has not passed away. As I say, it is a particular cruelty that can still tear at hearts that have long been hardened to such sorrow.

I am speaking, of course, of Miss McInnery's – Cher's – absence. It was keenly felt by all of the women in her crew, but most painfully, I believe, by Miss Movita Watson. I myself never permitted my heart the luxury of an intense friendship such as the one these two women shared. What one does not have, one cannot lose. And yet, given the new circumstances of life at Jennings, I found my resolve to protect my heart was weakening, and quite before I knew what was happening, it seemed as if I was now a member of Miss Watson's crew. I shared meals with these women, shared dreams with these women, and after many years of willful solitary exile, I felt at home with these women. It was so very good – and so very hard to witness their loss of their dear Cher. They did not speak of her – as many primitive cultures refuse to speak of the dead – but the sorrow of her absence was keenly felt by all.

Imagine then, the delight, when the cagey Miss Cher somehow managed to slip a communication past the prison postal officials and into the hands of a nearly ecstatic Movita Watson. It came as a simple tourist postcard from New York City – fittingly with a picture of the Statue of Liberty – and bearing this message:

> *Girls –*
> *Having a wonderful time – wish you were here! I'm looking good, feeling good, and taking my own personal bite out of the Big Apple and enjoying every minute of it.*
> *Love from Lady Liberty*

Miss Watson put on a brave and defensive show of snorting disregard and ridicule of the message, and yet I could not

help but note that she held tight to that postcard throughout the dinner we shared that evening. Everyone was talking about Cher – speculating about Cher – and in doing so,
bringing Cher back into their presence, if only for that
moment.

It was Miss LaBianco who first suggested that we collec-
tively return correspondence to Cher. She strongly opined
that given the new leadership and conditions at Jennings,
we, too, were looking good, feeling good, and – while not
taking a bite out of the *Big* Apple – enjoying more fresh
fruit in our diet than ever before. All agreed that we should
share with Cher just how nice it had become to be imprisoned. I'll admit that I was intrigued. However, as no one
knew of Cher's whereabouts, it was impossible to send our
greetings (and, may I say, our gloatings?) to her.

It was Miss Watson who then informed us that she, having access to the Warden's files, could easily find a mailing
address for her friend. I recognized the address at once as
being that of an infamous mailing service that enables the
pretentious to lay claim to an Upper East Side address. So
exactly where Miss Cher was actually residing could not be
determined, but I can assure you that it was not on East
Seventy-third. However, that was the address we had, and
so it was decided that we should – in flagrant violation of
the regulations – post a letter to Cher.

It fell to me to pen this epistle, as I was the only resident
at Jennings to possess both personally engraved stationery
and (if I may be so immodest) a most beautiful calligraphic
mastery of penmanship. Although my Mont Blanc had
long ago run dry, I managed with an inexpensive disposable
ballpoint to compose a lengthy letter to Miss McInnery in
which I shared each of the 'crew's' personal taste of this

heretofore rotten – but now considerably rosier – apple we
know of as Jennings. I share it with you now.

My Dearest Lady Liberty,

*Greetings from 'The Crew'. We were so delighted to
receive your most welcome communication. We too, wish
we were there. However, as you are no doubt aware, the
privatization of Jennings has led to numerous
improvements in our living conditions, and so while we
cannot be there, being here is not nearly so bleak an
experience as it once was. Each of the crew has asked that
I share some specifics with you.*

*I shall begin with Miss LaBianco, as it was at her
suggestion that this letter was written. Theresa has
brought her considerable business acumen to bear in the
development of an entire curriculum of instructional
courses covering all aspects of occupational training.
From composing curriculum vitae and practicing
employment interview techniques, then on to instruction
in modern business practices and telecommunications
skills and computer use, the course of study fully prepares
each participant to reenter the competitive employment
market. It is a pity that you could not have availed
yourself of this fine program prior to your release. I am
certain it would have been of great value in your efforts to
find gainful employment in New York City. Be that as it
may, Miss LaBianco is both a brilliant teacher and an
inspiring motivational speaker. Whenever a student voices
a doubt as to the efficacy of the class work – often citing
the problems inherent in applying for employment as an
'ex-con', Miss L. launches into one of her familiar
lectures. 'Problems?' she'll ask. 'You know what they say*

about problems, don't you? Problems are just opportunities to find solutions! That's what they say about problems.' She is absolutely right, you know. It is much better to believe that we have opportunities for solutions than to wallow in our problems.

Which brings me to Miss Conrad. She is the proud mother of a healthy baby girl she named Christina. Suki, too, is benefiting from the changes wrought here at Jennings. In addition to the aforementioned classes in professional training, there are numerous instructional opportunities for expectant mothers, both in pre- and post-natal care. These courses are part and parcel of an entire program of improved medical services. Full-time medical personnel are readily available twenty-four-seven, as they say, and, in addition to improved health care, we have instituted a fine program in preventative medicine as well: nutritional classes, exercise regimens, and effective treatments for substance abuse are available to all.

You do know, of course, that Miss Spencer is largely responsible for the improvements here at Jennings. While I recall that you and she did not always see eye to eye, I trust that you will agree that she has been a tireless champion of the women here. She continues to conceive, develop, and implement innovative programs and services that seek to rehabilitate rather than to punish. Her legacy is worthy of any philanthropist. She is quite a remarkable young woman.

As is, as you know, your dear friend Miss Watson. Now while I would not choose to write such sentiments myself, Movita has insisted that I quote her exactly: 'You tell that honky bitch that she'd better keep her snotty nose clean or else she'll be draggin' her sorry white ass right back in here!' I trust you can read beyond the harsh bravado of those words and see the underlying truth of her love and devotion for you. In addition to her continued service to the Warden, Movita has been instrumental in the development of improved visitation services, and, with the overnight facilities for families nearing completion, it won't be long before she will enjoy lengthy visits with her daughters. Miss Watson misses you dearly, and while I'm sure she does not wish it for you, be assured that should you ever drag your 'sorry white ass' back to Jennings, she would welcome you and it most warmly.

Which brings me at last to my own distinctive – if somewhat diminutive – contribution to the betterment of Jennings. I have drafted and introduced to both the staff and the residents a most thorough and rigid 'Code of Courtesy'. It is my hope that I shall live to see the day when we no longer refer to one another as B——s, c——s, and w——s. Instead, I have insisted that we treat one another with the respect that we deserve. The code calls for everyone – residents and staff alike – to use 'Miss' or 'Mrs' while addressing residents, and to use 'Officer' or whatever title is appropriate while speaking to staff members. While many have mocked and ridiculed this code, others have grown to appreciate the new civility and can now see the benefits of good manners and proper decorum. Miss LaBianco has suggested that I teach courses in deportment, and I believe I shall agree to do so.

And so, Miss Liberty, we remain your less-tired, less-poor, and not-so-huddled masses yearning to be free.
Sincerely,
Margaret Rafferty

I was especially satisfied with the closing. However, upon sharing the letter with Miss Watson, prior to its posting via my son's hand, she opined that Miss McInnery would well require the use of a dictionary to assist in her reading of the missive. In fact, what she said exactly was, 'We asked you to write to the bitch in English. She can't read no foreign language.' I thanked her for that pithy observation. But as a woman involved in education most of my life, I always champion any effort to broaden one's vocabulary. As one can probably infer, it is, in fact, difficult for me to articulate the renewed vigor that the changes at Jennings have brought to my life. I wake up without lethargy or depression. It is of no mean import to know that a life's sentence need not terminate one's life's work.

As for Miss Watson, I doubt I shall ever be as great a friend to her as Miss McInnery was. However, despite the difference in our skin color, our backgrounds, our vocabulary, *et al.*, given the shared nature of our incarceration, we shall never have to say good-bye to one another. In total fairness, I should say that I – being many years her senior – will likely never have to say good-bye to her. I trust when the day comes that she bids me farewell, she will understand and forgive my selfish devotion to her. She is my new friend.

45

Jennifer Spencer

Making it out there ain't no easy thing, honey. We're as good as lepers out there.

An older woman parolee. Kathryn Watterson, *Women in Prison*

'You know what they say about advice, don't you?' Theresa asked Jennifer. 'They say, if you can tell the difference between good advice and bad advice, then you probably don't need any advice. That's what they say about advice.' Theresa leaned back and let her words of wisdom sink in.

'What kind of advice is that?' Jennifer wanted to know. 'If I didn't need any advice, I wouldn't have asked for any advice.'

'That's what I'm trying to tell you,' Theresa explained. 'You've been asking for advice about this parole hearing from every woman in the joint, and has everyone advised you to do the same thing?'

'No,' Jennifer answered. 'In fact, it seems like everyone that I talk to has a different idea of how to act at a parole hearing. Some say I should be all passive and regretful, and

412

others say I should be confident and strong and really show them that I'm rehabilitated. And Flora said I should just stay quiet and only answer the questions.' Jennifer paused. She really was nervous about this. She could be out in weeks if the board passed her. But lots of inmates had told her that the board was reluctant to parole anyone on their first request. Jennifer was confused. 'I keep thinking, if they all know so damn much about it, why aren't *they* out on parole? So the point is, I don't know what to think. That's why I'm asking *you*. What's *your* advice?' She looked at Theresa, who wasn't an idiot, though she sounded like one sometimes.

'I just gave it to you.' Theresa smiled. 'You have to figure out whose advice is good advice and whose advice is bad advice, and then you won't need any advice at all.'

'I can't believe you actually made millions talking like this,' Jennifer said in exasperation. 'You just talk in circles.'

'Okay, fine,' sniffed Theresa. 'Let *that* be my advice. My advice is "What goes round, comes round." It all goes in circles.'

'That doesn't tell me a thing either,' Jennifer sighed.

'Then try this,' Theresa continued as she fit another damn piece in the puzzle. '"It is in pardoning that we are pardoned." That's right from the mouth of St Francis, and you don't get much better advice than his.'

Jennifer didn't say anything in response – not right away. She was giving serious thought to what Theresa had just said. 'That's great advice, Theresa,' she finally said, 'but who is it that I'm supposed to pardon?'

'Who are you pissed at?'

Jennifer's brow furrowed as she considered Theresa's question. Who was she pissed at? Tom? Not anymore – not really. She hated his guts, she despised everything he stood for, and she was sorry as hell that she had ever met the guy. But she wasn't really pissed at him anymore. She didn't have the time to be pissed at Tom. Donald? Same story. That sorry son-of-a-bitch would get his eventually. She just hoped that she would be there to watch it happen. Donald Michaels had played her for the fool that she was, and if she was pissed at anyone, it was herself. She was pissed at herself for idolizing a monster, loving a weakling, and letting them both bring out the absolute worst in her. And she was pissed for being stupid, greedy, and gullible. 'Me,' she finally said in answer to Theresa's question. 'I'm pissed at me.'

Theresa just smiled. 'Well, my advice still applies. It is in pardoning that we are pardoned. Go in there and tell that parole board everything that you're sorry about, and then tell them that you've worked damned hard to forgive yourself, and then tell them you would appreciate it if they would forgive you, too.' Theresa paused for a moment, then asked, '*Are* you ready to pardon yourself, honey?'

'Yeah,' Jennifer answered. 'Yeah,' she said again, 'I think I am.'

'Then you shall be pardoned,' Theresa concluded – and then, like the Pope, she actually blessed Jennifer with the sign of the cross. 'Now go, my child, and sin no more.'

'*That's* why you got paid the big bucks,' Jennifer laughed. 'You really are good at this shit. You know that, don't you?'

'Well,' Theresa demurred, 'you know what they say about modesty, don't you? They say modesty is the art of letting other people find out for themselves just how wonderful you are. That's what they say about modesty.'

'I'll remember that, Theresa,' Jennifer said. 'You are pretty wonderful.'

'You are, too, honey,' Theresa replied. 'You are, too.'

That afternoon, when the time finally came for Jennifer's parole hearing to begin, she was not surprised to discover that everything that Theresa had told her was absolutely true. It all had to start with Jennifer forgiving herself.

As she walked down the hall, she smiled. She couldn't believe that she was about to go to a major meeting without first spending several hours deciding what to wear. Never in her life had she ever gone before any kind of board meeting without her hair styled and her makeup done. But she couldn't do any 'homework' for this meeting, and she hadn't prepared one single thing to say. Two years ago she would've never forgiven herself for being so badly prepared, but today she knew that she had to forgive herself for having been so *mistakenly* prepared in the past. The Jennifer Spencer that stepped into that parole board hearing had forgiven herself for being herself. She could only hope that Theresa was right, and that others would be willing to forgive her, too.

'I've never given a more heartfelt and forceful recommendation for parole in my life,' Gwen Harding said. She was waiting outside the meeting room to take Jennifer in. 'And it wasn't easy for me, Jennifer,' she said, wiping away a tear. 'If I could have my way, you'd never leave here. I don't know how I'll do it all without you.'

There wasn't time for Jennifer to reply to Gwen's words. The bailiff opened the door and instructed her to 'appear before the Westchester County Board of Parole'. Gwen reached out and took Jennifer's hand between hers and gave it a squeeze. 'Good luck, Jenny,' she sniffed. 'Good luck.'

There were five of them. Three men and two women. They all looked so severe as they sat perched behind the long wooden table. They were all dressed in various pastels and plaids, and before each of them was a high stack of papers. The older of the two women gave Jennifer an encouraging smile, but the other remained quite grim and said, 'Have a seat, Ms Spencer.' The three men all cleared their throats in unison, then one of them asked, 'Are you ready to begin?'

'I am,' Jennifer said quietly as she sat in the chair in the middle of the room.

The proceeding began just as everyone said that it would. There was a painful retelling of her crime, her arrest, her trial, and her conviction, and when it was over Jennifer was asked if what she had just heard was complete and accurate. She nodded and said that it was. Her record of incarceration came next: her work record, her time in the SHU, the various reports that Byrd had written up – it was all there. And again, she was asked if the record was complete and accurate, and again Jennifer nodded and said that it was. Jennifer's mouth was so dry that her tongue was sticking to the roof of her mouth and all she could think about were the five pitchers of ice water that were on the table where the board members sat. 'May I have something to drink?' she asked them.

The youngest of the men stood and brought her a glass. Jennifer thanked him for it, drank deeply, and then held the glass in her lap, waiting for the hearing to continue.

'Warden Harding just presented a glowing review of you, Ms Spencer,' the older woman said. 'She assures us that you have been a most cooperative visitor here, and that in her mind, you are both remorseful for your crimes and fully rehabilitated. Would you agree with that assessment?'

'Yes, ma'am,' Jennifer replied. 'I would agree.'

'Do you have anything to add to that?' the other woman asked.

Jennifer was unsure as to what she should say. She hadn't heard Gwen's review, so she didn't know whether something had to be added or not. 'I – uh,' she hesitated. 'I'm not sure what Gwen – I mean, I'm not sure what Warden Harding told you,' Jennifer said, 'so I'm not sure what to say.'

'What would you like to say?' the older woman asked.

Jennifer thought for a moment. What would she like to say? She didn't really know. All she knew was that she just wanted to be released on parole. So that is what she said. 'I'd like to be granted parole, ma'am,' was her answer. 'That's all I really have to say.'

The older woman and the handsome young water-bearer chuckled softly. He was the next one to ask her a question. 'And why do you believe you should be granted that parole?' he asked with a smile.

'Because there's nothing left for me to do here,' Jennifer answered without thinking.

The members of the board seemed to be dumbstruck with her answer. The older man poured himself a glass of water, while the other one shuffled his papers. The kind old woman smiled and leaned back in her chair, but the younger one leaned forward in hers and studied Jennifer's face. This time, it was the very severe middle-aged man who spoke up.

'Do you believe that you were sent to this facility to do mission work, Ms Spencer?' he snapped at her.

'Excuse me?' Jennifer asked, looking at him. He might've

been Donald Michaels's brother. There was that same smug, self-satisfied and all-knowing smirk on his face.

'Do you *know* why you were sent here?' he wanted to know.

'Yes sir, I do know,' Jennifer answered. 'You have read my records, we have agreed that they are accurate. There is no question of why I was sent here. It was my understanding that today was going to be about why it was time for me to leave.'

'Please, Ms Spencer,' the older woman counseled. 'Do not jeopardize your freedom by responding so harshly.'

'That's right, young lady,' the older man echoed. 'It is our responsibility to determine whether or not your behavior warrants parole. It is not in your best interest to behave badly, don't you agree?'

'Yes,' Jennifer replied, 'I do agree.'

'Then would you like to reconsider your answer to my question?' the young man asked her.

Jennifer blushed. 'I'm sorry. I can't remember what your question was.'

The Donald Michaels clone and the snippy younger woman both let a snort of disgust, while the older woman just shook her head in despair. But now the old guy was almost chuckling, and the young man smiled broadly as he repeated his question. 'Why do you believe you should be granted parole, Ms Spencer?' he asked. 'Why do you think you should be released from this prison?'

'It's not a prison,' the young woman snapped. 'It's a correctional facility.'

Jennifer let out an involuntary chuckle.

'Did you find something amusing, Ms Spencer?' the woman asked.

'I'm sorry,' Jennifer answered. 'But you see, it doesn't matter what you call this place. We used to call it a prison, or the pen, or the clink. Now we call it a correctional facility. I guess it's the difference between believing in punishment and believing in rehabilitation. I don't know.' Jennifer stopped. She fully expected to be silenced at any moment, but it appeared as if she had their undivided attention. She continued. 'I do know that when you're on the Inside, the difference is between feeling like you've been *thrown away* like a useless piece of trash, or feeling like you're being *recycled* into something that resembles a "law abiding and productive member of society". But whatever you on the Outside call it, when you're locked up on the Inside, it all feels pretty hopeless – and not just for us inmates, but for the warden and the staff as well.'

'Why hopeless, Ms Spencer?' the old gent asked.

'Because rehabilitation is damned hard work when you don't have the tools you need to do it. You can't rehabilitate in a place that's set up to punish. You're going to have to decide if you want to punish us or rehabilitate us – or even both. But just be honest about it.'

The snorting man snorted again. 'Thank you for that advice, Ms Spencer.' He smirked. 'I'm sure everyone here will value your wise words on honesty.' The bastard was almost dripping with irony.

'Well, you know what they say about honesty, don't you?' Jennifer asked. 'They say that honesty is the best policy. That's what they say about honesty. And honesty is the new policy here at Jennings. I can tell you quite honestly that I was guilty as charged. And I can tell you quite honestly that I have been severely punished. And I can also tell you that I am quite honestly rehabilitated. This "pinstripe mama" will never wear Armani again.' Jennifer was standing by now.

'Did you know that we can pay a nurse a full month's salary with what it cost to buy just one Armani suit?' she continued. The man only glared in response.

'That's why I think I should be granted parole,' Jennifer said. 'Because I came in here wearing Armani and I thought that made me invincible. I was wrong. I'd trade all the Armanis in the world for a full-time medical staff. I'd sell every silk Kirman I could find if I could have the money for educational programs. My shoe budget alone could keep all of Unit C well fed and healthy. That's why I think I should be granted parole. Because now I know the difference between right and wrong – and between Armani mamas who can read a balance sheet and the real mamas who just want to be able to read to their children. No, sir, I wasn't sent here on a mission. I was sent here to be punished. But I lucked out. The missionaries were waiting for me when I got here.'

Jennifer collapsed into her chair. She couldn't believe that she had lost control. She'd never get out of Jennings now. Never. She lifted her hands to her face and began to sob uncontrollably. Theresa would be so disappointed in her.

And then – she heard clapping. Just the slow, rhythmic sound of one hand slapping against another. And then she heard some more. And soon it became applause. She braved a look between her fingers. Her handsome young water-bearer was on his feet applauding! The old woman rose to her feet as well – and then, so did the old gent. They were applauding her and smiling. And even the snippy one was smiling, too. But Donald's look-alike wasn't pleased. No, not at all. As the others stood and smiled, he angrily swept up the pile of papers before him, threw them into his brief-case and slammed it shut in disgust. Grim-faced, he glared at Jennifer. But she didn't mind. She couldn't please them all – and you know what they say about pleasing all of the people all of the time?

Theresa was going to be so proud.

46

Gwen Harding

Times change, and we change with them too.

Anonymous Latin translated by John Owen in *Epigram*

Gwendolyn Harding sat in her office, looking out the window at the blue sky and smiling at her own thoughts. She'd just heard that Officer Roger Camry had given Suki Conrad an engagement ring.

It was crazy, she knew, but she felt maternal pride. She had no children of her own and, as prison warden, she had always felt that she was running a home. Suki was as close to a daughter as she'd ever have. This was a good thing. She had no regrets.

The fact that Suki had been incarcerated because she'd let some man get her into trouble made the situation even more poignant. The girl deserved a break and hopefully she was getting one.

'I think Camry's okay,' Gwen said to Movita, who sat at a desk working a little distance from her.

'Unfortunate that the baby is that bastard Byrd's,' Movita replied.

'Look, Movita, I know how difficult the whole situation was, but Byrd's gone and Suki really loves this baby!'

'I know, but it still doesn't make the whole thing right.'

The Warden looked at Movita with concern. 'I'm hoping he loves her. I don't want her to marry him if he doesn't!'

Movita grinned. 'I'm sure you don't have to worry about that, Warden. He's a good man.'

Warden Harding reached for Suki's file and began to browse through it. The girl was actually twenty-four. And of course she was a mother twice over. Camry seemed caring – no – besotted with her. The warden had done little about their 'misdemeanor'. If she'd been so blind as to not know about Conrad's rape or pregnancy, she could close her eyes to their innocent love. Let there be one happy story to come out of Jennings. Love is such a powerful force that even the head of a prison can't control it.

What the Warden was interested in now was the wedding and the happily ever after. Deep down, she knew that Movita was of the same mind as she was. Between the two of them and with the help of the 'crew', they could give Suki a nice wedding, even if it had to take place within prison walls, and keep it low-key. But the Warden thought she'd first have another talk with Roger Camry. Gwen had him come to see her in the office. The young man looked a little shamefaced when he arrived. 'I think it's time to stop looking guilty, Roger,' Gwen said to him. 'You're soon going to be a married man with a daughter.'

He turned a shade pinker and Warden Harding decided he would probably make Suki a decent husband. He was no cavalier but he was no rogue either.

'So let's get down to business,' she continued. For a moment she wondered if he was as clueless as Suki. 'You're going to need a best man.'

Roger beamed. 'My best friend, Barry White.'

'Good,' she said.

Then Suki came in to talk about what she would like, which gave Gwen a chance to hold little Christina. 'We want to give your mommy a nice wedding,' she said to the infant, who stared at her, puzzled, and then started to cry.

'I'd like to invite my family,' Suki said, taking back the infant. 'Would that be possible? How many can come?'

'Make a list of them and bring it to me. We'll invite as many as we can. Of course your mother will come.' Suki nodded.

'Sure my mom'll come. She wants to come the night before.'

'I was wondering what you're going to do about a dress.'

Christina began to cry again and Suki opened her shirt to feed the little girl. 'I have two cousins who got married this year and both of 'em have dresses. They're gonna send me pictures so I can decide.'

'Real wedding dresses?' the Warden asked.

Suki looked surprised. 'Of course,' she answered. 'You can't get married in no other kind of dress.'

'Of course,' the Warden answered, amazed for a moment at how the world outside functioned.

'We'll get a justice of the peace to do the ceremony. Is that fine with you?'

'As long as he dresses proper and isn't fat.'

The Warden was puzzled. 'What do you mean "isn't fat"?'

'When my sister Doreen got married three years ago, the guy who did the wedding was so fat that everybody laughed. It practically spoiled the whole thing.' She looked up at Gwen as little Christina nursed on, her tiny mouth moving confidently. 'Doreen had a *gorgeous* gown. It was satin. But it turned yellow in a year so nobody else could wear it.'

The Warden looked down at the file on her desk. She knew Suki's father was dead and that there was a brother a few years older than she was. But something told her not to mention him. He'd never visited her. 'Have you thought about who you would like to give you away?'

Suki looked unhappy for the first time. 'No,' she said. 'I don't know who should.' She paused. 'I'd ask Bobby but there's no way he'd ever do it.'

'Why not?'

'He doesn't like me.'

It was the first time the Warden had heard her say a negative thing about her family. Rather than probe, she looked down at Christina.

'Why don't you take her back to your room and sit on your rocker,' she said instead. 'You'll both be more comfortable.'

Suki smiled. 'Okay.' She took her breast out of the baby's mouth gently, but the little girl frowned and whimpered.

'Okay, quit fussin',' Suki said gently, kissing a chubby cheek. 'I love you.'

What a sweet girl, Gwen thought. At that moment Warden Harding decided that she wanted to give Suki away at the wedding. She wouldn't exactly offer, but she'd tell Movita the idea and maybe she could suggest it to Suki. Maybe Suki had someone else, maybe there was some uncle or other who she would want to walk her down the aisle, but she sincerely hoped it could be her to do it.

Once Warden Harding had granted permission for the wedding of Roger Camry and Suki Conrad, the crew decided to have a little 'springtime' party for Jennifer and have the ceremony at the same time. Low-key all the way. When the Warden gave her blessing to the affair, preparations began in earnest. Everyone who was going to attend had to have something to wear. And everyone wanted to give Suki something special. These are difficult tasks Outside, very difficult Inside a prison.

But the crew outdid themselves preparing for the event, and Movita and Jen came to the Warden with their plans.

'We want to have it in the visitor's room,' they said.

'Why not the cafeteria? Like the fashion show?' the Warden suggested.

'Since we can't have any visitors here we don't need that much space,' Jen said. 'I know how much Suki wanted her family here for this but maybe sometime later they can renew their vows.' But in the end, there really was no place else.

So with the help of Theresa, Flora, Springtime, Maggie, and Mo the cafeteria was decorated again. Gwen smiled when she walked in, remembering the fashion show and how much the inmates had enjoyed it. But this little soiree was going to be a very mixed bag of emotions. Gwen was going to play mother to Christina while the ceremony took place. She would be teacher when it came time to organize the inmates for the gathering and then nurse when it came time to comfort the women when they said their good-byes to Jennifer Spencer.

Springtime had taken some flowers from the new green-houses and decorated the small altar they had made out of the stainless steel table at the far side of the wall. Movita had a few extra yards of fabric to lay out on the floor as a 'red carpet' for Suki to walk down.

As for the guests, Gwen thought it best to make the attendees only the immediate crew, and it was understood by Suki that it had to be done this way. But in her innocence and happiness she was pleased to be allowed even to have the marriage take place.

After the justice of the peace concluded the vows, Roger gave Suki a quick peck on the lips – most certainly he wanted to be more passionate, but due to the stipulations Gwen had put in place, he was more than understanding about it.

Everyone went around the cafeteria and hugged and kissed Suki, and Gwen handed little Christina off to Roger to hold. 'Here's your daddy, little girl.' The baby cooed at him as if she knew who he was.

Then it came time for everyone to approach Jennifer Spencer, the newly paroled inmate at Jennings. All the women had such great admiration for her, the work she had done to get Jennings to be a more humane place to have to stay in.

Movita, Maggie, Theresa, and Suki were sitting at the table waiting for Jennifer to finish talking with Roger and playing with Christina. As she came to join them, they greeted her with strangely subdued enthusiasm. They had mixed feelings about Jennifer leaving. They were jealous, they were envious, they would miss her terribly, and they were unselfishly happy for her. All of them had all the feelings.

'Oh God, girlfriend,' Movita said, giving her a hug. 'I'm gonna miss you!'

'Let's not say good-bye yet,' Suki cried, tears filling her eyes. 'Not until we have to.'

'Okay,' Movita said, 'let's eat. You won't believe what we made for the bride and groom and the parolee!'

'Come and sit down,' Maggie said. 'Theresa and I will bring it out.'

The table was set with paper place mats decorated with crayon drawings.

'Movita, these are adorable,' Jennifer said. 'I see another business here.'

'If you're not careful,' Warden Harding warned, 'Movita's going to buy this prison out from under you.'

Movita laughed. 'Then I'll throw myself out!'

They all laughed; Jen slapped the table in her hilarity. Gwen could see the happiness bubbling up inside her eyes like an eruption beginning deep in a volcano. The woman was intoxicated with the thought of freedom so close.

Maggie and Theresa came out of the kitchen carrying trays of covered dishes, which they set down with a flourish. 'Macaroni and gravy!' Maggie cried. 'What do you think of that!'

'It's our favorite,' Suki and Jennifer said simultaneously.

Their raptures were interrupted by the noise of the cafeteria door opening. For a second they all feared an unpleasant interruption. Then they saw that it was Warden Harding carrying out a tray full of flavored crushed-ice drinks. 'To help the cake go easier,' Frances said as she popped her head out from behind the Warden. 'I figured you'd want one last ice delivery.'

The small group laughed and Warden Harding set the

tray down in the middle of the table. 'Drink up!' she said.

Everyone grabbed at the drinks. There was no argument over who got what color, since they were all green. There was silence for a moment as they sporked up the ice pellets. 'It's really too bad you can't find Cher when you leave and let her know how we all are doing,' Movita said.

There wasn't a dry eye at the table after that, and Theresa was the only one who could speak. 'The food's getting cold,' she said softly.

'Wait, I have something else,' Movita said, and disappeared into the kitchen. She returned with a two-tiered cake. It was signed by the entire crew in colored frosting.

'It's got a bride and groom on it,' Suki said.

'And look at this, they put "Good Luck Jen" on the back side of it.'

Gwen cleared her throat and lifted up what was left of her ice drink. 'To the future!' she declared, and everyone raised their cups in unison.

47

Jennifer Spencer

He hath sent me to bind up the brokenhearted, to proclaim liberty to the captives, and the opening of the prison to them that are bound.

Isa. 61:1

After serving almost a year of a three-to-five-year sentence for investment fraud, Jennifer Spencer was finally leaving the Jennings Correctional Facility for Women. In many ways she was as terrified to leave the place as she had once been to come to it.

As she waited nervously for her release to be officially processed, she remembered so clearly the day of her incarceration. She was so sure of herself back then – so arrogant, so certain that she had everything under control. She knew – or thought that she knew – exactly who Jennifer Spencer was. But what she didn't know was what *prison* was, and she didn't know what prison could do to her. Now, ironically, she knew prison life all too well, but she wasn't so sure that she knew herself. Who was Jennifer Spencer now? And what would life outside prison hold for her? The only thing she knew for certain was that neither she nor Jennings was the same. Jennings was a far better place – and Jennifer wanted to believe that she was a far better woman. A better woman with the permanent record that the nuns always said she would have.

Jennifer smiled as she remembered how they had meted out detentions and demerits for each and every minor infraction of their Byzantine rules. Then, even after you served your time and suffered your punishment the nuns always threatened, *This is going on your permanent record!* Jennifer had never once believed that such a record actually existed – until now. Now, the complete account of her arrest, trial, conviction, and prison sentence – along with her fingerprints and mugshots – were part of a nationwide law enforcement database. Jennifer Spencer was an official ex-con. She left Jennings with a permanent record – but little else.

It came as no real surprise that the bag bearing Jennifer's name held no trace of the clothing or personal belongings that Cher had bagged and tagged on the infamous day of Jennifer's incarceration. Jennifer was neither surprised nor outraged; she didn't really want to leave Jennings in an Armani suit anyway. Probably whoever took over Cher's job in Intake managed to confiscate her clothing. What the hell, Jennifer thought, they wouldn't fit me right anyway – she'd lost weight during her stay in Jennings. Jennifer was going to be on the Outside – and she didn't have a damn thing to wear.

'Oh, Jennifer,' Gwen sighed when they discovered the thievery, 'there's nothing in your bag except someone's old torn blue jeans and a T-shirt.'

Jennifer just laughed. 'Give 'em to me,' she said. 'If they fit, I'll wear 'em. It doesn't matter.'

'But you can't wear these,' Gwen protested. 'Do we have time to call Lenny and ask him to bring you something from your apartment?'

'It's fine,' Jennifer said as she changed into the clothes. 'And besides, these match my record, don't you think?' The sneakers in the bag were far too large for Jennifer, and it was decided that she could wear the shoes issued from the prison. 'I'll return them,' Jennifer assured the Warden, 'I promise.'

Gwen just shook her head ruefully, then offered her hand for a handshake. The handshake turned into a clumsy embrace, but Gwen insisted that Jennifer should not get all maudlin and sentimental. 'I would like to believe that we both learned a great deal from each other,' she said warmly.

Jennifer nodded, wiped her eyes, and watched as Gwen Harding hit the final 'enter' button that sent Jennifer's record to every computer in every prison, police station, and precinct house in America. The theme song from *Cheers* popped into Jennifer's head, and even though she didn't have anything she'd come in with – or a purse to put it in – she walked out of Jennings with a smile. She hummed the theme song. Perhaps everyone would know her name, but she would be free, and that was all that mattered. She didn't want the things she had thought she wanted. Clothes and furniture and Sub-Zero refrigerators were not important. What was important was her freedom and though most people took it for granted, she would never forget that.

Roger Camry was there to unlock the gate for her, and Lenny was waiting next to his car. 'What are you singing?' he asked Jennifer as she approached him.

'It's too warped to explain,' Jennifer told him. 'C'mon, let's get out of here.'

'Are you wearing that?' Lenny asked in surprise.

'It's all I have,' Jennifer said with a shrug. 'Are you embarrassed to be seen with me?'

Lenny blushed. 'No,' he said softly. 'It's just that I brought you a gift.'

Jennifer shyly accepted the gift and eagerly opened it right on the spot. Inside was a beautiful silk scarf that she lovingly lifted out of the distinctive gift box from Gucci. 'Oh Lenny,' she cried, 'it's lovely.' And she brought the scarf to her face and caressed her cheek with the luxurious silk. 'It's lovely, Lenny,' she said again, 'really so lovely.' Then, with a flourish, she expertly tied the scarf about her neck and said very haughtily, 'Jennifer Spencer has always been a trendsetter. I predict that in less than a month every woman on Wall Street will be wearing silk with denim.'

'Every woman on Wall Street will probably be *here*,' Lenny joked.

'Oh,' Jennifer sighed sadly, 'haven't the people here suffered enough already?' As she opened the door to step into Lenny's car, she saw Springtime in her flower bed. 'It's looking real good, Springtime,' she shouted and waved. Springtime's smile was no different than it had been the day it first sent shivers down Jennifer's spine, but now Jennifer knew her; now the smile had a name, and that made all the difference in the world.

'What's a little old lady like that doing in prison?' Lenny asked.

'She had fields and fields of pot growing north of Albany,' Jennifer laughed. 'She sold it to her friends with glaucoma.' Jennifer took a final long look at Springtime, her flower bed, and the prison walls, then she turned to Lenny and said, 'Take me home now. I'm ready to go home.'

Jennifer and Lenny's eyes met for just a moment, and as always, Lenny nervously looked away. But he didn't move from where he stood next to her. 'It's going to be okay, Jennifer,' he said, looking at his feet. 'Everything will be back to normal before you know it.'

'I don't even remember what normal is,' Jennifer told him.

Lenny lifted his head and stared into her eyes. This time, neither of them looked away – nor did they say anything. Jennifer smiled at Lenny. 'Let's go,' she said, and she opened the door and sank into the front seat of his car. It was the softest thing that she had sat on in almost a year. She closed her eyes, heard Lenny start the engine, and never looked back as they turned out of the prison drive.

As they neared the city, Jennifer kept her nose almost pressed to the window to take in every sight along the way. It was almost too much. After a year of dusty rose, dirty green, and battleship gray, the rich and wonderful hues of New York were almost dizzying. It wasn't long before she felt right back at home. All the stores, all the people, all the traffic. It was all wonderful. 'Hey,' Jennifer shouted, craning her neck as they drove through the street, 'I think that woman back there used to be at Jennings.'

'Lock your doors,' Lenny said reflexively. 'This is a rather rough neighborhood.'

'Bigot,' Jennifer reprimanded him. 'I bet a person isn't any more likely to be robbed on this street than she is on Wall Street.'

'Touché!' Lenny conceded.

It wasn't long before Jennifer realized that they were headed for her loft in Tribeca. She felt her stomach knot in nervous anticipation of her return. How many times had she dreamed of being home? How many times had she returned to this place in her imagination? Now again, she closed her eyes and envisioned her loft. She could see the living room, the kitchen, the bedroom. Nothing was changed – everything was there. But now, in the living room she saw Movita, in the kitchen stood Theresa, and in the bedroom she saw another bed, and on it lay Suki. She opened her eyes and smiled sadly. She was going home – and yet, she feared that she was still going to be homesick.

'You're home,' Lenny said as they rounded a corner and pulled up in front of Jennifer's building. He cut the engine, jumped out of the car, and came around to open her door. 'What's wrong?' he asked when Jennifer made no move to get out.

'I'm afraid,' she replied with a whisper.

Lenny held out his hand. 'Come on,' he said softly, 'there's nothing to be afraid of.' Then he added shyly but with genuine valor, 'I'm right here with you.' He helped her from the car, then took her arm and walked her to the door. 'I don't have my keys,' Jennifer said suddenly as they neared the building. 'When they went looking for the clothes and things I checked in with, all of my stuff was gone,' she said.

'Don't worry,' Lenny assured her. 'I have keys and I made another pair, just in case.'

They let themselves into the building and rode the rather cumbersome, but atmospheric, freight elevator up to Jennifer's loft. Had she ever really lived in this place? Jennifer thought, as the ride brought back memories of a life she thought was gone forever. She tried to remember being here, living here. She tried to recall the nights of making love with Tom. Had he ever really loved her? Did she love him? She didn't know. She supposed the answer was no – and yet, she had enjoyed his company and she did care deeply for his well-being. She could've probably made a marriage to Tom Branston work. Their kids would've been terrific, she thought ruefully. The elevator clanged to a halt and Lenny lifted the wooden gate and escorted her to the familiar door.

Lenny took his key, and without hesitation opened the door and gestured for Jennifer to walk in. The sight of all her beautiful furniture before her caused her to want to cry out in happiness. She reached for Lenny's hand to help her calm herself and to keep from collapsing. She walked around the living room caressing the tabletops and the upholstery fabric. She picked up a throw pillow or two and hugged them to her chest. She walked into the kitchen and ran her fingers over the stove top. A real cooktop. No more hot plates. Then she went into the television room. When she opened the door she was taken aback. 'What are you doing here?' Jennifer asked more calmly than she expected. 'Why are you in my apartment?'

Lenny came over and stood behind Jennifer.

'A friend of yours said I could stay here until you got back,' Cher said, mustering her familiar bravado.

'You're lying,' Jennifer spat back at her.

'No, I'm not,' Cher answered calmly. 'And besides, this isn't what it looks like. I've been looking after your place for you until you got out.'

'And by the looks of you you're taking care of my clothes, too,' Jennifer snapped. 'You took my things from Intake didn't you?'

'Hey, you weren't going to need them anytime soon,' Cher said.

Then there was noise from the bedroom and a man's voice – a familiar one – called out. 'When are you coming back in here?'

'Oh, and you decided to have houseguests too? How convenient,' Jennifer said.

'Well, it's not like he's unfamiliar with the . . .'

Just then the bedroom door swung open and Tom walked into the room wearing nothing but his expensive blue silk boxers. 'Are you going to join me?' he asked and then looked up.

Jennifer stared at him in dumbstruck amazement. She was almost glad that he was giving her yet another reason to despise him. She just looked at him.

'Jennifer?' Tom said in horror, 'Jenny – is that you?'

'Yeah, Tom,' she said sadly, 'it's me.'

'I'm uh – I'm sorry, I uh – didn't think you'd –' he fumbled.

'What's the matter? Aren't you glad to see me?' she said angrily.

'You uh – you, well – you . . .'

Jennifer didn't speak. She felt herself slipping into a rage, and she didn't want to relinquish control of this moment just because she was angry. After taking a deep breath she said quietly, 'I cannot believe that you have done this, Tom. Haven't you hurt me enough already?' There was no more rage left in her, no more hurt – only a deep and powerful sense of indifference. It was, perhaps, the most terrifying emotion she had ever known. She felt Lenny take hold of her hand, and once again she was grateful for this man who had seen her through the darkest days of her life.

'This must be very uncomfortable for you, Jenny,' Tom finally said, breaking the silence.

'And are you comfortable, Tom?' she asked.

He sighed heavily and hung his head. 'No, Jenny, of course I'm not comfortable,' he answered her.

'Please don't call me Jenny,' she said coldly.

Tom only nodded in consent.

'I want to explain what's happening here,' Cher said calmly from where she sat. 'I know you ain't gonna believe this,' she continued, 'but I really am very sorry for what I've done.'

Jennifer snorted in disbelief. 'You've apparently stolen everything that I had,' she said angrily, 'and what you didn't steal you ruined. What gave you the right to do that?'

'What gave you the right to have it?' Cher shot back, standing up to face Jennifer.

'I earned it,' Jennifer snarled at her. 'I earned everything that I had and you took it.' She willed herself not to give in to the sobs that were threatening to erupt from her clenched and aching throat.

'I said I was sorry, Jennifer, and I meant it. I was just watching over everything for you. Trying to help you out.'

'Help me out?' Jennifer repeated, and in spite of her every effort, she burst into tears. 'You've taken over my home, you even took my old boyfriend.' She hated how ridiculous those words sounded. She felt as if she were back in junior high. Her old boyfriend!

'I did not take your boyfriend,' Cher said. 'You gotta let me explain.'

'Explain?' Jennifer snapped. 'There's nothing to explain. I'm not blind. I can see what the two of you have been doing.'

'It's not what it looks like,' Cher insisted.

Lenny had remained silent through this all, but now he

let go of Jennifer's hand and stepped between her and Cher. 'Stop it,' he said with uncharacteristic disgust. 'You two are spitting at each other like a couple of alley cats over a guy who isn't worth the time it would take to run over him with a car.'

Jennifer couldn't believe that Lenny had spoken the words that she heard.

Cher, on the other hand, was laughing. 'You're damned right about that,' she said, and she sat back down on the couch.

Jennifer stared at Cher and considered what she said. Cher had used Tom – just like Cher used everyone. But Jennifer wasn't worried about Tom. 'How have you been managing to live here, Cher? Did you rack up my credit cards? Did you take money from my bank accounts?'

'I did what I had to,' Cher answered.

Jennifer sighed and said nothing more.

'I'm sorry I did it,' Cher offered again.

Jennifer looked at her, then she looked at Tom, then she looked back to Cher. 'I'm sorry you did, too, Cher,' she finally said.

Jennifer looked around at the place she called home. Somehow it didn't seem to matter to her anymore. 'Let's go,' she said to Lenny, then grabbed his hand and led him to the door.

48

Jennifer Spencer

Few rich men own their own property. The property owns them.

Robert Green Ingersoll, address to the
McKinley League, New York

Her fury, Jen decided, was actually a good thing. She left her apartment with Lenny and she was shaking with rage, but that gave her the motor she would use. In the meantime, Lenny took her shaking hand. 'I'm so sorry,' he said. 'It's my fault. I should have gotten into the apartment. I should have . . .'

She looked at him. He was a truly good man and his sense of responsibility was, unlike most men's – deeply overdeveloped. 'No permanent harm done,' Jennifer said. 'I'll take care of it tomorrow.'

'We'll take care of it,' he said. She looked at him and nodded. 'So what do you need right now?' he asked.

'Something clean to wear. Some new shoes. A bath in a big tub with good bath salts, a haircut and a room in a hotel.' She looked around Greenwich Avenue. 'Let's go to Soho,'

she sa~
asked if she ~
walking outdoor~ few blocks away, and though Lenny
She thought of poo~nothing felt better to Jennifer than
ing from the outer corne~ ~t line for as long as she wanted.
then back again. 'You know w~ making her endless spiral-
'Maybe the day after tomorrow?' H~ yard to the center and
'I'd like to walk from Broadway down h~ like to do?' she said.
the Cloisters!' ~d for her to go on.
~l the way up to

Lenny laughed. 'That's over two hundred blocks,' he said.
'You'd have to walk through Soho and the Village, the
Flatiron District, Midtown, the Upper West Side, Morning-
side Heights, Harlem, Washington Heights –'

'Yeah,' she said. 'Wouldn't it be great? I'd end up at the
Cloisters.'

'You'd end up a cripple,' Lenny said.

'Nah, I'm no softie. I'd grease my feet and I'd get a new
pair of Nikes and I'd just go.' She looked around West
Broadway. 'And there would be shops and cafés and restaurants and businesses and apartment buildings. There would
be doormen and people at bus stops and window boxes and
garbage and Korean fruit stands and shoe stores and probably nine Gaps and about fifty Starbuckses and I swear
I'd have a good cup of coffee in every single one along the
way. Boy,' she said, 'you really come to appreciate the little
things.' Then a dress in the window of a shop caught her eye.
It was a pinkish red, and out of a silk that seemed to shine
with a subtle iridescence. 'Oh,' she said, 'that's what I want.'
She'd never had a dress like that in her life. It was girly and
sexy and absolutely inappropriate for business. But it wasn't
cheap. It had a subtle fluid motion to it; the fabric had been
cut so that, simple as the dress was, the slight iridescence of

441

the material seemed to make that move. 'I
want that,' she said.

said, took her arm and

'Then you shall have it
led her into the shop.

at Otto Tootsie Plohound, makeup
at Sephora,
They bought her underwear and a beautiful nightgown at
Joovay and a
sat down, both of them exhausted, at Penang, a restaurant
where the shrimp was fabulous and the décor transported
you to Southeast Asia. They had their own little booth, a
sort of opium den made of bamboo, so small there was
hardly room for the two of them and all their bags.

Lenny had insisted on paying for everything. And once
she had realized that her credit cards were useless – since
Cher had had access to everything – she allowed him to.
'I'm exhausted,' she said. 'But in a good way.' She looked
down at their leftovers. 'I wish Movita and Theresa and
Suki could taste this shrimp,' she said. 'They wouldn't
believe it.' She closed her eyes for a moment and while they
were closed Lenny must have reached out to her, because
she felt his hands enclose hers. She opened her eyes, and he
kept his hands wrapped around hers. It felt really good. 'I
want to thank you,' she said. 'For being such a good friend.
For really being there for me.'

'Oh,' he said, 'come on. You know what really happened.'

'Did I miss something?' she asked. 'I thought that was
what really happened.'

He shook his head. 'I've wanted to be closer to you for
years. Almost since you came to the firm. Your misfortune

was just an opportunity for me to get to know you better. It seemed in a way like taking unfair advantage.'

She laughed. 'Oh, yeah. Those visits in that stinking room were really unfair to me.'

'You know what I mean,' he said.

'Let me tell you what I mean,' she said. 'You saved my life. I don't know how I would have gotten along without your help. I don't think I would have. Thank you, Lenny. Thank you for everything.'

He smiled. 'You're welcome. You know,' he said. 'I'm a little bit frightened that I won't get to see you much now that you're out and free. I'm ashamed to admit that, but it's true.'

'Oh, don't worry,' she said. 'You're going to get to see a lot of me. After all, we have a business to run.' She took a deep breath. 'God, I'm tired,' she said.

He shook his head. 'I'm so sorry about the apartment, I –'

'Don't be ridiculous. I don't think I'd want to go there right now anyway.'

'Well, you're welcome to come to my apartment.'

'Where is your apartment, Lenny?'

'On the Upper East Side,' he admitted. 'Kind of in a boring neighborhood.'

'Does it have a really big bathtub?' she asked.

'I don't think so,' he admitted. 'I shower.'

She nodded her head. 'Yeah, guys shower,' she agreed. 'But I have to have a really good long soak. You know, we only got showers once every three days. And we were watched the whole time.'

Lenny shook his head. 'I'm so sorry.'

'Don't be,' she told him. 'You know it was good for me. It's made me a different person.'

'Well, I like the person you were before,' he said. 'But I think I love the person you are now.'

She grinned at him. He was awfully shy. She figured he didn't have much experience with women, and if she slept with him and it was bad it would be so upsetting, so mortifying to both of them. She wondered for a few minutes about men and women and what was important, and then realized that a few lifetimes wouldn't be enough to figure that one out. It was probably safest for them to just go on with the friendship, working together and enjoying each other, because if she slept with him and then rejected him, it would be too hard for him to take. No man could put up with that. She thought back to her nights with Tom. He was so tall and his shoulders were so broad. She had felt like a little doll when he wrapped his arms around her. Lenny was perhaps five foot eight or nine. His shoulders and hips were narrow and she doubted that he weighed twenty pounds more than she did. But she liked his long, narrow nose and the compassion and feeling in his dark eyes. 'I think I'd like to check into a hotel,' she said. 'Maybe the Mercer has rooms.'

The Mercer Hotel in the very center of Soho has a kind of Zen elegance. The rooms are not large and the décor is a soothing one with dark woods and white walls and luxe but discreet upholstery that doesn't call attention to itself but makes you feel immediately relaxed. The attraction for Jennifer, however, was the bathroom: double doors swung open to reveal an enormous white ceramic tub in the very center of the room. The tiny white mosaic tiled floor seemed to go on for an acre around it and the white marble double sinks, the closets, the Egyptian terry cloth towels as large as bedsheets along with a whole range of FACE shampoos, conditioners, shower gels, bubble baths in big, simple containers instead of those tiny little annoying froufrou sample packs.

'Oh, yes!' she cried as she ran to the tap and started to fill the tub. My God, you could swim half a lap in it or, alternatively, have half the swim team bathe with you.

'My God,' Lenny said as he set the bags down on the bed. 'Is that a bathtub or a sarcophagus?'

'Either will do for me,' Jennifer told him. 'I want to soak for hours and if I die, well, it would make a great last resting place.' She poured all of the bath salts into the swirling water of the tub and looked over at him. He was shifting from one foot to the other. He looked suddenly very uncomfortable. Poor Lenny. He was a nice looking man, his face long, his jaw square and shadowed now with the beginning of the need for a second shave of the day. Maybe that's why his skin was so nice. She had read somewhere that men's skin benefited from being exfoliated by shaving. She walked toward him.

'I guess I'll have to go now,' he said, obviously regretful.

She made a serious face. 'But Lenny,' she said. 'You hate wasting money. I'm paying for a double room. There's a double bed.' She swung open the closet door. 'And there are two robes. I can't wear both of them.'

He looked at her for a moment, not comprehending. Then the implications of her words sank in.

'You can stay over,' she said. 'And you can make love to me. And we can sleep together all night and we can have a room-service breakfast together and read the paper together. But you have to make me two promises.' He nodded. 'The first one is, if we never do it again you'll still be my good friend.'

'Of course I will,' he said.

'Oh, don't speak so quick. Men's egos, you know.' Meanwhile she thought, what the hell? He might not be a very experienced or good lover but he was an experienced and good man. She could at least try it. After all, she'd been in prison for the last eleven months. It had to be better than that.

'What's the second promise?' he asked.

'That I get to take my bath for as long as I want all by myself.'

Lenny smiled. 'Can I at least watch?'

'You have to watch,' she said. 'And maybe you have to wash my back.' He was just her height and he took her face gently in both his hands and brought her mouth to his. His lips were soft, gentle. He tugged at her lower lip with his own, then bit lightly. They both smiled, looking at each other. From that close, he was blurry. She closed her eyes again, letting herself be pulled into those soft lips. She tasted his breath, fresh, like sweet corn. It was so long since she'd kissed a man! Now they kissed harder. The pressure against her lips felt so good. This *was* good, she thought as she reached up to touch his neck. She brushed his cheek, feeling the bristle, caressing it for a moment, scruffy, manly. Then she held on to the back of his neck, his head, caressing his hair. She found it was softer, finer, than she'd expected.

He was caressing her back now, massaging her, pulling her close to him. She felt as if she'd come alive all over. She could go on like this for a long time. This was *very* good.

What a surprise! The man really knew how to kiss. Maybe he knew more . . .

Then, as Lenny pulled away for a moment to touch her cheek, she opened her eyes and saw the tub behind him about to overflow. 'Oh, my God!' she said. 'Oh, my God!' The two of them got there in time to turn off the taps and to throw towels down to take up the water that had overflowed. They laughed hysterically, half from nerves and half from the fun of it.

The bath she took was warm, luxurious, exciting, and relaxing. And she liked having Lenny watch her and soap her back, prolonging the anticipation. Then, when she was fully dried off – the fluffy white towels of the Mercer Hotel were so luxurious after the skin-scraping rags she'd become accustomed to – she let herself be enfolded in Lenny's arms and pampered some more. At first, everything was soft and gentle and all about caressing her and soothing her aching body, but then things suddenly turned. He touched her nipples, gently, then harder and harder until she moaned. When she opened her eyes he smiled at her. It was a wicked, teasing smile. 'You like teasing?' she asked, and she moved her hand down to him, touching him until he was so hard she could feel his pulse. Then she withdrew. Her teasing made him vigorous and energetic, and she found herself tangling with him on the bed, almost sparring. He held her shoulders down, at last, and rolled on top of her. She was surprised and delighted to find such voraciousness beneath Lenny's calm exterior. And her own full-body participation, as well as his passion and teasing skill, brought her a welcome release after so many months of unfulfilled longings.

49

Jennifer Spencer

*As long as possible live free and uncommitted. It makes
but little difference whether you are committed to a
farm or the county jail.*

Henry David Thoreau

Jennifer woke up in the big bed of the Mercer Hotel, Lenny
lying beside her, and for a moment – a long moment – she
didn't know where she was. She wasn't home and she wasn't
in prison. Had it all been a dream? Or was this a dream?
Then she remembered not only their day together, but their
night, and smiled. In that mysterious way that lovers have
Lenny must have sensed she was awake because his eyes
opened slowly. She'd never noticed before what long lashes
he had. 'Hello, gorgeous,' he said.

'Hello, sexy,' she told him.

Before they had a chance to compliment one another
any further the phone rang. She looked at him. He
shrugged. 'Does anyone know you're here?' she asked.

He shook his head. 'Are you kidding? It must be the
desk,' he said. 'They'll call to see if we're checking out.'

'At this time of morning?' she asked.

'What time is it?' he asked.

'I don't know,' she said.

They both laughed and he reached over for the phone. He listened for a moment and his eyes opened wider. 'Oh,' he said. 'Hello.' And looked over at her. 'It's Cher,' he mouthed.

Jennifer grabbed the phone. 'You have nerve,' she said. 'How did you know we were here?'

'Oh, please,' Cher said. 'You think I don't know Lenny's credit card numbers? You think I can't find out where anyone is if they've charged something?' Jennifer threw Lenny a look of disbelief and shook her head. 'What do you want?' she asked Cher.

Cher's voice was insistent. 'I'd like to meet with you and explain a few things . . .'

'You're a thief and a bitch. No explanation needed,' Jennifer cut her off. She heard Cher sigh on the other end of the line.

'Well,' Cher said. 'Both of those things are true, but it's my motivation that you have to examine.' She paused. 'I did it for you,' she said.

Jennifer laughed out loud. Lenny looked over at her as if he were ready to get on the line and end any problems she was having. Jennifer waved him away; she could handle this herself. 'Thanks, Cher. That might work on morons but not on me.'

'Listen, I've gotten into Tom's portfolio and files, as well as his pants and your apartment,' Cher insisted. 'I've bankrupted him. He doesn't know it yet, but he's penniless.'

Jennifer reconsidered. Still, it was probably just Cher's selfish motivations that made her steal the money. 'Well, thank you for that. It was very selfless of you,' Jennifer said sarcastically.

'Hey, don't go off on me,' Cher told her. 'Your boyfriend is a bad guy as well as a bad fuck. I think you ought to meet with me.'

Jennifer sighed. She wished this was all over with and she could just have her home back. But there was nothing she could do. 'Okay,' Jennifer agreed.

An hour later, Jennifer found herself sitting across from Cher at a stylish, minimalist table at the Mercer Kitchen, the restaurant in the hotel. She couldn't get over how different this was from camping out over a simple home-made dinner in Movita's cell. The silverware, the napkins, the service, and the delicacy of the Euro-Thai cuisine were a continual shock to Jennifer. Unfortunately, Cher was distracting her with a play-by-play of her bad love life with Tom.

'Didn't you ever take the time to teach him how to go down on you?' Cher asked in disbelief. 'Okay, at his age he should know how, but you were engaged to the dumb fuck. You were going to live with that boring tongue action for the rest of your life? Is he a man or a Labrador retriever?'

Cher looked great. All of Jennifer's clothes seemed to suit her, and Jennifer didn't know whether Cher had started going to Angelo or not but her hair looked fantastic as well. It had been cut two different lengths but was now straight and shiny. She had something that had seemed missing before. Not that Cher was ever stupid, but now she seemed, well, classy. Jennifer had never believed that clothes made the man but in this case they seemed to have made the woman into a lady. No wonder she could fool everyone, Jennifer thought. She was a chameleon. If I didn't know where she came from, if I didn't know for sure about prison, I would never believe it.

'Look,' Cher said. 'I know I haven't treated you well and I know you probably don't like me or trust me and I don't blame you. But you can't blame me for the way I used to treat you because you used to be a bitch.'

Jennifer stiffened. 'What's your point, Cher? Did you drag me out to insult me?'

'No, I mean you changed.' Cher calmed her down. 'When you first got to prison you walked in it like you were God's only child and we were dirt. And I'm willing to admit that I took attitude against you but I think you can understand why.'

Jennifer interrupted. 'Well, you were a real bitch to me when I first came in.'

Cher nodded. 'I know I was, and for that I'm sorry. Once I saw you being so good to Suki and to Movita, and then when I saw what you did when you found out about what those bastards were up to at JRU, I was really impressed. And I don't impress easy. You jumped right the fuck in.'

Jennifer couldn't stop herself from smiling. She'd never heard Cher praise her before.

Cher continued. 'I know you took a risk doin' that. It was good of you. And what ya' done since, well I don't think no one but you coulda done it. Oh, the Prez, she woulda wanted to, but she didn't know how.'

'Cher, if you were so impressed with me,' Jennifer had to say, 'then why'd you get out and take over my life?'

'Let me finish,' Cher insisted. 'I gotta tell my story my way. That's just the way I am.'

Jennifer signaled the waiter for another glass of wine. She was going to need it.

'You took the best each person had to give and you found a way to make it work for the good of everyone,' Cher continued. 'And there wasn't nothin' in that for you. I thought you were a selfish bitch, and suddenly, to tell you the truth, I had to admit you'd changed. By the time I stole you that cell phone and got it set up for you, I was startin' to kinda like ya'.'

Jennifer was getting a little tipsy from the wine. 'I liked you too, Cher. You know I couldn't have done it without that cell phone.'

'Oh, you woulda found a way,' Cher insisted. 'Anyway, you don't have to believe me or nothing. I can disappear long before you can stop me. But the point is I didn't do this to hurt you or steal from you.'

'How can you say that when you're sitting there in my suit?' Jennifer protested. Suddenly, she looked around the restaurant, wondering if anyone was overhearing this crazy conversation. She bet that the Mercer Kitchen had never been witness to a conversation between two ex-convicts before.

'Okay, okay,' Cher admitted. 'At first I needed a place to crash and I thought maybe I'd wear your clothes for a little while, but then, well, I heard what you were doing and I just thought someone should do something for you.'

Jennifer almost spat up her wine. 'What? How is living in my place for free and stealing my clothes and my boyfriend your idea of a reward?'

'Shit, girl, I wouldn't fuck him for money.' Cher took a swig of water. 'I established myself. It didn't take me long to get a new social security number and a new name and I got a job. I'm working on the Street.' She lifted her eyebrows. 'Not as a prostitute, on Wall Street. I found a boiler room a friend of mine had set up and from that I moved up to a discount brokerage firm, but I was sellin' so much goddamn stock that the sons-of-bitches kept moving me up and now I'm managing portfolios.'

'Cher!' she said. 'What do you know about portfolio management?' She couldn't believe her. But it was an even crazier story to make up.

Cher grinned. 'I know enough to get your boyfriend to put his money in my hands.' Jennifer raised her brows. Tom was greedy, but he was very cautious. 'I doubt that,' she said.

'Hey, look. We got an expression: No one easier to con than a con.' She paused. 'Okay, I admit I had to have him put a few other things in my hands, but it was a small price to pay.'

'A small price to pay for what?' Jennifer asked, completely out of patience.

'For watching him go broke,' Cher said with a deeply satisfied smile. 'He doesn't know it yet but I've put him into every bad deal I could find. I've given him positions even a contortionist couldn't survive.' She laughed. 'But that isn't all,' she said.

Jennifer laughed, too. She couldn't take all this in. 'What do you mean? There's more?'

The lunch crowd had begun to thin out and Jennifer was on her third glass of wine. It was going to her head more than in the old days, before the eleven-month abstinence of prison.

Cher nodded. 'I also got copies of all of Tom's files and I have the goods on him and Donald Michaels on your deal and a few previous ones. In writing: contracts and memos signed by them.'

Jennifer shook her head. 'But how did you gain Tom's trust? Didn't he find you in my apartment?'

'I just told him I was a friend of yours, and once I got set up at my new job, he believed me. It's amazing how gullible these smart guys can be,' Cher shrugged. 'Hey, Jen – were you ever raped in prison?'

Jennifer turned white. She'd heard too many stories. 'No, thank God.'

'Well, Tommy boy is a little too pretty for his own good. I'm tellin' you once we get his lily ass in prison, that bitch is gonna be cleanin' somebody else's house.' Cher smirked. Then she reached into her pocket. She took out a big wad of cash. 'Look, I owe ya' this from when I first moved in. I had to use some of your charge cards and shit and here's all the rent I woulda paid ya'. I'm not even askin' for a discount.' She handed Jennifer a wad of bills. All hundreds.

Jennifer looked down at the roll and wouldn't count it right then, but there had to be ten, maybe fifteen thousand dollars, maybe more. She stuffed it into her new purse. And to think she had been worried about money when she shopped yesterday afternoon.

'Thanks, Cher,' Jennifer said finally. 'I didn't expect this.'

'I know ya' didn't,' Cher said. 'But listen, if you still want to turn me in you can call the police, or Tom, or my parole officer, who – by the way – I'm fuckin' too, and he knows how to do it.'

'No, Cher, I would never –' Jennifer started.

Cher cut her off. 'Good, 'cause what I'd like, what I'd really like is for you to just get back at these guys who rail-roaded you and then maybe leave me in my job without blowin' the whistle. I never thought I'd say it, but I kinda like being legit. Not that it's all that different from what I used to do.'

The waiter came by to see if Jennifer wanted more wine. 'Actually, I'll have a Cosmopolitan,' Jennifer said. This sounded like a celebration.

Cher made eyes up to the ceiling. 'Oh, Christ, Deb. Nobody drinks those anymore.' Cher ordered a top-shelf, single-malt scotch on the rocks.

Jennifer just had to sit there for a few minutes to take it all in. 'So, I still don't get something.'

'You need me to tell you the whole friggin' story again?' Cher asked.

'No,' Jennifer said. 'Just tell me again, how did you get Tom to trust you?'

Cher laughed. 'Oh, come on. These kinda guys never think women have enough brains to screw them. We're the screwees. All I had to do was offer it up and hang around for the ride. If ya' keep your mouth shut most of the time except when you're praising them or they've got their dick in it, they'll believe anything. Don't pretend you don't know that.'

Jennifer stared at Cher and then she began to laugh. 'You,' she said, 'are a real piece of work.'

Luckily, their drinks arrived just then, and they were able to toast to that.

'Duh,' Cher teased her. 'And you just noticed, huh? No wonder they could railroad you so easy.'

Jennifer didn't take offense. It was true, so she began to laugh and laugh and then for a few minutes she actually couldn't stop. It was a little frightening, but all of the adjustments that she had had to make in the last twenty-four hours, from leaving Jennings to her shock at the apartment to her spending spree and her incredibly wonderful night with Lenny upstairs at the hotel were, she had to admit, a bit much for any girl.

Cher pushed her hand from across the table. 'Don't you go off on me,' she said. But then she started to laugh, too. 'Friends?' she asked.

'Oh, yeah,' Jen said. 'Friends. But let me tell you about the little plan that I've worked out that you might want to help me with.' She leaned forward. 'Do you really think Movita and Suki and Theresa should still be in prison?' she asked.

'Holy shit,' Cher said. 'I am not getting involved in a fuckin' jail break.'

Jennifer laughed again. 'Oh, come on, Cher. I appreciate the compliment but I'm not that bold, or that stupid. Still, I do have a plan.' She leaned forward again and quietly began explaining.

50

Jennifer Spencer

*You're so sure you're not going back to the same crowd.
But pretty soon you be hanging out with the same ol'
crowd again, just to feel like you belong somewhere.*

Theresa Derry, an inmate at SCI Muncy, Pennsylvania.
Kathryn Watterson, *Women in Prison*

Jennifer went over every detail with Lenny to make sure that she hadn't left anything out. He had to admit two things: that the plan could work, and that he wouldn't mind staying on at the Mercer for a little while. 'It's just for the towels,' he said.

Jennifer laughed, grabbed him around the neck with the crook of her arm and pulled him down onto the bed. 'Miss Spencer,' he said. 'What are you thinking of? The chambermaids just made this bed.'

'Dumb move,' she said, and then she showed him a few of her own.

Later, stretched out in the bathtub, she thought she'd never take a bath again without appreciating it. Now, when she looked back, she realized that she had thought she knew

Lenny, but she hadn't appreciated him. She shook her head, wetting her hair. Well, she'd have a professional cut today to prepare her for this evening's showdown. She thought for a few moments about what other preparations she might need. Cher promised to have the written records and the computerized ones of the questionable Hudson, Van Schaank transactions ready. Lenny, she was sure, could serve as a witness with a lot of clout since, unlike herself and Cher, he was not a convicted felon. She allowed her feet to float in the deep tub and stared up at the ceiling. She wondered why these rooms, so simple as to almost be stark, were beautifully pleasant while the rooms at Jennings were so hideously ugly. She stared up at the white ceiling and let her entire body float on the warm pillow of bath water.

Lenny lay asleep in their bed. He was an amazing lover, and she wondered if he always had been or if this was a special effort inspired by her. If it was the former she'd just been stupid and blind; if it was the latter she was touched and grateful. Speaking of touched, she felt her fingers pruning up. Underwater they looked like white raisins. Perhaps she'd been in the bath long enough. She looked over at the white freesia that Lenny had bought for her. She could smell them from the tub, though they weren't splashy or even particularly rare. They were just beautiful, the green of their stems so perfect, long and thin as dancers, the white of their blossoms creamy, and the graceful way the blossom moved horizontally across an extension perpendicular to the stem, with each flower or bud getting smaller and smaller. Oh, it broke her heart that she had gone without a single blossom for almost a year. She stopped and counted. Well, there had been the chrysanthemums at Christmas and Springtime's marigolds, but she didn't think she could ever like those flowers again.

Prison had wasted more than eleven months of her life, but wouldn't they have been equally wasted at Hudson, Van Schaank? All she'd been doing, her apartment, her antiques, her Kirmans, and her portfolios . . . When she'd been sent to Jennings she had been a selfish, narrow young woman. She had lost touch with her old friends and didn't have any new ones – except for her so-called fiancé and her boss, both of whom turned out to be . . . she searched for Lenny's term. Oh yes, yellow rat bastards. Her judgment, her values, her goals, and her viewpoints had all been questionable. Prison had set her free. She knew the most important thing wasn't how much money she made, or how successful her next deal was, or how many people envied and respected her, or how powerful her friends were. She shivered, though the tub water was still warm. She had taken for granted all of life's most important pleasures and she had been a pouting child when they'd been taken away from her. She had never admitted her guilt, nor taken responsibility for losing her way as she had. Jennings had been dreadful, but through imprisonment she'd found freedom. She was no longer afraid. She didn't need to keep a big apartment, or a large paycheck, or a big wardrobe. She needed to keep her friends, and her freedom. She wanted to be free of fear.

Though she had changed, one thing in New York certainly hadn't. Balthazar was still the hottest restaurant in the city and dinner there on a Friday night wasn't easy to plan. The room was massive and the crowd was loud. The décor was such a perfect re-creation of a French bistro that she had heard the O'Malley brothers had actually imported French dust that they had ground into the tile floors. The red banquettes with chairs opposite were desirable, but not as desirable as the semicircular seating on the east and south wall. Above them hung squares of old mirrors pieced together to form large mirrors, ornately framed. The ceiling, a dark beige pressed-tin, still had a few playing cards stuck to it where previous parties had taken place. Jen remembered a Christmas party where Donald Michaels had reserved the whole restaurant for a soiree. A magician had been hired and one of the tricks was to have a participant sign his name to a random card in a deck. When all the cards were thrown into the air the only one that stuck to the ceiling was the one that had been signed. Jen looked down at her own feet as she and Lenny entered. Her foot was beautifully covered in the new Otto Tootsic Plohound shoes. The floors were beautifully covered in tiny mosaic tiles. They walked through the crowd to the deep mahogany bar, but it was so crowded that Lenny took her to the back where all the luscious seafood was laid out on beds of crushed ice.

It was a good place from which to observe the crowd, a combination of downtown hipsters, Wall Streeters, beautiful women, and the occasional rich family or older couple celebrating some anniversary or event. Despite the crowd it was easy to spot Tom and Cher when they came in. Cher, who seemed to have given up her flamboyant style, still managed to glow. While she had adopted a patina of pampered grooming there was still something raw and vibrant about her that shined through. For a moment Jennifer could hardly bear to look at Tom – not because she still loved him but because she was ashamed that she had ever thought she did. He looked so untouchable and self-satisfied that for a moment she really wondered if she could pull this off. His harsh judgment of Lenny and his off-loading of her weren't justified by his smooth good looks, his perfectly tailored suit, and his aura of impeccable breeding. Then she pulled herself together and got ready.

They were seated at table fifty-three – one of the best circular banquettes – by Zuair, the maitre d'. 'Let's go,' she told Lenny, and took his hand for a moment. He gave her hand a squeeze, as if he knew she'd been shaken. She led the way through the crowd.

'Well, hello,' she said, looking down at the two of them. Tom looked up and for a moment his face froze. Then he managed a smile.

'Oh, surely we're not going to have another scene, Jennifer.' He looked over at Lenny and registered surprise, or was it . . . contempt? Whatever it was, it enraged her.

'A scene?' she asked. 'Certainly not.' And she slid into the banquette next to him while Lenny slid beside Cher. There was no way he could get out, short of ducking under the table and scrabbling away. She knew Tom well enough to know that he'd rather die than make a public spectacle.

'I don't remember asking you to join us,' Tom said. 'Lenny, why don't you take Jennifer out of here.'

'Why don't you listen to what Jennifer has to say,' Lenny told him.

Tom turned to Cher. 'I'm sorry about this,' he said. 'It's almost like having a stalker.'

'Shut up, you motherfucker,' Cher told him.

Tom blinked. 'What?' he managed to ask, as if his ears couldn't take the obscenity in.

'Shut the fuck up, you douche, and listen to Jennifer before I get your knees broken.'

Tom blinked again. 'I don't understand,' he said.

'Well, it's necessary that you do,' Jennifer said. 'Now listen, I'll cut to the chase: I have all the documentation I need to put you in prison for the next ten years at least. And believe me, it won't be a country club.'

'Don't be ridiculous,' he said.

'I'm talking about the Anderson deal, the Thompson acquisition. I'm talking about your insider position on the Bayler-Crups merger. I'm talking about the secret purchases you've made for Donald. That's leaving out how you perjured yourself and misrepresented my case. It's also leaving out Donald, and how he'd throw you to the wolves in a heartbeat – if he had a heart. If it would protect his ass from the FCC.'

'I have more,' Lenny added 'And some of it I witnessed. I can testify under oath.'

'Do you think you're scaring me?' Tom asked.

'I don't really care how you feel,' Jennifer told him. 'I'm just telling you the drill: You go to Donald. You get me the money he owes me – the money he promised me – as well as a pardon from the governor.' She handed him a piece of paper. 'And you get a pardon for these women as well.'

'I will not even discuss this,' Tom said. 'I am an attorney. You're talking about privileged information . . .'

'Well, I'm a thief,' Cher interrupted him to say. 'And I've stolen quite a bit of privileged information myself. All of your portfolio statements, your files, your correspondence on the Thompson and Bayler-Crup deals. I even have a few tapes of you and Donald talking about your latest scheme, that Canadian petrochemical company.'

'What are you talking about?' Tom asked. 'What do you mean you stole this information?'

Cher yawned. 'I mean that I went through your mail and your desk and your briefcase. I have copies of your phone bills, I duped your laptop files.'

'How, how could . . .'

'It was my pleasure,' Cher said. She reached over and took Jennifer's hand. 'Anything for a pal,' she said, and smiled real wide at Tom.

He got very pale. Jennifer could see the perspiration forming in tiny pinhead drops on his upper lip and just over his brows.

'The only reason why a woman – other than dumb Jenny here – would fuck you, pencil dick, is because she needed access to your wallet, your contacts, or your data bank. Make sure you remember that the next time you climb up on top of some little heifer, 'cause you've climbed up on me for the last time. Thank God.' Cher looked over at Jennifer. 'Please, promise me I don't have to fuck him again. It's so damn boring I'm afraid my heart will just stop beating. Even as a favor to you it's been tough to swallow, you should pardon the expression.' She smiled brightly at Tom. 'My friend here wants you to be the intermediary with your boss. I suggest you do it. I tell you, I know a lot of men in prison and I think you'd dislike getting fucked by them even more than I disliked getting fucked by you.'

Just then the Balthazar waiter approached the table. 'Would you like to hear the specials?' he asked.

'No, thank you,' Jennifer said. 'I've just gotten out of prison and I have an enormous craving for seafood. Could we get the triple crown and a vintage bottle of Veuve Clicquot? I didn't have any champagne in prison either.'

The waiter laughed. 'Any other drinks?' he asked.

Cher shook her head and indicated Tom with her chin.

'He doesn't get any choices,' she said. 'And the funny thing is, he pays the bill. But I'd like a bottle of champagne, too.' She turned to Tom and smiled. He seemed to be in a state of shock, speechless, or maybe beyond speech. 'He'll just watch,' Cher said.

51

Jennifer Spencer

Injustice is relatively easy to bear; what stings is justice.

H. L. Mencken, *Prejudices: Third Series*

'But I wanna come.'

'And I want to be an astronaut. But it's not going to happen in this lifetime,' Jen told Cher.

'But why? I did so good with Tom.'

Jennifer put down the blow-dryer and checked out her makeup in her bathroom mirror. She and Cher were both there, though Cher had found her own apartment in Chelsea and was moving in on the first of the month. 'You know, Cher, I don't want to hear the details of what you did with Tom,' Jen said.

'Oh, come on. I did it for you. Please, please can't I come to the meeting with Donald Michaels?'

'No, you can't.'

'Just give me one good reason.'

'Because you tried to set him up as a future mark.'

'Okay. Point taken. But give me another good reason.'

Jennifer hated to admit it, but she actually liked having Cher at her place. And though she did have a real concern that at any moment the bunko squad might knock on the door and take her off in cuffs, she was proud of Cher for going so far toward legitimacy. (The fact that Cher, with all of her predatory traits, was thriving on Wall Street was only another indication to Jennifer that perhaps it wasn't tragic that she would no longer be permitted to be in that line of work.)

In fact, she had almost definitely decided that she wanted to continue working with women in prison. She wasn't sure how yet, but she knew she didn't want to go back to a life where her comforts and her plans were the only important things in it. Jennifer looked at herself in the full-length mirror. She wasn't wearing one of her business suits – that was over. She instead had on a pair of black slacks and a simple white shirt.

'You look great,' Cher told her. 'Like you just got outta prison. So give me one more reason.'

'I am not giving you another reason. It's something I have to do on my own.'

'Don't bullshit me,' Cher said. 'And put on a little more lipstick. You don't have to look like a dyke.'

Jennifer picked up a tube of Nars and remembered the Adobe Red Cher had handed out at Jennings.

'Lenny's coming with you,' Cher said, and sounded exactly like a four-year-old.

'No, he isn't,' Jennifer told her. 'This is something I have to do myself. But if I need reinforcements you and Lenny will be the first two people I'll call.'

'You suck,' Cher said.

'This, from a woman who had sex with my ex-fiancé,' Jennifer responded, then picked up her purse and went out the door.

Nothing in Donald's office had changed, least of all Donald himself. He sat, well buffed, well coiffed, well dressed, and well fed, his feet – well shod as ever – up on the desk and crossed at the ankles as usual. The only time his feet came down from the desk was when he had to walk to his limo or kick someone's ass, Jennifer thought. Somehow, staring at his shoe sole – certainly the only soul he possessed – bothered her more than coming into the Hudson, Van Schaank & Michaels building, going past the receptionists and ex-coworkers, waiting in Donald's private reception area or even seeing Tom, slightly pale, enter the room. She had once read that, during his presidency, Lyndon Johnson used to go to the toilet and defecate during meetings, expecting his cabinet members to follow him while he continued the conversation. Somehow staring at the bottom of Donald's shoe was like that.

'I want it very clear that it is only as a courtesy that I am seeing you,' Donald began. 'Tom came to me with your demands, and I want you to hear this very clearly, Jennifer: You have no grounds for these allegations and I am not intimidated. Now, if you have something else to say, say it, because I have a meeting – an important one – in ten minutes.'

So it was going to be like that. Jen just shrugged. 'I don't have a wire on,' she told Donald. 'You don't have to bother with your broadcast to the troops.' Jennifer stood up and in less than three seconds opened her shirt, unzipped her pants and dropped both to the ground. She turned around briefly. 'There,' she said. 'See?' One thing prison had done for her was buff her up. She wanted to show these two jerkoffs something perfect they'd never have. She didn't look at the two men's reactions. She merely bent down, pulled up the slacks, buttoned the waist and slipped back into her top. After the group showers and everything else she'd been through at Jennings, this was no big deal, but it made a hell of an impression on the two of them.

'Are you offering yourself to me?' Donald asked.

Jennifer actually laughed aloud. 'Yes, and I've converted to Islam,' she said, then sat down and crossed her legs. She shook her head. 'Don,' she said, consciously using the nickname he hated. 'Don, I wouldn't fuck you with Tom's dick. Now, let's get serious. I don't know if you are recording this, but that nonsense about blackmail can be disregarded. Let me make this short and sweet. We made an agreement. I took the fall for you and you were going to pay me.'

'Jennifer, there was no wrongdoing on my part,' Donald began. 'You know perfectly well.'

'Don, say that one more time and I'm going to have to make you strip. I'll take off my clothes and start to scream rape. So just cut the crap and let's get down to cases. You owe me eleven months' salary, bonuses from two Christmases, and the down payment on a larger apartment. You never promised me that last one, but since prices appreciated while I was in prison, I'm adding it instead of interest. Consider it the vig.'

Donald was silent for a minute. 'What else?' he asked.

'I want him out of here,' she said.

'You mean, fired?' Donald asked, looking at Tom.

'Hey,' Tom said. But neither of them was paying much attention to him.

'No,' she said. 'Although it's an interesting idea. I just want him out of here now.'

'Is that really necessary?' Donald asked calmly.

'Donald, as your counsel, I . . .'

'Shut up,' Jennifer told him. She looked directly at Donald. 'This is not negotiable,' she said.

'Thomas, would you excuse us?' Donald said, as smooth as marble and just as hard.

Tom tried to object but Donald made the movement of his hand that meant no discussion was possible. Slowly, reluctantly, Tom stood and looked at Jennifer, the expression in his eyes the one she had waited for for almost a year: fear. It took all of her willpower not to smile. He stood up and walked hesitantly to the door. She didn't allow herself to turn around, but she watched Donald's hand and knew that Tom had tried to speak before he closed the door.

She sat for a moment and let the silence build. Before prison she never could have tolerated the pressure but now talking to Donald – Don – was NBD. She waited and then waited. He spoke at last. 'All right, Jennifer. What's it going to be? I'm not saying that I'm committing to anything but at least let me hear your demands.'

'I don't look at them as demands, Don,' she said calmly. And she felt calm. 'I look at them as choices. Choices for you to make.' She reached into her purse and took out several dozen pages. She put them at the edge of his desk so he had to put his feet down to get at them. He rifled through them and, though he was famous for his poker face, she thought she saw a flicker of concern. He put the papers down and his feet back up.

'Is that your whole hand?' he asked.

'Oh, no,' she said. And she told him all of the information

that Cher had gathered, along with the corroborating evidence that Lenny Benson and others would give. 'We've been through all the files,' she said. 'And accessed your computer. And you've been very negligent in the trades you've been making in the last year and a half with Peter Grant.' She handed him the file on those. 'The SEC will be calling you on that,' she said. 'Sooner or later.'

Donald looked down at the statements. 'I didn't do these trades,' he said.

'And I didn't do your crime,' she told him. 'But I did do your time. Hey, it's your name, social security number, and your code word. By the way, how is Grendel?'

'My dog?' he asked. And she saw the light dawn in his eyes. 'How much more of this stuff is there?' he asked.

'Plenty,' she told him. Though in truth her quiver was just about empty. Still, it would serve.

'Jennifer, you know the money isn't an issue. So what is it you want?'

She handed her last sheet of paper to him. 'Gubernatorial pardons for those three inmates. You have their numbers and the pertinent information.'

'Jennifer, one of these women is a murderer. I couldn't even get *you* a pardon.'

'You didn't even try,' she told him. And when he began to argue she made the hand motion he always used. 'We've had an election since then, and I know that your contributions got him reelected.'

He stopped. 'Is that it?' he asked.

'There's one more thing,' she told him, and allowed herself a smile. He waited. 'About Tom,' she said.

52

Movita Watson

*All that we know who lie in gaol is that the wall is
strong.*

Oscar Wilde, *The Ballad of Reading Gaol*

'I don't like this, Theresa. I don't like this one bit,' I said,
looking at the paper in my hand. 'I think this has got to be
baaad news!'

Theresa had the same kinda paper as me and was
readin' it like I was. It was a summons to go to the
Warden's office. I don't mean an official summons, like to
go to court. I mean that the Warden was tellin' us that we
had to come in there. Now I see her nearly every day and if
she's got any news for me of a decent sort, even if it ain't
great, she just tells it to my face or sends someone to bring
me up there. But this was a note – handwritten by her, and
signed.

'Don't assume,' Theresa said. 'It makes an ass of you and
me.' I swear I almost tole her to take her happy little readin'
away with this worried expression.

471

'What do you think it could be, Movita?' Suki asked, holding her baby and an envelope just like ours.

It was just what I was afraid of. I threw my summons down onto my bunk. 'You got one, too. I'm almost sure that it has to do with Suki and Christina. That child's gonna be twelve months old and that's about the limit for keepin' her in here. She's gonna have to let her go.'

'Oh, no!' Suki moaned.

'Are you sure?' Theresa asked.

It was all I could do not to cry, seein' 'em there happy and so much a part of each other. I told Suki my idea as quickly as I could. She went through all kinda expressions on her face as she listened and then broke into tears and hugged Christina to her.

'I know that's what it's about,' she said. 'I been sick about it.'

'Well you bein' sick ain't gonna do no good at all,' I whispered loudly.

'Then why does she want to see *us*?' Theresa asked.

'Obviously 'cause she don't want Suki to be by herself,' I said. It irritated me when Theresa didn't just listen when I knew somethin' for sure. 'It's like havin' the family in. She wants us there helpin' the girl. Me because I went through it with my kids, and you because you're so damn fulla wisdom.'

'How terrible! Suki's going to be heartbroken.' Theresa looked at me with that look she's got like a helpless animal. For someone who's always tellin' others not to give up, she gives up awful fast herself.

'Not if it don't happen,' I said. 'We got to think of some way for her to keep her longer. She's up for parole in a little over a year.'

I went over to the sink to wash my hands, and got one of those pangs that I always get over my own kids. Damn it all to hell, I thought, it never changes. I'm always wantin' so bad what I can never have.

'I think we should tell the Warden that Christina is sick,' I said, turning around to Suki and Theresa, 'and that for the time bein' she needs to stay with her mother.'

Theresa looked at me and then the baby, real doubtful. 'That child is the picture of health,' she said.

'Sick children don't always look bad,' I answered. 'Besides, the way I see it, the Warden favors Christina and Suki both and if she could think of an excuse to help keep the baby in here, she would do it. We just got to give her one.'

'But a doctor is going to have to see the baby. And you can't fool a doctor,' Suki cried.

I snorted. As if. 'Yes, you can,' I said, tucking my shirt in. 'The child can't speak, so you'll just say that she has some kinda symptoms during the night, like cramps or something.'

Theresa shook her head. 'I don't know . . .' she said.

'Theresa,' I warned, 'we gotta try. That child is still just a baby and needs to be with her mother. It's barbaric to separate 'em and you know it. The Warden knows it. Now c'mon!'

We called Officer Mowbry over and told her we were ready to go. She unlocked the door and we all walked to Warden Harding's office, but we walked real slow, like it was the last mile. During the time we did, I tried to think of more possible symptoms we could say that Christina had. I was rememberin' my own kids' problems, like with teethin' and colds and stuff, but none a that was serious.

Suki started to cry and that started Christina fussin'. Which was no bad thing, if Suki would shut up.

'Now stop that,' I tole her. 'Act like it's all a surprise. And you gotta think a some way that Christina's sick.'

Suki just kept on cryin'. By this time not only her and Christina but Theresa had tears in her eyes, too. We were a miserable-lookin' group when Warden Harding opened her door and asked us to come in. We walked in like goin' to the gallows. And then the confusin' thing was that the Warden herself looked happier than the day we got the prison back from them JRU bastards. She just started cooin' at Christina, which I thought was a damn cold thing to do, considering she was about to see her handed off to foster care.

'How's my favorite little girl?' she asked, lookin' at the baby and positively radiatin' happiness. I was about to scream, thinkin' that maybe the Warden liked the idea of Christina leavin' the prison.

The Warden gave Christina back to Suki and sat down. She looked at all of us, still smilin' like crazy.

'I have news for all of you,' she said. 'Very important and very good news.'

None of us said a word or moved a muscle. I swear, even that baby was still. What could it be? 'Our friend Jennifer Spencer has done it again,' the Warden said. 'She has secured unconditional pardons from the governor for all three of you.'

I musta been crazy right at that moment. I know it's a sin to admit, but I got a feelin' of terrible, terrible sadness, thinkin' that the three was Theresa and Suki and Christina, and that only I was goin' to stay there forever. But the Warden was smilin' at me most of all, and there were tears in *her* eyes, but not of sadness.

'You too, Movita,' she said, as if she read my mind. 'You're free to go home.'

I have never in my life felt anything like I did that moment in that office, not even when I was sentenced to life without parole by the judge. It was as if what the Warden said had to go through my whole body, like a physical thing, before I could even hear it. It started at my shoulders and moved down my arms like some kinda pain. Then my legs were weak and I couldn't a stood if I had to, and then it went to my stomach and I bent over in the chair and felt as if I was goin' to be sick. Then finally it went to my head and I heard the words. But I didn't believe them. I got the horrible thought that she was just lyin' to me.

'Oh, please, Warden,' I groaned, still bent over in my chair. 'Don't say that if it ain't true.'

'It's true, Movita. I'm sorry.'

I knew that was kinda funny, her apologizin', but I couldn't laugh. I was starting to feel a tiny kinda happiness creepin' on me, but then I was afraid, real afraid like this was just another dream and I'd wake up and see the pink wall again. I still couldn't straighten up. My mind was somethin' like paralyzed. I heard Theresa talkin' and Suki cryin'. I was far, farther away. They were huggin' each other and someone touched me, but I could hardly feel it.

'Oh my God!' I heard Theresa say. 'How did she do that? Oh my God, that girl is a saint. I would've been here two more years before I maxed out. I'm going to faint.'

Suki was cryin' away, rockin' Christina, sayin' 'We're gonna go home, baby. We're gonna go home, baby.'

I still couldn't believe I was goin' home. I just sat there and listened to the Warden goin' on about what Jennifer had done.

'She got you all unconditional pardons, which means you are *out of here*,' she explained. 'You don't have to go before any board. This is *not* parole. You may not know this, but it also means you can be in touch with each other on the Outside. It means you won't have to check in, or be checked on.'

I straightened up and looked around the room. Theresa was sittin' on the edge of her chair as if she was already on her way out, and Suki also had a different look about her already. Like she was a more important person.

The Warden stood up and told us to go and pack up our things, whatever we wanted to take, and to come back to her office. And then I got really afraid.

'Do you mean now?' Suki cried. 'We can leave now?'

The Warden laughed. 'To tell you the truth,' she said, 'after twenty-four hours I'm going to have to throw you out. You are no longer inmates here.'

I'd never fainted in my whole life, but after Warden Harding said that and everyone laughed I got woozy in my knees, like I wasn't sure they'd hold me up no more, even though I was sittin' in a chair. And my face and hands got all hot, like I was burnin' up. I could feel beads of sweat breakin' out on my forehead and under my arms, and when I looked at the light over the Warden's desk – that light I've seen maybe a million times – it suddenly got real bright and started to drown out the whole room. I looked over at Theresa and Suki, maybe for some help, but they was gettin' whiter and whiter, and seemin' further and further away. They was lookin' at me like they was worried, but before I could say anythin' they faded into the light and I felt myself slide sideways off the chair. Then everythin' just seemed to stop.

I woke up on the floor with the Warden and Theresa fussin' over me. The Warden was holdin' somethin' strong-smellin' under my nose. Theresa had some ice. I pulled myself up but I didn't say nothin'. I couldn't say nothin'.

'Come on, Movita,' Theresa said to me. 'Pull yourself together. Let's go to our cell. I'll help you.' Her voice was real serious. Somehow she musta known what I was goin' through.

The Warden put her arms around me. 'It's gonna be okay, Movita,' she said real quietly. 'In fact, it's gonna be more than okay. Go get your things and come back here. That's all you have to do.'

I got up and told Gwen I was all right. Theresa hugged me, and so did Suki, and Gwen Harding – she was just beamin'.

'Go on back and take it in,' she told me. 'Then pack yourselves up.'

I thanked her and nodded and we left the office. Once we got to the long corridor I started to cry but kept walkin' along with Theresa next to me, Suki in front. I sobbed on and on like I would never stop. I was sadder durin' that walk than I ever been in my life, which sure was strange. It was as if I was suddenly thawed out or somethin' and thinkin' that maybe I was not some kinda rat that is supposed to be kept in a cellar. I didn't think those words then, I couldn't think any words, but that's what I remember the feelin' bein' like. I think I let myself cry for all the times I didn't all the years before.

Back in our cell, Theresa started sortin' through her stuff. I had stopped cryin' but I couldn't move. She told me to just take what I wanted, and leave the rest. I think it was one of her stupid slogans, but for once it was useful. I took the pictures of my children and the pack a letters they sent me, and I don't know what else.

'Now where are we goin'?' I asked Theresa. I stopped cryin' and was just kinda numb by this time.

Theresa stopped what she was doin' and looked at me. 'That's actually a good question. I don't know,' she said. 'And how will we get wherever we go?'

Then she smiled. 'Look, I'm sure the Warden will help us. We get our money – everything in the canteen fund plus what we earned working plus a hundred dollars. And then, if we sell our stock, we're rich. Don't forget that.'

'But it all takes time.' Crazy as it sounds, I think I was scared.

'She knows we can't just walk out of here.' Theresa made like she was lost in the universe, wavin' her arms and lookin' at the ceilin'. She was jokin' but it was how I really felt, and I bet she knew it. She had sisters and all kinda family to go to. I had the girls but . . .

She came over and looked at my little pile of stuff.

'Don't you want to take anything else?' she asked me. 'What about a few clothes? You'll need something to wear.'

So I started puttin' together a bundle but the pants and shirts that I'd designed now just looked useless to me. Toothpaste and washcloth. I was finished in a minute and went and stood by the door, like I always used to, but this time when I leaned against it, it moved.

'Theresa!' I said. 'Ryan didn't lock the door!'

She came up behind me and pushed it open. 'We are no longer inmates of this prison, Movita. We're outta here.'

I followed her out into the corridor holdin' my stuff, and then turned around and looked back. I looked at my bunk and the sink and the wall without my kids' pictures on it. It was the most horrible lookin' place I ever saw, but I stared at it for a minute, 'cause it was where I lived for all those years.

In a kind of a daze we went to Suki's cell, 'cause she had a lot more stuff to carry than we did, all the baby paraphernalia and the baby – who was sleepin' quietly in her bassinet. I realized I didn't want to say good-bye to nobody who wasn't gettin' out right then with us because it would be too damn cruel. Then Ryan escorted us back to the Warden's office. I was afraid maybe she'd say 'April fool' or something, but she didn't.

'Come with me,' she said, puttin' her arms out like she wanted to hug all of us at once. 'I'm going to walk you Outside.'

We followed her out, walkin' along as if we were just visitors at Jennings, like the JRU groups and the tours that sometimes came through. Everybody we passed was lookin' at us different than they had the day before. You can't never keep a secret in a woman's prison.

'But where will we go, Warden?' Suki asked. 'I can go to Roger's but . . . well . . .'

I knew she was feeling sorry for me. I hate that. 'I'm not sure I got a place to go,' I admitted.

'Oh, I don't think you have to worry about that,' she said. 'There's someone picking you up Outside and we're all going out for lunch. After that we'll take care of where you're all settling down.'

Well, I may be crazy but I ain't no dummy. I knew it'd be Jennifer Spencer waitin' out there for us. Still, it was the greatest feelin' in the world to come out into the actual Outside and see her standin' there. It was then that I knew it was for real.

And of all the amazin', outrageous things, she had come with a huge stretch limousine! Must have been six windows on each side. And when the driver opened the door, about fifty helium balloons poured out and up into the air.

'Freedom!' Jennifer said.

This just started me cryin' all over again. I was so grateful that I couldn't even speak, so I just hugged Jennifer. Then that bitch Cher stepped out of the car! 'You like her better than you like me?' she asked. I swear, I was bewildered, but I hugged that girl and let everyone else do the talkin'. Cher told me later that this was the only time she ever saw me bein' quiet.

Everybody climbed in the big car, even the Warden, and we drove away from Jennings. For a moment everybody was quiet as we pulled through the gate. I was waitin' for the Warden to say somethin' about Cher and Jennifer bein' in violation of their parole – they weren't supposed to be together. But ol' Gwen said nothin'. Me and Theresa looked out the tinted window, but Suki didn't 'cause she was busy with Christina. After that I just looked at Jennifer. To me she was the best and most beautiful person in the world and I knew I'd never live a day without thinkin' of her and bein' more grateful than I could ever say. Didn't matter she was white. She was my sister. I don't think anyone can understand how it feels to be released. Even I don't understand it and it happened to me.

Jennifer couldn't get over how Christina had grown. She had to wake the child up to admire her. 'She's gotten so big! Honestly, Suki, she's the cutest baby I've ever seen!' she said. 'She's a big chubby doll!' She took out a box, all wrapped nice. 'Here, I have something for her. Why don't you put it on her now?' I just loved that the box was wrapped up beautiful and *not* rewrapped. I noticed right away.

Suki opened the box and inside was a little flowered dress with a sweater to match. She took off Christina's rompers and put on the new outfit. We were all just overcome by the beauty of the child. We began laughin' with pleasure, 'cause smilin' and words were just not enough.

Then Jennifer told us what we were goin' to do. First we would have lunch, after which the Warden would have to go back to Jennings, and we would go into New York City. She said we could all stay at her apartment for the night and then the next day we would go home. She'd arranged for drivers. It was like a dream, I was thinkin', and I bent my head down so that I wouldn't faint again.

We went to lunch at some fancy restaurant, which I thought was the most beautiful place I'd ever been in, and I said so. I was also the only African American sittin' down, though there were several waiters and service people. I forgot how white the world Outside was. But I was so happy, nothin' could spoil it. But when I got the menu I kinda froze up. Too many choices. I felt my fingers tighten on the card. How to choose? What to eat, what to drink? It was way too much.

Jen saw my problem. 'Let's all have the Cobb salad,' she suggested. I had no damn idea what the Cobb salad was, but I said sure, and to this day that blue crumbly cheese is the taste of freedom to me.

'Missy, I'm gonna take you places that make this look like nothin'!' Cher said to me. But I shook my head. I don't think any place is ever gonna look so beautiful to me. Still Cher was full of fun, and she looked the bomb, and a lot younger than when she was in with us.

But the best came last. When we came out of the restaurant, there in the parkin' lot was another limo and out
of it poured three of Theresa's sisters, Roger Camry, his
mother, and then, one by one, my girls: Jamorah, Talitha,
and Kiama, all dressed real nice.

'Mama!' Jamorah cried, and ran across the tarmac, her
arms open wide to give me the best hug of my life.

53

Maggie Rafferty

*I suppose society is wonderfully delightful. To be in it is
merely a bore. But to be out of it is simply a tragedy.*

Oscar Wilde, *A Woman of No Importance*

One by one they had become dear to my heart and one by
one they left me. First Jennifer Spencer was paroled, then
Miss Watson, Miss LaBianco and Suki Conrad along with
dear little Christina – all were pardoned. I didn't resent
their new freedom, but I did miss them. Of course, I was
very busy in my new, expanded role as inmate coordinator.
Dozens and dozens of women needed counseling, direction, a chance to share their grievances, and an intercessor.
I filled the bill. And I wasn't abandoned by my friends
because they were pardoned, so all of them were free to
write and visit me, and they already had – and frequently.

I had begun to take my meals alone again, but the food
was now so much better in the cafeteria that I frequently
picked it up there and then brought it to my cell. It was a
peaceful respite for me after dealing with people all day

long. But when I heard the rumor that Warden Harding was leaving, and then heard it confirmed by a CO, I felt a pain that pierced my heart. Two, or sometimes three, times a week we had been having tea and sharing gossip and inmate problems in her office. Now that would be denied me, too, and I felt deeply bereft. It wasn't that my days were empty – to the contrary, they were filled with interesting and useful activity. There were many young women I had already come to like, and with the clearly psychotic housed in their own wing, I was no longer troubled by the screaming, cursing, and bizarre behavior that could so often disrupt a meal, sleep, a class, or even a conversation. I had also come to have deep affection for Springtime, whom I worked with each morning in one of the new gardens. She rarely spoke, but her presence was soothing and I believe that somewhere in her troubled consciousness she felt the same about mine. Springtime had finally stopped trying to escape, and would have been outdoors, nursing her plants and flowers or in the new greenhouse with her seedlings twenty-four-seven, as they say here, had it been allowed.

Since the yard had been grassed and the young birch trees planted, recreation had been extended to an area all around the perimeter of the building. I no longer had to walk in circles, figuratively and literally. A whole team was working on landscaping what we called the 'woods walk', a winding path all around the prison that would be visible from the guard towers (so no mischief could take place there) but would give the illusion of something approaching Arcadia to the walker. Already about a third of it was completed, and the azaleas, rhododendrons and plantings of annuals and perennials looked both natural and inviting.

Many of the inmates had become really interested in landscaping and nursery work as a career and I had made sure that Flora, who had inherited my job at the library, was collecting a significant selection of horticultural books and books on careers in the nursery and gardening fields. The perimeter walk was one of the new privileges at Jennings and it was so coveted that good behavior had certainly increased among the inmates to ensure their outdoor time.

The news, though, of Warden Harding's departure shocked and upset me in a way I simply wasn't prepared for. Of course, it was only a rumor, but I called her office and asked if I might come up to speak with her. The dull Miss Ringling had at last been replaced by a pleasant older woman named Ethel Schutz. No one, of course, could take Movita's place. But a new young woman named Tulip had been, at my suggestion, given a chance. Tulip put me on hold and came back on to tell me that I could come right up. That was a comfort, but when I got there I had to wait almost twenty minutes, and the phone calls and the faxes seemed to indicate that the rumor might be true. I could, of course, ask Tulip, because she did owe me a favor, but I didn't like to use that kind of ploy. I merely sat, my hands in my lap, and looked down at them.

They were the hands of an old woman. It was clear that they had done a lot of labor and the speckles on them showed that I was well past menopause. They were hands that had raised two boys, diapered and burped them, hands that had touched a man with passion, hands that had gestured and demonstrated and remonstrated to countless students, and they were hands that had killed a man. I stared and stared at them, going into an almost trancelike

485

state. Well, I thought, they were hands that would have to do without the warmth of a cup of tea with Warden Gwendolyn Harding.

When the intercom buzzed Mrs Schutz looked up and politely told me I could join the Warden. I walked into her office expecting the worst and prepared for it. 'So,' I said, 'is it true, Gwendolyn?' After years and years of calling one another by title, we had only recently gotten onto a first-name basis (although I was always careful not to use her first name in any setting but her office).

'Yes, Margaret,' Gwendolyn said, smiling broadly. She seemed not to have the slightest regret that she was moving on. Well, I couldn't blame her.

I tried not to show my disappointment. 'Congratulations,' I said, and smiled back at her.

'You seem troubled, Margaret. Are you okay?' Gwendolyn asked, concerned.

'I'll be all right. Really,' I tried to reassure both of us. 'Do you know who'll be coming in to take over for you?'

'Take over for me?' Gwendolyn asked. 'What makes you think I need to be taken over? Haven't we been through that already?'

'Well, if you're going to be Director of Corrections, I merely assumed that . . .'

'That I was leaving? No. I made the agreement to take on the job only if I could use this office as my base.' Gwendolyn paused. 'Oh, dear. If you think I'm leaving so does everybody else,' Gwendolyn shook her head, then leaned back in her chair. 'I'm sorry if you've been worried about all of this, Margaret. But I'm not going anywhere. Yes, I've been given more responsibilities and a new title but I'm still going to be based here at Jennings. They'll have to lease an administrative building nearby, but I thought that you might be very involved in that work.'

I instinctively hugged myself. Tears rose in my eyes. 'Oh, thank heavens! You don't know how much that means. I . . . just don't think I could take any more change around here.'

'Well, there will be changes, but they'll be good ones. Speaking of changes, did you get one of these?' Gwendolyn handed a white envelope to me.

I took it, struggled to pull out the enclosure, and glanced at it. It was an invitation to Jennifer Spencer's wedding. 'No, I haven't gotten one, yet. I can't say I'm surprised, though. Lenny is a lovely man.'

'But won't it be fun?' Gwendolyn asked.

Perhaps I was muddled over the reversals of the morning. All I know is I said, 'She deserves every happiness. Still, it doesn't much matter since I can't go to it anyway.'

'Actually, you will be able to go,' Gwendolyn said.

'Gwendolyn, you can't let me leave the grounds to go to a wedding. She's not even a relative. I know things are different, but they're not *that* different.'

'Have wedding, will travel,' Gwendolyn said, and chuckled. 'Look at the invitation, Margaret. Former Inmate 71036 is coming here to be married!'

'Here?' I asked. 'Where? Where will it be?'

'Margaret, you'll have to go out to the shed.'

They hold a lot of weddings at men's prisons. I don't pretend to understand the phenomenon, but it's surprisingly common that a woman will correspond with a prisoner, become involved, and marry the criminal, even if he's guilty of a heinous crime. Perhaps, as my friend Gwendolyn opined, it's because when your husband is in prison at least you always know where he is. I think the situation feeds into a woman's need for fantasy and 'romance' – if he's not around underfoot, if you can see him only briefly, if the sex is rare or actually impossible and only imagined, a woman is capable of turning any frog into a mental prince. But weddings in women's prisons are virtually unheard of. And women love weddings. So, you can imagine the stir that the event made at Jennings.

The garden shed had been converted into a bower of flowers. White lilacs, roses, lisianthus, lilies, and ivy covered it. Seats had been put outside, with white ribbons streaming from them. Inmates had volunteered to work on a long white runner, hand hooked, that ran from the shed to the entrance of the yard. The wedding was truly beautiful. Jennifer looked radiant. Her dress was simple; a white swath of silk designed by Movita, covered with tulle that created a ghostlike effect as it shadowed the dress beneath. Jen also had what seemed like miles of tulle flowing from her simple headdress, and a wreath of flowers prepared by Springtime. Leonard – I was the only person who refused to call him that undignified name he was known by – looked very elegant in a simple black suit. I regretted, a bit, that it wasn't Bryce or Tyler Jennifer was marrying, so that she could actually become a member of my family – until I realized that neither of my boys was good husband material, and she was a member of my family anyway. I will never lose track of her or she of me.

Before the ceremony I had helped prepare the bride along with the other 'girls', Movita, Suki, Theresa, and Cher. Jen had asked that I give her away and, as she had neither mother nor father, I was pleased to do it. I had spent years serving *in loco parentis,* and I probably was more loco than parental at this point.

I was a little worried about misbehavior on the part of any of the inmates but I had two weeks to prepare them and I was delighted that their deportment was excellent. I have no idea what Leonard Benson's mother and aged father thought about the venue, but I could see that they were delighted with their new daughter-in-law.

I hadn't been to a wedding since my Tyler was married and that had been some fifteen years ago. And I couldn't attend any ceremonies for either of my boys anymore so this was definitely going to be an extra exciting time for me. The wedding march had started to play – the warden had brought in a CD player – and all the girls and I got in line and waited nervously for the right time to enter the yard. Theresa and Cher walked out first as the bridesmaids, then Movita as the maid of honor. The flower girl was Christina, who was accompanied by Suki for assistance. They were all stunning, dressed up in their lavender dresses, wearing real makeup, with their hair done beautifully. Once the girls had gotten twenty steps out – I had to try to keep count as they walked away – I gave Jennifer's arm a little squeeze and she smiled down at me through her veil. 'Let's get outta here,' she said, and gently took my hand.

When we stepped out of the doorway and into the sunshine and fresh air I felt like it was the first time I had ever been outside. A sound, something between a sigh and a gasp, came from the many inmates and guests assembled. I felt rejuvenated. The colors of the maid of honor's and bridesmaids' dresses against the green of the lawn and trees was breathtaking. As we approached the pastor I squeezed Jennifer's arm again. I didn't want to let go of her at the end of the white runner but I did. As I let go, Gwendolyn came up behind me and helped me to my seat. 'Isn't she ravishing?' I asked.

'Without a doubt,' Gwendolyn whispered.

The ceremony was emotional for everyone. Even the bulldaggers cried.

When the pastor pronounced the two of them man and wife, Leonard leaned forward and took Jennifer's face in his hands. I was right next to them and I had never noticed what lovely, long, strong fingers he had. He tilted her face toward him and the kiss that he gave her was as deep and long and passionate as I hoped their marriage would be. Jennifer colored, and the blush was one I remembered from the days when Riff was exciting in a good way. She was a wise and good girl, Jennifer Spencer Benson. She had picked her mate, a decision always fraught with the potential for catastrophe for a woman. She had picked her mate wisely. Leonard clearly cherished her and I had the strongest sense that he would continue to do so.

And when it came time for Jennifer to throw her bouquet, I must say it was the hungriest, most eager group that I had ever seen. Jennifer, with Lenny's help, stood up on a chair, closed her eyes, and threw her flowers. As the bouquet was released, arms shot up into the air as if the women were waiting for the delivery of packages from home. Several of them used basketball blocking moves. The bouquet suddenly disappeared from the air and the women were scrambling. I couldn't see who caught it and no one was holding it up in victory. Were they ripping it into pieces so they each got some? What were they doing?

Then I saw the bouquet come out of the crowd. Behind the flowers I saw a dark leathery face and loony bright eyes.

I was distracted for a moment by Jennifer, who was still standing up on the chair, and who had started to laugh and point. When I looked back to the group of inmates still collected, I spotted what Jennifer was laughing at. Behind the colorful flowers I saw Springtime with the biggest grin on her face, the recipient of the bridal bouquet.

Epilogue

> If I had been present at the creation, I would have given
> some useful hints for the better arrangement of the
> Universe.
>
> Alfonso the Wise, King of Castile

I didn't feel sorry for myself despite all that I had gone
through. And I didn't feel sorry for Tom Branston when he
was disbarred, or when he found out that he was virtually
penniless due to Cher's shenanigans. I never spoke to
Donald again, and I never asked for a pardon from the
governor, because I was guilty. Not as guilty as Donald, who
has never been punished, but if I had learned anything at
Jennings, it was that there may be plenty of laws but there's
very little justice.

I have been luckier than most. I was born with a good
brain, I was raised by my own mother, I managed to get into
university and even graduate school. That it was the wrong
one, and that I wasted some years on Wall Street, doesn't
seem like a major mistake compared to the mistakes that
other people make with their lives. And I did learn how the

system works as I combated the system. Certainly, my time at Jennings wasn't wasted. I learned the value of liberty, something I had always taken for granted. I learned about injustice, and how prevalent it is. I had the chance to reevaluate the importance of money versus human needs. In this country, in this century, financial considerations will virtually always win out over human ones, but Jennings put me on another path. My work now is focused on helping other women, women not so lucky as I.

Mostly, I raise funds. Movita Watson is now the director of the outreach program that we've created. My husband has worked hard to get us the not-for-profit status that we need. He's started his own practice, which makes his time as flexible as mine is. Sometimes, on very busy days, he'll watch the twins. Otherwise I take them to the office or drop them with Suki, who is running a day-care center. Roger's quit his job as a correctional officer and is now a guard for Brinks Security.

Cher is still on Wall Street. So far she hasn't been arrested for stock fraud, insider trading, or alienation of affection. At last count she'd had three affairs with moguls, and she's a big contributor to our outreach program. 'Nobody ever gave me nothin',' she says, tough as ever, 'but since it's tax deductible, I may as well.'

Theresa has opened a restaurant with one of her innumerable sisters, or maybe it's her cousin, or her sister-in-law. It's in Brooklyn, and we all get together there at least once a month and eat 'macaroni and gravy' and drink too much red wine.

Gwen Harding now heads the State Corrections Authority and is engaged to be married! And to a judge! We could hardly believe the news when we heard it but Gwen says she can hardly believe it either. Movita was the first one to meet him and she says he's a pretty good guy for a judge. We all expect to meet him at a party they're throwing in Albany next month.

And finally, there's Maggie Rafferty. I visit her regularly, and she seems happy and busy in her many roles at Jennings. She runs our outreach program from Inside and feeds inmates into our programs as they become ready for them. If I have any regret at all, it's that I couldn't get Margaret Rafferty out of prison. But her case was simply too high profile and other members of the Rafferty family (not her sons) were too politically connected to allow it. While men murder their spouses at an alarming rate, women who kill the men in their lives are rarely forgiven. It's dreadful to imagine that Maggie will end her life in Jennings, but she does seem adjusted to that fact, and to be, to some extent, at peace.

The sale of JRU back to the state made Maggie a tidy sum of money, but she donates virtually all of it to various programs protecting women caught in the legal system. And, in the last two years or so, a change has come over her. She seems, in a way, to have transcended her physical boundaries. I don't know if it's my imagination or if it's true, but she seems to have found some kind of peace that makes me think of the saints I read about back in parochial school. She seems not just satisfied but actually fully realized, and, although incarceration is a cruel punishment, after all these years it seems as if Maggie Rafferty has found a mission and a raison d'être. She's godmother to both of my twins as well as Christina, and I know Suki plans to ask her to be godmother to the new baby as soon as it's born.

Movita's eldest, Jamorah, has just aced her SATs – with

a little help from her friends – and plans to become an attorney instead of a fashion designer as she had once planned when she was younger. Talitha has also been doing well. The youngest, Kiama, has been diagnosed with a learning disability. Now she's being tutored three times a week.

As I said, I have no regrets. I'm not as optimistic as Theresa, who believes that everything is part of God's plan, but I do know that serving time in Jennings has brought me my life's mission, my husband, my best friends, and my little boys, Tyler and Bryce. Needless to say, Maggie dotes on them and is their honorary grandma, since my mom is dead.

I think now that my mother would be proud of who I am, and though I know I can never do enough, at least I'm doing something. I'm busy all the time. Of course, there are times when I'm overwhelmed, depressed, particularly exhausted, or upset. But those are the times that Lenny reminds me of what Thomas Jefferson wrote: 'Eternal vigilance is the price of liberty.'

Acknowledgments

Of all of the novels that I have written in my career, I must admit that *Insiders* has been the most difficult. *You* try to write a charming, uplifting, funny, and empowering story about a woman who wrongly goes to jail! I wrote this book to expose some of the evils and inequities that exist in the prison system, but I felt certain I could find the fun and dark humor of strong women being taken advantage of by a bad system (as I have previously done in *First Wives Club, Flavor of the Month, Fashionably Late,* and *Young Wives*). But in doing my research for *Insiders* I found there was very, very little that was charming, uplifting, or empowering in prison. What I learned within prisons, from prisoner advocates, prison superintendents, inmates, and correction officers has helped in the creation of this novel, but a great deal of pain and misery had to be jettisoned. The characters are, I hope,

497

lifelike, funny, and inspiring; but their situations (except for the most desperate parts) are far better than what real inmates experience. It is important for readers (and all women) to be aware of our incarcerated sisters and to know that:

- Women are the fastest growing sector of the entire prison population. Since 1980, the female inmate population nationwide has increased more than 500 percent.
- Health care for female prisoners is incredibly insufficient. (Pap smears, mammograms, annual gynecological checkups, are almost nonexistent.) It is common practice for prisoners to be denied medical examinations and treatments.
- Every time a woman is incarcerated her innocent children are also punished. They are sent to family members or – tragically – sent out to foster care.
- Women prisoners spend, on average, seventeen hours a day in their cells with only one hour outside for exercise (far less than for male prisoners).
- Despite the minimal services, it annually costs more to send a woman to prison than to Harvard University.
- Privatization of prisons is creating a female slave labor force. (Prisoners are forbidden by law to unionize or strike.) Unprotected by minimum wage laws or the Fair Labor Standards Act, they cannot voice complaints or even refuse to work without receiving *severe* retaliation.

It takes a special kind of person to do good work in a prison, jail, correctional facility, or whatever you choose to call the walls that incarcerate women. To choose to be locked inside a building full of misery, addiction, illness, and pain, where there is virtually no privacy, and where you – as an employee or volunteer – experience the heartbreaks of so many women, takes tremendous courage. To witness the pain of the return of a previously released inmate, when family or friends don't arrive for visitor's day, when early release is jeopardized by a single mindless act, or when bad news from the Outside is received, is more difficult than most people can imagine, much less bear. Without the assistance of those listed below, I wouldn't have been able to interview inmates, tour facilities, obtain necessary statistics or the 'insider' information that I needed to write this book. So, special thanks to:

Randy Credico of the William Moses Kunstler Fund for Racial Justice, a hero who has worked at freeing more unjustly imprisoned women than anyone else I know.

Kathyrn Watterson, author of *Women in Prison*, for the definitive book on the subject, as well as her generous permission to quote from it.

Andi Rierden, author of *The Farm*, a human and humane look at female prisoners.

Robert Gangi, executive director of the Correctional Association of New York, for his insights, as well as his entrée to prisons and halfway houses in New York and elsewhere.

Jennifer Wynn, director of the Prison Visiting Project, for her help in doing the difficult work necessary to get clearance for me to visit women prisoners.

Mishi Faruquee, director of Women in Prison Project. Keep up the good work.

Margaret Owens, executive director of the National Center for Women in Prison. Thanks for being there, and for the tremendous job you do.

New York State Senator Velmanette Montgomery of the 18th Senate District in Albany. Thanks also to Sandy Stewart, her able administrator.

Superintendent Eleine Lord of Bedford Hills. Her savvy, compassion, and wisdom impressed me enormously (and I'm not so easily impressed).

Superintendent Wayne Strack of Fishkill Correctional Facility for allowing us to tour the Beacon, New York, women's prison.

Superintendent Susan Schultz of the Beacon Correctional Facility for Women, who not only gave us a tour but also gave us lunch and free access to talk with inmates.

The Prison Activist Resource Center of Berkeley, California. Their tremendous work on behalf of prisoners all over the U.S. and the statistics that they have gathered were absolutely invaluable.

Nan Robinson, my able and loving (as well as much beloved) editorial assistant, who toured many facilities with me (and the Cheshire County Department of Corrections in Westmoreland, New Hampshire, without me).

Superintendent Richard N. Van Wickler of the Cheshire County Department of Corrections for giving Nan Robinson a personal tour of his facility and for taking the time to explain procedures, observation areas, Special Holding Units (which I am glad to report have been turned into storage closets), and for answering so many of our questions. Thanks too, to the staff: Kerry, Penny, Julie, and the many COs, and the medical staff Nan met during the tour.

Nan would like to extend a special thank-you to the group of women who were housed in the Cheshire County

Department of Corrections at the time of her visit for allowing her to walk through their wing, watch a little television, and – most important – to be interviewed during their lunch time.

The book is, unfortunately, unworthy of the subject. So, most important of all, I would like to thank the women inmates who took the time and made the effort to talk with me despite cynicism, depression, or fear. Ironically, I cannot give copies of this novel to any facilities until it comes out in the paperback edition because hardcover books are considered contraband (items can be hidden in the book binding). But in the meantime, women on the Inside need to be visited by women from the Outside. And while I took small gifts to many of the women I visited, I received so much more than I gave.

Special thanks to the inmates in the Beacon Horticultural Program who gave me the terrific houseplants. They are still going strong, despite my black thumb. I have one on my kitchen windowsill and I like to think of the plants as expressions of the strength of the women who helped to start and nurture the seedlings.

A final thanks to Tracy Fonville, an inmate sentenced to an unjust twenty-three-year sentence, and who was released early. Our joy at meeting in front of Rockefeller Center had to be experienced before I could write about newfound freedom with any truth.

On the last page I list a few books that I recommend to readers who want to be more aware of the prison problem in America. And I remind us all that:

Olivia Goldsmith

He that judges without informing himself to the utmost that he is capable, cannot acquit himself of judging amiss.

John Locke, An Essay Concerning Human Understanding

Recommended Reading

Books:

The Farm: Life Inside a Women's Prison. Andi Rierden. University of Massachusetts Press.

Women in Prison: Inside the Concrete Womb. Kathryn Watterson, Meda Chesney-Lind. Northeastern University Press.

The Celling of America: An Inside Look at the U.S. Prison Industry. Daniel Burton-Rose, Dan Pens, Paul Wright, eds. Common Courage Press.

Criminal Injustice: Confronting the Prison Crisis. Elihu Rosenblatt, ed. South End Press.

Live from Death Row. Mumia Abu-Jamal. Avon.

Lockdown America: Police and Prisons in the Age of Crisis. Christian Parenti. Verso.

Race to Incarcerate. Mark Maurer. New Press.

States of Confinement: Policing, Detention, and Prisons. Joy James, ed. Palgrave.

Articles/pamphlets:

'The Prison Industrial Complex.' Eric Schlosser. *Atlantic Monthly,* December 1998.